MAGICAL FOLK

The History of Fairies

Simon Young and Ceri Houlbrook

Editors

London

GIBSON SQUARE

This volume is dedicated by the editors to
one of our greatest living folklorists,
John Widdowson

And see ye not yon bonny road
That winds about the fernie brae?
That is the Road to fair Elfland,
Where thou and I this night maun gae

EDITORS' NOTE
&
ACKNOWLEDGEMENTS

We have sought to bring together a blend of introductions and scholarship on the subject for the enjoyment of the general reader and the interest of folklorists. Where no author is mentioned, the words are ours as editors of this volume. We gratefully acknowledge permission to reproduce the illustration of Chapter 2, copyright Pollyanna Jones; the illustration of Chapter 3, copyright Peter Hall; the illustration of Chapter 9, Copyright Andy Paciorek, blurb.com/user/andypaciorek.

This edition first published in 2023 by Gibson Square.

rights@gibsonsquare.com
www.gibsonsquare.com

Papers used by Gibson Square are natural, recyclable products made from wood grown in sustainable forests; inks used are vegetable based. Manufacturing conforms to ISO 14001, and is accredited to FSC and PEFC chain of custody schemes. Colour-printing is through a certified CarbonNeutral® company that offsets its CO2 emissions. Copyright holders are kindly invited to come forward.

Contents

FAIRIES TALK

The Scottish soldier and writer John Stedman (1744-1797) had many extraordinary adventures in his life. He fought in the jungles of South America; he supped with poet and visionary William Blake; he had a long and passionate love affair with a slave, Joanna; he got involved in drunken brawls. But for sheer bizarreness nothing comes close to his run in with a supernatural being in the 1790s. Stedman had taken an evening coach going from Hammersmith to the centre of London: Hammersmith is, today, deep within the metropolis, but, in the late eighteenth century, it was mostly green fields. As Stedman was enjoying the ride he heard a strange whistling noise. He looked out of the coach window and was flabbergasted to see 'a little fellow, about two feet high, dressed in a full suit of regimentals with a gold-laced cocked hat'. Even stranger the small man was strolling along, at about nine miles per hour, or twice the average walking speed of a man! The fast pace was apparently creating the noise Stedman had heard and Stedman stared gobsmacked as this impossible humanoid overtook the stage coach, swinging his cane.[1] Stedman had encountered a fairy, one of the magical folk in the British Isles.

We often think of fairies as inhabiting our islands' wildest Tolkienian landscapes—the west coast of Ireland; the Scottish islands; the Cornish hedgerows...—and there is something to this. Certainly, no country in Western Europe has as many fairy records as Ireland: important studies published through the nineteenth century; vast (and still largely untapped) records of fairy sightings and fairy belief in Irish newspapers in the 1800s; and tens of thousands of pages of folklore with matching index cards heroically collected by the Irish Folklore Commission from 1935. Nor is it just a question of the quantity of documentation: there is also the intensity of fairy belief. In 1838 a Co. Limerick court attempted to prosecute fairies for an illegal meeting, a meeting which had been witnessed by scores of people.[2] In 1864, in Co. Tipperary, a local witch convinced several dupes that she could bring their dead relatives 'back from the fairies'.[3] In 1895, an Irishman Michael Cleary, from the Clonmel area, burnt his wife (with the partial collusion of the wife's family) because he believed that she was a fairy who had taken his real wife's place.[4] In England there were fairy beliefs but, by the 1800s, they rarely caused men and women to act in such a dramatic fashion.

Indeed, as the nineteenth and twentieth centuries progressed, fairies were increasingly seen as a 'Celtic' phenomenon. A crucial moment in the development of this idea came in 1911, when an American bohemian and mystic Walter Evans Wentz published *The Fairy Faith in Celtic Countries*, with Oxford University Press. *The Fairy*

Faith, based on three years of field work in Brittany, Cornwall, Ireland, Man, Scotland and Wales, is perhaps the strangest academic book ever published in Britain (which is saying something). As well as proving—to his satisfaction—that fairies exist, Evans Wentz's Oxford University Press monograph also offered insights into the reality of Atlantis and gave us our single most interesting collection of fairy encounters. Evans Wentz restricted himself to 'the Celts' because he believed that they had a special mystic faculty, not given to materialist Anglo-Saxons. His beliefs proved influential, as the *Fairy Faith* was, in the postwar period, republished in cheap paperback editions. Today the idea that fairies are Celtic has gone mainstream. As the author of the most important fairy study of the last decade concedes: 'the notion that Wales, Scotland and Ireland have a particular claim on [fairies] is deeply ingrained in the consciousness of the English-speaking world'.[5]

But—as chapters in this book will show—fairies are also sighted throughout Britain and not just in the rugged west and north. They have, up to the present, turned up deep within England and are as English as Shakespeare. Indeed, if you run a fine comb through even the most urbanized of the modern English shires fairies will come tumbling out. In the spirit of Stedman's experience let's return to what is certainly the most difficult place to hunt for fairies in Western Europe, the area today covered by Europe's only world city, London. A fairy tree once stood—and was still feared by locals in the seventeenth century—very close to what is today Crystal Palace.[6] (Another fairy tree perhaps stood at Windsor Park: at least it did according to Shakespeare's *Merry Wives of Windsor*.)[7] Locals in the Greenwich area, meanwhile, take their children to the Fairy Hill Recreation Park, named after a local fairy mound or possibly a Fairy Hall in the area. It could be argued that these are just fossils from before London's 'red rust' crept out into the Home Counties: and that fairies are no longer associated with the patch of concrete that covers the grave of the fairy tree or Greenwich's moribund fairy hill. But the remarkable thing is that fairies continued to be seen within London itself; not admittedly in the thoroughfares or roads of the centre, but in London's parks and gardens.

Thus, in the 1880s, a little girl watched scores of tiny fairies flying from water lilies to the trees in Kew Gardens, before her father ordered her away.[8] In the late 1920s, artist Ivor Innes created the Elfin Oak in Kensington Gardens (today a Grade II listed structure), inspired by the fairies he saw play there and by memories of Peter Pan.[9] In the years before the Second World War a couple driving by Richmond Park watched a deer cross the road ridden by 'a little man about three feet high, clad in a jerkin and hose'.[10] A clergyman's widow had a conversation with a small green fellow in postwar Regent's Park: the little green man took away a pain in the widow's foot.[11] In 1987, an eighteen year old slept the night on Hampstead Heath and woke to see '[a]round 50 to 60 little dryads staring down from the leafy boughs'.[12] There have also been visions in private London gardens: in wartime Harrow one woman watched several glow worms in her allotment resolve themselves into gnomes, 'some in green coats and hats, some in red coats and hats, others in mauve'.[13]

It is only now possible to retrieve these stories and others like them because of one of the happiest innovations of the last generation—the digitisation of printed works, which are scanned and their texts stored online. The digitisation of millions of pages of British and Irish newspapers and magazines means that many local traditions, beliefs and stories can now be reclaimed from hundred- or two-hundred-year-old pages of ephemera. The digitisation of books in Britain and Ireland, particularly books about parishes, villages and towns, in Google Books and Archive.org, means, likewise, that it is feasible to find scarce and isolated references to folklore in works from the eighteenth and nineteenth centuries, when fairies were more commonly sighted. This is transforming the study of the British and Irish supernatural. For those interested in fairylore, particularly, we are living a similar moment to that experienced by Cold War historians in the early 1990s: after decades of having to rely on redacted documents, the archives in the west and the east were simultaneously thrown open.

The work that follows has uncovered a series of human characters whose lives became enmeshed with the fairies, and whose stories would not be known without digitisation. There is Fanny Bradley, a dwarf who was widely said, in the Yorkshire community in which she lived, to have been kidnapped by the fairies of Almscliff Crag as a baby.[14] There are the terrified boys who venture into a Cumbrian fairy cave, taking an eighteenth-century pistol with them to kill any fairies that they might meet.[18] There is Joyce Chadwick who watches pixies, on a holiday in Devon: they change shape in front of her, one even transforming itself into a long furry roll that spins along on the ground.[16] There is Kittie Crowe who tells stories about riding the rails with fairies, hobo style, in the American Midwest.[17] Then, most dramatic of all, there is Roderick, who tells how he was picked up and whisked across the Atlantic from Prince Edward's Island, Canada, to Ireland by fairies who kept dunking him into the waves as they flew: 'see here, boys, there may be ghosts or there may not; but if there are none, there are fairies, and they are worse'.[15]

If digitisation is one new and rich seam in fairylore, another is contemporary fairy sightings. Fairy experiences continue to this very day, both in England and along the Celtic fringe. However, most folklorists and historians have been unwilling to grapple with new fairy experiences. There is among some, an unspoken rule that anything later than the publication in 1920 of five photographs of fairies taken in Cottingley near Bradford can be ignored. These photographs are to fairy studies what the birth of Christ is to history: there is 'before' and 'after'. The five Cottingley photos were sponsored by Sherlock-Holmes author Arthur Conan Doyle (a fairy believer) and had been taken by teenage cousins Elsie Wright and Frances Griffiths; Elsie and Frances finally confessed to their fakery in 1983. Over a century since the first photographs were taken, the reluctance to engage with new fairy encounters is slowly changing. In the last years there have been four surveys of fairy experiences (two undertaken by authors in this book). Some chapters report on the latest of these, The Fairy Census, the first published scholarly survey of contemporary fairy sightings. The Fairy Census gathered almost five hundred different fairy experiences from Britain and Ireland and beyond from people who had striking and sometimes life-changing meetings with the 'little people' or the not so little people—one record from Scotland has a fifteen-foot fairy standing next to a sycamore....[19] Such experiences may be difficult to unravel for the modern mind, but they are part of the continuing fairy story and modern fairy sightings are, consequently, woven into this book.

The Fairy Census has several particularly striking episodes and patterns. For example, a couple reported an encounter, in the 1990s, with a supernatural being on the edge of Dublin that strongly echoes several (little known) nineteenth-century experiences with an Irish goblin named the Pooka.[21] There are other intriguing findings, too. How is it possible—to choose one account—that a six-year-old girl in Texas had an experience which recalls the early modern witch's Sabbath?[22] Perhaps, most exciting, though, there is data to chew over for psychologists, psychiatrists and neurologists. Why is it that so many fairy sightings occur while we are in bed? Why do so many children see fairies? Is it significant that several of these children remember being sad when they saw the fey? Why do so many drivers observe fairies, sometimes running along beside their car? Why do people watching television glimpse fairies in their peripheral vision?

Fairies have changed, of course, through history, as, not least, the Fairy Census shows. We have records of British and Irish fairies going back almost to Roman times: there were the elves, gnomes and trolls of Germanic and Celtic Europe in the Middle Ages, then, the child-sized, light-carrying, musical fairies of Shakespeare's England. And twentieth-century media has influenced popular perceptions of fairies, not least by moving fairies away into the realms of child-lore. Ever since Tinker Bell followed Peter Pan to Hollywood, modern sightings show that Disney's fairy visions have left their mark and that fairies are often today seen as small winged sylphs, wheeling through the heavens (though Tinker Bell, on the stage, had originally been nothing more than a fairy light and a bike bell). Yet the first fairy wings, for example, appear only at the end of the eighteenth century in paintings and were an invention of a cabal of British artists rather than a feature of traditional folklore. It took seventy more years for fairy wings to be mentioned in fairy tales, then another fifty for the first claims that people had seen fairies with wings. Another example: all our medieval and Elizabethan historical records of fairies describe human- or child-sized beings. There are no butterfly-sized fairies, which we arguably owe instead to the imagination of Elizabethan dramatists and poets.

How can we best define these strange beings that fascinated and sometimes terrified our adult forebears? They are certainly not tiny fluttering winged elves who guard flowers and trees and who live in the deep woods spreading pixy dust and kindness over a desolate world. Human neighbours were so terrified by the fairies' potency that they referred to these morally ambivalent, unpredictable, havoc-creating beings as 'the Good People', or 'the Gentry' because the word 'fairies' apparently annoyed the fey. The fairies, meanwhile, assaulted and tricked and, in some cases, murdered and kidnapped their way through human populations.

What are (if we dare use the term) fairies then? A simple but efficient definition is that traditional fairies are 'magical, living, resident humanoids', who dwell exclusively in Britain, Ireland and in some of the lands that British and Irish migrants settled. 'Exclusively' because the continent has its own magical folk, and these have their own characteristics; *'fée'* (France) and *'fata'* or *'fada'* (Southern Europe) or more exotically *'maitagarri'* (among the Basques) and *'keijukainen'* (Finland). 'Magical' because fairies do not, of course, obey the normal rules of physics. They rush through the air, they appear and disappear, time has no hold on them, and, they can change the environment around them with a wave of their hands. 'Alive' in the sense that they are not ghosts. It is true that there are some claims, not least in Irish tradition, that the dead go to live with the fairies, but this is an exceptional view. Fairies are 'resident' in that they are tied to places. Sometimes these places are natural: a wood, a hill, a vale… But sometimes these places are human constructions: a bridge, a prehistoric mound, a house or a church. Finally, fairies are 'humanoids'. The vast majority of descriptions are about beings that look like humans or that are human-like; as noted above they are also usually of adult- or child-size.

After this very general definition we run, though, into problems; the principal of which are regional variations. Indeed, the first rule of the fey is that all fairylore is local: hence the approach adopted for this book. The first clue to these differences are the names that fairies go by in different parts of Britain and Ireland. In Cornwall they are piskeys, in the Channel Islands pouques, in parts of southern and midlands England pharises, in Orkney and Shetland trows, in Ireland (or at least in parts of Ireland) the *sídhe*…. Nor is this just a question of different labels for the same thing. The fairies in the different areas are also notably different in their habits, characteristics and in their appearance. Take fairies' relations with humans. A human neighbour would probably survive a run in with fairies in Cornwall. He or she might be led a merry dance, pinched or, worst case scenario, dunked in a marsh. Offending the fairies in the Scottish Highlands or Ireland might end, instead, with deaths in the family.

Of course, there are things that these different fairy tribes hold in common, and there are also parallels with their cousins on the continent. For example, fairies have, in many parts of Britain and Ireland—or at least they did until recent times—the evil habit of stealing babies and replacing them with fairies disguised to look like the stolen child: this is the changeling tradition, referred to often in the pages that follow. There are also similar stories told about fairies in different regions. For instance, the tale of the broken spade—a broken tool is mended and a reward is given—appears in three different chapters in the present volume: Cumbria, Sussex and Worcestershire. But, and this is crucial, there are local variations even within these common traditions. The tale is told one way in Cumbria, where a human mends a fairy's broken tool, and another way in Worcestershire, where fairies mend humans' broken tools.

If *Magical Folk* offers an unashamedly local or regional take on fairylore, often while using exciting new sources, it also brings another valuable thing to the mix: contemporary traditions. It makes the point that fairies are still encountered in our time. In some areas—Ireland and Atlantic Canada stand out—we have fairy traditions dating back generations, beliefs that are still, in some quarters, taken seriously. In other areas—think of fairy money trees in Scotland, underwater gnome villages in Cumbria and pagan rituals at prehistoric stones on the Channel Islands—there are traditions that have only surfaced in the last few years; we might add fairy wings and fairy doors to this list. Some may want to ignore these late traditions as being inauthentic. But the truth is that believed, half believed or enjoyed, they stand as useful examples of modern fairylore: twenty-first-century successors to the elf bolts and fairy flights of our ancestors.

THE FAIRY CENSUS

The Fairy Census is a world-wide (ongoing) scholarly online survey in which people recorded the weirdest, most intimate fairy experiences they lived through and started in 2014. Those who participate often confess that they had told no one, or practically no one, about what they had experienced. While 'told' folklore and 'lived' folklore differ, surprisingly, they also bleed into each other in a way that matters when editing a book about fairy lore alive in specific regions.

Usually the participants had some knowledge of told folklore. For example, while shooting a film in a wood in Arkansas (response §221 of the survey), electrical leads keep knotting. The respondent takes off his jacket and turns it inside out, thus confounding the mischievous fairies as he remembered this remedy; and the wires untangle. It is remarkable that a middle-aged American man in the early 2000s would think to do this. At the same time, he clearly knew about the tradition of turning pockets or coats against fairy wiles.

Some of the most curious incidents recorded in The Fairy Census, however, contain fragments of 'unknowing tradition'. In these instances the individual had a fairy experience that echoes fairy lore—yet they themselves had no apparent prior knowledge of it. Here are three of the best illustrations so far:

§338 US (New York State): 'They came to me in my sleep, very often and the purpose was always the same. To take me to fly above the rooftops and treetops throughout my neighborhood as a very exciting treat. I thought for years it was just an odd recurring dream but the details of the things I saw from that bird's eye view would be impossible to have been a dream. In later years. I was able to understand and recall more emotional details…. They were fluid-like beings that were dressed in material that barely covered and was white and thin and always flowing as they too never touched the ground although [they] had legs and feet. I went willingly and trusting as I knew it was under my control where I was to fly and when I was to return. I now feel there was an exchange that occurred. I feel they (as many as five or six) absorbed the excitement from me.'

§376 US (Texas): 'I was playing in the empty lot next to my house and suddenly, I was in a forest. The fairies were tall and they fed me a drink and cakes that were very sweet and seemed to be made of light. It was dark, but it wasn't because it seemed like light emanated from the trees. After a couple of hours a woman told me I had to go back. I didn't want to go back and complained. She told me I had to because I had a purpose. Suddenly, I woke up on the floor of my living room. I don't remember getting there or leaving the open lot where I was running around and playing. I felt like I had lost time.'

In the seventeenth and eighteenth century, in many parts of Europe, witches were made to confess their midnight meetings at the Black Sabbath. There has long been the speculation that the 'Black' Sabbath was the local church's take on a folk tradition called the 'White' Sabbath. Most folklore records of these White Sabbaths come down through the filter of legal documents recording the prosecution of witches: this was an occasion where men and women would fly at night to feast with the fairies and seal a pact, whereby the humans would serve the fairies and the fairies would give the humans power in return.

The two respondents' cases—§338's memories of perhaps age six to ten and §376's of age six—are effectively stories about socialising with the local fairy population and there are hints of an exchange. Both involve some kind of dream (the White and the Black Sabbath took place during sleep with the dreamer travelling in the spirit) and they appear to be first-hand experiences of folklore. The respondent from Texas also report having 'regular' supernatural experiences as an adult.

Here is a second example, also reported from the US. Mermaids, of course, seduce sailors into the sea. But freshwater monsters are, generally speaking, even worse. Take, for example, 'Jenny Greenteeth' in the Midlands and North of England, who pulled children into canals and pools so that she could devour them in her underwater lair. Consider this fairy experience from the US, which is perhaps the darkest one from the entire Fairy Census.

§343 US (North Carolina): 'I was on a rock in the river reading while my husband fished on up-river. I was across from a park, people walking with kids and dogs. There were two young boys walking on the trail with their dad. They began moving down towards the water, when it started coming up the river moving through the water towards them. It was pale-skinned water-logged looking with black hair and sharp serrated teeth showing in a smile. It paid me no attention, but was focused on the boys. They were pointing at it with sticks and could absolutely see it. The dad finally ushered them away from the edge of river seemingly unaware of it being feet from his kids. It watched them move up the trail away with a creepy look on its face and then moved on up-river out of sight. Did not look friendly to me.'

A third example of 'unknowing tradition' also has an American connection.

§148 Ireland (Co. Dublin): 'While traveling at night, on a road that ran up some mountains, we saw a shapeless white form that appeared to be a white shopping bag blowing around in the wind moving quickly up the mountainside. It was moving against the wind, however. Uphill. We had pulled off the road, at a lay-by, to look at the view of the city lights down below, when we noticed the shape jumping from tree to tree towards us. It was about two- or three-square feet in area, and a matte bluish white color. Like a large pillowcase or, like I said earlier, a shopping bag. No markings or features, not shiny at all, looked more like a strange cloth than a plastic. Both myself (American) and my fiancée (Irish) had a feeling that whatever it was, its intentions were not good.'

In Ireland there is a nineteenth-century tradition about the Pooka, a mischievous imp who runs around the countryside. The poet W.B. Yeats (1865-1939) knew, for example, of a Kilkenny pooka that 'takes the form of a fleece of wool, and at night rolls out into the surrounding fields, making a buzzing noise that so terrifies the cattle that unbroken colts will run to the nearest man and lay their heads upon his shoulder for protection.' There are a number of these rolling fleeces recorded in the tradition of not just Ireland, but of north-western Europe generally.

There are already some interesting statistics at the time of writing this book. 76% of the respondents were women and 24% men, and education is no indicator of whether or not you see a fairy: professors, scientists, doctoral students, engineers, psychologists have responded with their own experiences. Only 33% were Brits living in Britain, while most sightings were from the USA at close to 40% with New England and California as leading areas, but they were certainly not the only ones in the US. More significantly, only some 20% of the experiences dated to childhood and 80% to teenage years and above. At the time of writing this book, over 50% of participants were aged over 40. More importantly, 76% report seeing fairies 'regularly' and almost half of this number see them 'frequently'.

Modern fairy experiences are typically quick, out-of-the-corner-of-your-eye incidents. 35% lasted less than a minute, and many of these for mere seconds. But 9% reported fairy experiences lasting several hours. They can be hugely impactful. 24% say that the fairy sighting marked a turning point in their life. Among these respondents are an atheist gave up his objection to beliefs and a young woman dedicated her life to psychic questing.

27% of respondents described the fairies they experienced as unfriendly or even hostile. Only half of the experiences mention wings. Nor are modern fairies woodland creatures only. 5% of modern sightings took place in or around cars. A number of sightings even took place while people are watching television and one was spotted on the new Heathrow runway in London, England. Only for a small number of respondents, intoxicants were part of the sighting. Nor are sightings strictly experienced on one's own. In 23% of the cases, filings had two or more witnesses seeing the same fairy. Some of the most interesting cases were mothers and children. The Fairy Census—if not this volume—makes clear that new fairy lore continues to manifest and shape itself in the 21st century.

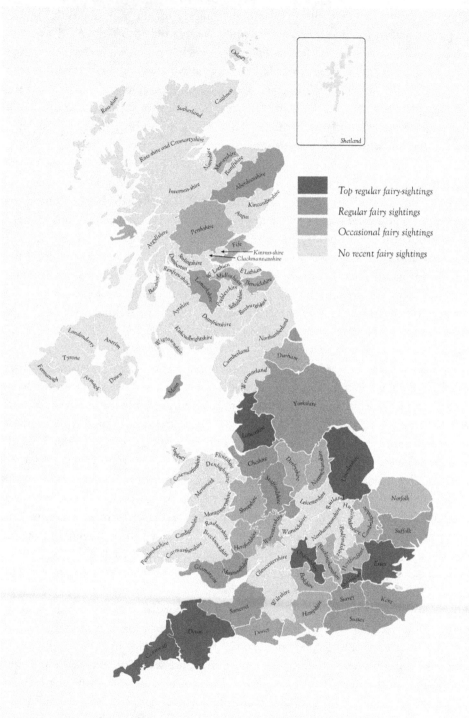

Top regular fairy-sightings

Regular fairy sightings

Occasional fairy sightings

No recent fairy sightings

20TH- AND 21ST-CENTURY FAIRY SIGHTINGS (detail, Great Britain)
Source, The Fairy Survey (organised from 2014 by Simon Young)

AIRY TRIBES

Channel Islands: The fairies of the Channel Islands include the pouques and the faiteaux. These island fairies are tied to local prehistoric monuments, which they both inhabit and guard. The Guernsey fairies particularly have a violent reputation: they are said to have slaughtered the first human inhabitants of the island in a dimly remembered invasion. The Jersey fairies are believed, meanwhile, to have escaped from human concerns to, of all places, the moon.

Cornwall: Across the Tamar the fairies are known as 'piskeys'. These fairy vagabonds steal babies, and even cows from human neighbours. There are also, in Cornwall, knockers, the spirits of the tin mines. The fairy miners warn those at work of coming disasters and help them to find rich seams. Knockers followed, in the nineteenth century, the Cornish tin men to the mines of America. There they would become the most famous of all New World fairies.

Cumbria: Like their Scottish cousins to the north, Cumbrian fairies often raise hell. It might be a question of sabotaging a local railway, highway robbery, or shooting, for sport, arrows at human and bovine neighbours. They dwell in the great free-standing rocks that pepper the Lake District; and, occasionally, too, in Cumbrian caves. One man was only saved from being dragged off a horse and into their lairs because he had, in his pocket, some pages from a Bible.

Devon: The pixies of Devon, as the fairies are known there, are typically found in the wilds where they dwell in rocks and caves like the Pixies' House. They are most famous for their tricks in pixy-leading. They disorient men or women and then take them on a merry dance through moors or woods until their human victims are ready to collapse from exhaustion. The only effective way to break this pixy-spell is to turn your pockets inside out and hope that the pixies will vanish.

Dorset: Fairies, goblins, pixies and poukes…. The fairy folk of Dorset go by many names. Legends tell how a number were driven out of the county by church bells: church bells act as fairy disinfectant. But the survivors get up to numerous tricks including pixy-riding, where they take out a horse in the night and have their fun racing it around the fields. The farmer knows his horse has been roughly used when he finds, in the morning, a sweating, restless steed with 'elfknots' woven into its mane.

East Anglia: Despite its lack of reputation as a home of fairylore, East Anglia should not be dismissed. Commonly known as farisees, ferriers or ferishers in Suffolk, Cambridgeshire and Essex, and more obscurely as 'hikey sprites' in Norfolk, the fairies of this region engage in an eclectic range of seemingly ever-changing activities. These range from the traditional act of stealing babies to the enticing of young women for marriage proposals through the elaborate giving of gifts. This range does however decline in the twentieth century, where traditional beliefs about fairies settle, becoming largely confined to the bread oven and the stable.

Ireland: The Irish fairies are known as the *sídhe*, the 'people of the mounds'. These powerful spirits kill or maim mortals who transgress their rules: don't build a house on a fairy track; don't fall asleep on a fairy fort; don't throw slops out on passing fairies; don't cut branches from a fairy tree.... Wily human neighbours, then, often leave small offerings for the *sídhe*, to keep them contented: including poteen and potatoes. Unusually Irish fairies are described as being of human size.

Isle of Man: There are a whole host of Manx fairies including the Buggane, the Fenodyree, the Glashtyn and the Mauthe Doog. Many accounts describe fairy music on the island including one horseman who heard, while crossing a river, one night, 'the finest Symphony' for three quarters of an hour. Manx fairies are clearly very demanding in musical terms. A human fiddler was left 'bruised and hurt' after playing tunes that offended the island fairies.

Orkney and Shetland: The trows are the fairy-folk of the northern isles. They trace their descent not to Celtic or Anglo-Saxon ancestors but to the trolls of Scandinavia: they arrived in Orkney and Shetland with the Vikings. They are known as 'the grey folk' and live in fairy mounds and have 'long, dark, bedraggled hair'. Curiously, when seen by women they walk backwards and they are notorious for stealing things left out in the open by human neighbours.

Scotland: Fairies in Scotland are known as: hill folk, siths, fanes, the seelie and unseelie courts and the klippe. They live under aristocratic rulers and the wild landscapes in which they dwell seem to make them fiercer than their English kin. The Scots, sensibly, seek magical charms to keep the fairies away including anything iron, four leafed clovers, and burnt bindweed. Most at risk are human babies, which the Scottish fairies sometimes kidnap, leaving a decrepit fairy in their place.

Sussex: In the South Downs live the pharisees. These Sussex fairies have, as elsewhere in Britain, both helped and plagued their human neighbours. The most famous encounter with these little people came when poet and visionary William Blake, walking in his garden one night, ran into a fairy funeral. 'I saw a procession of creatures, of the colour and size of green and grey grass-hoppers, bearing a body laid out on a rose-leaf.'

Wales: The Welsh fairies are the *tylwyth teg* ('the fair family') or *bendith eu mamau* ('their mother's blessing'). The mortal enemies of the non-conformist clergy, who came to dominate Wales in the eighteenth and nineteenth centuries, Welsh fairies are seen dancing at oaks, their favourite trees, but they also sneak into human houses during poor weather. Woe betide the owners if clean water is not left out for them to wash themselves and their young in!

Worcestershire: The most remarkable feature of fairy life in Worcestershire is the frequent presence of fairy lights or will-o'-the-wisps. There is also Poake, the great grandchild of mischievous Puck in *A Midsummer Night's Dream*, who Shakespeare heard of in his childhood in a neighbouring county, Warwickshire. Worcestershire fairies may also have been the inspiration behind J.R.R. Tolkien's hobbits.

Travelling Fairies

Canada: The Atlantic Coast of Canada has more fairies than any other region of North America. A melting pot of the fey from different region of Western Europe are to be found including: elves, lutins, leprechauns, co-pixies, little-johns, dalladadas, hollies, jackies, mickadenies and dawnies. By whatever name they go, their greatest sport is to mislead human victims in the swamps and woods of Newfoundland and Nova Scotia. Only some stale bread in your pocket will keep them at bay.

Irish America: Relatively few Irish fairies crossed the great water at the time of the Famine as 'the huddled masses' of Ireland fled from hunger. Some even blamed the potato famine on the Irish fairies. But occasional migrant fairies from the old country are glimpsed in the New World from Irish taverns in New Hampshire to Irish tenements in Dubuque, while the banshee, of course, continues to warn Irish families of impending deaths in the Americas.

New England: Some intrepid European fairies made their way over to New England. We have records of pixies (probably from Devon) and bogles (from Scotland) in Marblehead, Massachusetts, in the eighteenth century. These newcomers, though, had to come to terms with an older resident population of Indian fairies. Take, for example, the fearful Pukwudgy, who can transform himself into a forest animal and who lures travellers into swamps and over the edge of cliffs.

IOGRAPHIES

Dr Francis Young is a UK based historian and folklorist, who specialises in the history of religion and supernatural belief, monasticism, saints, the history of magic and ritual (especially exorcism), early modern Catholicism, fairy beliefs and European paganism. Two of his books were shortlisted for the Katharine Briggs Folklore Award, and he regularly appears in the media.

Francesca Bihet is a PhD student at the University of Chichester and grew up on island of Jersey. Her area of research covers folklore, fighting and fairies, and explores the changes in the theoretical treatment of fairies by The Folklore Society between 1878 and 1945.

Dr Jenny Butler is based in the Study of Religions Department at University College Cork (UCC) where she teaches on new religious movements and Western esotericism. She received her PhD in folklore and ethnology from UCC. She is a specialist on folk religion and researches traditions about non-ordinary beings, such as fairies. She has carried out ethnographic research in Ireland on beliefs and attitudes about fairies, as well as a comparative ethnographic study of fairylore and legends connected to the landscapes of Ireland, Iceland and Newfoundland.

Laura Coulson studies folklore, mythology and folklore and maintains a blog, faeryfolklorist.blogspot.co.uk.

Jo Hickey-Hall is a Bristol folklorist, researcher and social historian with a long-held interest in the relationship between supernatural experience, local landscape, and oral tradition in rural communities. Born in Jersey and of Irish parentage, she received a masters degree in history from the University of Bristol on *sídhe* in Medieval Irish literature. Her research project Modern Fairy Sightings collects and preserves contemporary experiences and explores the resistant cultural taboo surrounding disclosure at scarlettofthefae.com.

Jeremy Harte is a researcher into folklore and archaeology, with a particular interest in sacred space and tales of encounters with the supernatural. He graduated from Cambridge University and worked in the archaeological section of the Dorset County Museum in Dorchester before training as a curator. At present he runs the Bourne Hall Museum at Ewell in Surrey. Jeremy has written widely on folklore, industrial archaeology and local history in Dorset. He has written several books and his *Explore Fairy Traditions* was winner of the Katherine Briggs Folklore Award (2005).

Dr Ceri Houlbrook (EDITOR) is an Early-Career Researcher in folklore and history at the University of Hertfordshire. She received a PhD in archaeology from the University of Manchester on the folklore and history of coin-trees in Britain and Ireland (forthcoming as a monograph, *The Roots of a Ritual*, from Palgrave Macmillan) and co-edited *The Materiality of Magic* (Oxbow, 2015).

Ronald M. James studied at the Department of Irish Folklore at University College, Dublin, and at the University of Nevada, Reno, where he was adjunct faculty while also serving as the State Historic Preservation Officer. His dozen books on folklore, history, architectural history, and archaeology include his *The Folklore of Cornwall: The Oral Tradition of a Celtic Nation* (University of Exeter Press, 2018). In addition, he has served as chairman of the USA National Historic Landmarks Committee.

Pollyanna Jones is a writer based in Redditch whose special interest is local Worcestershire history. She is also more widely interested in folklore traditions of Britain and Ireland, mythology, folk magic, and maintains a blog, pollyanna-jones.co.uk.

Stephen Miller's research interests are Manx folklore and folk song in general, the histo-riography of British folkloristics, and the Scottish folklorists, William George Black and the Rev. Walter Gregor. He previously held a post at the Austrian Academy of Sciences and was an occasional lecturer at the University of Vienna.

Peter Muise has degrees in anthropology from Bates College and Brandeis University. He blogs weekly local folklore at newenglandfolk-lore.blogspot.com from his home near Boston, and makes frequent excursions in search of strange places and unusual stories. He is the author of *Legends and Lore of the North Shore* (2014) and has appeared on the History Channel's Mysteries At The Museum.

Mark Norman is a folklore researcher and author based near Dartmoor in Devon. He is widely interested in folklore and tradition, specialising in black-dog folklore, and is the author of *Black Dog Folklore* (2016), the first academic monograph on the subject. He contributes articles to a wide variety of magazines and websites, is a committee member of The Folklore Society, and the creator and host of thefolklorepodcast.com, a twice-monthly podcast.

Jacqueline Simpson is one of Britain's leading folklorists. She studied English literature and medieval Icelandic at Bedford College, University of London, and has been, at various times, editor, secretary, and president of The Folklore Society. She was appointed Visiting Professor of Folklore at the Sussex Centre of Folklore, Fairy Tales and Fantasy, at the University of Chichester (2010). She has a special interest in local legends—as opposed to international fairy tales—and has published collections of this genre from Iceland, Scandinavia in general, and England. Her books include *The Folklore of Discworld* (Corgi, 2009) with Terry Pratchett, *The Lore of the Land* (Penguin, 2005) with Jennifer Westwood, *Icelandic Folktales and Legends* (Penguin, 1971, 2004), and *A Dictionary of English Folklore* (OUP, 2000) with Steven Stroud. She lives in West Sussex.

Dr Richard Sugg has lectured on Renaissance literature at the universities of Durham and Cardiff. He has written articles on corpse medicine, cannibalism, vampires, witches, ghosts, poltergeists and mummies for newspapers and magazines, including the *Guardian, The Lancet,* and *Der Spiegel.* In 2011 he and Tony Robinson made corpse medicines on Saturday night television. He is the author of many books, including *Murder After Death* (Cornell University Press, 2007), *The Smoke of the Soul* (2013), *Mummies, Cannibals and Vampires* (2015), *A Century of Supernatural Stories* (2015), *A Century of Ghost Stories* (2017), and *A Singing Mouse at Buckingham Palace* (2017), and *Fairies: A Dangerous History* (Reaktion in May 2018). He lives in Cardiff.

Richard Suggett is Fellow of the Learned Society of Wales and Senior Investigator of Historic Buildings at The Royal Commission on the Ancient and Historical Monuments of Wales. He is author of *A History of Magic and Witchcraft in Wales* (2008) and lives in Aberystwyth.

Chris Woodyard is the author of the best-selling *The Victorian Book of the Dead,* a look at the popular and material culture of Victorian death and mourning as well as nine books on the ghostlore of Ohio and several collections of Victorian forteana. She took her degree in Medieval and Renaissance Studies from The Ohio State University. She blogs on Fortean topics, Victoriana, and the ephemera of fashion at hauntedohiobooks.com and mrsdaffodildigresses.wordpress.com.

Dr Simon Young (EDITOR) is a British historian based in Italy where he teaches in the University of Virginia Program in Siena. He has written several books (including *The Celtic Revolution,* Gibson Square, 2010) and published extensively on folk beliefs in such journals such as *Folklore, Béascna,* and *Supernatural Studies.* From 2014 to 2017 he ran The Fairy Census, the first-published scholarly survey of modern fairy sightings, gathering over five hundred records and their traditional and psychological determinants (fairyist.com/survey/).

FAIRY QUEENS AND PHARISEES

Sussex by Jacqueline Simpson

Since Victorian folklorists defined their field of study as being old traditions surviving unchanged in undisturbed rural communities, they concentrated their attention on the fringe areas of Britain, ignoring counties close to London as being too strongly influenced by industrialization, city life, and education. This no doubt explains why so little was written about Sussex lore, and why information about its fairies is scanty and scattered.

The Fairy Queen at Rye

The earliest mention of fairies in Sussex is to be found in the incomplete and somewhat confusing records of testimonies submitted at a trial held at Rye in 1607. Two women, Susan Swapper and Anne Taylor (also known by her maiden name of Anne Bennett), were accused of 'counselling with and feeding wicked spirits in order to obtain treasure', this being a capital offence under the Witchcraft Act of 1604. Susan was found guilty and sentenced to be hanged, but was in fact simply imprisoned; Anne's case was deferred and she was later further charged with causing the death of Thomas Hamon, Mayor of Rye, by witchcraft. She was acquitted of all charges in 1609, and Susan was released from prison in 1611.

The case has been thoroughly analysed by the historian Annabel Gregory on the basis of documents held in the East Sussex Record Office and her research into the social structure of the town;[1] she shows that the accusations were motivated by a local political rivalry, and that Anne Taylor was the primary target. Diane Purkiss, selecting different passages from the same documents, highlights their relevance to fairy beliefs.[2] There also exists a single page document, seemingly copied from the trial records and describing Susan Swapper's visions, which was published by G. Slade Butler, a believer in psychic phenomena.[3]

Susan tells how once, apparently a few years prior to her trial, as she was lying in bed at midnight, 'there appeared unto her four spirits in the likeness of two men and two women', whose looks and clothes she describes. Next night they came again, and one, a woman in a green petticoat, said, 'Sue, come and go with me or else I will carry thee.' At this, being frightened, she woke her husband, crying, 'Here is a thing that will carry me away'. He could see nothing, and the visions vanished. Next time they came, the woman in the green petticoat told Susan to go to her neighbour Anne Taylor, dig in her garden and plant sage there, 'and then you should be well'.

The following afternoon Susan and Anne started digging, but there is no more mention of planting sage; instead, they searched for a buried treasure which Anne thought she was heir to. They found nothing, but Susan recovered from her sickness. Some weeks later she saw the four spirits again, and they told her to take Anne to dig in a certain field, which had once belonged to her, where they would find a three-legged pot full of gold. There, Susan again saw one of her spirits, who pointed out a man in black and a woman in green walking in the field. Susan asked who they were, and the spirit replied that 'the woman is Queen of the Fairies, and that if she would kneel to her she would give her a living.' Susan refused to do so, the Queen vanished, and Susan went home very sick and frightened.[4] Later she told Anne, who declared that she herself had seen 'eighty or a hundred' such spirits, 'and they were all fairies'. However, at her trial Anne and her husband George gave a very different interpretation: they now said Susan's spirits were angels coming 'to cut off the wicked from the earth' and that 'at eleven months' end there should no man living be left to tread upon the Earth'.[5]

Obviously it would be safer for Anne, being on trial for witchcraft, to say Susan had received a religious message from angels rather than following instructions from fairies, and the vagueness of the terms 'spirit' and 'fairy' made the evasion possible. As Emma Wilby has pointed out:

[T]rying to make any hard and fast distinction between categories of spirits in early modern Britain is impossible…The term 'fairy', for example is a misleadingly broad generic term which, in the period, covered a wide range of supernatural entities.[6]

In Susan's own account, however, her visionary visitors have nothing angelic about them, nor do the angels of religious belief have any association with treasures hidden underground. But the fairies of early modern England did, as Diane Purkiss points out,[7] and especially the Fairy Queen. So strong was the belief that petty crooks could exploit it; in Hampshire in 1595 a thieving woman promised her dupes that the Queen of the Fairies would reveal a treasure buried in their garden.[8]

There is no indication whatsoever that Susan intended to exploit her visions in order to cheat or rob the Taylors; her crime, in the eyes of the law of 1604, was to 'consult… feede or rewarde any evill and wicked Spirit'. This she had undoubtedly done, and so had Anne Taylor. Susan told the court that once when she went to Anne's house, the latter:

> [D]id make four Nosegays and delivered them unto this examinate [i.e. Susan] to give unto the Four Fairies as she termed them, the which Nosegays she did lay in the window for that the familiars were not there at her coming. And afterwards they were taken away as she thinketh by the spirits, for that no body else could come there, the doors being shut.[9]

As for Anne, one of the witnesses reported a conversation in which she said she had once given Susan an apple to offer one of her spirits who was with child, 'and a piece of sugar too.'[10] In legal terms, 'spirits' and 'fairies' were simply 'familiars' and anyone who had dealings with them could be charged with witchcraft.

A Fairy Funeral

Our next Sussex fairy encounter could hardly be more different. It occurred one summer day sometime between 1800 and 1803, when the poet, artist and visionary William Blake was living in Felpham, and he later described the experience in conversation with a fellow guest at a dinner. He describes the following scene as he was purportedly sitting in his garden:

> There was great stillness among the branches and flowers, and more than common sweetness in the air; I heard a low and pleasant sound, and I knew not whence it came. At last I saw the broad leaf of a flower move, and underneath I saw a procession of creatures, of the colour and size of green and grey grasshoppers, bearing a body laid out on a rose-leaf, which they buried with songs, and then disappeared. It was a fairy funeral![11]

Here it is no longer a question of spirits which appear realistically human in their size and clothing, but of tiny, whimsical sprites such as Shakespeare described in *A Midsummer Night's Dream*—a concept which was highly popular among later poets and painters, and which persisted well into the twentieth century, e.g. in the 'Flower Fairy' paintings of Cicely Mary Barker. However, the notion that fairies occasionally die and are buried does have some basis in folklore, as is attested by Charlotte Latham for

Sussex:

> There is a tradition in the parish of Pulborough of a fairy's funeral, and the very
> place is pointed out to you. It is at the top of a green mound, known by the name
> of the Mount, and it would be hard to find a more fitting place for such a train
> to assemble at.[12]

Farmers and Fairies

Writing in 1854, the Sussex antiquarian and historian Mark Anthony Lower noted
that 'Several well-connected fairy stories were current, from ancient tradition,
towards the close of the last [i.e.eighteenth] century; and we are enabled, through the
aid of one who, himself a native of the South Downs, has now passed the "three-
score and ten" of life, to preserve one or two of these all but obsolete legends'—and
proceeds to give two of them 'as nearly as possible' in the words of his informant.[13]

This informant Lower identifies as 'Master Fowington', thus indicating (by using
'Master' rather than 'Mister') that Fowington was a working-class man; Lower renders
his words with spellings which attempt to convey a thick rural accent, and notes that
he lived in the Cuckmere Valley in East Sussex.

But Fowington did not claim personal knowledge of the two fairy encounters he
told of. One allegedly happened to his uncle's grandfather ('I've heerd uncle tell de
story dunnamany times'), and the other to 'an ol' brother of my wife's gurtgran'-
mother'. To set the events two (or three) steps backwards in time is a useful narrative
device, reminiscent of the notorious friend-of-a-friend who is the 'source' for so
many contemporary urban legends; it gives the teller the apparent support of an
informant who is close enough and respectable enough to be trustworthy, yet is not
actually available for questioning. The two stories themselves are given in minute
detail, both as regards the scene-setting and the dialogue, smoothly and fluently,
much as one imagines a confident raconteur would tell an anecdote he had repeated
many times over the years.

The first tale describes a friendly and mutually helpful encounter between
human and fairy. Fowington's great-great uncle, whose name was Chols [Charles]
Packham was out with a friend called Harry, ploughing a field near some medieval
ruins known as Burlow Castle. This was 'a hem [hell] of a place' for fairies, and
nobody liked to go near it after dark for fear of them. When the two men break
off their work for their mid-morning snack, Chols is frightened to hear 'a queer
sort of noise right down under the ground', and tells Harry (who has heard it
too) that he reckons it is a 'Pharisee'—for in Sussex dialect, as in some other
regions too, the plural of 'fairy' is 'fairises', and this became confused with the
similar-sounding Biblical 'Pharisees'. But Harry mocks him: 'Derea'nt no
Pharisees now. Dere was once—at Jerusalem; but dey was all full-growed people,
and has been dead hundreds o' years.'

The noise comes again, this time more plainly; it is a shrill little voice calling,

'Help, help, help!' Chols, though scared, asks what the matter is, and the voice replies, 'I've broken my peel, and I dunno what to do.' (A peel was a long-handled wooden shovel used for handling loaves in an oven; if it were broken, the bread could not be removed when cooked, and would eventually burn to ashes.) Chols says he will try to mend it, and a little peel 'no bigger than a bread-and-cheese knife' is thrust up through a crack in the ground. It is so small that he almost laughs, but keeps quiet, 'for he knowed of old how dangerous 'twas to offend any of dem liddle customers'. Using his knife and some tintacks Chols mends the peel and puts it back down the crack. Harry, meanwhile, had had his back to all this, and refused to believe it when Chols told him, for the parish clerk had assured him there were no Pharisees nowadays.

Next morning the two men are at work in the same field; at the mid-morning break Chols hears the little voice again, and finds a small bowl of very good liquor by the crack in the ground. He drinks it, and means to show Harry the bowl as proof, but it suddenly slips from his hands and is smashed, so Harry laughs at him again. Then comes the moral of the tale:

> But howsomever Harry got sarved out for bein' so unbeleivin', for he fell into
> a poor way, and couldn't goo to work as usual, and he got so tedious bad dat
> he fell away to mere skin and boän, and no doctors couldn't do him no good,
> and dat very day twelvemont he died, at de very same hour dat de Pharisees
> was first heerd, and dat he spoke agin 'em.[14]

The second of Master Fowington's tales must have been very widespread in Sussex, since not only was it recorded by Lower in the 1850s but versions are also given by W.D. Parish in his *Dictionary of Sussex Dialect* (1875) to illustrate the meaning of 'pharisee',[15] by Charlotte Latham in 1878,[16] and by Arthur Becket in 1909.[17] It tells of how fairies secretly help a farmer by working for him during the night, usually by thrashing or stacking his wheat, but in Parish's version by feeding corn to the carter's plough-horses; this continues until one night the foolish man, curious to know what is going on, hides and spies on them. The fairies are so small that he can hardly prevent himself laughing, and when he hears one shrill little voice exclaim, 'I'm sweating, Puck, are you sweating?', he quite loses control. Jumping up from his hiding place, he bellows (in Lower's version), 'I'll sweat you, you liddle rascals! What bisness ha' you got in my barn?'—or, in Parish's, 'Dannel ye! I'll make ye sweat afore I've done wid ye!' The result is of course disastrous. As the fairies rush out of the barn, the farmer feels a heavy blow on his head and falls senseless, and within a year he is dead; the carter's horses become so thin and poorly that he can't bear to be seen with them, and leaves the district.

Just how small these fairies are is indicated in Becket's account, where it is the effort of dragging a single ear of wheat which makes one of them sweat—an interesting detail, paralleled in Scandinavian versions,[18] with the explanation that this one ear is magically equivalent to the weight of the whole fine harvest which the farmer would have received, had he not lost it because of his rude laughter.

Puck and Dobbs

Nowadays we think of 'Puck' as the personal name of an individual fairy, as in Shakespeare's *Midsummer Night's Dream* and Kipling's *Puck of Pook's Hill*, but in Sussex dialect it is a word for any member of a particular type of fairy—the kind that lives in or near human habitations, can be helpful to humans, and is never more than mildly mischievous, as opposed to the more dangerous forest, river, or mountain fairies.

It is an intriguing word, of unknown origin; it has close analogues both in Celtic and Germanic languages, so its etymological development is unclear. It also has a range of meanings. In Old and Middle English it denoted a devil, or even Satan himself, as its Icelandic equivalent, *púki,* still does; but from Elizabethan times onwards, it merely meant a mischievous or tricksy fairy, especially one which bewilders travelers so they lose their way.[19] It survives in this sense in the dialect of various regions.

A number of Sussex place-names, past or present, appear to incorporate this word, though in some cases it might simply derive from the surname of a human landowner: Puke's Farm, Puckscroft, Puckroad or Puckride, Puckstye, Pook Pit, Pookhill.[20] Listing some of these names, A.A. Evans says they convey a sense of dread, referring to something eerie, uncanny, or evil, for a puck is a sinister goblin, bogie or elf, always out to make mischief.[21] However, traditional narratives such as Becket's prove that a puck can be helpful, provided nothing is done to annoy him. He thus belongs among the 'household fairies' known in most parts of Europe, for instance the German Kobold, the Danish Tomte, the Norwegian Nisse, and the Russian Domovoy.

The Pookhill mentioned above is near Alciston, but the same name is also attached to a spur of Downland visible from the windows of Rudyard Kipling's house at Burwash. Naturally, it is often assumed that this precise spot inspired the title of his children's book, *Puck of Pook's Hill* (published in 1906). However, there are indications that the name was once more widely used in the neighbourhood, for the census returns from the 1850s record 'Pook's Hill' as a district on the edge of the Weald near Burwash which supported several dwellings, one actually called 'Pook's Hill Cottage'.

It should also be noted that, in Sussex, there is a personal name for a helpful household fairy: Master Dobbs. The name is obviously related to the more common 'Dobby', used in Yorkshire and Lancashire for a harmless hobgoblin.

There was a common Sussex saying in the nineteenth century, complimenting a woman who had completed her work quickly and well: 'I see Master Dobbs has been helping you', while anyone who was having difficulty churning butter could induce him to help by repeating an old charm three times:

> Come, butter, come,
> Come, butter, come,
> Peter stands at the gate
> Waiting for a buttered cake,
> Come, butter come![22]

A more recent writer says she was once told that Dobbs used to wear a tattered old hat, so one night the farmer, grateful for his help, set out a fine new one for him, and waited to see what would happen. Dobbs took it eagerly, and cried out, 'New hat, new hat! Dobbs will do no more good!'—after which he never worked there again.[23] This is a version of 'The New Hat', a widespread international legend.[24] according to which, rather mysteriously, a household fairy will always depart if given an item of clothing.

Although the fairylore which survives in Sussex is only fragmentary, it conforms to story-patterns and motifs which are well known in other parts of England.

PUCKS AND LIGHTS

Worcestershire by Pollyanna Jones

Introduction

Worcestershire is to be found in the heart of the English Midlands. Gloucestershire stands to the south, Warwickshire to the east, Herefordshire to the west, Shropshire to the north-west, and Birmingham and Wolverhampton, some of the most urban areas in Britain, to the north. Crowned by the Malvern Hills, this is a land of rolling hills, ancient woodland, orchards, and pastoral landscapes with magnificent rivers: the Teme, Arrow, Avon, and the Severn wind through the county on their way to the Bristol Channel. Famed for Worcestershire sauce, fruit farming, asparagus, and Edward Elgar, many older customs have survived in Worcestershire. Agricultural festivals are still celebrated in villages and towns with May Day fetes, Morris dancing, mumming, mop fairs, and harvest festivals punctuating the year. It should come as no surprise, then, to learn that Worcestershire has a rich tradition of fairylore. Worcestershire fairies are, today, considered to be pretty little dainty beings, dressed in bright or woodland colours, and often said to have wings. This image owes more, though, to the Victorians and popular culture, than to older Midland traditions. In pre-twentieth-century accounts, Worcestershire's fairies often appeared, in fact, as lights. They proved also skilled shape-shifters, who led villagers astray.

Puck

Much of this mischief was attributed to Puck, or 'Poake' in Worcestershire dialect. Puck, Shakespeare's Robin Goodfellow, is one of the most ancient figures of British folklore and a central character in the region's fairylore. His name comes from *púce* in Old-English or perhaps *pwca* in Welsh, and he may be pre-Christian in origin.[1] So popular was Puck or Poake in Worcestershire that he features in many place-names. Take, for example, Upper Puck Hill and Lower Puck Hill in Acton Beauchamp, Puck Pit in Abberton, Upper and Lower Puck Close in Feckenham, Puck Meadow in Hallow, Puckley Green Farm in Martley, Puck Piece in Abbot's Lench, Puck Hall Field and Far Puck Hall Piece in Hartlebury, Pug's Hole Allotment in Bromsgrove Parish, Puck Hill in Himbleton, Puck Croft in Powick, and Puck Lane in Stoke Prior.[2]

Puck often plays the part of a trickster. Stories of Puck leading people off into ditches are common, particularly in the southwest of the county. Thanks to the work of Jabez Allies, a nineteenth-century Worcestershire folklorist (and the inspiration for much of this chapter), we have many examples from Alfrick, a village and civil parish in the shadow of the Malvern Hills.[3]

Allies wrote in 1852 that the rural folk of Alfrick were sometimes 'Poake ledden'; a term used for those waylaid in the night by a sprite. Encounters with Poake would usually follow a similar pattern. A carouser staggers back from a farmhouse or tavern late at night in the darkness. With his belly full of cider, he would then follow the ethereal lights of an *ignis fatuus* (meaning 'foolish fire'), and stray from the road. Elsewhere known as a Jack-o'-lantern or Will-o'-the-wisp, these lights were believed to be Poake himself or Poake carrying a lantern. The victim would next be taken on a merry dance across the fields, before they came a-cropper in a marsh or pond. Poake would then disappear laughing.[4] We can certainly imagine how being 'Poake ledden' would be widely used as an excuse employed by drunken husbands after collapsing in a ditch after a night of drinking!

These lights may sound like the product of too much alcohol, but there are, certainly, numerous accounts of them from the region. A witness submitted a statement to Allies in February 1834:

> One of the cottagers, named Thomas Booth, of the age of 67 years, then residing at Old Storage (Modern Old Storridge), in Alfrick, and who had lived there about the last 34 years, told me that he had frequently seen 'Hobany's Lantern,' in the course of his life, at Alfrick, Knightwick, Lulsey and other parts. That it appeared after wet weather, in boggy sour places, in the winter season. That the last time he saw it was in December, 1833, when it appeared in a damp place on the top of Storage Common, at about thirty yards distance from him, and that he looked at it for about three minutes. That it moved up and down for some time, and then fell to the ground and vanished away. That he had seen it most frequently in two meadows, one called Lamaste Meadow, and the other Pivany Meadow, at the north-

west side of the brook at the bottom of Old Storage, near the Mill Pond, and sometimes at the boggy parts in the woods at Storage. That the first time he saw it was a great many years ago, about midnight in some coarse ground called the Stocks Gorse, at Raffnal's Green, in Lulsely, where he went to fetch home the wagon-horses to the Upper House. That it appeared to rise out of the ditch, and pass across before him and the horses, into the copse, at about eight yards distance, which frightened the horses as well as himself. That he, at the time, was satisfied it could not be a person with a lantern, because it went so swift, and also because it did not cast any shadow as it passed the trees. That he mentioned the circumstance at the Upper House, the next morning, when he was told that he had seen a 'Jack o' Lantern.' That upon another occasion, namely about eighteen years ago, at a boggy spot in Pivany Meadow, he was within three of four yards of a 'Jack o' Lantern,' and thought he smelt something like sulphur, but it immediately afterwards flitted away, and he saw no more of it. That the light of them is just in appearance, like, and about as strong, as the light from a small horn lantern, such as are used in stables, and by country people. That sometimes they appear near to the beholder, and then, in the twinkling of an eye, at a considerable distance. That at other times they will stay for some time near one place, and flit up and down and also move about horizontally, like as if a person was looking about for something with a lantern.[5]

Allies lists several witness statements. He even observed the lights himself, on occasion, over the winter of 1839. He described how:

The light of this *ignis fatuus*, or rather these *ignes fatui*, was very clear and strong, much bluer than that of a candle, and very like that of an electric spark, and some of them looked larger and as bright as the star Sirius; of course, they look dim when seen in ground fogs....[6]

These lights have been observed by separate witnesses in other parts of the county. Interestingly they continue to be seen today. Take this 2003 sighting from Rubery:

We were walking through the old hospital grounds, before Joseph Sheldon Hospital had been knocked down. You know, where the cinema is now, in the area called Great Park. It was about 8:00 pm on an Autumn evening. It was dark, but a fairly mild night; cool but not frosty. The weather was damp, but there was no mist or rain. We was [sic] walking along the path from Rubery Lane towards Rubery town itself through grassland. We had reached a spot on the path near the river Rea, when we saw it. It was ball-shaped, misty, and glowed with a white light. It appeared on the path, at about head-height and hung in the air, perfectly still. It didn't move. Naturally, it was quite a worrying sight and we didn't know what to think of it. We just turned around and walked back the other way![7]

There are many alternative names for the *ignis fatuus*, one is the Pinkett. This fairy (if it can be called that) dwells in the Badsey area, in the bountiful Vale of Evesham where much of Worcestershire's fruit and vegetables are grown. The Pinkett is a type of elf-fire or a Will-o'-the-wisp: it is quite possibly linked to Pinck who served Queen Mabin in a poem by Drayton.[8] Whilst most *ignes fatui* are referred to as being male, the Pinkett is typically referred to as a 'she'. Place-names that might be relevant here include Pinkett Coppice near Wickhamford, and Pinkett Street at Badsey. Roughly nineteen miles north-west of Badsey in the city of Worcester, there is also a Pinkett Street. On this evidence the Pinkett was once known more widely.

Ignis fatuus is also known as 'Hobberdy's Lantern' (see the account above), 'Hobany's Lantern', or simply 'Hob and his Lantern'. Worcestershire dialect often includes Hob in its family of fairies. Hob is as mischievous with his lights as Puck, but while Puck is associated with graceful fairies, Hob is earthy and grotesque in appearance.[9] Hob, like Puck, often appears in Midland place-names, including, in Worcestershire, Hob Hill, Hob Meadow, Hob Rough, and Little Hob Hill near Portway. Then there is also Hob Moor in Chaddesley Corbett, Hob's Hole in Offenham, Hobden in Stoke Prior, Hob Well in Great Malvern, and Hob Acre in Frankley (not to be confused with 'New Frankley' in Birmingham). On the northern fringe of the Cotswolds, there is the small village of Abbot's Lench tucked within the pretty hillside region of the Lenches. A local name for this village was Habbe or Hob Lench.[10]

A thirty-year-old J.R.R. Tolkien visited a family farm in Worcestershire in 1923 whilst recovering from a bout of pneumonia. Owned by his maternal aunt, Jane Neave, Dormston Manor Farm was known jokingly to the family as 'Bag End' as the lane was a 'cul-de-sac' (from the French for 'bottom of the bag'). The local folklore caught his attention and Tolkien decided to write his aunt a story about elusive beings that lived in the hedgerows there: the house name certainly later appeared as Bilbo Baggins' home.[11] A few years later, Tolkien sent her a first edition of *The Hobbit*; Bilbo can perhaps then be called a Worcestershire fairy!

Puck is occasionally described as whickering or neighing, whilst in horse form, to lead horses into bogs and marshes, or to confuse farmers into wandering into the mire in search of a distressed animal that simply isn't there. Such mischief is mentioned by Shakespeare in *A Midsummer Night's Dream*,[12] where Puck describes some of his pranks to a fairy friend:

> I am that merry wanderer of the night.
> I jest to Oberon and make him smile
> When I a fat and bean-fed horse beguile,
> Neighing in likeness of a filly foal

The *Dream* was probably written in 1595 or 1596 and Shakespeare arguably took his fairylore from nearby Warwickshire, suggesting that such shape-shifting beliefs have long been held in the English Midlands.[13]

The names 'púca' (Old English) and 'pwca' (Welsh) also take us back into the past. Welsh legends (and had they survived we might surmise Anglo-Saxon legends) describe Pwca taking many forms including horse, cat, rabbit, goat, goblin, and dog.[14] Of course, not only fairies but ghosts, witches, and even doomed souls can, according to tradition shape shift. The village of Alfrick, for example, which was so carefully studied by Jabbez Allies, has its own legend about a shape-shifting black dog.[15] Puck does not seem to have a particular animal guise in Worcestershire, though the braying of an ass, the neighing of a horse, the hooting of an owl, or bleating of a lamb, were traditionally interpreted as his laughter.[16]

Fairies and Fairy Superstitions

Perhaps it is the Malvern waters, but there certainly seems, in supernatural terms, to be something special about Alfrick. As one of Worcestershire's more rural areas, it was of particular interest to Jabez Allies, who saw it as a repository of traditional lore. To this day the area is largely unspoiled, with much of the land there protected as a Site of Specific Scientific Interest. There are many local legends, and Alfrick has the reputation of being one of the most haunted villages in Worcestershire. No wonder, with frequent sightings of the magical lights described above. It was commonly believed that the region was fairy-plagued, with Alfrick being 'elf-reich' or fairy land.[17] The district's name is, as it happens, more likely to mean 'dwelling (or farm) of Ealhred', after an Anglo-Saxon landowner. However, the area features delightfully named spots such as 'Fairy's Cave', in a ferny woodland gorge in the Knapp and Papermill Nature reserve.

It is a great pity that the rest of the county was not subject to as thorough a study as Alfrick, as much of Worcestershire's pre-twentieth-century fairylore has now been forgotten. So much of our fairylore is actually relatively modern. One superstition likely to have originated in the romantic nineteenth century was the idea that drifting seeds of rosebay willow herb and thistle are fairies floating in the breeze.[18] Catch one, make a wish and let it go, and the wish *might* just come true. This is charming but probably no more traditional than the fairy doors that have appeared, in the last years, on trees throughout the county.[19]

There are some older beliefs in Worcestershire, though. Flint arrow-heads, for instance, were thought to be elf-shot: in fact, Anglo-Saxon evidence for this belief may come from Worcestershire.[20] The elves used these shots to lame a horse, or to cause a traveller to suffer from stitch or even illness.[21] Certain fossil outcrops were seen as petrified fairy gardens, as with sites in Martley and around sedimentary areas near the Malvern Hills, where outcrops of limestone are filled with fern-like shapes. Old coins, dug up, were relics of the fairies, as across the border in Bolitree, and Kenchester in Herefordshire, imperial coins from Roman Ariconium and Magna Castra were treasured as the currency of these magical creatures.[22] Coins discovered in Worcestershire are said to be 'pennies from heaven' or 'fairy money'; especially if these coins disappear soon after discovery. The fairies had simply taken them back! I wonder whether the Tooth Fairy doesn't have links with this belief, as money left in exchange for a tooth 'magically appears' in the morning under a child's pillow.

Bad language is, to this day, to be avoided in a Worcestershire household, and arguing and discord in the home is bound to upset the fairies. Midland fairies do seem to like their peace and quiet. Sure signs that they have been angered include mysterious and sudden breakages, milk turning sour, food going off quickly, and a general run of bad luck. Likewise the mysterious loss of shiny objects, or objects that disappear and then reappear in the same place might also be a clue that fairies are about. Bread dipped in milk or honey is offered by some to appease the fairies in the hopes that the missing item is returned soon, and also to offer apologies in instances where the fairies have been offended.[23]

Circles of mushrooms or toadstools are very common in the county, and these are still called fairy rings. Such rings may be linked with stories of fairies dancing in a circle under the light of the moon; these mushrooms and toadstools (which often appear overnight) were perhaps believed to track fairy footfalls. It is considered very bad form to break a fairy ring; seven years of bad luck await anyone who kicks fungi in Worcestershire. Many people will avoid walking inside fairy rings, some believing them to be portals to another world.[24]

Fairy-Human Relations

Fairies and humans sometimes live in harmony, one helping the other. Take, for example, the fairies of Osebury Rock, sometimes called Rosebury Rock, located in Lulsley near the Malvern Hills. Now protected as a Site of Special Scientific Interest, the Rock has long been famous as a haunt of fairies, sometimes known in Worcestershire dialect as 'pharises' (pronounced 'faira-zees'). They dwell in a cave, which is also known as the 'Witches' Oven', overlooking the banks of the river Teme. A local legend describes how a man and boy ploughing a field near to this cave went to the aid of one of the fairies in his hour of need:

> Once upon a time, as a man and boy were ploughing in an adjoining field, they heard an outcry in the copse on the steep declivity of the rock; and upon there going to see what was the matter, they came up to a fairy, who was exclaiming that he had lost his pick, or pick-axe; this, after much search, the ploughman found for him; and thereupon, the fairy said they would go to a certain corner of the field wherein they had been ploughing, they would get their reward. They accordingly went, and found plenty of bread and cheese, and cider, on which the man feasted heartily; but the boy was so much frightened that he would not partake of the repast.[25]

This wasn't the only human neighbour to have had a close encounter with the pharises. Another account describes how a fairy came out into the field to find a ploughman. Again, he asked for help. Perhaps with the first pair being so kind, the fairies grew bolder with the locals? The fairy is said to have exclaimed, 'Oh, lend a hammer and nail, which we want to mend our pail.' Fairy-human relations were, according to such tales, amicable. If a human woman was to break her wooden peel—a kind of shovel used for baking bread—she would leave the damaged tool in the Fairies Cave at Osebury Rock where the fairies would mend it for her. This, it might be noted, is a reversal of the more widespread British legends where humans mend fairy peels.[26]

Upton Snodsbury, near Worcester, is another village where there were stories of cordial human-fairy relations. A fairy had apparently broken his chair or 'bilk':

As a countryman was one day working in a field in Upton Snodsbury, he all of a sudden heard a great outcry in a neighbouring piece of ground, which was followed by a low, mournful voice, saying 'I have broke my bilk, I have broke my bilk; ' and thereupon the man picked up the hammer and nails which he had with him, and ran to the spot from whence the outcry came, where he found a fairy lamenting over his broken bilk, which was a kind of cross-barred seat; this the man soon mended, and the fairy, to make him amends for his pains, danced round him till he wound him down into a cave, where he was treated with plenty of biscuits and wine; and it is said that from thenceforward that man always did well in life.[27]

Scary Fairies and the Wild Hunt
Whilst fairies seem to live quite happily with humans, there have been instances when they object to our activities. This account from Inkberrow, near the Warwickshire border, describes how the fair folk sabotaged efforts to build a church in their territory:

In days of yore, when the church at Inkberrow was taken down and rebuilt upon a new site, the fairies, whose haunt was near the latter place, took offence at the change, and endeavoured to obstruct the building by carrying back the materials in the night to the old locality. At length, however, the church was triumphant, but for many a day afterwards the following lament is said to have been occasionally heard:
                'Neither sleep, neither lie,
                For Inkbro's ting tangs hang so nigh.'[28]

There are many British stories where fairies and other magical folk are disturbed or even driven away by the sound of church bells. Indeed this theme is common throughout Europe; in Scandinavia, for example, trolls are similarly believed to flee from church bells.[29]

Suckley, near the Herefordshire border, is home to a terrifying breed of fairy known as a whistler. Local folklore describes them as heralds of doom. These beings fly overhead at night and are heard making whistling noises in the air. This statement was recorded by Allies in the nineteenth century:

I have been informed by Mr J. Pressdee, of Worcester, that, when a boy, he used to hear the country people talk a good deal about the 'Seven Whistlers,' and that he frequently heard his late grandfather, John Pressdee, who lived at Cuckold's Knoll, in Suckley, say that oftentimes, at night, when he happened to be upon the hill by his house, he heard six out of the 'Seven Whistlers' pass over his head, but that no more than six of them were ever heard by him, or by any one else, to whistle at one time, and that should the seven whistle together the world would be at an end.[30]

So far, none have heard all seven at once, but I imagine that many a child has been kept awake at night by the eerie sound of whistling in the wind near Cuckold's Knoll.

The Seven Whistlers are reminiscent of a wider European belief in a spectral or fairy hunt. Also known as the Wild Hunt, lore around this supernatural host is common across Britain and further afield. In some instances, the hunt is led by a deity: examples include the Germanic Woden or the Celtic Gwyn ap Nudd with his fairies. Others are led by cursed humans, such as Eadric the Wild of Long Mynd in Shropshire.[31]

One such hunt in Worcestershire was led by a certain Callow of Feckenham. His territory was the hamlet of Callow Hill, adjacent to Hunt End, presumably the boundary of his hunting grounds. Feckenham Forest was once a huge wooded area, which provided a rich hunting ground for humans and fairy folk alike. Whilst humans found their sport in hunting animals, fairies would find their sport in claiming souls, denying them a place in heaven. Some believed that if an unbaptised child died they would be claimed by the fairies and become elves themselves.[32]

Whether Callow's hunt carries him farther afield, we do not know. However, a place named Callow's Grave is marked on maps near to Tenbury Wells, in the far west of the county near the border with Shropshire. There may also be some crossover with legends of Herne the Hunter, recorded by Shakespeare in *The Merry Wives of Windsor*, as Herne too was said to roam the forest of Feckenham. It is not clear whether there is any common superstition about the consequences of witnessing Callow's hunt, though another Wild Hunt over the Lickey Hills near Rednal is said to be a portent of death. Harry-ca-Nab, the cursed huntsman of Halesowen, rides a winged horse or wild bull over the Lickey hills on stormy nights, and woe betide anyone who sees him.[33]

And are the fairies quite gone from Worcestershire? A 2006 sighting from Bretforton, near to Evesham, suggests not. I collected one report from two witnesses who described how they were enjoying a pint of ale at the Bretforton Inn one summer afternoon when they saw something most unusual. Gazing through the pub's small orchard towards the end of the garden, they were astonished to witness a small creature, about the size of a human toddler, with gangly limbs, climb over the fence at the bottom of the orchard and then disappear into the field beyond. They referred to it as a 'goblin'. Its skin was nut brown and the creature was quite naked. Neither man had drunk more than two pints and both seemed quite sure of what they had seen...
[34] Fairies may or may not dwell in Worcestershire, but there is no question that people still see them.

3

PIXIES AND PIXY ROCKS

Devon by Mark Norman and Jo Hickey-Hall

Introduction

The wild and rugged landscape of Devon, in south-western England, provides a perfect setting for fairy beliefs. Even in the fast-paced twenty-first century, time seems to pass more slowly amongst the desolate moors and verdant valleys. It is no surprise that there's such a wealth of folk- and fairylore here, weaving curious patterns through land and time. In Devon tradition there is little attempt to split fairies into types: fairy, pixie, imp, sprite or elf. All become interchangeable. Though note that this may not have always been the case; in the mid-nineteenth century, for example, a record of a war between fairies and pixies (also known as piskeys) was reported![1]

The origins of the fairy races in Devon are impossible to trace today. However, various theories have been put forward. The late and great Devon folklorist Theo Brown made a few promising suggestions: that they were the remains of some form of prehistoric race (or alternatively the ghosts of the same); or that they were a diminished form of a pagan deity.[2] Thinking of the prehistoric race, the term 'pixie' has been tentatively connected to the Picts of northern Britain.[3]

The proof of the popularity of pixies is there in the Devon landscape. There is, for example, the tale that a member of the Elford family, who lived in the moorland town of

Tavistock, managed to hide from Cromwell's troops in a Pixie House (a fissure), which is still visible on Sheepstor. There is another 'Pixie's House' located at Chudleigh Rocks—known instead as the 'Pixie's Hole' in 1812[4]—though in this case the name has varied slightly over time. A small race were said to have lived here at one time, also using a hollow inside the rocks which became known as the 'Pixies' Parlour'.

Lady Rosalind Northcote told a story of a gamekeeper who lived in this area with his wife and two children. The eldest was said to have become lost one day and could not be found despite a search of many days by her family, and local residents with dogs. She was eventually discovered by two men, naked, but quite happily playing with her toes. It was assumed that she had been abducted by the pixies but subsequently returned: the child presumably got lost and the pixy stories were wheeled out to explain the event.[5]

Back on Dartmoor, it was even claimed that the pixies attended church. A rock, long since blasted, was said, by Anna Eliza Bray, a mid-nineteenth-century writer with an interest in south-western folklore and traditions, to have been named Belfry Rock or Church Rock. The name came from the fact that, on a Sunday, if you placed your ear to the rock it was said that you would be able to hear the sound of bells calling out for service. The rock became known as Pixies' Church because of this phenomenon, which we must imagine was due to some natural echoing of the sound from Tavistock church itself: the bells were said to ring at the same time.[6]

To this day, in Ottery St Mary in east Devon, there is a calendar custom which commemorates an old tale concerning pixies, bell-ringing and the landscape. In this case, however, the pixies were responsible for abducting the bell-ringers, not ringing the bells themselves! The story allegedly dates back to 1454 when Bishop Grandisson was said to have had a set of bells commissioned for a newly constructed church in the town. The pixies, concerned that the new church and bells would mean an end to their rule of the area, set out to divert the monks who were bringing the bells back from Wales where they had been constructed.[7]

Their plan ultimately failed and the pixies were said to have fled from Ottery St Mary to a local sandstone cave which became known as the Pixies' Parlour. The legend is still celebrated and every year, on the Saturday closest to Midsummer's Day, the local cubs and brownies dress as pixies and 'abduct' the town's bell-ringers (or in some years, the town council). A reconstruction of the Pixies' Parlour is built in the town square and abductees are imprisoned within it, before being rescued by the vicar. Fairy folklore is clearly alive and kicking in contemporary Devon.[8]

Pixy-Led

The pixies are most famous for pixy-leading, tempting travellers astray. The earliest pixy-leading story concerns Sir John Fitz, an astrologer and astronomer who lived at Fitzford House in Tavistock. Fitz and his wife were said to have been pixy-led whilst riding on Dartmoor and were saved only by finding a natural spring, the water of which both provided sustenance and appeared to restore their sense of direction. Sir John Fitz built a memorial in stone over the well around 1568 in order to show his gratitude. The location is still known as Fitz's Well.[9]

The possibility of being 'pixy-led'—as reported by Sir John Fitz—caused great unease among locals and travellers alike. This is illustrated in antiquarian Thomas Westcote's historical and topographical *A View of Devonshire* in the early seventeenth century, where the author quite routinely used the expression, 'I shall… lead you in a pixy-path by telling an old tale…'[10] A quarter of a millennium later, being pixy-led evidently remained a real risk. A surgeon based in Kenton wrote to the *Exeter Mercury* in 1883 to describe the local residents' 'hidden but cherished opinions'.

> The first hint I received that the superstition of the old times lingered in the place was the discovery that messengers, sent to summon me at night, would never come by a certain lane, called the Kenn-lane, about a mile in length, but travelled by a rougher and more hilly road. I was told that the lane was 'Pixie led', that a man returning at night to his home lost himself at the beginning of the lane and found himself sitting under the hedge at the end of it, and that he must have been carried by the Pixies rapidly through it.[11]

One might offer alternative explanations as to how a man could lose his way home late at night, and no doubt the account amused many readers of the time. Yet, this type of fairy enchantment was still believed locally in the late nineteenth century.

Pixy Tales

There are many Devon pixy tales, which have been handed down to us. One story, known as 'The Fairy Ointment', has a nurse in Tavistock, who was very fond of money, being taken by the fairies to tend to a fairy mother and her newborn child. In the course of her work she was given ointment to rub on the baby's eyes in a bottle, which she inadvertently takes back to the human world after her year of work with the fairies. She ends up, in a twist recounted in other chapters, putting some on her left eye, with which she is then able to view the fairy realm. However, the fairy king discovers this fact and blinds her in the offending eye for her disobedience. Here the pixies punish the curious.[12]

The fashion for collecting native folklore in rural communities reached a peak in the mid-nineteenth century. One of these collectors was Anna Eliza Bray, referred to above. The following story, preserved by Bray, has a fairy deployed to make a moral point.

> Two serving damsels of this place declared, as an excuse, perhaps, for spending more money than they ought upon finery, that the pixies were very kind to them. In the house where they worked near Tavistock, they had discovered that silver would be dropped overnight into a bucket of clean water, if they were careful to leave this in the chimney corner before they went to bed. But one night they forgot to put the bucket out, and the pixies came rustling indignantly into their room. The girls woke up and heard what was going on; one of them thought they should get up immediately and set the hearth in order, but the other yawned lazily and said they

should not stir themselves, not for all the pixies in Devon. Well the hard-working girl got up, and filled the bucket, where a handful of silver pennies were found waiting for her in the morning; but the lazy one was afflicted with a lameness in her leg, and this lasted for seven years.[13]

This is a nice glimpse of two young women working in an industrial boomtown, when access to wealth and success, it seems, went hand in hand with supernatural beliefs.

Back on the moor, William Crossing, another nineteenth-century folklorist, had 'gathered from the peasantry' a collection of pixy stories.[14] One example in *Tales of the Dartmoor Pixies* (1890) describes how a labourer had begun ploughing at dawn and by breakfast time had grown hungry. As he worked the field back and forth he came closer to an ancient granite standing stone.

As the ploughman passed near this rock on his way across the field, he was startled at hearing voices, apparently proceeding from beneath it. He listened, and distinctly heard one, in a louder tone than the rest, exclaim, 'The oven's hot!' 'Bake me a cake, then,' instantly cried the hungry ploughman, in whose mind the very mention of an oven had conjured up thoughts of appetising cheer; 'Bake me a cake, then,' He continued the furrow to the end of the field, when, turning his plough, he set out on his return journey. When he approached the rock, what was his surprise and delight at seeing, placed on its surface, a nice cake, smoking hot. He knew at once that this was the work of the obliging little pixies, who evidently had a resort under the rock, and who had taken pity upon his hunger, and provided him with a morning meal.[15]

Compared to the Tavistock servants' tale, it is a playful anecdote.

In another of Crossing's tales, brother and sister Jimmy and Grace Townsend were said to live in a cottage on the moor. Jimmy was a sociable sort of fellow, 'not particularly fond of labour', and though Grace took care of all the housework, he maintained to friends that he 'lived wi' a pisgie'. He blamed her for all manner of life's setbacks and vowed that a pixie had taken her place in the cradle as a baby, 'vor her frawed up sich across tempered little mortal as you ever zeed, an' whoever's got anything to do wi' her will sure to come to some harm.' Though his companions did not share his view, Jimmy could not let go of his convictions, even when Grace left home to get married. In fact, Jimmy continued to blame Grace for his brother-in-law's misfortunes.[16]

The story illustrates how belief in fairies provided for some control over family members. Supernatural anecdotes were still an important part of rural home life in the early nineteenth century. Crossing's description of fairy tale telling in a typical Dartmoor family of 1830 is rendered in modern terms by folklorist, Jeremy Harte.

As the family sit round the hearth, talk turns to the pisgies—"they've a got their own ways 'bout everything an' us can't understand mun" The children sit wide-eyed and scared; the others are more inclined to say that it is all stories, but when a sound is heard outside they all jump, and as the man of the house goes to the door his wife looks troubled. But no, it is only a neighbour who has been pixyled on the moor. By now the servant girl is quite worried, and the farmer's son insists on taking care of her, and brings her to his side, behind the settle.[17]

Modern Belief

When did belief in pixies die out? In 1868, fieldwork was undertaken by the Devonshire Association to try to ascertain the extent of pixie-lore in the county. In the Association's *Reports and Transactions* we can read how, rather than making the life of country folk difficult, Devonshire pixies were busy assisting those whom they favoured. In the mid-nineteenth century one north Dartmoor yeoman discovered flail-wielding pixies threshing corn in his barn. Making their escape, one tripped and was imprisoned for some time in the farmer's lantern.[18] The farmer's brother reported this to the Devonshire Association in 1868 in good faith, noting his brother's take on the pixy helpmates:

'Niver did I zee zuch drashers as they was. They were talking and laughing among themselves as busily as they were working. One said to another, I twit (sweat), don't you twit?'[19]

On another occasion, Association Members found one old lady, on the edge of Dartmoor, who had seen a pixie in her youth:

'I did zee one once, when I was a little maid—I did zee a pixie man'. Claiming that he was about eighteen inches tall, she described his dress as '...a little odd hat, and a pipe in his mouth, and he had an old jug in his hand—not like the jugs us uses now... I never zeed but that one, and I du think they've gone to some other part of the world'.[20]

Her belief that the pixies had moved on and that they inhabited another place was shared by many locals. In this way they relinquished their faith in Dartmoor fairies (perhaps for shame of ridicule from outsiders), without denying their existence altogether. While belief had remained strong up until the mid-part of the nineteenth century, it then waned. This was aided in no small part by the sensationalist treatment of many folklore subjects in the Victorian age, which rendered them so implausible as to be embarrassing.

By the end of the 1800s, belief in the fairy folk was considered to be something found exclusively in rural areas and among the 'uneducated'. Writing in *The Windsor Magazine*, described at the time as 'an illustrated monthly for men and women', Archibald S. Hurd suggested that, 'though the children of Dartmoor are still ruddy of cheek, strong of limb, and unkempt, no self-respecting boy or girl believes to-day in Pixyland, that unknown country beneath the bogs where the fairies hatch their schemes of good or ill'.[21] This was in 1896. However, the following year Mrs G. M. Herbert had an experience, which she, thirty years later, recalled in the *Reports and Transactions of the Devonshire Association* in these words:

> Though I am a grown woman with three sons, I still firmly believe in pixies and in
> fairies. When a child of seven I saw a pixie, and in recent years I have been 'pisky-led'
> on Dartmoor. I saw the pixie under an overhanging boulder closer to Shaugh Bridge
> (on the southern edge of Dartmoor) in the afternoon. I cannot say more definitely as
> at to the time, but I remember running in to my mother after an afternoon walk and
> saying I had seen a pixie—and being laughed at. This was in 1897. It was like a little
> wizened man about (as far as I can remember) 18 inches or possibly 2 feet high, but
> I incline to the lesser height. It had a little pointed hat, slightly curved to the front a
> doublet, and little short knicker things. My impression is of some contrasting colours,
> but I cannot remember what colours, though I think they were blue and red. Its face
> was brown and wrinkled and wizened. I saw it for a moment and it vanished. It was
> under the boulder when I looked, and then it vanished.[22]

People continued to report fairy encounters throughout the twentieth century. Many of
these took place in Devon, and Dartmoor in particular continues to provide a rich
backdrop for fairy sightings. An example was given by a Mrs Violet Tweedale, a noted
mystic, and recorded in Sir Arthur Conan Doyle's book *The Coming of Fairies.*

> One summer afternoon I was walking alone along the avenue of Lupton House,
> Devonshire. It was an absolutely still day—not a leaf moving, and all Nature seemed
> to sleep in the hot sunshine. A few yards in front of me my eye was attracted by the
> violent movements of a single long blade-like leaf of a wild iris. The leaf was swinging
> and bending energetically, while the rest of the plant was motionless. Expecting to see
> a field-mouse astride it, I stepped very softly up to it. What was my delight to see a
> tiny green man. He was about five inches long, and was swinging back-downwards.
> His tiny green feet, which appeared to be green-booted, were crossed over the leaf,
> and his hands, raised behind his head, also held the blade. I had a vision of a merry
> little face and something red in the form of a cap on the head. For a full minute he
> remained in view, swinging on the leaf. Then he vanished. Since then I have several
> times seen a single leaf moving violently while the rest of the plant remained
> motionless, but I have never again been able to see the cause of the movement.[23]

In November 1930, meanwhile, a seemingly well-informed Devonian, Paddy Sylvanus,
wrote to the *Morning Post* in response to an article by a Mr Park, which sought to invalidate
Dartmoor superstitions.

> I have lived for ten years on the borders of Dartmoor. I could and would introduce
> Mr James P. Park to a bridge that cannot be crossed at midnight; to a dell where fairies
> are still seen to dance; to a dangerous locality where an earthbound spirit dwells,
> causing terrible accidents; (and) to a well-known and universally respected lady who

has seen a pixie and heard the wish-hounds. I could take him to visit a witch in her cottage, at the risk of being overlooked.[24]

The impression was that Devon fairies were very much alive and well. I wonder if Mr Park ever took Mr Sylvanus up on his offer? The public were certainly interested. Imagine the satisfaction of the editor of *John O'London's Weekly*, a literary magazine, when a request for first-hand fairy accounts was answered by Joyce Chadwick. Her letter, which was published in March 1936, describes a very matter-of-fact observation of a 'pisky'.

A few years ago on the Cornish-Devonian border, I was surprised to see on the cliff above me the figure of a tiny man, dressed in black, strutting round in a rather vain-looking way. So incredulous was I of the existence of the 'pisky' people that I said to myself, "In a minute I shall see what he really is—a bird, or a shadow." But no, he went on being a tiny man—until he changed into a quite indescribable thing (are not piskies' Irish cousins known as the shape-changers?); something with the appearance of a long, furry black roll, which gambolled about on the grass and then disappeared. A few minutes later, however, two more little shapes became visible—slightly larger and more rounder than the first pisky-man. They were sitting one on either side of a gorse bush, making movements similar to those made in sawing with a two-handled saw. Curiosity impelled closer investigation—but the short cut I took up the cliff ended in unclimbable steepness and rubble, and I was obliged to return to the shore. By the time I had reached the gorse-bush by the usual path the pisky-sawyers were gone. Nothing except a form of air, though, could have sat on air as the sawyer on the sea side must have been doing—for the bush hung some inches over the cliff edge.[25]

We do not know the exact location and are not told whether Joyce was a Devon resident or simply visiting—her address was given as London—but the description of two busy piskies is teamed with an unusual account of shape-shifting.

It's interesting to note, meanwhile, that fairy sightings were fairly standard in the village of Postbridge, near Hartland. In 1938, a Mrs E. D. Pethybridge wrote to inform the *Western Morning News* that 'many people in the village have seen the pixies; even dogs are credited with seeing them sometimes.' Nonetheless, technological advancement had denied Mrs Pethybridge an encounter of her own, 'my home is far too modern… I have an electric light plant and a car, so I cannot expect to even glimpse them, you see.'[26]

Post-War Experiences

Pixy experiences continued after the Second World War, at which time—perhaps due to the growing discord between modernity and the old superstitions—a handful of folklorists were renewing their interest in collecting these kinds of accounts. In Diarmuid MacManus' *Irish Earth Folk*, a Mrs C. Woods described an encounter near Haytor Rocks, Dartmoor in 1952. While out walking, she saw a three-foot-tall elderly brown-capped or brown-haired figure, dressed in a smock of the same colour tied with a waist cord. He seemed to be shading his eyes from the sun as he watched her. As she moved closer to get a better look, he quickly disappeared between the stones.

> I had no idea at first that he was a little man; I thought rather of some animal until I got much nearer, and then I just stared and said to myself, 'This is no animal, it is a tiny man in brown.' I felt and still feel so convinced.[27]

The clothing described is archetypal and is repeated in the following fairy sighting. In *The Witchcraft and Folklore of Devon*, the author Ruth St Leger-Gordon describes a talk she gave in 1960 regarding pixies. One lady declared, to the author's incredulity, that her friend had seen:

> ... four of them one day emerging from a bracken stack in one of the little rough field enclosures near Widecombe-in-the-Moor. All four were little men, two being somewhat taller than the others and less pleasant looking than the smaller couple. All wore the traditional costume of red doublet, red pointed cap and long green hose.

Ruth was later informed that on Dartmoor, '...the incident was not considered unusual.'[28]

Veronica Maxwell of Devonshire reported to mid-century fairy folklorist Marjorie T. Johnson that she knew of a woman who had ventured into the woods of Berry Pomeroy Castle. Having settled herself onto a log, she spotted a movement 'out of the corner of her eye'. A pixie, wearing a cap and jerkin, seemingly incensed to find somebody sitting there, ran along the log towards her, slapped her face and disappeared.[29] The pixie's behaviour highlights the fact that not all fairy encounters are charming, or predictable.

One might be surprised to learn that even vicars are not immune to interaction with the little people. Holidaying at a Devonshire cottage in 1962, a cleric and his wife returned from a day's outing expecting to dine on bread and cheese, only to find that a fire had been lit and a previously uncooked stew was now ready for eating. 'The fire was alight and the stew was hot,' the wife explained. 'We had been within sight of the house all day. We had seen nobody go there, nor had we seen any smoke.' If that wasn't inexplicable enough, some days later, when the dinner had been left unchecked, cooking on the stove all day, the couple were surprised to find that their meal had, very considerately, been taken off the heat, rather than burnt to a crisp.[30]

The authors of this chapter themselves collected a Devon pixy sighting involving food, this time from a late twentieth-century kitchen in Chagford. Harpist Elizabeth-Jane Baldry was busily preparing for a concert one evening, whilst making dinner for her two young sons. In her haste, she discarded some potato peel into the bin rather than take it out to the compost as she would have ordinarily done.

> I felt bad when I did that, because it's not something I'd usually do. A minute or so later I had to throw something else away. I opened the bin and there was such a bright

shining light sitting on the potato peelings in the rubbish bin. It was actually quite frightening because it's something you don't expect. I knew it was a fairy. I couldn't see a physical humanoid form, I just knew it was a fairy. I looked up and around and thought, 'is there anything shining into this bin?' But it was such a dark little cottage and there was nothing shining into it, it was just there. I watched it for a while, until I got scared and put the lid down.[31]

Food is certainly an important part of many fairy encounters and the stories of fairy feasts which are glimpsed and heard at night, and then disappear when the human percipient tries to approach are well known. Interestingly, an account, known as 'The Chagford Pixies', tells of a gentleman who, driving towards Chagford at night, spies lights in the meadow, hears pretty music and witnesses a whole gathering of fair folk eating, drinking and making merry. It is only the sound of a cockerel and dawn that causes the whole vision to fade from his sight.[32]

Had the fairy in Elizabeth-Jane's story taken umbrage at a momentary recycling lapse? Fairies can certainly show their displeasure, particularly when humans enter their territory, as we learned in the Berry Pomeroy Castle encounter. Looe resident and author of *West Country Faerie*,[33] Diana Mullis, recounted to the authors how, during a recent visit to the Wistman's Woods on Dartmoor, she felt an overwhelming sense that she and her companions should not go in. 'You must listen to yourself and sense whether it is right or not. Because it's not based on *your* terms, it's on the fairies' terms and you'd soon know if what you were doing wasn't right.' To illustrate the point, Diana tells us of a man who visited the woods and upset the supernatural occupants: 'He went to Wistman's Woods, climbed one of the boulders and got pushed off it. It wasn't as though he fell, he actually said, "it felt as though somebody had pushed me off". "Well," I said, "they probably did!"'

We might agree that fairies were well within their rights to take ownership of such enchanted settings as Wistman's Woods. But what if fairy visitors frequented your land? In around 2002 author Michael Howard was told of a Devon farmer who by all accounts was 'the most rational and sceptical person you were ever likely to meet.' The story goes that in dismantling an old barn he lit a fire and placed the timbers upon it, keeping it blazing all afternoon. As twilight approached, he went out to tend the fire.

As he approached the fire, the farmer was amazed to see in the light from the burning embers a circle of small green figures standing around it. He immediately rushed indoors to tell his wife and bring her outside to witness the strange sight. She predictably reacted with incredulity when her husband told her what he had seen and said he must have been mistaken. Naturally when the couple went back to the fire the mysterious green visitors had gone.[34]

Evidently pixies are still active in the county of Devon...

FAIRY MAGIC AND THE COTTINGLEY PHOTOGRAPHS

Yorkshire by Richard Sugg

Traditional Fairies

Once upon a time, Britain was alive with everyday magic. Down to the close of the nineteenth century many people lived in awe or outright terror of witches, fairies or cunning folk. Yorkshire was no exception. In spring 1804 one Robert Sutcliff of Blackshaw, apparently beset by a poltergeist, applied to a cunning man called John Hepworth. Attempting counter-magic, Hepworth filled an iron bottle with human blood and hair and threw it onto Sutcliff's fire. The bottle exploded, blowing out the windows and killing Sutcliff.[1] At the other end of the century older Yorkshire villagers still believed that anyone seeing a white rabbit at night would soon meet their death. A writer of 1891 recalled a stonemason who, spotting a white rabbit whilst out netting sparrows one night, had gone home to bed and died of sheer terror.[2] The same fate could meet those who chanced on the supernatural dog, known as the padfoot or barguest, a creature sometimes associated with the fairies themselves. Around summer 1880 a Horbury man spied a strange white dog, and found that on striking it, his stick passed clean through. He too took to his bed and died.[3]

In this context, fairies were not graceful miniature princesses, twitching glittered wings at small girls. Like witches, fairies were at worst terrifying, and at best powerful and useful. Neatly enough, a witch-craft prosecution of 1677 captures all these qualities. 'A Yorkshire white witch', we are told, 'supplied the sick with a white powder which effected wondrous cures and which he alleged was periodically given him by fairies'.[4] In other contexts, a person exploiting that contact might well be valued as a 'fairy man' or woman, or a 'fairy doctor'. The dark power of this kind of association is brought home when we learn that, over the Cumbrian border in Lamplugh between 1656 and 1663, four people had allegedly been 'frightened to death by fairies'.[5]

Two hundred years later, Yorkshire fairies were as powerful and ubiquitous as the moorland winds and mountain torrents—and to be treated with similar respect. Around 1891 J.C. Atkinson, vicar of the moorland parish of Danby, wrote bemusedly of how Peter, his own parish clerk, had as a child feared being taken by fairies when playing in the 'fairy rings' (circles of darkened grass produced by fungal action) near his home at Fairy Cross Plains. Demanding to know if Peter really believed in such dangers, Atkinson was told, 'Why, yes, we did then, sir... for the mothers used to threaten us, if we weren't good, that they would turn us... out of doors at night, and then the fairies would get us'.[6]

If Atkinson felt his clerk to have too much of the pagan about him, he would have been yet more disturbed to know that, even as he wrote, the mothers of children with whooping-cough were still taking their infants into a hob-hole or cave near Runswick, where they prayed to the hobgoblin to cure the afflicted bairn.[7] What Peter also reminds us is that, having drunk in fairy beliefs with your mother's milk, you did not easily lose them. Ever after, the fairies were in your head. Day by day, you heard them, sensed them, inferred them from their activities—and sometimes even saw them.

Just what could you hear? At various wells and springs fairies washed both their clothes and their butter—typifying the way that their lives and habits so precisely mirrored those of human beings. Around Claymore Well on the coast, the sound of their clubs beating on laundered clothes could be heard up to a mile away.[8] Other eavesdropping was more deliberate and more intimate. Popular legend had it that the mound known as Pudding Pye Hill, near Thirsk, had been raised by the fairies, who lived beneath its turf. If anyone should run nine times around the hill, stick their knife into its top, and then place their ear to the ground, he or she would hear the fairies talking within.[9]

This was a world in which the numerous fairy place names (from Hobcross Hill and Hob Holes, through various Hob Lanes, to Sheffield's Grymelands and Kexborough's Scrat Hough Wood) were much more than pretty folklore.[10] The fairies really were there beneath your feet. In the 1890s the folklorist and author Richard Blakeborough knew an old lady who assured him that the fairies had 'most beautiful houses at a great depth below the surface'. Echoing kindred beliefs across Britain, this notion neatly allowed the fairies to be both proximate and invisible. Nor was the old woman's idea merely vague or fanciful. '"Nobody nivver cums across 'em when well-sinking, mining, or owt o' that soart"', she told Blakeborough, because 'the little folk possess the magical power of transporting [their homes] to a distance in an instant, should there be the least likelihood of their being disturbed'.[11]

A similar precision was evident when Blakeborough had as a boy excitedly showed to an old man the flint arrow head he had found during some amateur archaeology near Blois Hall. The old man told him that this was 'an elf-stone, declaring that the elves were evil spirits, who in days past used to throw them at the kine [cows]'. Moreover, 'the elves got them out of whirlpools, where they were originally made by the water spirits', and the man 'knew of several instances in which both cattle and horses had been injured by the elves'.[12] How could you shake beliefs as entrenched, intertwined and holistic as this? When they were so beautiful, would you necessarily want to?

Elsewhere, the butter which fairies had made or washed at fairy wells might be flung in elvish mischief at your gates or window-frames; for 'fairy butter' was the name given to a northern fungus, known to rot wood, and now more mundanely termed *exidia glandulosa*. Yet this kind of nuisance was mild compared to what fairies could do to your children. As well as routinely switching human babies with their own, leaving fairy changelings behind, Yorkshire fairies might occasionally pull more unusual tricks. In 1884, Mr J. Cocksedge of Brighouse, West Riding, recalled how as a child he had often looked in wonder at hat-maker Fanny Bradley, the tiniest woman he had ever seen. Fanny's brother Tom was similarly small—the reason being that as infants the two had been snatched by fairies whilst their mother reaped corn in a field near Almscliff Crag. In reality, it seems that the pair had simply wandered off, and returned when they heard her crying. The result, however, was that the Bradley family (and doubtless others) invested the siblings with that uncanny status for the rest of their lives.[13]

If you had seen the Bradley children during their adulthood, you might already believe that you had seen fairies. But there were stranger cases than this. An old woman once told Atkinson of seeing a green man with 'a queer sort of cap' disappearing along a ditch; and more precisely of a 'fairy bairn' found in a local hayfield. Beautiful at first, this infant presently dwindled away and died—because, the woman explained, its fairy mother could not do without it any longer.[14] Intriguingly, this sounds like a real baby which had been abandoned by its mother. When it died, it was believed (as so often across Britain and Ireland) to have been taken into fairy-land.

Around 1815 William Butterfield, the attendant of the Ilkley Wells baths on the slope of another Yorkshire moor, arrived to open the building one midsummer morning. After having unusual trouble with both lock and door, Butterfield finally heaved open the latter, and...

... whirr whirr whirr! such a noise and sight! all over the water and dipping into it was a lot of little creatures, dressed in green from head to foot, none of them more than eighteen inches high, and making a chatter and a jabber thoroughly unintelligible. They seemed to be taking a bath, only they bathed with all their clothes on. Soon, however, one or two of them began to make off, bounding over the walls like squirrels

and, with the astonished Butterfield now shouting at the top of his voice, all bounded off head over heels, making a noise like 'a disturbed nest of young partridges'. Unlike more obviously mythical sightings, this was not repeated with variations down the years. It seems to have been a one-off. Butterfield himself was very reluctant to talk about it; and down to at least 1878 there were still locals who would vouch for his honesty and sobriety.[15] Here, we may be in the kind of bewildering territory which so often confronts readers of Marjorie Johnson's remarkable collection of sightings, *Seeing Fairies*.[16]

Cottingley

Just over a century after Butterfield's experience fairies seemed to be losing their earthy density and organic roots. To most Britons in 1917, surely fairies meant *Peter Pan*, and Rose Fyleman's whimsical children's poem about fairies at the bottom of the garden. And yet, improbably enough, as two Yorkshire girls fell asleep to the sound of the waterfall one Friday night that July, they were about to reinvent fairies in a way which charged them with new kinds of beauty, power and danger, and whose capricious energies would flow through yet one more eventful century.

One hundred years ago two cousins, nine-year-old Frances Griffiths and sixteen year old Elsie Wright, catalysed one of the biggest hoaxes in Britain's history. In July and September 1917 the girls took two fairy photographs at the beck beneath their home in Cottingley, near Bradford. Because Elsie's mother, Polly, was interested in Theosophy, these presently caught the attention of Edward Gardner, a prominent member of the Theosophical Society, and next that of Sir Arthur Conan Doyle, creator of Sherlock Holmes. Although Doyle was initially sceptical of these first two photographs, his interest in fairies was already strong. Accordingly, he arranged for Gardner to travel to Cottingley in summer 1920, where the girls presently managed to take three further fairy photographs. By late November 1920 the fairies were staring out at bemused Londoners from the pages of the *Strand* magazine, and come 1922 Doyle had published a remarkable book, entitled *The Coming of the Fairies*.

Doyle seems to have gone to his grave, in July 1930, still believing the images to be genuine. Others thought so for decades afterwards, with both the fairies and the adult cousins playing an artful game of cat and mouse until one fateful day in September 1981, when Joe Cooper met Frances at a coffee shop near Canterbury cathedral. 'Frances eyed me' (writes Cooper) 'with amusement. "From where I was, I could see the hatpins holding up the figures. I've always marvelled that anybody ever took it seriously."' More public confessions followed from both women, with the story breaking in the press in March 1983. 'The reputations of the world's most famous fairies and Sir Arthur Conan Doyle ... are in tatters', wrote David Hewson in *The Times*, adding that Doyle had taken one hatpin for a fairy's navel.

As we will see, even this basic story is rich with ambiguities and uncertainties, as the girls-turned-women continually hurled fairy dust into the eyes of interviewers across more than sixty years. Did they really see fairies? Was the fifth photograph (included at the head of this chapter) actually real? And if so, who took it? No less intriguing than these essential questions, however, is one broader one: just what did the Cottingley fairy photographs *mean*, to those most closely involved, and to the wider world?

For Doyle and Gardner and many peers the photographs were closely bound up with Theosophy, Spiritualism, and anything else which offered alternatives to an increasingly stark and materialistic world-view. Lamenting that 'Victorian science would have left the world hard and clean and bare, like a landscape in the moon', Doyle at times became almost messianic in his response to the pictures. They must be 'either the most elaborate and ingenious hoax ever played upon the public, or else they constitute an event in human history which may in the future appear to have been epoch-making in its character ... The recognition of [the fairies'] existence will jolt the material twentieth-century mind out of its heavy ruts in the mud, and will make it admit that there is a glamour and a mystery to life'. When Doyle went on to compare the affair to the European discovery of the Americas, he nicely echoed May Bowley, who in June 1920 had written to him, stating: 'if they were really taken ... the event is no less than the discovery of a new world'.[17]

The Theosophical Society (founded 1875) must in part have been a reaction to Victorian science. Yet for Doyle and so many peers 'those heavy ruts in the mud' had been more recently carved out by tank tracks in the ravaged fields of France and Belgium. The man who would also claim to have photographs showing 'massed spirits of dead soldiers hovering over the crowds' at the Whitehall Cenotaph had lost a brother and a son to World War One; whilst Polly Wright admitted that Theosophy had 'rescued her from atheism'.[18] Even the fairy-poet Rose Fyleman, just a few months after her famous fairies down the garden, would write a new poem, entitled 'There used to be fairies in Germany'.

If the war for many typified masculine violence and cruelty, as opposed to feminine grace, gentleness and nurture, then who better to open a door into 'a wonderful new world of possibility and beauty' than two cousins who combined femininity with the innocence of childhood?[19] Doyle and Gardner saw the youth of the girls as playing a vital scientific role in the whole affair. It was believed that the girls, especially when together, helped the fairies to materialize, and also that children could see fairies, when most adults could not.[20] In 1921 Elsie stated that, 'in their more recent appearances the fairies were more "transparent" than in 1916 and 1917, when they were "rather hard"... You see, we were young then".'[21]

At less conscious levels, femininity infused this story in much subtler and more powerful ways. Both Doyle and Gardner, like so many men, were probably prone to idealise the innocence of young girls; and even the no-nonsense Arthur Wright (who always dismissed the photographs) seems to have lent the girls his precious camera just because Elsie, at age sixteen, knew exactly how to get round her daddy.[22] When the girls were initially given pseudonyms, Elsie's new name was Iris, and the first, most iconic photograph similarly fuses femininity and nature. Behind the gracefully capering female fairies, Frances stares dreamily from under her crown of flowers, whilst the waterfall pitches down in a white blur over her shoulder. A caption beneath the purely sepia original has the girls describing the fairies' true colours as 'very pale pink, green, lavender and mauve'.[23] Behind all this girlish artifice, there may also have been some real feminine compassion for Conan Doyle. When the truth finally broke in 1983 Elsie would state: 'I was feeling sorry for Conan Doyle because the press were giving him stick about the supernatural… he had lost his son in the war and I felt that he was trying to comfort himself through unworldly things'.[24]

What else did the Cottingley fairies mean for Frances and Elsie? Most obviously, the photographs and all the stories spun from them were an extraordinary source of personal power. 'Forget Bailey and Lichfield' (wrote *The Times* in 1998): 'Probably the century's most famous British photographers are two mischievous Yorkshire cousins….'[25] By this point, the cut-out sprites and gnomes themselves had long been widely acknowledged as 'the world's most famous fairies'; whilst Frances had once remarked to Cooper, decades before the internet and its viewer statistics were dreamed of: 'I've heard it said that every hour, somewhere in the world, someone makes a reference to the Cottingley fairies'.[26] Such power occasionally gained a sharper edge, as when Elsie, in 1978, wrote to Cooper of the sceptical presenter who had interviewed the cousins back at Cottingley for Yorkshire Television in September 1976: 'That day up at Cottingley Beck you could have slain Austin Mitchell in five seconds from the right angle'.[27]

Curiously enough, when Elsie said this she was urging Cooper to believe in that fifth, most controversial photograph. Curiously, because in 1986 Elsie would publicly and firmly deny the existence of fairies, and in 1983 had already claimed that she had fabricated and taken this picture, which 'was all done with my own contraption'.[28] By contrast, Frances had always insisted that she took this picture, that it was genuine, and that on one trip to the beck she had seen a fairy man materialize on a willow branch: 'he looked straight at me and disappeared'.[29]

This clear split between belief and disbelief might lead us to suspect that, in 1917 and 1920, it was the older, more cynical Elsie who led on and even exploited her younger, fairy-believing cousin. It is at this point, however, that we need to remind ourselves of the realities of class in post-Edwardian Britain. It has often been argued that the two lowly rural girls were intimidated by the likes of Gardner and Doyle, and therefore unable to disappoint them. There may be some truth in this. Yet even Elsie, in 1983, put her behaviour down to compassion rather than fear. What is more interesting, in class terms, is the distinctly upper-middle-class background of Frances. 'When we lived in Johannesburg', she told Cooper, 'going out to the opera … was wonderful … I had a little fur cape—my father was a sergeant major in the army and we had servants… it was horrible coming to Cottingley and wartime and black bread, and sleeping all crammed up with Elsie in the attic'.[30]

Did Frances really see fairies at Cottingley? She clearly wanted to. For her, the 'glamour and mystery' which Conan Doyle yearned for had originally been very worldly things. Deprived of these in the backwater of Cottingley in 1917, she helped Elsie create some suitably modish female fairies, thus fusing the new glamour of Johannesburg society with some older British magic. From this angle, the Cottingley fairies look more like an attempt to escape the confines of the Yorkshire countryside than a celebration of it. The apparently worldly Frances would also tell a 1971 interviewer that Elsie was 'young for her age. She used to play with my dolls'—a detail which reminds us that, though only just turned ten in September 1917, it was Frances who managed to take the second photograph. Ironically, one of the biggest advantages of the girls' 'youthful innocence' may have been purely legal. At one point Doyle wished the cousins to sign an affidavit affirming what they had seen. But this idea was dropped. Was that because even the older Elsie was, in 1920, still technically 'an "infant at law"?'[31]

One other detail about their supposed childish innocence must also be added. Simon Young shrewdly notes how the three-year gap between the two sets of photographs is often ignored. Yet clearly it was vital, both in terms of the cousins' increased maturity, and their basic intentions. They had had little control over the strange accidents which sent their first two pictures to Gardner, Doyle, and the *Strand* magazine. But in 1920 they certainly did not have to create and photograph their new fairies. As Young rightly puts it, 'in 1917 Frances and Elsie were out to trick their family, in 1920 the world'.[32]

Cottingley's Afterlife

With the 1983 confessions of both women, many might have assumed that the fairy tale was over. It had indeed been a thing of beauty, power and danger—the latter most conspicuously for Doyle, whose association with the rigorously forensic Holmes never quite recovered from this embarrassment. But the cousins had somehow created a new kind of fairy folklore. As much as anything, folklore is about the power of stories. Some stories are tough. They manage to continually recreate and re-energise themselves; and the Cottingley affair did just that. Even the apparently disbe-lieving Elsie seems to have felt that widespread public belief had given the girls' paper cut-outs a curious sort of life, rather as religious faith does to its gods and saints. Tellingly, her first response to Frances' confession in March 1983 was: 'I am sorry someone has stabbed our fairies to death with a hatpin'.[33]

She would probably have been delighted to know that, at a hundred, the Cottingley fairies are still leaping about with surprising vigour. Since the deaths of Frances and Elsie (in 1986 and 1988 respectively) we have had, among other things, Steve Szilagyi's 1995 novel, *Photographing Fairies* (filmed in 2004); Emma Carroll's ecologically-conscious children's book, *In Darkling Wood* (2015); and Hazel Gaynor's new fictional re-imagining, *The Cottingley Secret*, which hit the bookshops in July 2017.

And in 1997 and 1998, two inter-related phenomena showed how much the

Cottingley affair had become a kind of British National Treasure. First, we have Charles Sturridge's film, *Fairytale: A True Story*. As the playful title suggests, this version is in part self-consciously ironic—but how much so is a tricky question. *Fairytale* has the seventeen year old Elsie played by Florence Hoath, who had only recently turned thirteen when the movie premiered in October 1997.[34] It also plays up the idyllic rural side of Cottingley in a way which is less than faithful to its more urban qualities. Perhaps most strikingly, it introduces a severely wounded soldier, missing almost half his face, who is first met by Frances on a train; and who later rescues the innocent girls from a slimy reporter. When the soldier's notably tremulous query to the girls about the truth of the fairies is answered in the affirmative, the force of his relief ('I knew it; I just knew it') is almost metaphysical. This invention not only highlights the sense that, after a certain point, the cousins could not bear to disappoint all the believers they had created, but again underlines the impression that the whole potent fusion (fairies, girls, unspoiled nature) offered something free and pure, something worth fighting for and living for, once the smoke of war had faded.

It was still being fought for, a little more prosaically, in 1998, when Arthur Wright's original cameras and 'assorted memorabilia' came up for sale. *Fairytale* had been produced by Mel Gibson's company, Icon Productions, and Gibson himself makes a fleeting uncredited cameo appearance in the film. He now bid £20,000 for Wright's Cottingley artefacts, thus threatening to take part of the British National Treasure abroad. Touchingly, Geoffrey Crawley, who owned the cameras and prints, agreed to let them stay in the UK provided £14,000 was raised. This sum was reached with public help, and donations from Canon, Jessop and Olympus; and in June 1998 the Midg and Cameo cameras which had shot the fairy photographs were given to Bradford's National Museum of Photography 'in front of a 2,000 strong crowd chanting "Fairies coming home".'[35]

In 2011 Cottingley unveiled a £73,000 sculpture garden as a memorial to the cousins. It holds an annual Cottingley Fairy Fest, and now contains a housing estate with closes named after Titania and Oberon. But the dangers of the affair still linger on. The centenary had barely opened when an article titled 'The Curse of the Cottingley Fairies' appeared in the British *Daily Mirror*. The victim, now, was not Conan Doyle but Joe Cooper. Cooper's invaluable factual account, *The Case of the Cottingley Fairies*, was a labour of faith and love, originating in the early 70s, and published only in 1990. He clearly wanted to believe in both fairies and the Cottingley photographs, and of Frances' face-to-face confession he would later write: 'My world shifted a little and I had no words'.[36] Speaking in January 2017, his wife Shirley revealed how Joe, having told his family nothing of the confession, suddenly vanished in July 1982. His daughter Jane believed him to have suffered some kind of breakdown, and on his return his twenty-three-year marriage to Shirley came to an end.

The posthumous reputation of Arthur Conan Doyle had ultimately suffered after 1983; but he had arguably been lucky to die with his own belief intact. By contrast

Cooper, a hero of World War Two's Bomber Command, allegedly broke under the strain of losing his belief. Not only that, but for Jane Cooper the cousins had broken the faith of believers across the world. 'They should', she insisted, 'have taken their secret to the grave so it could have been one of those great mysteries like the Loch Ness Monster'.[37]

Oddly enough, Frances seemed to have felt much the same, just after Cooper had written up her confession in an article of December 1982. 'You're a traitor' she burst out, before slamming down the phone.[38] As we know, a traitor is usually someone who betrays their country—or their country's National Treasure… But the truth of this treachery was more complex and ironic than centenary press reports imply. Cooper wanted to believe in the photographs. He wrote up the truth only after Frances had confessed it to him. And Frances herself did not confess voluntarily. In fact, she essentially jumped before she was pushed. Shortly before she met Cooper in Canterbury, she had learned that Elsie had confessed (albeit privately). Why? Because in August 1981 her son, Glenn Hill, had confronted her with a 1914 fairy picture which he suspected she had used as a model.[39] Could any fairy tale ending be more poetic than this? The mischievous girl who had sought to deceive her parents was finally exposed… by her own child.

Girlish innocence and childish mischief; a daughter of the Empire and a Scottish knight; a Yorkshire war hero chasing fairies through the archives for almost twenty years; and the once ubiquitous pagan elves of Britain trapped within five flat picture frames… if ever the twentieth century boasted a British National Treasure with something for everyone, the Cottingley Fairy Photographs was surely it.

5

FAIRY BARROWS AND CUNNING FOLK

Dorset by Jeremy Harte

South-West England can be busy with visitors in the summer, and Dorset is particularly crowded. The tourist board, which adds up these things, reckons that the county received three million visitors last year. I don't know how many came a century before, but enough to justify a trail of old guidebooks, their light learning illustrated with scenic watercolours. Then as now, most people wanted to see Hardy Country, paying homage to the author who had made imperishable literature out of the lives of country people. A more select few came with their copies of William Barnes, the finest of English dialect poets. The collectors of folksong made their rounds, and were not disappointed.

So Dorset is not *terra incognita* for the study of rural culture. But unfortunately the ethnographic record does not contain much about fairies. We have only names, beliefs, turns of phrase, the stubs of one or two stories. Still, this paucity of evidence does at least sharpen our focus on the sources. And these show that, although people have been talking about fairies in Dorset for eight hundred years, it is not at all certain that they have always been talking about the same thing.

The Pūca

After all, the earliest evidence comes from place-names, and these refer to a being about whom we would otherwise know nothing, the *pūca*. At least sixteen places in Dorset contain the name of this spirit, who survives in later forms as the Elizabethan puck, the Welsh *pwca* and the Irish *púca*. These are all of them trickster spirits, but this does not necessarily tell us what the name originally meant: often in fairylore a word continues in use but changes its meaning. We know that the *pūca* was being talked about as early as the tenth century, since a spring called *pucan wylle* appears in a Somerset charter of that date.[1] The first name to be recorded in Dorset (although place-names can be much older than the document in which they appear) is a thirteenth-century *Pukefurland* in Radipole.[2] *Puckysbarry* and *Puckysway*, both recorded at Winfrith Newburgh in 1471, are, for good philological reasons, from Middle English *pouke* rather than Old English *pūca*.[3] In any case, we know that the word was still current in Middle English, because it was being used to coin surnames; John Puke of Bovington near Wool is mentioned in 1280, and several men of this name lived around Shaftesbury a generation later.[4]

John evidently looked like a *pouke*, or maybe he was just famous for his practical jokes. Either way, it is clear that these spirits were not shapeless presences; they had a character of their own, and you could see their likeness in a familiar neighbour. They were to be found out in the fields, not far from the village; we have already seen a furlong-strip named after them, and there was also an arrish or stubble field at Cheselbourne and a hay or enclosure at Compton Abbas. At three more places (Wool, Osmington and Puddletown) there was a pit, meaning—as usual in place-names—a rough hollow. But most often they were to be found near water. There was a well, or rather a spring, at Beaminster; a marsh at Arne; moors at Motcombe and Cann; and three separate instances of a lake (which in Dorset means a stream, not a body of water) at Langton Matravers, Halstock and Chideock. Add a lane at Shaftesbury, the barrow at Winfrith, and a stone at Studland, and we have sixteen names in all.[5]

Those moors and streams sound like the abode of mischievous spirits who, like the puck of later tradition would lead the traveller astray, laughing when he stumbled floundering into the water. In that case there may be a connection with *puxy*, a West Country dialect word which has been used for quagmires and muddy patches in the roads since at least 1604.[6] On the other hand, the Puckstone at Studland is not deceptive at all; it is a large mass of conglomerate rock, forming a useful landmark for travellers over the heath. We are to understand that anything so large and odd must have been placed there by the supernatural intervention of a *pouke*, and in fact the neighbouring Agglestone was said, in later tradition, to have been thrown into position by the Devil.[7]

Two further names introduce us to a *pūcel*, or 'little *pūca*'. One of these, at Portesham, is applied to a moor, which supports the case for water-loving spirits. The other is more curious: a field at Wyke Regis was called *Pokulchurche* in 1460.[8] This is an unfamiliar turn of phrase, but not unique, for there were other churches of the *pūcel* in Gloucestershire and Wiltshire.[9] The name is an imaginative one, using the idiom of Old English kennings—a rhetoric in which whale's road means 'the sea', by a kind of logical parallelism: as road is to men so sea is to whales. In the same way, as the church is to men so this place Pokulchurche was to the *pūcel*. No doubt it was an outcrop of the local limestone in which imagination could see a tower and pinnacles.

It's a fanciful name; no-one ever supposed that the *pūcel* really did meet up with his companions here for Evensong. Perhaps we should not press too hard for a literal understanding of other fairy place-names, either, since names can fit a whole spectrum of belief, from 'that stream where you see the *pouke* at nights' to 'that muddy stream where you can fall in suddenly, just as if you were the man in the story who was tricked by a *pouke*'. If some of these names are fictive rather than literal, it would explain why they use literary language. At Portesham there was a *Gobelynshole* in 1461, even though the word *gobelin* is Norman French and not English.[10] It was adopted by English writers in the fourteenth century, but never became part of local tradition.[11] In the same way, some rough ground at Milton Abbas was called *Alvysch Thornys* in 1319.[12] *Elvisch* originally meant 'of the elves', but in Middle English it had a more general sense of 'outlandish, eerie'. Twisted, black and old the thorn trees may have been, but they were not thought to be literally occupied by elves.

Elves

There is something surprising about this absence of elves. Leaving aside two or three conjectural etymologies, they are not found in the place-names of Dorset, nor in those of the neighbouring counties either. Indeed names in *ælf* (the Old English form of the word) are rare in southern England, although they are quite common in the North Country—where, however, names in *pūca* are almost unknown.[13] And yet the early literature recognises no other class of fairy being. Tenth-century herbal manuscripts from Winchester give cures for those who are shot by elves. La□amon in his native epic of Arthur has much to say on the lore of elves. The *South English Legendary* describes, in graphic detail, the consequences of having sex with elves. How come these traditions are not reflected in popular speech and place-names?

It seems that in Anglo-Saxon England the elite traditions of what folklorists have come to call the Seelie Court, with its fairy aristocrats, music, dance and laughter, had always referred to elves. The common people knew about this, but were more interested in the Solitary Fairies, those beings who haunted wild spots from which they emerged to mislead travellers, or sometimes to be cajoled into doing household labour: the word for these was *pūca*. After the Conquest, the French-speaking elite of southern England began to substitute *fay* and *fayrie* for *ælf*, while their English-speaking subjects expanded the sense of *pouke* to include other fairy traditions. But in the North, which was less awed by the new language, stories of elves continued to circulate among both rich and poor, whilst the word *þyrs*, which had originally meant 'ogre', gradually became the accepted term amongst Northerners for Solitary Fairies.[14] Finally as Middle English became the unified language of the kingdom, the name of 'fairy' replaced all other terms in southern England.

Fairies and Cunning Folk

Certainly 'fairies' is the word used in the first personal account of spirits in Dorset. This comes from John Walsh, who in the 1560s made a living as an amateur doctor in the village of Netherbury. Before that he had been the servant of a Catholic priest called Robert Drayton; with the passing of Queen Mary, Drayton's ministry was at an end, and he seems to have spent the last three years of his life in retirement, dying in 1561. He passed on his herbal knowledge to Walsh, together with a more equivocal bequest, the *Book of Circles*. For Drayton was no harmless old cleric, but a student of the magical art. Armed with this secret lore, Walsh was able to trace stolen goods and tackle the witchcraft that plagued his neighbours. When it came to identifying witches, he relied on advice from the fairies.

> Ther be iii kindes of feries, white, greene, & black. Which when he is disposed to use, hce speaketh with them upon hyls, where as there is great heapes of earth… Between the hours of xii and one at noone, or at midnight he useth them. Whereof (he sayth) the blacke feries be the worst.[15]

These 'heapes' are barrows; we must imagine Walsh glancing northwards from Netherbury to the green ring of hills which encompass Beaminster, and making his way by unseen paths to a consultation at noon or midnight among the tumuli of Beaminster Down. He was not the only one to practice such rites. His contemporary, Joan Tyrry of Taunton, had also learnt to inquire of the fairies if any man or woman was bewitched. They taught her how to heal both people and animals, and that was how she made her living, at least until the ecclesiastical authorities caught up with her.[16] When Elizabeth Homer was put on trial for sorcery in 1696 at Exeter, it weighed heavily against her that she had been seen 'three nights together, upon a large down in the same place, as if rising out of the ground'.[17] She had gone into the hills, to talk to those with whom a good Christian woman should not hold converse.

How many others did the same? It is not easy to follow cunning folk like Walsh into the secret places where they unmasked their dark opposites, the witches. There is a Fairy Barrow on the steep ridge above Abbotsbury, like Netherbury a town where the old clerical learning could be picked up without much difficulty.[18] We have already seen the *Puckysbarry* at Winfrith Newburgh. But other place-names hint at a more suspicious relationship with the Otherworld. A barrow at Milton Abbas was *Grymbargh* in 1385, and another near Corfe Castle preserved the name Grimberry into modern times.[19] The *grīma* was an ugly spirit, more spectre than goblin. Other barrows at Bere Regis, Cann, Portesham and Ryme Intrinseca were named after the *bugge*, a late medieval word for shapeless terrors.[20]

Cunning folk claimed a liminal status between good and bad for themselves, and for the fairies they consulted; others were not so sure. What kind of spirits were they pledging themselves to? Walsh's colour-coded fairies are like nothing else in folk tradition, but they resemble the angels described in the *Sworn Book of Honorius* and other magical texts. These, too, came in different colours and it was perilous to mistake the black company of Saturn for the green one of Venus. To the prosecutor it made no difference: they were fallen angels, all of them.

Three centuries later comes an echo of these early magical practices, from the music barrows on Bincombe Down and nearby at Culliford Tree, where 'the rustics say that if the ears be laid close on the apex at mid-day, the sweetest melody will be heard within'.[21] The source of the music is not made explicit, but since the same is reported from the barrow on Wick Moor at Stogursey, one of the most fairy-haunted places in Somerset, the connection seems clear.[22] Here, as at Beaminster, the fairies are to be visited at the magic hour of noon, but their occult communications have dwindled to a harmless humming.

Fairies and Christianity

Even in this diminished state, fairies kept their distance from any outward sign of Christianity. 'The pixeys lived down Neddyfield', said old folks on Portland in the 1860s, but 'when the church bells were put up on St George's Church all the pixeys went away'.[23] This is an attenuated form of a story in which the fairies complain that they can no longer live in their old home because of the noise of... those ding-dongs. Like spirits of another kind, they cannot bring themselves to name sacred things. The last demon-repelling peel of bells was rung in the mid sixteenth century; between then and the late nineteenth, when we are told with some regret that fairies were driven out by bells at Portland, Cadbury and Withypool, there seems to have been a softening of attitudes to the supernatural.[24]

Resistance of another kind was shown by the fairies of Castle Hill at East Chelborough, who took the church which was being built near their home and moved it down to the riverside at Lewcombe.[25] Put that way, the story suggests a fairy antipathy to Christianity, but it appears so tersely in our only source that it is hard to guess at the original intention. Tales about the supernatural movement of buildings are ubiquitous, but they do not always involve churches. The city of Winchester, for instance, was going to be built on Old Winchester Hill until fairies took a hand—or maybe, as others thought, it was the Devil.[26] Often these stories reserve judgement about the identity of their actors. Richard Warner, writing in 1793, tells us that Christchurch Priory was to have been built on St Catherine's Hill 'but as fast as they laid the stones in the day, so constantly were they removed in the night, by some supernatural power'. That is vague, but the accompanying poem supplies a clearer image, attributing the work to 'elfin shapes'.[27] People at West Dowlish were confident that their church was moved to Dowlish Wake, but by whom? The folktale collector was told different versions involving 'ghosts, fairies, pixies, druids, or "people who move at night".[28]

Pixies

As this recent account suggests, fairies and pixies have become more or less inter-changeable. But this may be misleading, since the present meaning of a fairy name is no guide to its earlier significance. The pixy name first appears in 1542, when 'Hobgoblin or Collepixie' is used as a general synonym for bugbears, followed by a theatre scene in 1611 when a roguish pedlar came on stage 'all tottered like coll pixci'.[29] Later we hear Hampshire traditions of a colt-pixy, who takes on the shape of a horse to mislead riders into bogs; but this may be pure invention, attempting to make sense of the name.[30] The New Forest had a Coldpixy's Cave, where the spelling suggests another distortion of the name.[31] In Dorset, fossil belemnites were called Colepexy's fingers, and sea-urchins Colepexy's heads.[32]

At Durweston there was a Pexy's Hole near the Rectory in 1784; 'hole' in these names has the same sense as 'pit', a rough overgrown hollow where unseen things can easily be imagined.[33] This is the only place-name of this kind in Dorset, but there are several in the New Forest, all from *pixy* not *pexy*. The earliest reference to people being led astray by pixy deceptions comes from Devon in 1630.[34] Devon and Somerset have pixy place-names, though most of these date from the 1840s.[35] There is an earlier example at Pixies Parlour in Ottery St Mary, a cave which inspired a youthful Coleridge to occasional verse in 1793: the first time that we hear about pixies as a particular race of fairies.[36] Before then, stories are as likely to refer to *the* Pixy, a solitary fairy. Clearly there is some overlap with earlier traditions; just as people used to say they were pouke-ledden, so they began to speak of being pixy-led. But etymo-logical links between the two words are tenuous, and an origin in *puca* fails to account for the early references to Coll Pixy. Perhaps this was an unrelated name which became popular in the sixteenth century, and was then adopted here and there in the south-west in curtailed form as a substitute for *pouke*.

If so, the fashion was not taken up by everyone. John Walsh and Joan Tyrry spoke of fairies, not pixies. The long barrow at Nempnet Thrubwell, just north of the Mendips, was still known as Fairy Toot in the 1780s.[37] When William Barnes wrote a glossary of Dorset words in 1844, fossil sea-urchins were called the faces and hearts of fairies, not of the Colepexy.[38] He was familiar with the word colepexying, but only as a term for beating down the last apples after the main fruit crop. Later on it seems synonymous with scrumping, and children are said to go colepexying in the orchards.[39] Barnes speaks of pixy pears and pixy stools as Somerset words for hawthorn fruit and toadstools; these are formations of the kenning type (as pears are to men, so are haws to the pixies), but they were not part of the idiom of his native Blackmore Vale, where people spoke instead of fairy rings. But Barnes' younger con-temporary Thomas Hardy, who grew up on the barren lands west of Puddletown, refers to people being pixy-led on the heath and knew the circles in the grass as pixy rings.[40] We have already met with pixies on Portland, and the word was also in use at

Lyme Regis.[41] On the other hand, 'fairy' is the only term used in the dialect of Newfoundland, which originates with Dorset emigrants from around Poole.[42] Throughout the nineteenth century, it seems, the western counties were patchworked into areas which had adopted the word 'pixy' and those which retained 'fairy'. In the end, it was tourist literature rather than local preferences which decided the lexicon: Cornwall was to be the home of the piskies, and Devon and Somerset that of the pixies, while Hampshire and Dorset would have… well, not much at all.

William Barnes and Fairies

The absence of stories about Dorset fairies hampered those who wanted to present the county's traditions to a growing folklore market. In his first collection of dialect poetry Barnes included 'Eclogue: The Veäiries': one of many dialogue poems (others deal with a ghost and a witch) whose conversational form allowed him to present traditional lore without an author's intrusive voice. Young Samel doesn't know much about fairies, and Simon is happy to enlighten him. The 'veäiry ring' is formed by little people dancing to the music of

> a little pipe
> A-meäde o' kexes or o' straws, dead ripe,
> A-stuck in row (zome short an' longer zome)
> Wi' slime o snäils, or bits o' plum-tree gum,
> An' meäke sich music that to hear it sound,
> You'd stick so still's a pollard to the ground.[43]

These are the tiny fairies beloved of Michael Drayton, Robert Herrick and other seventeenth-century fantasists who plundered the natural world in search of things small enough to furnish these diminutive fairies with tools, transport and so on. There is no other folklore involved. But this does not necessarily prove a learned origin, since the diminutive trope could have existed in oral tradition as well. After all, it is impossible to imagine a fairy ring being formed by anything except miniature dancers; and the use of the word *elferinge* as early as c.1300 shows that people were already thinking on those lines, long before the first night of *A Midsummer Night's Dream*.[44]

In Barnes' eclogue, Simon goes on to explain how a fairy encounter might come about:

> Why, when the vo'k were all asleep, a-bed,
> The veäiries us'd to come, as 'tis a-zaid,
> Avore the vire wer cwold, an' dance an hour
> Or two at dead o' night upon the vloor;
> Var they, by only utteren a word
> Or charm, can come down chimney lik' a bird;

> Or draw their bodies out so long an' narrow
> That they can vlee drough keyholes lik' an arrow.[45]

And then follows the family tradition of a fairy who came in with the rest one night, and joined them in tapping a keg of aunt's mead. He drank so much that he quite forgot 'the word he wer to zay to meäke en small', and so remained trapped behind the door until it was unlocked in the morning, when he could make a bolt for it.

This anecdote, presumably invented for the sake of the poem, is only a short one, but it draws on traditional themes.[46] Here is the division of time into the human day and the fairy night; the penetration of the house through tiny unguarded openings; the importance of the hearth, whose dying embers seem to provide the fairies with a warmth they cannot find anywhere else; and the appropriation of human food to nourish the fairies. All these motifs are familiar from lore elsewhere, and they can be humorous or anxious, depending on what people fancied or feared about the fairies in general.

Barnes was a kindly soul, who took a benign view of his tippling fairies. Others were not so happy with the thought of spirits raiding their hard-won stores of food. 'It is believed that fairies come down the chimney and do a deal of harm if you don't stop them', wrote Henry Moule of the County Museum. 'The way to keep them out is to hang a bullock's heart in the chimney'.[47] This piece of advice, halfway between pest-control and exorcism, was remembered in the 1880s when a bullock's heart was pulled out from the chimney of a cottage at Hawkchurch near Bridport. It was stuck through with nails, pins, and spikes from a hawthorn bush, and was recognised as a way of preventing witches or fairies from entering the house.[48]

Fairies were keeping bad company here, for the bullock's heart was normally a way to keep off witchcraft. It began as a counter-charm when cattle were overlooked by some witch, and began to die mysteriously; cutting out the heart of a dead animal, and hanging it up to scorch above the household fire, would mysteriously transfer harm back to the person blamed for sending it.[49] But by the early nineteenth century, it was being used as an all-purpose talisman against malicious things coming down the chimney-breast.[50]

Developments of this kind suggest a certain loss of substance in the object of belief. At first it is an actual, next-door witch; then a magical being, able to float down chimneys; and finally a vaguely conceived principle of bad luck. The thinner its identity becomes, the more likely it is that the strange being will be identified as a fairy. This could have advantages, especially for those who wanted to keep their identity secret.

Fairy Riders
C.V. Goddard, the folklorist of Chideock, refers to fairies seen up Peticrate Lane leading up to Langdon Hill. Elsewhere he gives a story which might explain this experience: when a horse was found in the morning standing restless, sweaty and

tired in the stable, it was put about that he was ridden overnight by the fairies, but in fact he had been borrowed by smugglers who were in a hurry to get their cargo inland.[51] Such is the story, and there may be something in it, since Goddard was writing in the 1890s, from a village which only a generation or so earlier had been the headquarters of a smuggling gang. However, these stories about smugglers disguising themselves with supernatural stratagems all date from long after the demise of the trade, and they gloss over the methods really used by gangs to ensure co-operation. Smugglers did not protect their anonymity by spreading stories about fairy riders, phantom coaches and ghostly lights. They protected it by cutting the throats of those who squealed.

Besides, horses could be found glistening wet with perspiration even in stables which were far inland. This was reported in the 1890s from Potterne Farm at Verwood, on the edge of Cranborne Chase, where the farm's cart-horses were found damp and disturbed in the mornings. The carter shrugged his shoulders and said 'Oh, the fairies have been out again'. He would point to tangles in the horses' manes, which were so knotted that they had to be cut out when combing would not release them. These were the footholds that had been tied by the fairies so that they could keep their precarious perch on the horse's neck.[52]

Like people who saw rings surrounded by mushrooms and fancied fairy dancers, the carter was observing natural phenomena and giving them an otherworldly explanation. Horses no longer show signs of mysterious sweats in the morning, probably because modern stables are better ventilated, but elfknots still appear in their manes, especially if the animals have been left to graze and not brushed down. It is a source of wonder to those who do not admit that wind and their own neglect are responsible.[53]

In Hardy's *Woodlanders*, the same phenomenon is given a different explanation: a horse is found exhausted in the morning, 'in such a state as no horse could be in by honest riding', and the stable groom has 'a whole series of tales about equestrian witches and demons, the narration of which occupied a considerable time'.[54] Hardy is playing with the reader's expectations here. Is the spun-out tale about spirits just rustic folklore? Superficially yes, but not if we recognise the underlying moral order of the novel. The horse has not, in fact, been honestly ridden; he has taken the young doctor Fitzpiers to secret assignations.

This moral subtext might account for Hardy's rejection from the 1880s onwards of fairies as supernatural riders in favour of 'witches and demons'. Fairies were just not serious enough. He evades naming them again in the late poem 'The Paphian Ball', subtitled 'Another Christmas experience of the Mellstock quire'. The quire are on their annual Christmas circuit, playing carols to the houses and farms around the village, when they are invited to provide dance music instead at a mysterious big house. They play until they are drowsy, and then by mistake strike up 'While shepherds watched....' Suddenly all around them vanishes, and they find themselves alone on the heath.[55] Almost anywhere else this would have been told as a story about fairies, but Hardy evidently had his reservations, and presents the mysterious house without naming it.

Child-Lore

By the early twentieth century, fairies were moving into the realms of child-lore. Udal in his *Dorsetshire Folk-Lore* has two traditions about fairy rings: a wish formed before dancing round one is likely to be fulfilled within the year, and if you can run nine times round a ring without drawing breath, a fairy will appear and bring you something good.[56] Both of these sound typical of the childhood dares which involve running round some spooky place three, seven, or nine times.[57]

The Blue Pool near Wareham is said to be the home of bad fairies, who make promises of perpetual youth to lure the unwary into the aquamarine water, and then ensure that they are never seen again.[58] This may be a parental fiction, warning against swimming in the pool at this popular beauty spot, where the slopes of clay make it hard to pull yourself out of the water. A story from the church of Stourpaine, just up the river from Blandford Forum, also has the air of something told to children. Early in the morning, fairies would go up the turret stairs, and ring the bells 'by using the fresh dew of the grass'. Bad luck awaited those whose footprints were seen in the fresh dew; but if someone were to approach the tower just as the grass had dried, they might run up the turret and see the dew drops scattered by the fairies.[59] This sounds like a story made up to satisfy curiosity about the small little-used doorway which leads into the turret.

Fairy Costume

Familiarity with imaginative literature helped to clarify what fairies looked like. No doubt there had always been some conventions of this kind, for Elizabethan audiences seem to have had no difficulty in recognising a fairy when one appeared on stage. But the spread of picture-book conventions made it easier to see fairies. Thus when A.R.T. Bruce, the curate of Sixpenny Handley, was out walking on Bottlebush Down and sat down on a barrow, he was astonished to see 'a crowd of little people in leather jerkins, who came and danced round him', but knew at once what they were.[60] The experiences of Mr Turvey and Mr Lonsdale, two clairvoyants from Poole, sound like the observations of a field biologist, or an ethnographer's first encounter. They were sitting in Turvey's garden at Branksome Park when:

> Looking closely, I saw several little figures dressed in brown peering through the bushes. They remained quiet for a few minutes and then disappeared. In a few seconds a dozen or more small people, about two feet in height, in bright clothes and with radiant faces, ran on to the lawn, dancing hither and thither.[61]

There are hints and echoes of these experiences elsewhere, in the old ladies of Puncknowle who often saw fairies or, at Langton Matravers, the 'green fairies seen at

Wilkswood in their Phrygian hats'.[62] The fairies appear, and that is all. The innumerable fears and hopes expressed in tradition about what they did were laid aside, for belief is everything.

Concluding Thoughts

But the canon of fairy legends was not closed. True, the fairies had disappeared from oral tradition, in which they seem never to have had a very secure hold; but they flourished in Dorset literature. Sylvia Townsend Warner was writing her *Kingdoms of Elfin*, and Llewelyn Powys included 'A Christmas Tale' in his *Dorset Essays*, a sentimental anticlerical piece in which a boy loses his heart to a river nymph and dies when the Church separates them.[63] Since then the story of Lubberlu has migrated back to folklore, being retold in more than one book of local legends.[64]

This is how tradition survives in the contemporary world; we generate new stories by commenting on the old ones. Connoisseurs of this process will appreciate Robert Newland's *Dark Dorset: Fairies*, a book which presents much of the lore we have been discussing so far, with a great deal of creative variation, and enhanced with a number of other stories which are presented as traditional but which do not appear in any known sources.[65]

In any study of this kind, there are two conflicting impulses. There is a natural desire to present a unified portrait of Dorset fairies; to make linkages, fill in narrative gaps, and generally unify the material to write the centuries-long biography of the Dorset fairy. And opposed to this are the critical, analytic methods of the historian, for whom everything is what it was at the time and not part of some larger whole. It is true that, as we have seen, there are recurrent associations in Dorset fairylore— barrows, bells, churches, dancing, hawthorn, midnight, music, noon, pits, ponds, and witches. But they have all meant different things to different story-tellers, and cannot be collated into a single timeless body of lore. This is not just a fact about fairies, of course. It has been the overall conclusion of folklore studies in the last fifty years.

FAIRY HOLES AND FAIRY BUTTER[1]

Cumbria by Simon Young

Introduction

Fairies have, from time to time, been sighted in contemporary Cumbria. In the early 1920s, fairy seer, Geoffrey Hodson, spotted, on his frequent visits to Kendal and the Lakes, brownies, rock gnomes, tree manikins, undines, lake spirits, nature devas, and memorably, on Hellvellyn, a god.[2] In 1941 a couple of hikers ran into fairies playing in the rocks at Borrowdale: fairies that disappeared as soon as the hikers went to investigate.[3] We have a postwar report from a woman remembering how, when a girl (before the war?), she saw 'pearly-looking beings' flying around a stream at Troutbeck.[4] Then, there are also twenty-first-century manifestations. There is a 'gnome village' at the bottom of England's deepest lake, Wastwater: divers put garden gnomes on the lake floor and, then, pose for photographs besides them.[5] There was, for two years, before vandals got to it, a fairy hamlet, built by a cycle path at Moor Row near Whitehaven.[6] Most charmingly, at Brampton, a fairy clan has taken to writing to the local newspaper: these fairies come out every spring, when perfectly carved fairy doors appear on trees in the nearby woods…[7]

These are all traditions worth celebrating. However, with great respect to Geoffrey Hodson and his successors, their fairies are different from the fairies that appear all too fleetingly in nineteenth-century folklore writing from Cumbria. Hodson's visions, the 'pearly-looking beings' and the doors at Brampton represent industrial, and now digital human beings reconnecting with the wilds that they have left behind. The poor rural populations that believed in fairies two or three hundred years ago in Cumbria had to live in those wilds and they knew how cruel the British countryside could be. These farmers and labourers, and their families, told tales, huddled together under the chimney wing on winter nights, to 'kill their tedious Spinning hours/with Witches, Ghost and Fairy'.[8] They collected elf shot (flint arrowheads) and fairy pipes, and, when they ran across them outside, they pointed knowingly at fairy butter (a fungi) and fairy beads (fossils). They believed that fairies were dangerous and they protected themselves with salt, rowan branches and with holy words. If we could have introduced them to modern fairies—the fairies, say, of Disney cartoons or New Age retreats—they would have been bewildered.

Their fairies, part of our medieval, perhaps even our Iron Age, heritage, have now vanished from Cumbria and this chapter is an attempt to recover as much as possible of the original North-Western fairy. In the pages that follow, to keep the focus tight, I have given myself three boundaries. First, I keep to the county of Cumbria: what the last fairy believers in the nineteenth century would have known as Cumberland, Westmorland, Lancashire North of the Sands and the West Riding around Sedbergh. I sometimes look for parallels from further afield, but only to illustrate Cumbrian fairylore. Second, I have limited myself to fairies: in Cumbria that means small humanoids dwelling in communities underground. I have reluctantly ignored: hobs (solitary house fairies); knockers (mine fairies); boggles, boggarts, dobbies and other walking monsters; mermaids and water dwelling demons. Finally, I have stuck to sources written in or using material from the period when Cumbrian fairies were still a matter of belief, very crudely, 1700-1900. Before 1700 no one cared to write about Cumbrian fairies (there is little recorded before 1820), while after 1900 belief in traditional fairies rapidly fades away.

Fairy Character
There are two good general descriptions of Cumbrian fairies. The first is from John Briggs, and was written shortly before his death in 1824. Fairies were, Briggs suggested:

> ... a race of beings between men and spirits. They had marriages and reared children, followed occupations; and particularly churned their own butter. Their habitations were in caves; and they were considered perfectly harmless, capable of being visible or invisible at pleasure; and generally of small stature. We have never been able to learn whether they were immortal or not, or whether they were liable to future rewards or punishments.[9]

Briggs, a working-class autodidact, made great efforts to get material from 'the lips of the old folks, independent of what writers may have said on the subject'.[10] His words on the subject should be taken seriously.

About thirty years afterwards (1849) an anonymous writer in the *Kendal Mercury* remembered fairies as fun-loving creatures:

[E]ven as late as the middle of the eighteenth century, the fairies were in the habit of holding wakes on the clouds and mountain summits, and on some particular state occasions, such as the coronation of George the Second, they would come down to the margin of a lake or a river and hold a pic-nic party among themselves. Whether they ever took any food or not, we cannot say; but they were reputed as excellent dancers, and had a sort of aerial music, which for rich and thrilling harmony far surpassed the most exquisite warblings of the Swedish nightingale. Their dress was a sort of short petticoat, and they had upon the whole a feminine appearance...[11]

As we shall see, there is another reference to clouds in Cumbrian fairylore: and fairies' dancing and music and even their celebration of national festivals ties in with wider British fairylore.

Neither Briggs nor the anonymous writer from the *Kendal Mercury* refer to the darker side of Cumbrian fairies: in fact, Briggs states flatly that fairies 'were considered perfectly harmless'. But people did sometimes die because of fairies. A miner named Simon at Coniston was gifted great mineral wealth by fairy friends until he shared their secret with others: the fairies, who resent their secrets being betrayed, cut him off and he died shortly afterwards.[12] One remarkable early eighteenth-century document from Lamplugh consists, meanwhile, of a list of deaths, copied from parish records. The writer of the list claimed that four parishioners had been 'frighted to death by the fairies' in just five years![13] It is a nice question what exactly this means: men and women who had a heart attack while out walking at night perhaps?

Fairies also went after infrastructure. There is a mid-nineteenth-century account of fairies tearing down a railway bridge at Shap: fairies hated railways for the noise they brought.[14] It has been suggested that this was all a local joke. But there is a similar case from elsewhere in northern England. A spirit named Dickie from Derbyshire was supposed to have sabotaged a section of track near the house he haunted.[15] Perhaps a collapse in bridge work at Shap had been handed off onto the most prominent diabolical force in the area?

It could be argued that these fairies were acting in self defence against bad faith, night walkers and din. But there is also a predatory side to fairies that emerges in the Cumbrian reports and that cannot be excused so easily. In other parts of Britain (in Wales, Scotland, Lancashire and Cornwall) fairies kidnapped children and even adults. This is one of the first parts of fairy tradition to fade, when fairylore disintegrates in a given region. However, the idea was still present in nineteenth-century Cumbria, if only just. There is, for example, a reference in a Cumbrian poem to the fairies stealing

'Sir Hartley's Bride': though I have not been able to establish who Sir Hartley was, nor what happened to his wife.[16] One mid-nineteenth-century story, allegedly based on a traditional tale, describes, instead, how a woman from Caldbeck married a fairy and had a child. The child was stolen by the fairies and when its mother went to rescue her boy, both were killed in the small dell where the Fairy Kettle (a pool) and the Fairy Kirk (a cave) stand.[17] Another story has a man returning along a road at night near Bewcastle and being dragged from his horse by fairies and hustled towards their den. By good fortune the man was carrying some pages of the Bible; this broke the fairies' spell and the traveller escaped.[18]

Fairy Place-Names

In the last paragraph I referred to a Fairy Kettle and a Fairy Kirk, and this brings us to one of the most underused sources for fairylore: fairy place-names. People have, of course, long given names to supernatural forces that they believe inhabit the landscape and they have long named the landscape after these forces. Thinking of the examples above, a particularly violent pool in a river might be called 'the Fairy Kettle'; a large and open cave becomes 'the Fairy Kirk' or Church, as forty or fifty fairies could gather there; while a deep pot hole comes to be known as 'the Fairy Hole'. The earliest fairy name from Britain is recorded in the 1600s and some of these Cumbrian names will also date back to the early modern period, while others will be more recent. I have found 32 Cumbrian fairy place-names: I have ignored only obviously 'touristy' names, for example, 'Fairy House' or 'Fairy Glen'.[19] These 32 are precious because they give us some sense of how Cumbrian fairies were imagined, not by the folklore professionals, with their prejudices and preconceptions, but by local people. There is nothing as democratic as a place-name.

Of these 32 names, twelve were for caves; eleven for bodies of water (three for wells, two for river pools, one for a pond, one for a spring, and four for streams); and seven were for impressive free-standing rocks. Cumbrian fairies, then, liked, on this evidence, underground places, and you went there at your peril. Some boys who ventured into the Fairy Holes at Lamplugh, c. 1800, sensibly took a pistol with them to explore the corridors where they believed the fairies lived.[20] The fairies were constantly around water: though we do not know why. And fairies were occasionally tied to unusual rock formations. Just as interesting are the names that do not appear. While there are no fairy place-names for prehistoric mounds or natural hills: yet in the Middle Ages fairies had often been linked to such places.[21] In fact, the only hint of a relationship with prehistoric monuments that I have been able to find in Cumbria are three cairns at Little Langdale, the Fairy Graves.[22]

The Cumbrian fairy place-names give us a very good sense of fairies' dimensions. Cumbrian fairies were, to judge by these names, small, but not that small. The fairy caves, particularly Fairy Holes, were typically difficult to get into for an adult; or could be penetrated only with a good deal of ducking and weaving. Larger caves were often called Fairy Churches (or Kirks or Chapels): for example, the Fairy Kirk at Caldbeck, which is some twenty yards deep. But these caves could never have functioned as churches for a human population: they are on a smaller scale. In any case, such names remind us that fairies were traditionally imagined as being child-sized. This is nicely confirmed by a place called the Fairy Steps near Beetham in southern Cumbria. Visitors to the Beetham Fairy Steps are challenged to walk up the steps, as the fairies did, without touching the sides; something quite impossible for an adult, but something that a gutsy infant might just pull off.[23] A more ghastly confirmation of the small fairy comes in a newspaper story from 1844. Three boys were playing in the countryside outside Carlisle when they came across the body of a 'fairy' in a plantation. They 'kicked' the 'fairy' around for some minutes before adults intervened: it was a naked newborn child, murdered by its mother.[24]

There are doubtless many other fairy place-names that I have not come upon while combing through county records. There are certainly other places that were associated with the fairies. So there were fairies at St Herbert's Island on Derwent Water.[25] There were fairies at Mallerstang.[26] There were fairies, too, in the grounds of Myrtle Lodge at Soulby.[27] There was a legend about a sinister fairy godmother at Maiden Castle just outside the village.[28] There were memories of a King Eveling, sometimes said to be lord of the fairies, at Ravenglass.[29] There were fairies at the Quarry Beck near Lanercost and at Elliotstowhiliolm. Indeed, in the early 1880s some still remembered having heard, many years before, the fairies' feet jingling in silver stirrups when they rode their small horses there.[30]

In most cases we know only that fairies dwelt in these places, but in some we know a little more. The Castle Rock of Trierman, for example, had a fairy population who would change the aspect of the rock as travellers approached it.[31] Frankhousesteads, a building at High Cross Tarn was 'a place reputed to be haunted by fairies' and a gang of robbers: robbers sometimes encouraged supernatural stories to keep the curious away.[32] There were fairies at Bewcastle Castle, or at least if you whispered your love problems to a stone in the castle wall, the fairies were supposed to help you.[33] There was evidently a population of fairies at Mossband, as well, because an old man had memories from his time as a scholar in the early nineteenth century. 'A fairy happened to be passing the school. There was a general rush to get a glimpse of the creature; and as he was too small to fight his way to the front, it got past before he could see it.'[34] Folklorists will know how he felt....

Fairy Artifacts
Another interesting aspect of fairies are their possessions, some of which they left for humans to find in the fields and the woods. Cumbrian fairies were, for example, assiduous but careless pipe-smokers. One knowledgeable author for East Cumbria writes: '[The fairies] smoked, too, and their little pipes were sometimes picked up'.[35] These fairy pipes, often, appear in Cumbrian sources. A Westmorland writer noted, 'fairies themselves are scarcely ever mentioned, except, indeed, when the servant lad, in turning over the soil, stumbles upon the large uncouth head of an ancient tobacco

pipe, with the exclamation 'here's a fairy pipe".[36] One miner, Robert Bell used to be teased by the fairies, but they would also bring him 'fairy pipes' as gifts.[37] What were these objects? They were probably clay pipes that had been discarded two or three centuries before and that looked quiet alien and abnormally small to the finders. 'Fairy-pipes', as one Cumbrian dialect guide has it, 'tobacco pipes, with very small and peculiar shaped bowls, frequently turned up with the plough. These pipes are of various dates, generally from the reign of Elizabeth to James II'.[38]

More mysterious is 'fairy butter'. Fairies in Cumbria seem to have had something of an obsession with dairy. They, for example, loved preventing the butter from coming: as a counter-charm maids would throw salt in the fire while they were churning.[39] But fairies not only sabotaged butter making or stole butter from humans; they also made butter. As Briggs noted in the passage quoted above: they 'particularly churned their own butter'.[40] Another writer recalled:

In Little Langdale the Busk and the Forge,… were regularly visited by fairies— harmless little beings it would seem, of the house-goblin class, for their principal occupation seems to have been churning butter after the family had retired for the night. They were, however, rather thriftless little folk, for near the Forge it was common to find bits of butter scattered in the woods, dropped, it would seem, by the uncanny churners in their morning flight.[41]

The butter 'scattered in the woods' was almost certainly 'fairy butter', a bizarre substance recorded in many parts of England and Wales. There is some disagreement as to what 'fairy butter' was. But, at least in the North West, it seems to have been a yellowish-white fungus, *Tremella mesenterica*, which grows on tree trunks and which has a gelatinous quality.[42] The first rule of interaction with fairies is that you should not eat their food[43]: a generally good rule for wood fungi, as well. However, one early twentieth-century informant from northern Cumbria insisted that: 'It's lucky… if you eat fairy butter.' He even told a story about a ploughman who had been left fairy butter by some fairy neighbours. One of the ploughman's horses ate the butter and thrived, one did not and died.[44] As it happens ingested *Tremella mesenterica* has no obvious effects on humans (or horses). It is apparently innocuous: the fungi is rubbery and flavourless.[45]

More sinister than fairy butter were elf arrows. These were Neolithic flint arrow heads that still today can occasionally be picked up in the English countryside and that retail for a pound or two on eBay. These objects were interpreted, in Scotland, as a sign that the fairies were attacking cattle or even people.[46] The same rules and fears operated in Cumbria. 27 June 1712, Bishop Nicholson of Carlisle arrived in Bowness on the Solway Firth: '[w]here we saw several Elf Arrows, too pretious (for the Cure of Cattle Elf shot) to be parted w[i]t[h]'.[47] The implication here is that the Bishop had asked members of his flock whether they might not give him the flint heads, but that they had explained they were useful: they would protect cattle from being shot by the fairies or cure those that had been. It would be interesting to know how the Bishop took this not particularly Anglican approach to cattle disease.

A final fairy artifact were fairy beads. These were found, like fairy butter, in various parts of England. But in Cumbria they were associated with a stream at Stainton called 'Fairy-bead beck.' '[S]ome years ago', this place, according to Sullivan, 'furnished an unlimited supply of curiously shaped pebbles, from which the stream received its name. They are described as of the size of large beads, partly shaped like the joints of a backbone, partly having a resemblance to ladles with handles, and to 'cups and saucers.' But they are scarcely to be found now, as if the fairies and their beads had disappeared together'.[48] Fairy beads are explained, by the *Oxford English Dictionary*, as being for Cumberland 'the crinoidea or enchrinal fossil', though this corresponds poorly to the description of the Stainton fairy beads.

Traditional Fairy Tales

There are only a handful of traditional Cumbrian fairy tales that have been handed down to us. The most famous is the Luck of Eden Hall. According to a legend, which was first written up in the late eighteenth century, and which was then elaborated, some fairies were feasting at the Fairy Well outside the hall. A man came among them and seized a valuable fairy cup (or in some versions the cup is left by fairies who flee). The fairies, however, warn the thief that should the fairy cup break then the family would fall: hence the name 'the Luck of Eden Hall'.[49] For many years the family kept the cup in a bank vault to avoid any danger of breakage. Now the Luck rests in the Victoria and Albert Museum. It is a work of fourteenth-century Arab glass-blowers and was perhaps brought back to Cumbria from the crusades.[50]

There are a series of stories from western Europe describing intrepid travellers who steal fairy objects, typically cups, from feasting fairies.[51] The story of the Luck, then, has antecedents. And this is true of four other Cumbrian fairy stories. Take the following tale about the ploughman who assists a fairy: a tale once well known across England as 'the broken ped' (a ped is a baker's shovel).[52]

In a paddock lying adjacent to the Fairy Kirk, two men were one day ploughing; by and by a sad lamentation was heard, something having evidently gone wrong in the domestic economy of the fairies, who, however, were invisible to the ploughmen. One of these took courage to ask what was the matter, when he was informed that the churn staff had broken. Bring it here, said the man, and I'll mend it for you! When he got to the end of the furrow, there lay the damaged article, also hammer, nails and everything necessary for repairing it. The man soon skillfully performed his self-appointed task and leaving the renovated churnstaff where he found it he returned to his work. When he again came to the end of the furrow, he found an offering of gratitude in the shape of a 'capital pot o' drink' which the latter worker scornfully declined any 'o' their fairy stuff'. He is said to have paid dearly for his contempt as 'he niver dowed after', but he who drank and approved throve ever after.[53]

The fate of the two men mirrors that of the two plough-horses in the story about fairy butter quoted above.

A third story, this time from North Cumbria, is also told with slight variations across Britain:

> There was a fairy that looked like a hare. It was a real fairy, but a man caught it for a hare, and put it in a bag, and thought he would have a nice Sunday dinner. While it was in the bag it saw its father outside, and he called to it 'Pork, pork!' and it cried out 'Let me go to daddy!' And then the man was angry, and said 'Thoo ga to thy daddy!' and it went away to its daddy; and he was very much disappointed at not getting his Sunday dinner.[54]

There are also usually two hunters, or more typically poachers, who accidentally bag a fairy only to drop the bag in terror when it begins to speak.[55] The Cumbrian farmer seems more bad tempered than fearful. I know of no other version where the fairy takes on the form of an animal.

A fourth story describes fairy crime on the mean streets of Ambleside.

> One old fellow told the writer indeed that in his young days strange were the reputed doings of the little folk in Ambleside fair and market. Dressed as common folk, they would mingle with the marketing folk, and then by blowing at the women at the market stalls they became invisible, and were enabled to steal things from the stalls.[56]

Here we have a confused version of a common European fairy tale, with versions that date back to the thirteenth century. A woman helps the fairies, often as a midwife. She, accidentally, splashes some fairy water on her eye and this allows her to see all fairies. The next day she spies them stealing in the marketplace and when she upbraids them for their dishonesty a fairy blinds her in the eye which had been splashed, often by blowing on the magic eye.[57] The 'old fellow' seems to have misremembered a story perhaps first told to him in the early nineteenth century.

A final story relates to the lands around Ullswater and was confirmed by the protagonist's aged grandson in c.1850, suggesting that the story was set about a century earlier.[58] It was the last time fairies were seen in this part of Cumbria.

> An inhabitant of Martindale, Jack Wilson by name, was one evening crossing Sandwick Rigg on his return home, when he suddenly perceived before him, in the glimpses of the moon, a large company of fairies intensely engaged in their favourite diversions. He drew near unobserved, and presently descried a stee (ladder) reaching from amongst them up into a cloud. But no sooner was the

presence of mortal discovered than all made a hasty retreat up the stee. Jack rushed forward, doubtless firmly determined to follow them into fairy-land, but arrived too late. They had effected their retreat, and quickly drawing up the stee, they shut the cloud, and disappeared.[59]

Here again we have a story that was told through much of Britain, the 'fairy's flit': made famous by Kipling in *Puck of Pook's Hill*.[60] However, usually the fairies simply march or ride away. This is the only example I know where the fairies ascend into the sky.

Non-Traditional Stories

So much for our handful of traditional Cumbrian tales. There are also a series of fairy stories that are best described as personal experiences. They are rawer, as a result, and more intriguing than the cookie-cutter yarns listed above. Take this experience told to Joseph Ritson:

> His informant related that an acquaintance, in Westmoreland, having a great desire, and praying earnestly to see a fairy, was told, by a friend, if not a fairy in disguise, that on the side of such a hill, at such a time of day, he should have a sight of one; and, accordingly, at the time and place appointed, 'the hob goblin,' in his own words, 'stood before him in the likeness of a green-coat lad', but, in the same instant, the spectator's eye glancing, vanished into the hill.[61]

The detail about fairies vanishing if you take your eye off them recalls Irish-lore about leprechauns.[62] It is not common in England.

Here, instead, we have an account of a low flying fairy cow.

> The tradition runs that the last fairy seen near Whitehaven was by a man standing on what is called the 'fairy rock,' near Saltom Pit. The man was looking towards the Isle of Man, when he saw a calf coming, at some height in the air, over the sea, and alight on the rock beside him. In astonishment he exclaimed, 'G——d! Weel loppen, cofe!' At the sound of the sacred name the calf disappeared, and no fairy has since been seen.[63]

Fairies do not typically appear as animals (though note the fairy hare above). They also do not fly in over the sea. However, the story of an innocent observer inadvertently protecting himself from the supernatural with God's name is well known.[64]

A further account comes from some young children who excavated a fairy house in the mid-nineteenth century. We are at Peelwyke near Keswick:

> [T]hree or four of the young sons [of the Watson family] were accustomed to play on the Castle Hill, which is believed to have been a British fort guarding the pass

or wyke. These boys made an excavation in the side of the hill and uncovered a neat hut roofed with slate. Dinner-time came before their exploration was completed, and they were called home. In hopes of having made a great discovery, they hurried back to the hill, but could not even find the place, for all was covered with soil and green sward as when they first found it, and no one has found the place since.[65]

In the south-west of Britain fairies often 'pixy-lead' their victims and trick them into getting lost.[66] There are no accounts of this from northern England (known to me). This form of fairy trickery is the closest we come. Watson senior, incidentally, once set a dog on 'two tiny people dressed in green in a meadow near Peelwyke', and his dog was, predictably enough, sent rolling over and over in agony.[67]

This next story took place at a four-lanes end, a crossroads, the place for many night-time visitations.

There was an old farmer at Lupton called Michael Black. He was coming back one night from Kirkby Lonsdale to Lupton, and when he came to four lane ends on the Kirkby Lonsdale-Lupton road, he found a hedge… across the road. A little gentleman came up to him and promised to help him if he gave him a pound of butter off his back. He would make him a road through the hedge. The farmer did, and he eventually got back home in the early hours of the morning, minus the pound of butter. And when the son went onto the road the next day he found the butter on the wall-top.[68]

The account of fairy highway robbery is also without precedent. Did an imaginative Luptonite just make it up to tease a folklorist? Perhaps, but there are a couple of details that suggest this is a genuine Cumbrian tale. Dairy foods appear again and again in accounts of Cumbrian fairies, as attentive readers of this chapter will have noticed. There is also the hedge across the road, which is echoed in a Cumbrian monster legend: the Dalehead Boggle blocks a road with a similar stratagem when a shepherd tries to pass.[69]

In the next story, Jwony goes to get his friends some whisky and is returning with a gallon and a half from an illegal still when he has an accident. He had already, it should be noted, imbibed a good deal.

On his way home [Jwony] had a brook to cross; and feeling uncertain whether he could safely cross by the stepping-stones, he took the wiser course to lay down on the bank, but eventually rolled into the stream, where fortunately it was shallow; and there he lay helpless. With more than common sagacity, the dog seemed to understand his predicament, and hurried home; and by its anxious gestures and continued whining, induced Betty, the wife, to accompany it to where her husband was left, and in time to save him. During the time he was in the water, he chanced to turn his head round, and saw a little man, of less than a foot high, dressed in green, and perched on his shoulder; he remained there till Betty came, and then he vanished. Jwony fancied the little creature had the power, and kept him down, and he used to say, 'If it hedn't been for Swan and Betty, I med ha' tofert in t' beck; for it was them 'at freetn't t' laal thing away.'[70]

Jwony seems to have been paralysed in the stream. There is one near contemporary example from Devon of a man paralysed in a wood blaming the pixies for his woes.[71]

A final intriguing case are the Soutra Fell sightings.[72] Soutra Fell is an extraordinarily steep and often rocky, scree-laden mount in the Northern Fells. In 1735, 1737 and 1745 spectral figures were seen on Soutra Fell from the farmlands below. In 1735 a farmer and his servant saw a ghostly marching army; in 1743 a servant watched an unearthly man and dog chasing after horses; and in 1744, 26 people observed a large body of mysterious horses parade for some two hours up and, then, over the Fell. The figures were very much on the mountain; they were not in the air. This was no Fata Morgana. But one of the witnesses stated that they could not possibly have been normal human beings. The man and his dog, for example, ran at an extraordinary speed. The horses went over places that horses could not go: there were carriages moving up rockfaces. The horses and human beings seemed to be a single entity. When subsequently the viewers went to the Soutra to follow the spectres' paths, they could find no clue that anything physical had been there: they found no thrown horseshoes or foot- or hoof-prints.

The word 'fairy' is never used to describe the Soutra spectres, but they are reminiscent of other fairy sightings; and there is the suspicion that had this happened in, say, Ireland or Wales they would have simply been described as fairy armies. Fairies were often seen marching or drilling out in the wilds.[73] Indeed, in 1744/1745, mysterious marching armies on the Lancashire hills were interpreted, quite naturally, as fairies.[74] There is also the date. All three sightings took places on Midsummer Night's Eve, a night that is particularly associated with fairy sightings. There was sworn testimony and the phenomenon was discussed as a scientific problem: these are not the kind of sources where the word 'fairy' would be used, especially in the eighteenth century. But it is very likely that those who lived in the shadow of Soutra will have referred to the spectres with that word.

Conclusion: Death of the Cumbrian Fairy

When did the traditional Cumbrian fairy die? In 1822, John Briggs wrote the following, about Westmorland, in the south of Cumbria: 'Fairies, which were once so plentiful in this country, are completely gone. Even those who believe they once existed, acknowledge they are now extinct'.[75] William Pearson, a learned friend of Wordsworth, confirmed Briggs' impressions, for the same region, twenty years later: 'As for Robin Goodfellow, Hob-thrush, and the Fairies, they are all gone—utterly vanished—'They live no longer in the faith of Reason.'[76] In 1856, the Rev James

Simpson wrote in a local newspaper: 'Fairies have I think long been strangers in [Westmorland] They seem to have lingered much longer on the borders than they did with us. I do not remember that I ever heard a story or tradition that fairies had been seen in our neighbourhood'.[77] Then, in 1857, Jeremiah Sullivan, in the first proper volume of Cumbrian folklore, insisted that fairies 'are now spoken of as belonging to the past'.[78]

However, these obituaries were premature. In 1901, a Mrs Hodgson of Newby Grange, in the south of Cumbria, read a short paper entitled: 'On Some Surviving Fairies'. Her piece is valuable, first, for recording precious Cumbrian fairylore, but, second, for reminding us of how easy it is for collectors to miss fairies.

> The injudicious collector who hunts [for fairies], so to say, with horn and hounds, will draw every cover blank; and even the aids to scouting formulated in folk-lore tracts may not always insure success... Fairies, it is well known, thrive only in moonshine.[79]

Did Briggs, Pearson, Simpson and Sullivan go charging in where a more gentle approach might have brought still living fairy experiences? Very possibly. By the early nineteenth century, traditional fairies were, in Britain, a sign of ignorance, a stigma even, and it cannot have been easy for agricultural workers to share experiences, with people of learning, particularly those, like Sullivan or Pearson, from a higher social class. Consider the following. The last Cumbrian fairy legend (the fairy highway robber) appeared in a survey in 1952, after a grandson recounted a fairy encounter that his grandfather had experienced, c.1855, at Lupton. Lupton, of course, is in the very region that Briggs had pronounced as being fairyless in 1822!

So when did the last Cumbrian fairy disappear, or, as at Martindale, climb up into the clouds? Though Mrs Hodgson did a wonderful job of searching out fairylore, at the turn of the century, she was clearly 'scraping the barrel'. It is difficult to believe that, even in the most isolated parts of the country, fairy belief continued much beyond the First World War, though the story from 1952 warns against overconfidence. However, the end of the Cumbrian fairy was a question, not so much of death as progressive neutering. We have seen in this chapter that traditional Cumbrian fairies had a malevolent and even murderous streak. Yet, most of the sources expressing this unpleasant side are early: for example, the reference to elf shot or the Lamplugh fairy killings both date to the early eighteenth century. In the bulk of the records we have from the nineteenth century, Cumbrian fairies show themselves, instead, in a kinder, at worst, mischievous light, throwing butter around or losing their pipes.

Sometimes we can see this neutering take place before our eyes. In one Cumbrian account, from 1859, an author notes that 'a fairy was a being who could dance upon a mushroom without injury to the delicate fungus'; our writer is here replacing the infant-sized Cumbrian fairy with something resembling a butterfly.[80] In another account, we read that Cumbrian fairies were: 'a delicate' (that word again) 'and graceful creation, something for the imagination to toy with, never interfering with the higher interests, or unsettling our relations with the life to come.'[81] Where, on earth, were these dainty, delicate fairies coming from? The chief point of inspiration was the fairy of Victorian children's books, of Victorian art and the Victorian theatre, where the fairy had become, by 1860, a British angel: traditional fairies, it should be noted, did not have wings.

We know for a fact that these dainty fairies made their way to the north west and the proof is not just in sentences like those quoted in the last paragraph. In 1867, for example, there was a pantomime put on at Whitehaven with 'Harlequin, Little Boy Blue and the Fairy of the Cumberland Fells'.[82] We have a record from Mill Row of a May festival, in 1892, where participants appeared as 'fairies and witches, reapers, gleaners and binders'.[83] There was, meanwhile, at Carlisle, in January 1897, a children's fancy dress party with 'fairies of night, a Highlander, Paddy, a jockey, a Spanish dancing girl, Japanese lady...'[84] Later that year children were dressing up again: this time as 'Spanish ladies, gipsies, and fairies'.[85] What did these fairies look like? They presumably resembled the fairies shown in Victorian theatres and in many Victorian books: they would have been white, winged and very possibly crowned. The traditional Cumbrian fairy had many enemies: railways, school teachers, supercilious vicars… But his most insidious foe was the new fairy, smiling in pictures from the *London Illustrated News* and dancing on creaking provincial theatre boards.

FERISHER AND HIKEY SPRITES

East-Anglia by Francis Young

East Anglia, which includes the counties of Norfolk, Suffolk and Cambridgeshire (and is sometimes extended to include the county of Essex) is England's easternmost region, jutting out into the North Sea. The region is renowned for its agricultural richness, its largely flat landscape, and its patchwork of attractive villages that still feel culturally remote from London, in spite of the region's geographical proximity to the capital. East Anglia has never had a reputation as a home of fairylore—perhaps because it lacks some of the landscape features (such as hills and caves) that are often associated with the fairies. As the East Anglian philologist Robert Forby mused in 1830,

> We partake of the mediocrity of our scenery; and we may fairly conclude that we never had any superstitions but such as are homely and domestic; and even these are fast wearing away. The very fairies would be forgotten, but for the rings in the meadows that bear their name.[1]

Forby's view seems to have influenced subsequent East Anglian folklorists, who made little effort to look for fairylore. But the region is by no means without its distinctive fairy traditions. Suffolk has by far the best recorded fairy traditions in East

Anglia—and some of the best recorded material in England, including some intriguing evidence for medieval fairy beliefs. Fairies in Suffolk, Cambridgeshire and Essex were commonly known as *farisees*, *ferriers* or *ferishers*, while Norfolk was home to the more obscurely named 'hikey sprites'.

Whether the sparseness of recorded East Anglian fairylore reflects an early decline of fairy belief in these counties, or is merely a reflection of the interests of East Anglian folklorists, is a matter of interpretation. On the one hand, the success of the Reformation in East Anglia and the rise of Puritanism in the region may have had a damaging effect on some aspects of East Anglia's traditional lore. On the other hand, where folklore collectors did make the effort to gather fairylore in the nineteenth century they were well rewarded, so it may be that a prejudice against the idea that East Anglia could have fairies at all conditioned the folkloric literature.

Place-names and dialect words

Place-names with definite fairy connections in East Anglia are few and far between, although Suffolk has one of very few place-names derived directly from the Old English word *ælf*: the village of Elveden, from *ælfadenu* ('valley of elves'). Unusually, the etymology receives some degree of confirmation in a twelfth-century hagiography that glosses the name Elveden as *vallem nympharum* ('valley of the nymphs').[2] A much later tradition recorded in the early twentieth century identifies the original 'valley of the elves' with a pit where an old woman reported hearing 'fairy music' as a child, but it seems likely this was a tradition inspired by the name of the village, rather than vice versa.[3]

Place-names derived from 'puck' are absent from East Anglia, with the possible exception of a house name from late medieval Stowmarket in Suffolk: 'Pokfennes', later recorded as 'Puckfens', first mentioned in the 1504 will of Thomas Gowle.[4] It seems unlikely that the Suffolk hamlet of Pixey Green (in the parish Stradbroke) has anything to do with the word 'pixy' (which is, in any case, more common in the west of England); a place-name recorded as *Phykessaee* in the same parish in the thirteenth-century may be related. One possibility, suggested by Keith Briggs, is that *Phykessaee* originally referred to a lake or pond stocked with pike.[5]

The Suffolk town of Southwold once had an area known as Fairy Hills (from Bronze Age tumuli now lost to coastal erosion).[6] Also in Suffolk, Thorington once had a Fairy Hill and Ashfield-cum-Thorpe a Fairy Farm.[7] Another Fairy Hill could be found at Ditchingham in Norfolk.[8] 'Hob' or 'Hobb' place-names may be fairy-related, but may also derive from a surname. A Hob Hole can be found at Pensthorpe in Norfolk,[9] and Simon Young has identified only one further 'Hobbs Hole' in East Anglia (at Great Warley in Essex), and several 'Bobbit'-derived place-names. Young suggests that 'Bobbit' is a regional variant of 'Hobb' specific to Essex, referring to some sort of bogey.[10] In addition, a Sprite's Lane can be found at Sproughton in Suffolk and a Spriteshall Lane at Felixstowe, although it is as likely that these names derive from surnames as from supernatural beings.[11]

A solitary place-name reference to Robin Goodfellow can be found in the Cambridgeshire town of March, where there is a Robin Goodfellow's Lane. The name is at least as old as 1830.[12] Robert Forby, writing about Suffolk dialect in 1830, noted that it was still proverbial 'to laugh like Robin Goodfellow' (meaning to laugh heartily), even though the identity of Robin Goodfellow himself was by then forgotten.[13] Furthermore, Forby recorded the name of a nursery bogey, 'Tom Poker', which may derive from 'puck'.[14]

Medieval Fairies

Fairies can be difficult to identify unambiguously in medieval sources because there was no consistency in the way medieval writers wrote about the fairies, or even in the words they used for them in Latin (the language of most medieval literature produced in England). However, some more or less clear-cut examples survive from medieval East Anglia. Between 1149 and 1172 Thomas of Monmouth, a monk of the cathedral priory of Norwich, told the story of a young woman who lived as a pious virgin in her father's house in the Suffolk port of Dunwich (then a large and prosperous town, before it was swept away by coastal erosion). The young woman was approached by a *faunus* (literally a faun, but in this case a synonym for a fairy[15]), who made the young woman a proposal of marriage, and 'produced rings, necklaces, collars, brooches, earrings and many things of the kind'. When the young woman refused, the *faunus* disappeared, but kept returning and pressing her, offering her 'Silken robes all glistening with gems, silver and gold, and whatever can be imagined most precious and fair in the glory of this world'.

The young woman told her parents, who concluded that her suitor was a spirit and set guards on her door, but to no avail. The *faunus* now turned to violence, while the parents had masses said for their daughter and sprinkled the bedroom with holy water, fixing a cross to her bed. This only further infuriated the fairy, who visited more frequently. Finally, one night the young woman received a vision of Bishop Herbert de Losinga, the founder of Norwich Cathedral, who told her to go to the tomb of William of Norwich, a boy supposedly killed by Jews in 1144. After praying at the tomb she was no longer troubled by the spirit.[16]

A similar incident occurred over a century later at Ingoldisthorpe in Norfolk and was recorded in the process for the canonization of Thomas Cantilupe in 1291-2. Christiana Nevenon was molested for five years by an 'incubus demon' (*a demone … incubo*) who transported her 'to a certain pleasant place, where she saw many marvellous things, among which there was also a table decorated and furnished with all kinds of delicious foods'. The incubus invited Christiana to eat, but she managed to make the sign of the cross and the scene vanished. However, the hand with which Christiana had made the sign of the cross atrophied and she was unable to move it until she prayed at the tomb of Thomas Cantilupe.[17]

Thomas of Monmouth's choice of the word *faunus* for the tempter of the young women of Dunwich may owe something to earlier English traditions of sexually seductive spirits, which are mentioned as long ago as the writings of Bede in the eighth century.[18] While the thirteenth-century account of Christiana Nevenon did use the term 'demon', the 'pleasant place' (*locus amoenus*) to which Christiana is transported by the incubus and his efforts to tempt her to eat otherworldly food suggest that he, too, may be a fairy—as does the link with muscular atrophy, which was sometimes blamed on the fairies (see below).

East Anglia is home to the earliest English example of a changeling story, the tale of Malekin, which was recorded in the early thirteenth century by the Essex chronicler Ralph of Coggeshall in his *Chronicon Anglicanum*. According to Ralph, 'a certain fantastical spirit' appeared in the household of Sir Osberne de Bradwell at Dagworth near Stowmarket, Suffolk, during the reign of Richard I (1189-99):

In the time of King Richard, at Dagworth in Suffolk, a fantastical spirit appeared many times and often at in the house of Sir Osberne de Bradwelle, speaking with the family of the aforesaid knight, imitating the voice of a one-year-old child, and she called herself Malekin. She said that her mother and brother lived in a neigh-bouring manor, and that she was often abused by them because she often presumed to leave them to talk to human beings. She did and said many things worthy of wonder and laughter and occasionally revealed a hidden act of someone. At first, the knight's wife and his whole family were exceedingly terrified by her conversa-tion, but having become accustomed to her words and the ridiculous things she did, they talked to her confidently and familiarly, asking her about many things. She spoke in English, according to the dialect of that region, but occasionally even in Latin, and discoursed on the Scriptures to the knight's chaplain, as he himself has truthfully maintained to us. She could be heard and felt, but hardly ever seen, except once when she was seen by a certain chambermaid in the shape of a very tiny infant, who was dressed in a kind of white tunic, and that not before the girl had begged and prayed her to show herself visibly. She would in no way consent to her request until the maid would swear by the Lord that she would neither touch nor hold her. She also said that she had been born at Lavenham and while her mother took her into a field, when she was eating with others, and had now remained seven years with the same; and she said that after seven more years she would revert to her former living with human beings habitation. She said that she and others made use of a certain hat, because it restored them to invisibility. She would often demand food and drink from the servants, which was left for her on a certain chest and not found again.[19]

At the heart of Ralph's Malekin story is a recognisable changeling narrative of a child stolen by the fairies in the fields near the Suffolk village of Lavenham, but the story is unusual (even unique) in portraying the human soul of the stolen child as a disembodied spirit. Indeed, the spirit in Ralph's account resembles the phenomenon much later called a poltergeist (a borrowed German word first used in English in the nineteenth century), which is not seen but plays tricks on the household and sometimes communicates with them. Katharine Briggs observed that Malekin behaved like 'a domestic spirit half-way between the brownie and boggart types which were later to become familiar', with the difference that Malekin 'is clothed in white instead of rags, and is rather unusual as being a female one'. Briggs presumed that Malekin's mortal body was occupied by a fairy (as a changeling) while Malekin was leading a disembodied existence with the fairies.[20]

If this interpretation is correct, it suggests an unusually sophisticated understanding of the changeling phenomenon, which was usually portrayed as the physical abduction of a human infant and its physical replacement by a fairy infant. In the case of Malekin, it was the infant's soul that was taken and a fairy soul left behind in the infant's body, rather like a possessing demon. Malekin herself resembles a demon in her ability to reveal 'hidden things' and speak Latin—abilities that her soul has presumably acquired from the fairies in a disembodied state. However, the fairies are never named in the tale of Malekin, and we are left to infer their identity.

Another story found in the pages of Ralph of Coggeshall—and also recorded by the chronicler William of Newburgh—is less clearly linked to fairylore. The story of the Green Children of Woolpit is probably Suffolk's best-known folktale: reapers in the fields near the village of Woolpit found a boy and girl, their hair and skin completely green, in a hole in the ground and brought the children to the local lord. They were unable to speak the native language nor to eat the food set before them, although they eventually ate green vegetables. The boy sickened and died, but the green girl survived and lost her unusual pigmentation, eventually telling the story of how she and her brother became lost in 'St Martin's Land', their world of perpetual twilight, and followed the sound of bells until they emerged in the human world.[21]

The Green Children of Woolpit have attracted a great deal of speculation since the sixteenth century, and both Briggs and Enid Porter interpreted the tale as an example of fairylore, citing elements such as the children's emergence from the earth and their inability to eat human food.[22] On the other hand, the children display no magical powers, and no other story clearly links green hair and skin with the fairies—unless we choose to interpret the Green Knight of the celebrated Middle English poem *Sir Gawain and the Green Knight* as a fairy. The Green Children, while they are otherworldly visitants, are not obviously fairies.

A snapshot of East Anglian fairylore at the end of the fifteenth century can be glimpsed in the records of an ecclesiastical trial that took place in Ixworth church in Suffolk in the summer of 1499. A young woman from Great Ashfield, Marion Clerk, claimed to have the power to heal, which she gained from the Virgin Mary and *les Gracyous Fayry* ('the gracious fairies'), who were 'little people who gave her information whenever she wanted it'. Marion's powers were linked to her mother Agnes, who was also on trial, and who claimed that as a child she conversed with elves ('Les Elvys') who promised she would one day have a child gifted with healing abilities (Marion). Agnes also claimed that the fairies gave her daughter Marion a magical cherrywood stick in order to find buried treasure hidden by Jews in Moyse's Hall, a stone building in Bury St Edmunds linked in folklore to England's Jewish community, expelled from the country in 1290.

It was only when the Clerk family brought the magical stick to the curate of Great Ashfield to be blessed, on Palm Sunday, that the church's suspicions were aroused. The case was referred to the Norwich consistory court where the Clerks were found guilty of 'heretical pravity', made to recant their deviant beliefs and sentenced to penance.[23] One feature of the Clerk case suggests that the family may have conflated the fairies with the mysterious Jews, since Marion Clerk said that both the fairies and Jews believed in God the Father. Such conflation between fairies and Jews as mysterious, magical and non-Christian 'others' occurred elsewhere in medieval English literature,[24] and it is striking that devotion to the antisemitic cult of William of Norwich delivered the young woman of Dunwich from the unwanted attentions of her fairy lover. Both Jews and fairies were linked to child abduction—in the case of Jews, through the 'blood libel' which claimed Jews kidnapped Christian children in order to parody Christ's crucifixion. Whether this medieval conflation of Jews and fairies was linked in any way to later confusion between the dialect word 'farisees' and the Biblical Pharisees must remain speculation.[25]

Marion and Agnes Clerk belonged to a tradition of 'fairy healing' that occasionally came to the attention of the church courts. One such case was heard by the Bishop of Ely's commissary in June 1566, when Elizabeth Mortlock of Pampisford, Cambridgeshire, confessed that she 'measureth the girdle or band of any such persons being sick [or] haunted, from her elbow to her thumb, and craving for God and saint Charity's sake that if someone be haunted with a fairy yea or no she may know'.[26] In 1562 the Suffolk physician William Bullein noted that people resorted to a cunning-woman named Mother Line in the village of Parham 'to have the fairy charmed, and the spirit conjured away' by Mother Line's blessed ebony beads.[27] As Owen Davies has shown, traditional healers of this kind both relied on the assistance of the fairies and claimed to heal people afflicted by fairy harm.[28]

Fairies and Imps

The counties of East Anglia were the epicentre of early modern witch-hunting in England. The earliest trial under the 1563 Witchcraft Act was held at Chelmsford in Essex in 1566, while an early campaign of witchfinding by the Essex magistrate Bryan Darcy resulted in the execution of ten witches at St Osyth in 1582.[29] However, the witch-hunt led by Matthew Hopkins throughout East Anglia in the years 1644—47 was the largest in English history, producing hundreds of victims and many confessions obtained under torture. A recurring theme in East Anglian witchcraft trials was the importance of 'imps', witches' familiars that often took animal form.[30] Like fairies, imps were embodied spirits, although in only one case (from Dorset) did a contemporary pamphlet specifically identify imps with fairies.[31]

Witch-hunters unhesitatingly identified imps with demons, but in truth they belonged to a 'homespun demonology' that cannot easily be reconciled with theology.[32] In some cases, the underlying influence of fairy belief can be discerned clearly in the testimonies of accused witches; Ellen Driver of Framlingham confessed to giving birth to two 'changelings' conceived by the devil,[33] and several Suffolk women claimed they were visited by imps in the likeness of children rather than animals. However, the idea that fairies can transform into animals features in later East Anglian folklore (in a Suffolk folktale collected in the 1870s fairies turned into white mice),[34] and by the nineteenth century imps were associated with magic as well as witchcraft—the benevolent Aldeburgh cunning-man 'Old Winter' was served by imps, for example.[35]

Belief in imps remained potent in the Cambridgeshire Fens into the twentieth century, with the hereditary witches of Horseheath inheriting a box of familiars resembling white mice—one of whom bore the fairy name 'Red Cap'—whom they deployed to spy on their neighbours.[36] Their close association with the human witch or sorcerer is one of the less fairy-like features of imps, who seem at times more like supernatural pets, but in other ways imps resemble fairies: they are spirits in corporeal form, possessed of magical power, and able to change their shape at will. The extent to which the imps of East Anglia belong to fairylore rather than to a folk demonology derived from the era of the witch trials remains difficult to assess.

Ferishers, Hikey Sprites and Traditional Tales

Judging from one story about the eighteenth-century highwayman Stephen Bunce (d. 1707), people in Essex were still intrigued by the idea of the fairies living underground in the reign of Queen Anne. On one occasion, Bunce tricked a man into dismounting from his horse by exploiting his unwitting victim's curiosity about the fairies. Bunce pressed his ear to the ground and claimed to be listening to fairy music, and when the man dismounted to listen, Bunce stole his horse and rode off to Romford.[37] The idea of the fairies as a secret, underground society was echoed by a Norfolk girl questioned by Thomas Keightley between 1828 and 1850, who spoke of fairies who 'dressed in white, and lived under the ground, where they constructed houses, bridges, and other edifices'. She added that it was unsafe to approach them when they appeared above ground.[38]

Most of our knowledge of East Anglian fairylore in the nineteenth century derives from one man, Arthur Hollingsworth (1802-59), who was vicar of the Suffolk town of Stowmarket from 1837 until his death. Brought up in Ireland,[39] Hollingsworth was the author of a detailed antiquarian history of Stowmarket in 1844, to which he appended a remarkable series of accounts of fairy encounters collected from elderly parishioners in Stowmarket and the nearby parish of Onehouse.[40] The seriousness with which Hollingsworth approached fairylore was unusual in East Anglia at the time, perhaps reflecting his Irish upbringing. The lore recorded by Hollingsworth included local versions of the widespread tales 'The Ploughman and the Fairies' and 'Midwife to the Fairies', as well as changeling lore. Most strikingly, perhaps, the 'Old Parish Clerk' of Stowmarket informed Hollingsworth that eighty or a hundred years earlier (1740s-

1760s) the fairies regularly came into the town at night, 'a large company of them dancing, singing, and playing music together'.[41]

In 1873 Walter Rye first recorded the Norfolk tradition of 'Hyter-sprites', whom he described as 'a kind of fairy rather beneficent than otherwise—a special habitat for which is a lane called Blow Hill, in Great Melton, prettily overshadowed with beech trees'.[42] Later authors characterised the hyter sprites (or hikey sprites) as more malevolent, and the research of Daniel Rabuzzi in the 1980s among older people in Norfolk suggests that the 'hikeys' functioned as bogeys to scare children away from lonely and dangerous places.[43] The hyter sprites were entirely confined to Norfolk, and even people on the Norfolk-Suffolk border (the Waveney Valley) knew about hyters only because they had heard about them from Norfolk relatives.[44]

Belief in the 'hyters' was concentrated largely on the Norfolk coast and in the Broads, and the name may be derived from Old English *hedan*, 'to heed/guard', suggesting the hyter sprites were originally guardian spirits of some kind.[45] In folklore research conducted among elderly Norfolk residents in 2008-13, Ray Loveday found no fewer than 23 variants of the name of the hyter sprites.[46] Loveday found hyter sprite lore connected with 77 different parishes in Norfolk, compared with Rabuzzi's 29 locations identified in the 1980s,[47] and parental threats to children about the 'hyters' or 'hikeys' seem to have been a routine feature of rural life in Norfolk between the wars.

In 1877 local journalist Francis Hindes Groome began publishing a series of 'Suffolk Notes and Queries' in a local newspaper, *The Ipswich Journal*. Anna Walter Thomas (née Fison) and her sister Lois Fison provided Groome with examples of fairylore derived from their childhood nurse, who came from Barningham in northwest Suffolk. One of the tales published by Groome, 'Tom Tit Tot', gained global fame as the English version of 'Rumpelstiltskin' (Tale Type 500), while another, 'Brother Mike', was a local version of a widespread story in which a farmer catches fairies in his barn.[48]

Other areas of East Anglia had their own distinctive fairy traditions. The Waveney Valley was known for its 'Sylham Lamps', trickster spirits that misled the unwary in the form of will o' the wisps, first mentioned by Richard Gough in his 1722 annotations to William Camden's *Britannia*.[49] Enid Porter believed that a decline in witchcraft belief in the Cambridgeshire Fens resulted in 'some Fenland housewives' attributing misfortune to the fairies instead. The influence of 'Irish neighbours' led Fenlanders to attribute the failure of butter to churn to the fairies; they also believed a door had to be left open in order to allow a fairy to enter and watch over bread dough set to prove before the fire, although food for the fairy had to be left beside the dough.[50] Porter gave no source for these solitary survivals of Fenland fairylore, although it is true that many Irish seasonal workers came to live in the Fens in the twentieth century and had a significant influence on the local area. However, the relationship suggested by Porter between witchcraft belief and fairy belief seems unlikely, since traditional belief in witchcraft persisted in the Cambridgeshire Fens for longer than most other places in England.[51]

The decline of East Anglian Fairies

'These ancient inhabitants of our homes and meadows are now all but forgotten', observed Charles Partridge, writing of Suffolk's fairies in *East Anglian Notes and Queries* in 1904.[52] Such pessimistic assessments of fairylore were common in the early twentieth century, and usually overstated; as Ray Loveday has shown in his study of hyter sprites, fairylore was still recoverable in Norfolk in the second decade of the twenty-first century. Nevertheless, it is undeniable that fairylore is an insignificant feature of the East Anglian folklore collected in the nineteenth and twentieth centuries when set beside the corpus of witchcraft lore and ghost lore from the region.

Before the First World War a group of boys in the Suffolk village of Saxmundham saw seven or eight mysterious dancers in a nearby meadow, dressed in diaphanous white garments, who disappeared after a few moments.[53] Tellingly, the witness who recounted this to the folklorist Joan Forman in the 1970s did not identify the beings as fairies; they were, rather, 'dancing ghosts', in spite of the fact that the incident almost exactly resembled one of the incidents recorded by Hollingsworth, when a man walking near Stowmarket in the 1820s saw mysterious dancers moving silently in a ring in a meadow whose 'dresses sparkled as if with spangles, like the girls at shows at Stow fair'.[54] In both cases, the witnesses reported they were unable to make out the dancers' faces.

Aside from rare fairy encounters, traditional fairy belief in early twentieth-century East Anglia was confined largely to the bread oven and the stable. People continued to place a 'farisee loaf' (an echinoid fossil) next to the oven in order to encourage loaves to rise, while holed stones were still hung in some stables to prevent the 'farisees' riding horses in the night.[55] In early twentieth-century Cambridgeshire, we encounter a solitary reference to a 'fairy-cart' that was supposed to carry off coffins for burial at Shingay, interpreted by Edward Conybeare in 1910 as a confused memory of the 'feretory' (bier) that carried bodies to be buried at Shingay during the Interdict under King John, when the Templar Preceptory at Shingay was exempted from the ban on burials in consecrated ground.[56]

There is little evidence for traditional fairy belief in East Anglia after the First World War, although sporadic encounters with fairies have been reported by people in East Anglia up to the present day. It is unclear whether these can be linked in any way to traditional folklore, or whether they are simply expressions of a more universal Romantic revival of belief in fairies sundered from previous traditions. However, the traditional portrayal of fairies as potentially malign and an object of fear is absent in most recent accounts, which often embody a self-conscious belief in fairies as guardian spirits of nature that is not found in the region's traditional lore.[57] Yet if the history of fairy belief in East Anglia teaches us anything, it is that perceptions of the fairy otherworld are subject to continual evolution and change.

THE *SÍDHE* AND FAIRY FORTS

Ireland by Jenny Butler

Fairies have long been strongly associated with Ireland and particularly Irish story-telling traditions. Fairy legends are interwoven into both the human and natural landscape, and Ireland's fairy place-names and folk memories of fairy encounters help to give a strong sense of place. In the Irish language, the word *sídhe* (the Old Irish spelling with variant spellings *síd* and *síde*, with Old Irish pronunciation akin to the English word 'sheath'; *sí* in Modern Irish, pronounced much as the English pronoun 'she') came to be translated into English as 'fairy'. With the Anglicisation of the country in the period of colonisation, *sídhe* was replaced with 'fairy'; today, with most Irish people being native English speakers, the term 'fairy' is typically used. However, some issues arise with this translation. The English 'fairy' is often whimsical and poetical: think of Edmund Spenser's *The Faerie Queen* and Shakespeare's *A Midsummer Night's Dream*. This is not true of *sídhe*. Medieval mythological writings give the term *aes sídhe* (or *aos sí* in Modern Irish), *aos* meaning 'people' and *sídhe* meaning 'mounds', as these are beings said to have inhabited Ireland in mythical prehistory, who had their residences underground;[1] another phrase is *daoine sídhe*, another way of saying 'people of the mounds'. *Sídhe* has different and interrelated meanings; it can refer to the 'fairy host of the otherworld', an 'otherworld hill or mound', and 'peace' (*síocháin* in Irish).[2]

The *sídhe* are often equated with a mythical people, the *Tuatha Dé Danann* ('the tribe of the goddess Anú'), who fled on the arrival of the Milesians, another mythical people sometimes said to have been the invading Celtic tribes. The Tuatha Dé Danann hid from the Milesians in their subterranean abodes, and their places of hiding included mountains and hills as well as the burial mounds associated with pre-Celtic peoples. In folklore, the *Tuatha Dé Danann* became associated with the underground fairies, while the descendants of the Milesians were the human beings living above ground. A precise understanding of these mythical peoples of ancient Ireland is not possible due to the way these stories have been handed down to us. Irish mythology was compiled by Christian scribes in the middle ages, so the beliefs and stories predate the assemblage of the material by hundreds if not thousands of years. It is important to be aware that the mythology of Ireland was not recorded comprehensively in early Irish manuscripts and did not survive the conversion of the land to Christianity intact; it was partially recorded and, in any case, mediated through a Christian worldview.

The mythological material is fixed forever in the time in which it was written down. The oral tradition, or folklore, on the other hand, has changed and continues to change. This has resulted in a multitude of stories, songs, phrases and beliefs about fairies that vary across time, as well as across the regions and counties of Ireland. In terms of folklore collections related to fairies, there have been two main phases and approaches, the first being 'antiquarianism' where collectors with an interest in 'antiquities' gathered local lore, created sketchbooks and collected stories. In the time that these collections of folklore were compiled, beliefs in fairies and other 'old' beliefs and customs were generally regarded as 'superstitions' (*piseoga*) rather than 'genuine' beliefs. These collectors viewed stories as quaint or humorous; rarely as sincere beliefs or as part of folk religion, as they might be understood today.

Many of the Romantic writers of the Anglo-Irish literary revival of the late nineteenth and early twentieth century were also folklore collectors, such as William Butler Yeats, Lady Augusta Gregory and Ella Young. Their era of writing has been described as 'The Celtic Twilight' (a phrase coined from one of Yeats' collections) and in this period the island of Ireland was romaticised and viewed as a 'mystical land'. Certain cultural characteristics were emphasised and folklore, especially fairylore, was employed in romantic nationalism, through which many of the aforementioned Anglo-Irish writers expressed their sense of connection to Ireland and a newly-constructed idea of 'Irishness'. Their interest in the mystical led them to focus on supernatural lore and places connected with Irish mythology. They collected stories largely in their own localities, which they then published in anthologies for an English-language readership; this entailed some 'translation' of native language as well as meanings. Similarly, the collectors of the Irish Folklore Commission (1935-1970) put more emphasis on story collections than on beliefs, and while information was collected on beliefs about fairies, these were not explored in much depth by way of interviews or other methods.

The Otherworld in Irish Tradition

In the traditional Irish worldview, the *sídhe* are part of the spirit realm or otherworld. In native Irish cosmology, the otherworld is a supernatural realm that is intertwined with the ordinary sphere in which human beings live. The pre-Christian conceptualisation of the otherworld, which has been preserved in mythology, is presented as a realm that is coterminous with the earth, and that is the abode of deities and other spiritual beings, and possibly the human dead. In Irish mythology, the afterlife and otherworld are sometimes conflated as one and the same location, although this is not explicitly stated.

We must, again, be aware, with interpretations of the otherworld, that we are looking through a Christian lens at the beliefs of pre-Christian peoples and that there are no extant first-hand accounts from the pagan inhabitants of Ireland. The ambiguity as regards the location and inhabitants of the otherworld in Irish mythology might thus be due to early Christian compilers and there is a likelihood that Christian concepts were added to the descriptions of the otherworld, and that other concepts from the older religion were omitted or obfuscated. Indigenous beliefs were perhaps deliberately obscured or it may have been the outcome of the mythological material being interpreted according to a Christian cosmology.

'Celtic conceptions of the realm of the dead are often close to but are not synonymous with those of the Otherworld'.[3] In Irish mythology, and in other Celtic mythologies, such as Breton and Welsh, the realm of the dead and the realm of supernatural beings are sometimes described in a way that hints that they are the same location. It has been suggested, indeed that the *sídhe* and the human dead are one and the same and that veneration of the ancestors carried on as customs of leaving offerings for the fairies. A traditional offering left for the fairies was some *poitín* (anglicised as poteen)—a distilled beverage that can be made from grain, cereals, whey or potatoes—poured on the ground. Another offering might be the colostrum or 'beestings' from a cow, which is the first milk drawn from the animal after she has given birth. In some cases, rather than being poured on the ground, the *poitín* or the first drops of milk from the cow would be thrown into the air for the fairies.[4] There are traditional beliefs that deceased humans can join the fairy realm, though it is not clear whether they do so as a human spirit or whether they become some other kind of entity after death. Similarly, in the folklore of other Celtic regions, beliefs about fairies and the dead are intermingled, but the exact nature of the realm in which they dwell is ambiguous. Folklorist Katherine Briggs made this connection between fairies and the dead, while emphasising the ambiguity that surrounds this lore:

At first sight the commonly received idea of fairyland seems as far as possible from the shadowy and bloodless realms of the dead, and yet, in studying fairy-lore and ghost-lore alike we are haunted and teased by resemblances between them. This is not to say that the fairies and the dead are identical, or that the fairies derive entirely from notions about the dead, only that there are many interconnections between them.[5]

There are frequent associations between fairies and dead humans in Irish folklore and this interconnection may stretch back to an ancient cosmology where humans were to join their ancestors in the otherworld after their earthly lives were over. The connection between fairies and prehistoric burial mounds would support the ancient provenance of such lore. In Ireland, 'bad deaths', associated with a sudden demise under tragic circumstances, were often connected with supernatural forces and the dead person was said to be 'in the fairies', which means they are residing in the fairy realm; especially if he or she died without a priest being present. This is a reminder of the way in which beliefs passed on from pagan times are meshed together with other beliefs, in this case those connected with the Roman Catholic 'Last Rites'.[6]

There are several names for otherworldly realms in Irish mythology, but it is not clear whether these are distinct realms or part of one otherworld, or, indeed, whether these realms are also the abode of the dead. One of the names for the otherworld is *Tír Tairngiri* or 'the land of promise' and another is *Tír na nÓg* meaning 'land of the young', described as a bright paradise where there is neither sickness nor old age. This delightful realm is not located in the heavens but underneath the ocean, or can be reached through caves and subterranean passages.

Fairy Places
Fairies are described as a community living alongside humans, their realm intertwined with the physical world and, in that sense, they share the natural landscape with their human neighbours. The idea of fairies as otherworldly 'neighbours', in close proximity but perhaps invisible to the human eye, gave rise to various traditions. There is an abiding belief, for instance, that fairies listen to the conversations of humans, and that one should not mention the name of these beings for fear that they might overhear. It is said that fairies dislike being seen or discussed by humans and are thus referred to euphemistically as *na daoine uaisle* ('the noble people') or *na daoine maithe* ('the good people'), the 'other crowd', or simply as 'themselves'. In Irish culture, fairies are both respected and feared.

Depictions of fairies vary widely. Sometimes they are described as 'wee folk' or 'little people' but 'the idea that they were smaller in size than humans was not general in Ireland'.[7] At times they are said to be the size of human toddlers; at others, the same height as adults. It should be highlighted here that phrases such as 'wee folk' are not always used in an endearing way. Irish fairies are not regarded as being all that different in physical form or appearance to the human race, 'except that they might be somewhat paler in hue and might be dressed in clothing of silk and satin'.[8] Fairies are also associated with wearing traditional Irish clothing from centuries past.

The fairies are often described as moving together across the landscape, as the 'fairy host' (*an slua sídhe*) and humans are unlucky to encounter the *sídhe gaoithe* or 'fairy wind', which can sweep people away with it into the otherworld. To avoid this, one should lie flat on the ground with arms and legs outstretched. In the unlucky event that someone has been carried off by the fairy wind, a way of dislodging the person from the fairies' grasp is to throw gravel or earth from under one's feet into the fairy wind:

> He remembered that he had often heard it said, if you cast the dust that is under your foot against [the fairy wind] at that instant, if they have any human being with them, that they are obliged to release him. He lifts a handful of the gravel that was under his foot, and throws it stoutly, in the name of the Father and Son, and Holy Ghost, against the whirlwind; and, behold forthwith downfalls a woman, weak, faint and feeble, on the earth, with a heavy groan.[9]

The Irish landscape is full of 'fairy places', including 'fairy hills', caves, 'fairy forts' and 'fairy trees' (particularly hawthorns), woodlands and particular rocks. As mentioned previously, many mounds are associated with fairies and are conceptualised as fairy dwellings and entrances into the fairy realm. 'Fairy forts' is the colloquial name for the archaeological remains of circular settlements called ringforts. These structures consist of a round wall, or walls, of earth or stone, sometimes with ditches between the walls. They are found across Northern Europe, some dating to the first millennium of the Christian era or later, while others date to the Iron Age or earlier, perhaps even as far back as the Late Bronze Age.[10] The Irish words for this type of settlement are *lios*, *ráth* and *dún*, all of which mean 'fort' and are 'traditionally considered a dwelling place of the fairy race'.[11] This is in line with the mythological tradition of 'the people of the mounds' and, as noted above, the Irish word *sídhe* can mean both the beings that inhabit the mounds and the mounds themselves; in fact, the inhabitants 'were thought to take their names from the mounds or *sídhe* in which they dwelt'.[12]

The forts, as entrances to the otherworld and as places where fairy encounters are much more likely, are dangerous places, where caution is advised. As places both in the fairy world and in the human world, connected by natural terrain, they are liminal sites, portals that connect realms; 'The remains of earthen forts and certain trees or places carry this notion, and were generally thought to be dangerous for any who interfered with them'.[13]

Ringforts are not to be confused with 'fairy rings', which are circles of fungus believed to be the fairies' dancing ground. Seeing fairies dancing, or hearing their singing, can prove lucky or unlucky for humans. In some cases, humans can join in the dancing and singing, but in others the fairies get angry at being watched or heard and punish the human. One such punishment is to be 'fairy touched', changed in some way that can be physical or mental; another is the 'fairy blast', which is believed to be caused by an often invisible fairy dart. The 'blast' results in swellings on the skin out of which ooze unusual substances of natural origin such as moss and thorns.

'Fairy paths' are the name given to the routes fairies are believed to take when travelling between forts. It is considered unlucky to make noise, speak profanely, or to disturb these paths by littering or building on them. Sickness and even the death of the occupants of a house built on such a path is believed to result, and similar explanations are given for a byre roof caving in or other mishaps with outhouses constructed on a fairy path.

Woodlands are associated with fairy sightings and specific types of trees are particularly associated with fairies. Hawthorn trees are known as 'fairy trees', also called whitethorn or 'the May' since it blooms white blossoms in May. These are also referred to as 'fairy bushes' and while *sceachgheal* is the Irish language name for hawthorn, the term *sceach* or 'thorn bush', used on its own, generally refers to a 'fairy thorn'. 'There are many stories of harm and even death coming to those who interfere with the fairy thorn'[14] and because of this, the tree is often seen on its own in a field where all other trees and foliage have been removed. Any intentional damage to, or meddling with, the tree often ends in the responsible party dying. The tree is credited with otherworldly powers, and its flowers are considered very unlucky, 'with death[15] resulting if brought into a house'[16]

There is a custom of tying little rags or ribbons to particular trees and this is thought to be a way of asking for help or healing from the fairies; this tradition has become interconnected with the same action in supplicating saints, the hawthorn having special associations with St Patrick. As well as being known as 'the fairy thorn', hawthorn is also called 'St Patrick's bush' and there are often legends about him where this tree grows.[17]

It is believed that fairies dislike the presence of humans and will try to dissuade them from coming closer by confusing them. One fairy stratagem to achieve this is changing the appearance of the landscape so that the person gets lost or trapped. There are many motifs in legends where someone gets lost in a familiar area, a farmer, for instance, who cannot get out of his own field. This is colloquially known as being 'turned around'. A way of avoiding this is for people to wear their coats inside-out when going near fairy places, since the symbolic inversion seems to protect the wearer from otherworldly influence.

Also associated with bad luck is the 'hungry grass', which are plots of unmarked famine graves out in the open. On walking across one of these, a person could become suddenly weak with stabbing hunger pains, and this is interpreted as a death omen. An alternative explanation for the origins of areas of 'hungry grass' is that they were 'in older belief, places where a meal had been taken and no share left for the people of the otherworld'.[18] This is interesting if the fairies are understood as ancestors, as there are customs of sharing food with deceased kin in various cultural contexts in different parts of the world.

Changelings

Encounters with fairies are often said to be unlucky or dangerous and therefore to be avoided. Many legends reveal fears of fairy abduction and of being trapped in the fairy realm. Customs have been recorded that involve warding off fairies and ensuring they don't interfere with humans or livestock. Fairies are said to 'hate iron, fire, salt and the Christian religion, and any combination of these mainstays of Irish rural culture serves to guard against them'.[19] Metal, particularly iron, can be employed as a defence against fairy aggression. It is believed that if individuals carry nails or pins in their pockets, they will be protected from being snatched by fairies and taken into their realm. It is believed, too, that the abductee is thereafter located in the otherworld, whether physically or in spirit; the lore also carries the idea that the person's physical form can remain in the human world but that this is in appearance only and the soul is ensnared and kept with the fairies. To retrieve the person from the fairies, it is said that throwing nails among the fairy host as they pass by will disperse them so that the human can be rescued.

Similarly, a metal implement such as a spade or tongs would be kept by a child's cot to keep the fairies away from the baby. A changeling is a fairy surreptitiously put in the place of a human or sometimes it is a log or a sweeping brush that is magically made to look like the human until the fairies return to their realm. The human being that is replaced is most often a baby or toddler, though in some cases it is an adult. For example, in 1895, twenty-six-year-old Bridget Cleary was, her husband claimed, abducted by fairies and a changeling left in her place. After an ordeal of two nights in which Bridget was accused by her husband, father, aunt and four cousins of being a changeling, threatened and commanded to reveal her true nature, she was burned alive by her husband in the presence of those same relatives in her home in Ballyvadlea in County Tipperary; the family members later claimed, in their court testimonies, that they were attempting to get rid of a changeling. The method of threatening and frightening the changeling was intended to get it to admit its fairy nature. It will, then, disappear or the other fairies will feel sorry for the abuse one of their own is suffering and thus switch back the human for the fairy.

Various ways of expelling a changeling are mentioned in stories. These include abandoning the changeling in remote locations in harsh weather conditions or placing it on a hot shovel or griddle, or stabbing it with a hot poker; again the combination of fire and iron, two things that fairies are supposed to fear. Another is to douse it with urine or to throw it on a dung heap and leave it there alone, since fairies are said to be fastidious and to hate dirt. The techniques used to intimidate and draw out the changeling, like questioning its true name and threatening with fire, are comparable to approaches to demonic possession in other cultures, and may have been influenced by Christian ideas about banishing demons.[20] A common motif in legends is that the 'changeling will rush up the chimney with a cry', when discovered.[21] In Irish culture, as in many other cultures, the chimney is a symbolic threshold between the dangers outside the house and the safety of hearth and home; other menacing creatures are associated with the chimney, such as the *Cailleach an Im* or 'Butter Hag'. This is a witch that climbs onto the roof of houses on May Day morning (May 1 or *Bealtaine*) and catches the 'first smoke' in a bag in order to magically steal the luck of the household, which is represented in the butter produced by the churning that traditionally starts on May Day. Since this is symbolically a time of vulnerability, and since it is believed that 'witches and fairies were unusually active at this time',[22] fairylore and witchlore became mixed together to some extent, especially in relation to the protections used against each.

More often, stories about changelings involve a baby being replaced by a fairy, which in many accounts is a sickly fairy child who continues to waste away, so that it looks pale and weak, and will not stop crying since it is pining for its own kind. In other cases, the substitute is an old fairy man and appears shrivelled up and withered. The substitute is described as being ugly, and sometimes hairy with yellowing skin. The idea behind the exchange of the elderly male fairy is that the fairies are placing an old member of their community into the human community, in the hopes that he will assimilate unnoticed, leaving the fairies with a strong and healthy human baby that they can raise as their own. Given that the fairy is mature, he must pretend to be a human baby and stories tell of the changeling, when he thinks he is unobserved, singing to himself, talking or doing something that no baby or toddler could manage: dancing, playing the fiddle, or jumping down out of the cot in order to look out the door or to fetch something.

In many legends the changeling's attention is drawn to something so that he is so engaged, he will exclaim in surprise at what is happening. An example of this is 'The Brewery of Egg-shells', documented by Cork-born folklore collector Thomas Crofton Croker. The mother of a baby, who has been replaced by a changeling, meets a 'cunning woman' and is advised by her to boil a large pot of water and to break a dozen newly-laid eggs, only keeping the shells, which were to be placed into the pot of water. As the mother of the child does what the cunning woman advised, the changeling asks, 'with the voice of a very old man, "what are you doing mammy?"' The implication is that the changeling has been distracted by the mother's unusual actions and forgets that he is pretending to be a baby. In fact, he subsequently cries out, 'I'm fifteen hundred years in the world, and I never saw a brewery of egg-shells before!'[23]

It is believed that humans who are in the otherworld should not eat any 'fairy food' they are presented with, for fear that they would be trapped in the fairy world for ever and no longer be able to communicate with their human family and friends. The converse of this, perhaps, is the belief that a changeling does not want to eat human food, or cannot digest it, and so does not suckle or ingest breast-milk; similarly adult changelings are said to avoid eating the food that they are given.

Encountering the Fairies

The idea that one should steer clear of situations in which one would meet fairies is not universal in Irish tradition and there are some accounts of the beneficial outcomes of such encounters. Indeed, 'those who are carried away are happy, according to certain accounts, having plenty of good living and music and mirth'.[24] Some people claim to be able to see fairies or to sense them and in the Irish context this is known traditionally as having the 'second sight'.[25] There are those who are believed to be able to communicate with the fairies and to receive help, healing or other 'gifts' from them, such as the 'wise woman' (*bean feasa* in Irish, from *fios* meaning 'knowledge') and the 'fairy doctor', usually male practitioners who dealt with afflictions of livestock and of humans, who were thought to have originated with the fairies.

Such figures were believed, in traditional Irish society, to be consorting with, and subsequently getting their powers from, the fairies. 'The curative powers of the wise woman are directly related to the fairy world'.[26] The plots of legends concerning the Irish wise woman figure contain motifs of her diagnosing and prescribing for a variety of physical ailments as well as other health issues.[27] Traditional healers in Ireland, as elsewhere, often contended that their knowledge or abilities came from the fairies: 'All persons who claimed supernatural powers naturally had to be willing to explain how it came about that they were so much more gifted than their neighbours. One explanation, to which numerous cunning folk resorted, was contact with the fairies'.[28] In this way, there is some intermingling of fairylore with magical practices and witchcraft.

Humans can meet fairies at any time, but at certain times an encounter is more likely or fairies are believed to have a stronger influence over human beings. Dawn and dusk, as liminal times of change—night into day, or day to night—are moments for fairy sightings. Certain times of the year are associated with fairies being in close proximity, especially the festivals of *Lá Bealtaine* or May Day on May 1 and *Samhain* or Halloween on October 31 through November 1, the traditional start of summer and winter, respectively. As times of transition, these are regarded as being dangerous, Halloween is viewed as a risky time to be outdoors, 'since the fairies were on the move from one dwelling to another and were particularly likely to abduct people'.[29] Halloween derives from a mixture of traditions from All Hallows Eve and the Catholic All Souls Day, but has its basis in the pre-Christian feast of the dead at *Samhain*. The correlation between the returning dead and fairies points again to the idea that fairies might be ancestral spirits.

Fairies and Modern Ireland

Some aspects of traditional Irish fairylore have continued and, for some people, form part of their worldview. There are also various adaptations of the beliefs and customs, whether these are intentional modifications or part of subtle cultural and social changes. In contemporary Paganism, an umbrella term for a wide range of spiritual beliefs and practices, practitioners often deliberately try to encounter fairies and to call upon them for guidance in magical rituals; these are new traditions in the Irish context, combining folklore sources with esoteric ones. The New Age Movement, a catch-all term for a multitude of spiritual expressions that are sometimes described as 'alternative spirituality', has also had an impact on the level of interest in, as well as understanding of, fairylore.

In his book *Running with the Fairies*, Dennis Gaffin explores what he refers to as the 'new fairy faith' in contemporary Ireland. The group under study are an informal social network based largely in Donegal, who are adherents of a type of Christian mysticism in which there is a shared belief in the reality of fairies as nature spirits, and humans as reincarnated fairies, and a sensitivity to 'fairy energy'. Both contemporary Paganism and New Age types of religiosity bring new ideas about Irish fairies with them. In the case of both New Age and Pagan belief systems, there are influences on conceptualisations of fairies from esoteric knowledge systems including Theosophy, which is an occult movement that originated in the nineteenth century with roots that can be traced to the ancient philosophical traditions of Gnosticism and Neoplatonism. Theosophical belief included the 'elementals', which are the spirits of the four elements[30]—Earth, Air, Fire and Water—and this influenced understandings of what fairies are within later forms of spirituality.

There has been a process of 'Disneyfication' of fairies and the effects of this have been felt in Ireland, as elsewhere in the world, with many portrayals of winged, cutesy fairies on television, in children's books and as toys. Advertising and marketing influence popular notions of what fairies are, one example being The Irish Fairy Door Company, which produces diminutive doors that can be stuck onto trees as well as miniature 'fairy houses', drawing more from Victorian and romantic literary notions of fairies than from traditional Irish lore. There are many complexities in Irish fairylore which can make it difficult to tease apart different layers of cultural meaning, but which also add to people's fascination with it. While some traditional beliefs seem to have died out in Ireland, like that of changelings, others continue, especially in relation to 'fairy places'. Others still are reinterpreted and combined with new cultural influences, new films and books and various commercial products, leading to new understandings and ideas about what fairies are and what 'fairy' means. Irish fairylore certainly endures at the heart of Ireland's cultural heritage, enmeshed intricately as it is with the landscape, beliefs, storytelling and a sense of place.

9
THE SEELIE AND UNSEELIE COURTS

Scotland by Ceri Houlbrook

Introduction

The waterfall cascades down the dark rocks and into the pool below. Sunlight glints off the water but the pool's edges, fringed by dense woodland and overhanging foliage, ripple in shadow. The bole of a tree brought down years before lies prone across the pool, half submerged, its bark encrusted with what at first glance appears to be fungi but, upon closer inspection, turns out to be coins. Hundreds of them. Each one jammed, lodged, or hammered into the fissures of the decaying bark.

A woman and her two daughters, aged six and eight, have been walking up the forested glen, making the most of a sunny Tuesday afternoon in the school holidays. They've been talking about an upcoming cinema trip to Inverness, but their conversation breaks off when they see the tree. The girls don't need to ask; their mother is already fishing in her purse for two pennies.

'Make a wish to the fairies,' she instructs them as they take the coins and slip them into the tree amongst the others. The girls close their eyes in solemn observance of the ritual—but it is only brief. Within seconds they're carrying on along the path, asking if they can go to Pizza Hut before the cinema.

This scene was observed by the author in early September 2012, in a place called

Fairy Glen, close to Rosemarkie, in the Black Isle, Scotland. The site has been identified as 'Fairy Glen' on maps since 1907[1] and local tradition avers that it once hosted well-dressing ceremonies, in which children would decorate the pool with flowers to ensure that the resident fairies of the glen kept the water clean. The fairies have clearly grown more economically minded; coins are now offered up instead of flowers, and tourists observe the custom as much—if not more—than the local residents. But the namesakes of the glen are still being appealed to, even if only in passing.

This beautiful and mysterious site, home to fairies, is far from unique in Scotland, which MacCulloch describes as a land that has 'always been a peculiar haunt of such beings'.[2] The Scottish landscape is replete with fairy glens—indeed, the Scots seem to have peopled many of their hills, meadows, caves, moors, and brooks with these creatures of folklore. The Schiehallion, a mountain in Perth and Kinross, is known as the fairy mountain of the Caledonians; a pair of chambered cairns on Cnoc Freicceadain, Caithness are described locally as Na Tri Shean, the three fairy mounds; and Tomnahurich Hill at Inverness is likewise described as accommodating a community of fairies.[3] These are just a handful of examples; maps of Scotland are festooned with fairy-themed place-names, whilst countless other natural features, which may not make it onto the maps, are known locally as fairy rings, fairy cups, fairy dishes, and so on.[4]

So closely interrelated is fairy belief with the Scottish landscape that the former is generally believed to have emerged from the latter. As was written in the prefatory note of the anonymously penned 1889 *Folk-Lore and Legends: Scotland* (hereafter *Folk-Lore and Legends*):

> The distinctive features of Scotch Folklore are such as might have been expected from a consideration of the characteristics of Scotch scenery. The rugged grandeur of the mountain, the solemn influence of the widespreading moor, the dark face of the deep loch, the babbling of the little stream, seem all to be reflected in the popular tales and superstitions. The acquaintance with nature in a severe, grand, and somewhat terrible form must necessarily have its effect on the human mind, and the Scotch mind and character bear the impress of their natural sur-roundings.[5]

The existence of fairies was accepted as fact by many Scots at least until the eighteenth century[6]—and, as is evident in the Fairy Glen anecdote, fairies continue to exist within popular perceptions of the Scottish landscape. So prevalent are fairies, indeed, in Scotland's legends and customs, both past and present, that this chapter cannot hope—and therefore does not attempt—to cover all aspects of this broad topic. Scotland has numerous and distinct localities each with their own blend of traditions. It likewise poses chronological challenges, with fairy beliefs inevitably altering over time. This chapter is therefore not intended as a detailed, in-depth study of Scottish fairy belief (which has, after all, been provided elsewhere, most notably by Henderson and Cowan 2004), but rather as a brief, and hopefully tantalising, overview of a vast and fascinating topic.

Sources

Evidence for Scottish fairy belief is frequently found in medieval and modern sources.[7] Robert Kirk's *The Secret Common-Wealth*, originally published in 1691, is the most useful text for pre-industrial Scottish fairy belief. Kirk, the minister of Aberfoyle, Perthshire, was said to have possessed the second sight—and therefore the ability to see fairies—and he believed that fairies were a race of beings 'of middle nature betwixt man and angel',[8] who existed everywhere but went unseen by most people. Arguing that folk belief and Christianity were not mutually exclusive, and that to disbelieve in fairies was to disbelieve in God, Kirk penned his treatise on fairylore, drawing on oral traditions, in the late seventeenth century. Owing to his strong opinions on fairy belief, Kirk's death in 1692 has become something of a legend in itself; it is said that his coffin remained empty and that he was taken away by the fairies to dwell under the Fairy Hill.[9]

Scottish witchcraft trials offer another invaluable resource to draw upon. There was little distinction made between fairy belief and witchcraft in Scotland; fairies and witch's familiars, for example, were viewed in similar terms in the popular imagination,[10] whilst the queen of both the fairies and witches was named NicNiven.[11] Unsurprisingly, then, many individuals who were tried for witchcraft were also believed to have encountered fairies; Bessie Dunlop of Dalry, Ayrshire, for instance, was tried in 1576 for communing with the fairy queen,[12] while Alisoun Pearson was tried in 1588 for 'haunting and communing with the guide neighbours and the queen of Elfland'.[13] This interesting relationship between witchcraft and fairies has been explored in numerous other works.[14]

Scottish poetry and ballads—usefully collated by Francis James Child[15]—are another important resource for fairies. Probably the best known is the tale of Thomas the Rhymer, which tells the story of Thomas of Erceldoune, a thirteenth-century laird purportedly carried off by the 'Queen of Elfland' and returned with the gift of prophecy.[16] This was the subject of a popular ballad in the fifteenth century, which later became a verse romance, expanded by Walter Scott into a three-part ballad at the start of the nineteenth century.[17] Walter Scott provides a particularly useful source for fairylore in his *Minstrelsy of the Scottish Border*, a collection of ballads first published in three volumes in 1802 and 1803, and in his *Letters on Demonology and Witchcraft* of 1830.[18] Together with poet James Hogg, Scott generated much interest in fairies, inspiring further works of art and the theatre.[19] Not least, J.M. Barrie, from Angus, launched his play *Peter Pan, or the Boy Who Wouldn't Grow Up* in 1904.

Henderson and Cowan, who detail the above sources, offer a useful warning: most of our sources on fairy belief come from the literate and the learned, 'forcing us to view the esoteric perspective through an exoteric lens'.[20] However, there is enough variety in the nature of our sources that we can be reasonably confident of gaining some insight into the more popular beliefs of the country.

A Description of Scottish Fairies

Fairies in Scotland are not always called 'fairies'. As well as being termed 'elves', they were given a plethora of names: hill folk, siths, fanes, the seelie and unseelie courts, the klippe.[21] People also employed a range of euphemisms when referring to them— the good people (*sluagh maith*), the good folk, the good neighbours, the honest folk, the fairfolk; flattering names employed to, as Kirk wrote, 'prevent the dint of their ill attempts'.[22] Occasionally individual fairies are named in legends: the Dame of the Fine Green Kirtle, a largely malevolent fairy who appears in many Highland folktales; the malignant Whoopity Stoorie whose name must be guessed to break a spell; the benevolent Habetrot, the fairy patron of spinning; Aiken Drum, the fairy subject of a Scottish nursery rhyme; and the queen of the fairies, NicNiven or Neven.[23] However, on the whole, fairies remain unnamed in legends and folklore, and are often referred to in the plural.

What the fairies actually are is up for debate. To some they were nature spirits; to others, mythological deities; to others, fallen angels; and to others, an actual race of people, the earlier inhabitants of northern Britain.[24] To Kirk, they were creatures between man and angel, described as 'intelligent studious spirits, and light changeable bodies (like those called astral), somewhat of the nature of a condensed cloud'.[25] However, regardless of their form or origins, to many they were a species closely related to death. It was a popular belief in Scotland that some fairies at least were souls of the dead; that when a person died, they might find themselves in fairyland.[26] As was written in *Folk-Lore and Legends*: 'Faces of friends and relatives, long since doomed to the battle-trench or the deep sea, have been recognised by those who dared to gaze on the fairy march. The maid has seen her lost lover, and the mother her stolen child'.[27]

Fairies were only seen by those with the second sight or, being liminal creatures, at twilight,[28] but descriptions differed from witness to witness. They rarely coincide with our modern-day image of the fairy: quaint, delicate, or overtly feminised, as seen in Disney's depiction of Tinker Bell, who Wood describes as having been given a 'curved adult body, modelled on that of Marilyn Monroe'.[29] Indeed, the common contemporary notion of fairies as being small and winged—spurred by that most famous fairy to have sprung from a Scot's imagination: Barrie's Tinker Bell—is, to my knowledge, never found in pre-industrial Scottish folklore.

Certainly fairies appeared to have come in many shapes and sizes, and to have possessed a range of abilities: some had super-human strength, for example, whilst others were able to turn invisible. However, while MacCulloch describes them as travelling 'through the air on an eddy of dust or a whirlwind',[30] they seem to have had no propensity for independent flight in early Scottish popular belief. And while some appear to have had the ability to change their height at will,[31] generally they seem to have been the same size as humans, to the extent that it is often difficult to distinguish between mortal and fairy.

One element that many sources agree on is that fairies were often clothed and their garments generally green,[32] a colour also associated with the devil and therefore of ill omen.[33] Green, however, probably demonstrates a connection less with the devil and more with the Scottish landscape: 'the usual dress of the fairies is green; though, on the moors, they have been sometimes observed in heath-brown, or in weeds dyed with the stone-raw or lichen'.[34] Similarly, their fashion sense is also perceived as a reflection of the Scottish people themselves, with Kirk observing: 'Their apparel and speech is like that of the people and country under which they live; so are they seen to wear plaids and variegated garments in the Highlands of Scotland'.[35] This idea has survived into the present day, with Margaret Bennett reporting a belief amongst the children of Balquhidder, Perthshire, interviewed by her in the 1990s, that fairies wear kilts.[36]

Within the race of fairies were various subspecies, detailed by Katharine Briggs.[37] There were the malevolent bogles; the mischievous bauchan; the kindly doonie who guide those in difficulty; the evil redcaps who inhabit the Borders between England and Scotland; the domestic urisk, eager to help with household chores; and the bean-nighe, the Scottish equivalent of the banshee who shrieks and wails in prophecy of death; the taunting Hobyahs from Perth (illustrated at the head of the chapter)—and this is to name only a few. There were also animal species of fairies: the each uisge (water-horse), the crodhamara (water-cattle), the roane (seals), and the fairy dog of the Highlands known as the cu sith.

Popular Pastimes of the Fairies
Kirk wrote of the fairies: 'They are said to have aristocratical rulers and laws',[38] and in later traditions especially they do appear to have been aristocratic in nature, often portrayed collectively as courts. In Scotland the good fairies were known as the 'Seelie Court', with 'Seelie' being the Saxon word for 'blessed'; while the more malevolent fairy sects were referred to as the 'Unseelie Court'.[39] Both were believed similar to royal households of the human realm, with their kings, queens, and hierarchies of nobles. Unsurprisingly, their pastimes reflected those of human courtiers. They loved to dance, leaving imprints of their activities in the grass: the fairy rings later identified and avoided by the wary human. Consequently they also loved music, and were gifted musicians, often capable of luring humans into their fairy rings with their eldritch melodies. And of course, as in any respectable court, dancing and music were complemented by feasts of good wine and lavish foods.

The women of their race were said to be particularly talented in spinning and embroidery[40] and most fairies appear to have enjoyed horsemanship. They would ride in invisible midnight processions, their presence only signalled by the ringing of their bridles or the music they would play as they rode by, when 'the sound of their elfin minstrelsy charmed youths and maidens into love for their persons and pursuits'.[41] These midnight processions, known as the 'Fairy Rade' are best described in the ballad

'Tam Lin', when Tam Lin himself is rescued from a rade by the heroine of the legend.[42]

To acquire their steeds, the fairies would often borrow from their human neighbours, and 'when such are found in the morning, panting and fatigued in their stalls, with their manes and tails dishevelled and entangled, the grooms, I presume, often find this a convenient excuse for their situation, as the common belief of the elves quaffing the choicest liquors in the cellars of the rich might occasionally cloak the delinquencies of an unfaithful butler'.[43]

As well as riding in the rade, fairies also loved the hunt, and a tale is relayed in *Folk-Lore and Legends* of a 'gentleman of Ballaflecther [who] had lost three or four capital hunters by these nocturnal excursions'.[44] Sometimes, however, more legitimate means were employed in acquiring horses; another story tells of a man living in the mountains who was asked by a little fellow if he could buy his horse. No sooner had coins and horse exchanged hands, then the little fellow rode the horse into the earth.[45]

So fairies appear, then, to have lived the hedonistic lives of courtiers, spending their nights dancing, feasting, and hunting, all the while led by their kings and queens. There is, however, one pastime that the fairies appear to have enjoyed even more than these decadent pursuits: interfering with their human neighbours.

Fairies as Friends

Some fairies were believed to be benevolent—or at least relatively fair in their treatment of humans. In the nineteenth century, what are described by Wilby as 'contractual relationships' with fairies were a common aspect of Scottish folklore.[46] Alliances were formed between mortals and fairies, whereby the fairy would undertake some work for the human in exchange for an agreed payment. Other accounts also tell of favours enacted by the fairies in response to past good deeds. A common formula involved the appearance of a fairy at a person's front door asking for some assistance. In a chapter of *Folk-Lore and Legends* entitled 'Fairy Friends', an example the author gives is of a 'little woman in green costume' requesting the loan of some meal from a farmer's wife who, in return for her kindness, was soon after presented with an equal quantity of everlasting meal.[47]

Another example from 'Fairy Friends' is used to demonstrate that 'It is a good thing to befriend the fairies': a poor man from Jedburgh was travelling to market in Hawick to purchase a sheep one day when he suddenly heard a cacophony of female voices. He could make out only a few words: 'O there's a bairn born, but there's neathing to pit on't'. The fairies were celebrating the birth of a fairy child, but were concerned that they had nothing to cover it with. The man duly removed his plaid and threw it to the ground, where it was immediately snatched up by an invisible hand, and the man went on his way to Hawick, where he bought a sheep for an unusually good bargain. 'He had no cause to regret his generosity for every day afterwards his wealth multiplied, and he continued till the day of his death a rich and prosperous man'.[48]

Fairies as Foes

As beneficious as it sometimes could be to engage with the fairies, it was generally wise to avoid such encounters. Fairies were often portrayed as morally ambivalent, mischievous, and capricious, and while some were benign, others were downright malicious. As Wilby observes, 'Scottish fairies were generally believed to be more prone to malice than the English'.[49] In his *Minstrelsy of the Scottish Border* Walter Scott considered why this might be, suggesting that it was the Scottish landscape itself that bred a more dangerous breed of fairies than those found in England: 'we should naturally attribute a less malicious disposition, a less frightful appearance, to the fays who glide by moon-light through the oaks of Windsor, than to those who haunt the solitary heaths and lofty mountains of the North'.[50]

A particular danger posed by Scottish fairies was their seemingly malicious intentions towards livestock.[51] If an animal was taken sick with cramp, for example, then it was believed to be 'elf-shot': shot by a fairy with an 'elf-bolt'. Such a belief no doubt arose from the plethora of such 'elf-bolts'—i.e. the triangular flint arrowheads of prehistory—littering the Scottish landscape.[52] One cure for such an afflicted animal was to chafe the affected body part with a bluebonnet,[53] but cures were not always effective, and in an agricultural society where the death of livestock had serious consequences for a family's livelihood, it is easy to understand why fairies were feared.

Then, humans were equally subject to the malign attention of fairies. Fairies were, for example, very territorial, and to accidentally stray into 'Fairyland' or 'Elfland' could have serious consequences. Once there, it was very difficult to leave. Even if the hapless wanderer followed the well-known rules for surviving Fairyland—don't eat or drink; don't speak; and don't accept gifts—and was able, or allowed, to escape, they might find themselves the victim of time distortion: one night in Fairyland could amount to years in the mortal realm.[54] They may find themselves still young whilst all those they had known had grown old or, worse, died. They may also find themselves geographically displaced. One tradition recounts the tale of a Scottish man in the seventeenth century, unwittingly caught up in the revelry of the fairies in a field, who found himself, the next day, in Paris. He was discovered in the cellar of the French king with a silver cup in his hand, severely hungover.[55]

There is much disagreement about where the Scottish Fairyland stands, though it is generally associated with the wilderness. Often described as a beautiful and other-worldly court of opulent halls and lavish feasting, Fairyland was notoriously transient, appearing one minute and disappearing the next. Invariably, it is a place best avoided—but dangerously easy to enter. The myriad fairy-hills, -knolls, -meadows, -caves, -moors, -brooks, and -rings were considered portals into Fairyland, and the unwitting wanderer could easily stumble across an unseen boundary and find themselves at the mercy of these capricious beings. Sometimes the mistake could be as simple as being in the wrong place at the wrong time; falling asleep under the shade of a particular rock or on the slope of a particular hill at sunset, for example.[56] So widespread were these demarcations of certain places as entrances into Fairyland that

Henderson and Cowan actually believe they 'may have served a larger social purpose: to protect community members from known, or presumed, dangers'.[57] 'Fairyland' was, consciously or subconsciously, employed as a scare tactic to prevent people from straying too far.

More often than not, however, mortals entered Fairyland unwillingly, spirited away by the fairies who coveted them for one reason or another. Love or desire were common motivations. A fairy, having taken a fancy to a particular mortal, would employ a range of means to get him or her into Fairyland. They may physically abduct them, but trickery was the preferred method; they could tempt mortals into their realm simply by enticing them with music, dancing, and food, or by promising them some form of material gain or magical knowledge.[58] Once there, the desired human could be in the fairy's amorous possession for a night; or for a lifetime. The ballad of Thomas the Rhymer details such a liaison. Thomas is seduced by the Queen of Fairyland and taken on horseback to her court, depicted as a limbo between Heaven and Hell, where he remained for seven years.[59]

In other instances, humans are coveted for the practical skills they possess. Music was one such skill; in the seventeenth century, for example, a boy known as the 'fairy boy of Leith' claimed that his talents with a musical instrument were admired by the fairies,[60] whilst knowledge of warfare was another prized skill. Isobel Gowdie of Auldeam claimed in 1662 that she had aided fairies with their fighting, as did Jean Weir of Edinburgh in 1670.[61]

The new mother was particularly vulnerable to the fairies because of her breast milk. Human milk was held in very high esteem by fairies.[62] The reasons for this are unclear, but the result was that women were taken to Fairyland to act as wet nurses for the fairies' young. Trows, the troll-like fairies on Orkney, were particularly keen on such abductions; legend had it that they were incapable of producing females of their own kind and so, in order to procreate, they needed to impregnate human women. However, once the baby trow was born, the human mother would die, and so the trow would require another human woman—a new mother—to nurse his newborn.[63]

Kirk maintained that:

Women are yet alive who tell they were taken away when in childbed to nurse fairy children, a lingering voracious image of them being left in their place (like their reflection in a mirror)…The child and fire, with food and all other necessaries, are set before the nurse how soon she enters, but she neither perceived any passage out, nor sees what those people do in other rooms of the lodging. When the child is weaned, the nurse dies, or is conveyed back, or gets it to her choice to stay there.[64]

More commonly, however, it was not the mothers who were abducted by the fairies, but their children.

Changelings

A particularly popular pastime of the fairies, as seen in many of this volume's chapters, was stealing newborn babies, with Briggs writing matter-of-factly that the 'thing that everyone knows about the fairies is that they covet human children and steal them whenever they can'.[65] The folklore indicates that parents greatly feared their baby being stolen, taken to be raised amongst—and as of one of—the fairies. And traditions did not give mere vague claims that fairies took newborn babies and new mothers; they went into great detail about it, including explanations for *why* fairies coveted them.

One reason given is that every seven years the fairies had to pay 'kane', or a tithe, by making an offering of one of their children to the Devil; they were, however, permitted to offer a human child instead, and so mortal babies were taken and sacrificed to ensure the safety of the fairy young.[66] Another reason given was that fairies wanted human babies to improve their stock.[67] It was believed that the fairies' young were stunted, ugly and discontent, and so their parents desired human newborns, strong and healthy, and would leave substitutes in their place. These substitutes are known as changelings.

The following extract is from Edwin Sidney Hartland's *The Science of Fairy Tales*, and recounts the story of a woman in nineteenth-century Scotland who saved her newborn baby from being exchanged for a changeling.

> A shepherd's wife living near Selkirk was lying in bed one day with her new-born boy at her side, when she heard a sound of talking and laughter in the room. Suspecting what turned out to be the case, she seized in great alarm her husband's waistcoat, which was lying at the foot of the bed, and flung it over herself and the child. The fairies, for it was they who were the cause of the noise, set up a loud scream, crying out: "Auld Luckie has cheated us o' our bairnie!" Soon afterwards the woman heard something fall down the chimney, and looking out she saw a waxen effigy of her baby, stuck full if pins, lying on the hearth. The would-be thieves had meant to substitute this for the child.[68]

In this case, the substitute is a 'waxen effigy' of the baby, but in other traditions it can be a model made from wood which, through fairy enchantment, resembles the stolen baby and deceives the human parents.[69]

However, most often it would be the fairies' own young who would be left in the place of a human baby. Although the changeling sometimes deceives the parents into believing nothing is amiss, most often they are noticeably different to their human counterparts: withered, loud, tempestuous, with insatiable appetites.[70] There are a plethora of tales told about changelings, with Marwick observing that: 'Changeling stories are in fact so numerous and so like each other that they can be extremely boring'.[71] The endings of these stories are sometimes happy; the changeling is either tricked or the parents manage to win back their stolen child. There were ritualistic methods employed in the winning back of these children; one involved the digging of a grave in a field and putting the purported changeling in it overnight. The parents would expect to find their child lying there in the changeling's place by morning.[72] Other stories are less happy: the human baby is never seen again, and the changeling stays with the human parents but often dies a premature death, rarely living past eighteen or nineteen years.[73]

Fairy Repellents

There were a number of measures taken by expectant parents in order to avoid the attention of fairies. Concealment was one such measure; writing of the Scottish islands, Marwick tells of 'the supposed necessity of keeping the secret [of pregnancy] from malevolent beings who could harm mother and child. It was unlucky to show preparations for the coming baby: the 'peerie [little] folk' would get to know'.[74] It was therefore advised to conceal pregnancy and any preparations for child-birth for as long as possible.

However, in the likely event that the fairies did 'get to know' about the coming baby, there were numerous other methods employed to keep them at bay, and these often took the form of protective devices (objects popularly believed to be supernaturally protective). Knives, scissors, and swords, for example, were particularly effective at warding off fairies—not for any physical harm they could do, but because fairies were believed to be afraid of metal. For the same reason, a row of iron nails should[75] be driven into the front board of the bed, and a smoothing iron or a reaping hook should be placed under the bed and in the window.[76] Fairies were also believed to dislike the smell of burning leather, so the wise placed an old shoe in the fireplace.[77]

Following childbirth, more measures were undertaken to protect the baby and new mother, and many of these involved the baby's cradle. For example, it was supposedly unlucky for newborns to be given new cradles; if an old cradle was not available, then the child's clothes had to be passed through the smoke of a fire in order to protect the child from fairies.[78] Numerous protective devices could be hung around the cradle in order to prevent fairy abduction. Burnt bindweed placed over the cradle was said to do the trick, as was a four-leaf clover, and amber beads.[79]

Again, metal objects were the most popular protective devices, their placements in or over cribs demonstrating greater fear of supernatural threats than the physical dangers of placing these metal objects—which included needles, metal tongs, knives, and swords—in a crib with a baby. An open pair of scissors were particularly effective because not only were they made of metal but they formed the shape of the cross, another potent fairy-repellent.[80]

Despite the folklore, even the 'magical' nature of these homemade charms and rites, they were often incorporated with elements from Christianity to increase their potency.[81] Kirk maintained that the fairies had no religion themselves and they 'disappear whenever they hear His name invoked, or the name of Jesus'.[82] An open Bible should always be kept close to the newborn child and, before their birth, the same book should be placed beneath the head of the labouring mother.[83] Firth, meanwhile, cites an example from 1887 of a new mother keeping, beside her in the bed, a Bible as well as a knife, 'the peerie [little] folk being equally as afraid of cold steel as of the Scriptures'.[84]

Demonstrative of this is the account given by a woman in Ballamodah, Scotland, in the early 1900s, as transcribed by Evans-Wentz:

> I have been told of *their* (the fairies') taking babies, though I can't be sure it is true. But this did happen to my own mother in this parish of Kirk Patrick about eighty years since: She was in bed with her baby, but wide awake, when she felt the baby pulled off her arm and heard the rush of *them*. Then she mentioned the Almighty's name, and, as *they* were hurrying away, a little table alongside the bed went round about the floor twenty times. Nobody was in the room with my mother, and she always allowed it was the *little fellows* (emphases in original).[85]

Other protective devices and rites appear to have been purely drawn from popular belief. In nineteenth-century Scotland, newborns were bathed in water into which a piece of gold had been deposited, known as *Uisge Or* or Long John, in order to protect them against fairies. Certain edibles were also prescribed to this end. While milk is naturally a large part of a baby's diet, in order to protect a newborn from fairies, they were given the milk of a cow which had eaten the pearl-wort (*Pinguicula vulgaris*). This is essentially a weed, but was widely held as a plant of virtue. In the Highlands it was custom to give the baby a large quantity of fresh butter just after birth, whilst giving the newborn sugar-water is a widespread practice, but for protection against fairy abduction it was specified that the baby's first sip of it had to come from a silver cup or spoon. For those who were too poor to have either, a shilling would be placed on a spoon and that would suffice.[89]

The power of familial bonds was also harnessed to protect babies. In 1910, MacCulloch wrote of the Scottish tradition of placing a father's clothing in a child's cradle in order to protect it from supernatural forces, 'the idea being that the father's influence protects the child through the proximity or contact of his clothes'.[90] This belief is evident in the account given by Hartland above, in which a shepherd's wife in Selkirk protects her baby from the fairies by covering him with her husband's waistcoat: 'The suggestion seems to be that the sight of the father's clothes leads "the good people" to think that he himself is present watching over his offspring'.[91] As Hartland observes, the malicious creatures of folklore are 'happily easily tricked'.

However, parents were also easily tricked. Fairies would often lure them out of their house, causing a disturbance amongst the cattle for example, in order to sneak in and abduct the baby.[92] The best advice for parents was, therefore, constant vigilance. It was advised that a newborn should never be left alone, and Keith Thomas believes that this rule 'could also be justified on more practical grounds of infant care'. Fear of fairy-abduction went hand in hand with the more palpable risk of human kidnappers, and the extra attention given by parents—whether motivated by natural or supernatural threats—would certainly have benefitted the child. 'In such ways,' opines Thomas, 'did fairy-beliefs help to reinforce some of the standards upon which the effective working of society depended'.[93]

Conclusion

By the late nineteenth century, belief in the fairies seemed to be waning in Scotland. Various communities were claiming to be the last believers; in *Folk-Lore and Legends*, the author tells of the vale of Corriewater in Annandale, for example, which in 1889 was 'regarded by the inhabitants, a pastoral and unmingled people, as the last border refuge of those beautiful and capricious beings, the fairies'.[94] By the 1970s, some communities, according to Ross, were claiming that fairies '*did* exist until comparatively recently but, like the great shoals of herring that populated the shores of the Hebrides, have now, for some mysterious reason, gone'.[95]

However, despite these claims of the endangered or extinct status of fairies in the Scottish landscape, they have proven indomitable. By conducting interviews with adults and children living in the Highlands and Islands of Scotland, particularly Balquhidder—the original home of Robert Kirk—Bennett has demonstrated that 'belief in fairies is alive and well' there—or at least that it was in the 1990s.[96] Stories are still told of them and their many dwelling places: *An Sithean* (the knoll of the fairies); *Cnoc-an-t-Sithean* (the little hill of the fairies); *Creag-nan-Seichean* (the rock of the fairies); and *Glen Shonie* (the glen of the fairy knolls), to name only a few.[97] Granted, however, traditions have adapted, allowing for more benevolent—if not Disneyfied— fairies, who are diminutive in size, grant wishes, and leave money under the pillow in exchange for a tooth.

Returning to the coin-tree in Fairy Glen on the Black Isle; fairies here are still resorted to for the brokering of alliances: the children offer a coin in exchange for the granting of a wish. Here, standing in the shade of the woods with the waterfall tumbling down in front of them, locals and tourists alike speak of fairies. Would they if the site were not called Fairy Glen? Possibly not. But this simply demonstrates how deeply ingrained fairy belief is in the landscapes of Scotland.

TROWS AND TROWIE WIVES[1]

Orkney and Shetland by Laura Coulson

Introduction

Orkney and Shetland are located to the north of the Scottish mainland, with Orkney comprising more than 70 islands and skerries, and Shetland about 100. However, the majority of these islands have no permanent population, at least no human population: though there are stories of islands mysteriously appearing and disappearing, under the powers of selkies, mermaids, and Finn folk. Orkney and Shetland are thought to have been continuously inhabited since Neolithic times, but are perhaps best known for their Viking residents, who arrived in the ninth century. Indeed, Orkney and Shetland only became Scottish in the fifteenth century and Norn, a variant of Old Norse, was still spoken there into the early nineteenth century. These northern islands are unlike any other part of Great Britain. Due to the high latitude, the summers are long with eighteen hours of sunlight at midsummer, but in winter there can be days of near darkness, with only six hours of daylight at midwinter. It is only natural that the supernatural life of the islands is also different to that of the mainland and by far the best known of Orkney and Shetland's supernatural fauna is the trow. 'This interesting race of supernatural beings', Saxby and Edmonston wrote in 1888, 'is closely allied to the Scandinavian Trolls, but has some very distinctive characteristics of its own. The trow is not such a mischief-making sprite as the Troll, is more human-like in some respects, and his nature seems cast in a morbid, melancholy mould.'[2]

But trows also bear some resemblance to the traditional fairy of Great Britain too. Trows, for example, kidnap children and women after childbirth, as well as stealing cattle. Both trows and fairies blind those who use their ointments and they are both fond of dancing and music. Some stories of the trows, indeed, have almost identical versions further to the south. For example, a passer-by enters a fairy or trow mound and a companion rescues them a year later. At times the words 'trow' and 'fairy' are used interchangeably in a tale. At other times there is a difference. A man of North Yell tells that 'faeries' were 'supposed to be a more, kind o' a gentle, gossamer being as what the trows wis… the faeries wis more or less a hairmless race… they were more up fir gaiety and all that… The trows wis… more closely associated til a earthly being,' at they could either be good or bad, according to whit way you dealt wi them.'[3] There are also similarities to Scandinavian folklore, and to the tales of trolls, drow, and draugr (the undead of Norse mythology). In some stories from Shetland, trolls are also mentioned alongside trows. To confuse matters further, some authors divided trows into different types. There were hill-trows and sea-trows. However, by the 1970s hill-trows, hill-folk and peerie (tiny) folk had become interchangeable terms.[4]

Perhaps the earliest mention of a trow comes in Jo. Ben's *Descriptio Insularum Orchadiarum*, a text usually dated around 1529. The word 'Trowis' appears in relation to a marine creature said to cohabit with women. There is even a story of a woman harassed by one of these creatures, which is said to be covered with marine plants and to resemble a horse. This recalls a nuggle or water-horse more than it does our modern idea of a trow. Perhaps this is what was, a hundred years ago, referred to as a sea or water trow? These were great rolling creatures who tumbled around in the waters and broke nets.[5] A Kirkness farmer was bothered by water-trows putting out his kiln fire and playing tricks on him, so he hid under some straw in his barn and hit the intruders with his flail scaring them off for good.[6] Mermaids and selkies were also occasionally referred to as sea trows. Hibbert believed that fishermen had misconstrued whales, orcas and porpoises.[7]

Another early mention of a supernatural creature that sounds like a trow comes in *The Court Book of Shetland 1615-1629*.[8] Katherine Johnsdaughter in Eshaness was burned as a witch. In her confession she admitted to having seen 'trollis' rise out of the kirkyard of Hildiswick and Holy Cross Kirk of Eshenes. She saw them on a hill called Greinfaill and claimed that they came to houses where there was feasting or 'great mirrines', especially at Yule. The connection with more recent trow-lore will become evident below.

What do Trows look like?
Physical descriptions of trows are usually quite vague, but often include the colour grey. Trows, indeed, are sometimes referred to as the 'grey folk'.[9] 'The Shetland Trow lives underground,—is nearly of human size,—or at least may adopt this form at

pleasure,—is always clad in sober gray and likes to interfere in human affairs'.[10]

One man who saw the trows whilst walking in winter along the cliff top at Tor Ness, in the Second World War, described the creatures as follows: 'These creatures were small in stature, but they did not have long noses nor did they appear kindly in demeanour. They possessed round faces, sallow in complexion, with long, dark, bedraggled hair. As they danced about, seeming to throw themselves over the cliff edge, I felt that I was witness to some ritual dance of a tribe of primitive men.'[11]

The size of trows also varies considerably. An account in Muir's *Mermaid Bride* from the BBC Radio Orkney Archives tells of a farmer at Sholtisquoy in North Ronaldsay who used to shoo the trows away when he went out at night: he was concerned about stepping on one, for they were, he believed, very small.[12] The inhabitants of Trowie Glen on Hoy were said to be no more than a foot high, though their leader 'Himsel' was taller.[13]

The following curious tale describes a creature that may or may not be a trow; in some respects it resembles the Scandinavian *draugr*. A farmer whose land included a large broch resolved to open this knoll, and found there ashes, bones, shells, and kitchen midden refuse; a graveyard, in short, from the past. One day whilst cleaning out the broch he saw an ancient grey-whiskered man dressed in an old grey tattered suit, patched in every conceivable manner, with a well-worn bonnet in his hand and aged shoes of horse or cowhide tied to his feet with strips of skin. The grey man addressed the farmer and warned him that if he worked on the broch any longer then he would regret it.[14]

Another tale, this one from Sanday, also provides a physical description of a trow-like creature. It tells of a farmer awakened at 3 am by a little fellow who stood in front of the box bed and asked for the loan of a 'piftanpiv'.[15] The little fellow was a lisping hill-trow or a hogboon looking for a sifting sieve. Marwick described the creature as small with long ears near the top of his head.

Trow Dwellings

A large number of trow sightings have taken place at Iron Age brochs or Neolithic mounds. 'They occupy small stony hillocks or knows, and whenever they make an excursion abroad, are seen, mounted on bulrushes, riding in the air'.[16] In the parish of Walls, an old woman's dog ran ahead of her. She eventually spotted her dog through a doorway in the hillside, leading to a warm and comfortable trowie house, where many trows were energetically dancing. A trowie wife stood washing a dish near the doorway and she caught sight of the dog and drove him out, then the music ceased and the light vanished.[17] Old Mac the tinker passed a mound and saw a small dark man standing at a door in the side. Mac advertised his wares and suddenly found himself in a large room inside the mound, and then suddenly he was back outside again sitting on top of the mound, his basket empty apart from five gold sovereigns.[18] Magnus Ritch saw a procession of little people at the Trowie Glen on Hoy and when he entered their cave he found a richly decorated hall where a dance was in progress.[19] The plantiecrue, a small circular drystone enclosure for growing cabbages, was another favourite haunt of the trows,[20] as were certain caves along the sea coast.[21]

Entering a trow abode is not advisable. A small hole on the summit of Liorafield on the Island of Foula is said to lead to the subterranean abodes of the trows. The story goes that several barrels of lines were let down without finding a bottom, and whoever opens the Liora or the vent there will die immediately.[22]

The destruction of a trow's home is, naturally, not to be undertaken lightly. A number of Roman Catholics pulled down a trow house to build the chapel of Gletna Kirk to prove to credulous natives how foolish and sinful their belief in trows was. But what they built each day was destroyed by invisible powers during the night. A devoted priest was the only one courageous enough to keep watch, but he was found dead the next morning. Many other kirks were also said to be trow-haunted, including, in Shetland, the Kirk-o'-Calvadell, Kirk-o'-Gunyester, and Kirk-o'-Underhool.[23]

Trow Behaviour

Trows are said to walk or skip backwards when seen by women. Men usually see them moving forward in the common way,[24] though one Shetland folklorist claimed that trows *always* walk backwards, facing the person watching them. If the sun rises while a trow is above ground, he or she has not the power to return home and must stay earth-bound, in sight of human neighbours until sunset.[25] Shetlanders once saw a little grey woman wandering as if in search of something, making a scolding noise in an unknown tongue. She was seen right through the day and about sunset one brave girl attempted to speak to her, but when the sun went down the woman suddenly disappeared.[26]

Trows cannot abide the mention of the word 'trow', much like many British and Irish fairies resent the word 'fairy'.[27] A herdsman sat beside an old fellow to strike up a conversation but when he described the man's snuff box as a 'vera trowy box' the old chap immediately vanished.[28] Note that the power to see invisible trows can be gained by washing your face with the first egg from a chicken.[29]

In some tales trows are given individual names. These include: Eelick or Alick, Bollick or Dollick, Gimp, Kork, Tring, Keelbrue, Bellia, Horny, Barnifeet or Bannafeet,[30] Tivla, Fivla,[31] Shankim, Hornjultie, Kannonjultie, Karl boggie, Peester-a-leeti, Truncherface,[32] Hill Johnnie, Eddy o' Annis, Peesteraleeti, Skoodern Humpi, Tuna Tivla, Bannock Feet,[33] Broonie,[34] and Hempie the Ferry-louper.[35]

Trows are said to klikk (steal) anything they can find, especially silver, though they are not allowed to steal from one of their own. A trow once stole a silver spoon from another trow and was banished from Trowland, condemned to forever wander the lonesome plains of the Isle, save for a brief visit to Trowland each Yule Day. He was seen rambling about clad in grey, weeping loudly. Kunal-trows are a sort of trow. They are very human in appearance but their nature is morbid and sullen. They wander in lonely places after the sun has set, and were seen at times to weep and wave their arms about.[36]

Trows are said to love fire, and always keep their underground dwellings well lit. If their household fire went out, they would renew them from the nearest human habitation, with some Shetlanders claiming to have seen a crackling rush of fire rushing towards their door.[37] Trows will punish anyone who forgets to lay the resting peat upon the waning fire.[38] Trows were also known to enter human homes to warm themselves by the fire. A woman in Northmavine was drying corn on the kiln in the barn one night when a very small man came in and squatted down by the hearth to enjoy some warmth. After a time the woman raked the fire and a number of embers fell on the strange visitor who let out a shrill cry and ran outside, losing a shoe. It was so small that afterwards she kept it as a snuff-box.[39] Trows would also enter human abodes to steal. One husband, tired of his oat cakes being stolen, hid himself in a corner to keep watch. To his surprise, one of the hearth stones slowly lifted upwards and through the opening came a trow hand. The hand snatched one of the broonies, the stone closing after it.[40]

One of the most curious stories comes from Alan Bruford. He tells of the Black Doctor, who would know when the fairies or trows came out:

> He'd suddenly spring up, he'd say, 'They're out! That's it!' He'd get dressed... maybe a wild night, he'd get dressed, oil coat, sou'wester, and take his—always took his heavy stick and he would set off... in the pitch blackness. He'd come home sometime durin' the night, all over covered of mud, all hacked... an' blood. He'd say, 'It was a tough fight,' he says, 'but I beat them.' Now where he'd been or what happened nobody knows, but he'd be out for hours on end, come back like that.'[41]

The trows bothered humans, but they also annoyed giants. A giant in the Kaem hills couldn't get any peace because of the trows, as they would climb over him, creep into his ears, and even pull his eyebrows. He made up his mind to put a stop to it and decided to construct a huge creel of straw and carry them over to Norway, leaving them there for good. He made the creel and then one moonlit night he found the trows and scooped them all up in his giant hands, and dropped them into the creel and tied the top up. But when he went to lift it he realised it was too big and he couldn't get it on his back, so he dragged it to the top of the hill to try lifting it from there. He nearly tore a hole in the creel from dragging it over the earth, and when he lifted it on to his back the bottom fell through and out came the trows, wiggling like fish.[42]

Property belonging to the trows is said to bring luck. A woman found a trow's kettle and she was very lucky while it remained in her house. Other trow items that have been found include a copper pan,[43] a wooden cog,[44] a beautifully carved spoon,[45] a small wooden cap with the power of curing jaundice,[46] an earthenware bottle with a healing liquid, which never depleted,[47] while a trow's bronze sword was found at Nordhouse, Shetland.[48] It was said that if a person was attacked by a trow, then the next time they visited the spot they would discover something valuable. One man returned and found a trowie dart, a talisman that served against all kinds of evil spirits.[49]

Trow Matrimony and Trow Children

There are, according to some authorities, no female trows. Trows marry human wives and as soon as the baby trow is born the hapless mother pines and dies, and no trow marries twice and no trow can die until his son is grown up. One trow tried to postpone matrimony and took up abode in a ruined broch, eating only earth shaped into fish, birds, cattle, and children. He eventually married a witch.[50] Tales of trow children are quite common, though whether these children are of the trow species or are stolen human children is not mentioned. One night the Guid man o' Taft found a strange wattled straw box in his yard. At first he thought it was a fiddle case so he flung it up on top of the box bed, before going to the byre to feed his cows. When he came back inside he heard, though, strange noises outside in the yard, a loud trampling sound mingled with a sound like 'foodle-dee-doodle-dee-doo, foodle-dee-doodle-dee-dee'. Then a small voice from the straw-box on the bed said 'Let me oot, mammie is crying for mulle'. Taft knew at once that there was a little trow inside the case; he quickly put it outside, and then there was silence.[51]

Maalie Coutt's grandfather had been digging peat turfs when he heard a voice shout 'Watch me heed!' and a boy, aged about eight and covered with hair, jumped out of a crack in the ground. The man offered to feed him and the boy replied that he ate heath and the black bull's bladder and that he was from between the Troils O Houlland in North Yell and the Grey Stane O Stourascord. The man took the boy home and warmed him, but the boy threatened to blow down the house if he wasn't released. He was a fairy changeling or trowie boy.[52]

A family in Yell also encountered a trow child. They were sat around the fire chatting one evening when they heard a child crying outside, and a few minutes later in walked a little girl. The older members of the family had no trouble recognising that she was of 'Da Gud Folk' and they resolved to treat her with kindness in case any harm should come to the house. They put her to bed with their own children and retired to sleep. The next day the child stayed and at night they heard a female voice calling outside as if looking for a child. As soon as the child heard their calls she disappeared, and the children, beside whom the trow had slept, prospered.[53]

The trows are said to require every hearth to be swept clean on Saturday night, and plenty of clean water must be left for them. This was thought to allow trows to wash their children: the trows also stipulated that they should be left in peace while they carried out their ablutions. When one boy neglected these duties, he awoke to a commotion and saw two trow-wives searching for water to clean their three-eyed baby. In revenge for his failure to put out water they washed their baby in a keg of swats, a Scottish oat drink, and then poured the mess back into the keg.[54]

A fisherman sat dozing by the fire when a soaking wet trow woman and child came in. He pretended to be asleep and she made herself at home, hanging the child's wet clothing on the man's foot. He stirred and the garments fell into the ashes, so she hung them back on, but he stirred and the same thing happened. The third time she struck him on the foot and in the generations that followed there was always someone who walked with a limp in the family.[55]

Occasionally a trow needed a favour from a human, especially during or after childbirth. Mam Kirstan was asked by the trows to look after and dress one of their babies, and one of the grey men gave her a box of curious ointment to anoint the child with. She wiped her own eye whilst doing this and so gained a sight so keen she could see a boat on the ocean twenty miles away, but when she accidently mentioned it to a trow he put his little finger in her eye and blinded her there.[56] Catherine Tammas's daughter met a similar fate; she used ointment meant for a trow child and saw a woman she knew to be dead. The dead woman asked which eye she saw her with and then blinded her in that eye using elf-shot.[57]

Trow Music and Trow Dancing

The trows are said to be great lovers of music, and they are especially fond of fiddles. Many a beautiful reel is said to have originated from the trows. An Unst man heard the trows playing inside a hill and listened until he had mastered their melody.[58] Another man learnt a trow air after he had heard, lying in bed one morning, a large company of trows passing his door accompanied by a piper.[59] One man was not so lucky. He heard the trows playing at a trow hill, but the 'peeric [tiny] misty men' guessed and from that night on his wits went 'a wool-gathering' and he could only babble of the trows and play their tune.[60]

Fiddlers were frequently invited to play for the trows, but often with unpleasant consequences. A fiddler of Yell was carried off by the trows on his way to a Halloween gathering. After playing for a considerable time he was allowed to leave, but, on returning home, found his house a crumbling ruin and he knew none of his neighbours. Years and years had passed and when he went to church the next day he crumbled into dust.[61] Tam Bichan the fiddler met a peedie (small) man dressed in grey with a long grey beard and dark mischievous eyes, who invited him to come and play for him and his friends. Tam followed him through a door into the great mound of Dingieshowe in Deerness and they went down a long steep tunnel and into a huge room. The Trow served Tam with heather ale and he played the fiddle for them, and when he left he found that many years had gone by, though he had not aged at all.[62] William Cooper prospered after playing at a trow bridal gathering, but when he spoke of it to his neighbours his cattle died, his crops failed, and he became blind and fell into poverty.[63] Some fiddlers were more fortunate. When the Fiddler of Flammister played for the trows they promised that nine generations of his bairns would carry a fiddle and so they did.[64]

The trows were also very fond of a good dance, and they were said to 'hink' or 'limp' when they danced, a word that appears in some trow sites including the Henkisknow.[65] They squatted till their knees were doubled up in front, their hands tightly held between the thighs and the calfs of the legs, and then they hopped about like pinioned fowl.[66] A Fetlar man saw a number of trows performing the 'halt', a dance, and he dared to argue with them. One threw a hedderkow (heather stalk) at him that hit his heel. He was crippled in that foot from then onwards.[67]

Trow Thefts and Kidnappings

The trows were once greatly feared, with many a tale of trows stealing cattle and humans. New mothers were particularly vulnerable: the new mother could in fact appear to be at home, but part of her was removed, leaving her pale and absent.[68] Children were also taken away to the hills in order to be play fellows to the trows' offspring.[69] People under the power of the trows were said to be 'in the hill'.[70] When a trow would steal girls in infancy they would come back in 'maiden prime with a wild unearthly beauty and glamour on them, and an unbroken silence regarding the land of their captivity'.[71]

A new father was returning after taking the midwife home when he saw a trow in the meadow, heading towards his house to steal his child. He threw a razor on to the green path to the door and the trows at once dispersed—trows, like most fairies, fear iron. But the following morning he discovered that they had taken his best milk cow instead.[72] The trows would often leave a likeness or wooden stock behind when stealing a cow or human. A Shetland crofter was returning home when he met a gang of trows carrying a bundle between them. When he entered his cottage he saw that his wife was gone and an effigy left in her place. He seized the effigy and flung it into the fire; it rose in the air and vanished through the chimney in a cloud of smoke. The wife soon afterwards walked through the cottage door.[73] A Sandness woman died in childbirth and her husband later remarried, but one day he came across a door in a hillock near Stoorbro Hill and inside he met his first wife, who told him she had been taken by the trows and an effigy body left behind. She warned him not to eat food whilst there, and he obeyed but his refusal angered the trows, who boxed one of his ears and he remained deaf in that ear for the rest of his life.[74]

Two women travelling on Mainland in Orkney stopped at a cottage and whilst resting there saw a repulsive looking creature with large unblinking eyes, making unearthly grunts. The housewife lamented how one morning she had gone to pick cabbages from the yard and when she came back she had found her own boy gone and a trow changeling in his place.[75] A blacksmith retrieved his kidnapped son by first collecting hearth ashes in eggshells, causing the changeling to laugh and give himself away, and then by throwing burning straw into the bed, causing the changeling to disappear in a blue flame. When he retrieved his son he found he had been employed working iron for the trows and had acquired the art of tempering scythes.[76] Another changeling gave itself away after a tailor employed at a farm was woken by music and saw a large company of fairies dancing. Suddenly a trow changeling jumped up and joined in their gambols, showing a familiarity with the movements of the dance that only a hill-dweller would know.[77]

Not all changelings were disagreeable. One overworked servant lad was advised by a changeling child to go to a trow knowe and say he had been sent to fetch 'So-and-So's Flail'. He obeyed and retrieved the flail from a very small wrinkled woman and when he returned, instead of an ill-thriven child he found a well-built young man who took the flail and threshed the corn for him. The strong man admitted to being the real human son, who had been stolen as a child by the trows and replaced with the changeling. He advised the servant that whenever he found himself in trouble he could call the young man for help. He then departed with his flail and the peevish child reappeared in the cradle.[78]

Trows were said to be fond of human food, particularly beef and mutton.[79] When Mam Kirstan saw the trows rolling something that resembled a cow along the way, she threw her bunch of keys into the heap without the trows seeing. When she got home she found her own cow dead, and when they opened the beast they found her keys inside.[80] A farmer of Kwitigirt, who was having a particularly bad harvest, said he would give his best cow if he could rise in the morning and find his corn shorn. Sure enough the next morning his corn was in sheaves and his best milk cow was missing. A neighbour said he passed at midnight and saw the trows at work.[81]

Trows at Yule

Yule was a special time for trows. Seven days before Yule, on 'Tul-ya's e'en, the trows would leave their homes in the earth and come above ground for the duration of the holidays.[82] They would steal mutton and pork hams unless a steel knife or fork was stuck in the flesh, and hold dances every Yule night.[83] They caused much trouble and it was very important that people remembered to bless and protect themselves and their property against the trows. Each member of the family washed their whole person, and slept in a clean, and if possible new, garment. The hands or feet were put into the water and three living coals were dropped in, or else 'the trows took the power o' the feet or hands'.[84]

Trows are said to be excessively fond of dancing, and very keen to join in the Yule revels, but they could only do so disguised as a mortal. Two small children were once left in their bed whilst the parents joined the dancing in the next house. The children were soon seen, however, gliding into the barn, with wide-open eyes and silent smiling lips. They danced with such marvellous steps that the merry-makers declared they must have been taught by the trows. But when the young mother spotted them she cried in horror: 'Guid save me, the bairns!' No trow can remain visible when a pious word is spoken, and the little strangers vanished at once. Everyone hastened outside to search for them in the snow, but to no avail. The mother had forgotten to bless her children, so the trows had taken the form of the children to go dancing. The children were found dead the next morning, in the drifts, wrapped in each other's arms.[85]

During one Yule celebration the drink ran low and an outspoken damsel named Breeta foolishly said she was not afraid to meet the trows. A youth named Josey offered to retrieve more drink and told Breeta that if she wasn't scared then she should come with him to see the trows slinking ower the braes. She agreed. Josey returned at last, alone with two empty whisky bottles, shouting madly: 'The trows have got the drink, and they've got the lass as well!' Her brothers found poor Breeta lying dead in the Moola burn. In her hand she clutched a bulwand, a type of marsh reed the trows use for horses. Josey was dead by the next Yule.[86]

Trows were very fond of drinking at Yule. A trow in Yell would visit all the houses looking for drink. He'd spend the first night in North Yell, then the next in South Yell, and if he found something he'd drink it. On one occasion he drank so much he was found lying on the ben (inner room) window ledge of a house. The people tried to grab him but he threatened them and beat a hasty retreat, fleeing for the north.[87]

On the twenty-fourth night of Yule the doors were all opened and there was much running around to chase out the unseen creatures. Their time of freedom was over and the trows retired to their gloomy abodes until the next year. At the Shetland festival of Up Helly Aa, iron was shown about as the trows cannot abide the sight of it, and there were marches through the town accompanied by a huge bonfire and much racket.'[A]mid noise and hearty congratulations the trows were banished to their homes in the hillsides. When day dawned after twenty-fourth night every trow had disappeared and the Yules were ended'.[88]

Protection from the Trows

There are many tried and tested methods for protecting yourself against trows and fairies and other methods for healing those affected by them. These included: laying crossed straws on the threshold or a circle of pins on the pillow,[89] iron,[90] a Bible under the cradle pillow or fastening the bed curtains with pins set in a circle,[91] a fire-brand borne three times around a person or an animal,[92] a black cock crowing,[93] silver coins or steel,[94] and a circle drawn on the ground in God's name.[95] In Shetland a dog with double back claws (dew claws) was considered a perfect safeguard against trows.[96] None, of course, should travel at night without a good steel knife in his pocket as 'whoever meets a trow should draw a circle around him and bid 'Gjud be about me' or lie down and stick a knife in the ground at his head'.[97] When a person became emaciated with sickness due to trows, a cunning man or woman would hang a triangular stone in the shape of a heart around the neck, or pour molten lead through a key so it assumed a variety of shapes, and then selected a portion which was sewn into the shirt of the patient.[98]

The farmers of Huip in Stronsay went out each evening to buil (pen in for the night) the trows who lived in a green mound to the west of the house. These creatures were scared away to bed by a circle of farm folk who closed in on the mound, banging milk pails and anything else that would make a noise. These trows caused great mischief about the house, and the story was told by a man in his eighties who had witnessed the penning of the trows as a boy.[99]

The Last of the Trows

A Yell fiddler played for the trows each Yule, but one year they failed to invite him. He went to the '*Trowie hadd*' to look for them but there wasn't a soul in sight apart from one old wife sat by the fire. She said a minister had come to Collyfa and the trows could not suffer his preaching and praying and they got no peace so they left.[100] An alternative version tells how the trows had moved to Faroe, but the old wife had stayed behind as she was too old to travel.

The trows who lived at the Knowes of Catfirth were forced to leave when quarrymen destroyed their homes. They were spotted one day leaving the knowes, weeping and lamenting. One had a kist on his back and a wooden tub in his hand, another had a kettle on his head and a three-legged stool under his arm; everyone carried something. When they reached 'Tammiesdik' they halted and stood in a circle, and an old man addressed the group, 'My dear children, lament no more. I have decided on a place to go, we shall go to Bijl-r-am O' Krun.' Then up spoke a young trow with a big yellow beard, who reassured the group that he had been there before and it wasn't a bad place, and advised them to hold their tongues and keep moving as daylight was coming in. They reached the knowes at the north side of Bijl-r-am and vanished.'[101]

Some say the trows have now abandoned mainland Orkney. They became dissatisfied with life and set on moving to a new dwelling beside the Dwarfie Stone on Hoy. At midnight they met at the Black Craig of Stromness and wove a rope from the bands used to thatch houses. A long-legged trow named Hempie the Ferry-louper made the enormous jump over to Hoy and attached the end of the rope to a rock, and a Trow at Stromness held on tight to the other end. The trows clung onto the rope and began crossing over the sea, but midway the trow in Stromness accidently let go and the others all tumbled into the sea and drowned. Poor Hempie was unable to go on without his friends and leaped into the angry waves to join their fate.[102]

According to Fergusson, when the older generations required their children to go somewhere on a dark night they coaxed them with 'A' the trows arc droned noo, they wunna fleg thee ony mair' (the trows are drowned now, they won't frighten you any more).Fergusson comments, 'This idea was generally very prevalent throughout the Orkney Isles, and the disappearance of Orcadian fairies is thus satisfactorily accounted for.'[103]

Lastly, just in case you were thinking of seeking out any remaining trows, a word of warning. 'It is told of a girl, that, in the saucy merriment of youth, she was wont to run to the fairy knowes, and call to the trows to come and fetch her to see their wonderful home. This she did frequently, and at last the irritated trows breathed upon her, and she became paralysed in the limbs, and remained so all her life'.[104] So perhaps it's best for all that the trows are left in peace....

11

THE FAIR FOLK AND ENCHANTERS

Wales by Richard Suggett

Introduction

'Our silly [=simple] people' have 'an astonishing reverence of the fairies'—so claimed the mid-sixteenth-century Welsh puritan, John Penry.[1] Fairies were commonly encountered spirits in early modern Wales. Indeed, the landscape was full of place-names that referred to the supernatural, including relatively recent arrivals like *pwca* ('puck') and *coblyn* ('goblin').[2] Fairies were the best known of many different sprites that tended to haunt the wild and were generally regarded as unpredictable or frightening, and were the subject of many stories which people accepted to a greater or lesser degree. The ways of the fairies (*ffordd bendith eu mamau*) were proverbially unknown and suspect.[3] The words referring to many of these spirits often do not occur in print before the eighteenth century. These spirits were part of the popular oral culture of early modern Wales, especially the stories of the fireside and other sociable situations that entertained and informed but also reproduced belief. In the eighteenth century there was a marked partition of belief as ideas of witchcraft and fairies were increasingly regarded as superstitious by the gentry and growing middle class. By the mid-nineteenth century these folk-beliefs had been rejected by the majority of noncon-formists as part of an 'old' unreformed Wales that had existed before the religious revival and belonged in the past. The beliefs described here may be considered part of a practical religion concerned with the nature of spirits, and by implication the nature of the person, which was almost exclusively oral but embedded in the landscape and expressed in numerous narratives of encounters with ghosts, fairies and other related beings.[4]

In England, Scotland, and in parts of continental Europe, there were similar beliefs. In England fairy beliefs were probably 'already ancient' by the Reformation and have been characterised as an amalgam of traditions of ancestral spirits, ghosts, sleeping heroes, fertility spirits and pagan gods.[5] In Wales, as elsewhere, the origin and chronology of fairy beliefs are difficult to establish, but fairy beliefs were probably relatively recent, displacing earlier and historically obscure traditions. The common but etymologically 'curious' Welsh term for fairies, *tylwyth teg*, literally the 'fair family', was probably an adaptation and mistranslation of the English word 'fairy'.[6] Its earliest use occurs in a poem of *c.*1500. A poet complains that his tryst has been ruined by an enveloping mist, which he likens to a magician flying from the abode of the fairies: 'Fal hudol byd yn hedge/ O barthllwyth y Tylwyth teg'.[7] It is interesting that the fairies were already associated with magicians, a marked feature of early-modern belief. The collective term was sufficiently ubiquitous to be included in Salesbury's short Welsh-English *Dictionary* (1547): 'tuylwyth tec [–] Fayries'.[8] The examination of the enchanter Harry Lloyd (discussed below), who claimed to have derived his knowledge from 'certaine fairies commonly called in Welsh 'y Tyllwith Tegg', provides the earliest surviving contextualised use of the term that was clearly entrenched by the early seventeenth century.

In south Wales (Breconshire and Monmouthshire certainly) the fairies were commonly called 'bendith y mamau' or 'bendith eu mamau', that is 'the (or their) mothers' blessings'. John Penry (1587) explained that the fairies were regarded as 'such as have deserved their mothers blessing'—accounted 'the greatest felicity that any creature can be capeable of'. The flattering terms for the fairies were 'propitiary names'. The same idea is found in the English 'good Robin' and more strongly in the Gaelic 'good people' ('sleagh maith') and 'les bonnes mères' of Brittany. The fairies were capricious and unpredictable, and flattering names were used to try and deflect their ill will. As Kirk pointed out, 'the Irish use to bless all they fear Harme of'.[9]

Many Protestant divines regarded the fairies as essentially evil spirits. Some Protestant writers referred to fairy beliefs in the most hostile terms, deliberately refusing to refer to them by their popular 'flattering' names. For them, sightings of fairies were an indicator of the success of radical Protestantism: as the light of the gospel prevailed, the fairies would hide. Morgan Llwyd, the puritan, announced in the mid-seventeenth century that as 'the day dawneth' the 'worms of darkness will hide.' Charles Edwards', in his history of Christianity (1671), claimed that the fairies (*tylwyth teg*) or 'neighbourly Devils' were not so bold as in the time of Popery, when they appeared as visible companies to lure people into familiarity with them. Edmund Jones, the Independent minister of Pontypool, wrote in the same tradition towards the end of the eighteenth century, claiming that 'the Apparitions of the fairies, and of other spirits of hell… have very much ceased in Wales since the light of the Gospel and religion hath so much prevailed, according as was foretold by the admirable Mr Morgan Lloyd of Wrexham'.[10]

Edmund Jones did not deny the reality of fairies—far from it; he provides a great deal of evidence about the vitality of fairy beliefs in the eighteenth century. Jones wrote in the didactic tradition of the Puritan divines of the later seventeenth century, especially Richard Baxter, whose work he mentions. Like his predecessors, Edmund Jones's purpose was polemical: by collecting narratives or 'relations' of apparitions he was concerned to demonstrate the reality of the spirit world and confound sceptics and 'Sadducees'. There was really no end to this type of collecting. Jones seems to have collected narratives from literate and illiterate informants alike for most of his adult life. The earliest related to events in the 1730s and he published a selection of these narratives in 1780.[11]

Fairy Characteristics

Edmund Jones's record of apparitions in eighteenth-century Wales helps define some of the attributes of the fairies when belief in them had vitality, and his work bears comparison with the quasi-ethnographic account of fairy beliefs in central Scotland by Rev. Robert Kirk (1691), the Presbyterian minister.[12] Like Kirk, Edmund Jones was rooted in the society whose traditions he faithfully recorded. His accounts of fairies and other apparitions are both numerous and detailed. Jones gives the source of each relation, clearly separating an account of the apparition from his gloss on it, noting details that he does not understand.

Edmund Jones, writing of his native upland Gwent, says that formerly (more so than at the time of writing, 1779) there were frequent appearances of the fairies in Wales. Fairies were still encountered, of course, and there was evidently a store of stories about the fairies which people enjoyed relating and which found their way into Jones's narratives. Fairies were seen and heard at all hours of the day and night, but more particularly in the night. Many saw them; sometimes several people at the same time. Many also heard their music, which was rather elusive, 'low and pleasant, but none could ever learn the Tune'. According to Edmund Jones, it was the general opinion in the past (when their appearances were very frequent) that the fairies knew whatever was spoken outside the houses, especially at night, but not so much what was spoken in the houses. The fairies thus had good knowledge of human affairs. Indeed they had fore-knowledge of disputes and altercations and were excited or agitated by this knowledge. Before any falling out in the parish of Aberystruth, the fairies would leap and frisk about making a serpentine pattern in the air. There were those who witnessed and tried to interpret these signs of contention, including Edmund Daniel ('an honest man, and a constant speaker of truth, and of much observation') who often saw the fairies after sunset 'leaping and striking in the air' before a quarrel.[13] The fairies were also heard talking, as if many were conversing together. The words were seldom heard distinctly, but the fairies seemed to 'dispute much about future Events, and about what they were to do'. The altercations of the fairies were one of their defining features, and their capacity for disagreement became proverbial. When people fell out in Blaenau Gwent, it was said, 'Ni chydunant hwy mwy na bendith eu mamau', that is 'They will no more agree than the fairies'.[14]

Fairies did not seem to have a consistent appearance. There is a revealingly unsentimental depiction of a fairy seen in Dyffryn Clydach, Glamorgan, drawn for a nineteenth-century folklorist before images of fairies had achieved their chocolate-box form, which shows a naked, alien-like creature with a perky expression (the image at the head of this chapter).[15] Other references suggest that they wore distinctly coloured clothes. According to Sir John Wynn (d. 1627), in the mid-fifteenth century a band of outlaws attired in green had greatly frightened people in Snowdonia who 'said they were the fairies and so ran away'.[16] About 1700 it was noted that 'our people clothe our feries in blue, as vulgar people commonly went in former dayes'.[17] Later descriptions of fairies clothe them in red. Fairies were not concerned with fashion. At any period, fairies seem to have been dressed in a style and (particularly) colour not favoured by the then current generation.[18]

The fairies appeared in different guises but generally collectively as 'dancing companies with music' and as funeral processions. The fairy funeral procession, complete with bier and black cloth, presaged a death. According to Edmund Jones, instances of this were so numerous that it was 'past all dispute that they infallibly knew the times of Men's deaths.' Jones attributed the fairies' foreknowledge to their superior astrological knowledge. When they appeared as dancers they sometimes tried to draw people into the dance. Those so enticed might remain with the fairies for some time, usually an entire year. Those who returned from the fairies were unable to give much of an account of their time, 'or they durst not give it', but said only that they had been dancing and that the time seemed short. Sometimes the fairies abducted humans for just a night but might transport them great distances, as sometimes happened in witchcraft cases. Edmund Jones related how in 1733 'infernal spirits' abducted his own brother from a benighted hunting party taking him from place to place until he was rendered insensible. Contact with the fairies was generally debilitating and those who returned from the fairies were sickly.[19]

Appearances of the fairies were generally witnessed by an odd number of people, one, three, or five persons, and so on. Fairies may have appeared more often to men than to women, but this was probably because men in the course of their work went to the places that fairies favoured. According to Edmund Jones fairies preferred dry ground, not far from the shelter of trees and hedges. They liked the shade of mature trees, particularly the large and branchy 'monarch' oak (*breninbren*), and there were several notable 'fairy oaks', including one engraved for Thomas Pennant. The fairies were sometimes called 'y tylwyth teg yn y coed', the fair folk in the wood, because they were seldom seen far from trees. Certain places were particularly favoured by the fairies. In Aberystruth parish the fairies most frequently appeared at Hafodafel and Cefn-bach, which were 'dry, lightsome, pleasant places'.[20] Other fairies lived underground. In the guise of 'knockers' they followed the veins of lead and silver, and through their knocking led miners to good veins. The Cardiganshire miners regarded the knockers as benevolent, and in the mid-seventeenth century it was said that there was 'nothing more ordinary' than to hear and after see these subterranean spirits.[21] Yet other fairies lived in lakes. Traditions of lake-dwelling fairies were found all over Wales. Occasionally humans ventured to speak to these aquatic and other fairies. An eighteenth-century diarist rather prosaically reported the death of a Glamorgan carpenter in 1794: 'It was he that talk[ed] with a she spirit a few years past'.[22]

Fairies lived in the wild but they would sometimes come into people's houses, particularly during stormy weather. This puzzled Edmund Jones, as disembodied spirits like the fairies should not feel the cold, wind or rain. However, he supposed that bad weather made their favourite places less pleasant. The 'poor, ignorant people' for fear of the fairies made them welcome in their houses by providing fresh ('clean') water, and—an importantly specific detail—by taking care that no knife, or other iron instrument, lay near the fire. Iron was hateful to the fairies and those who neglected to do this might be injured by them. The fairies were welcomed into Morgan William's house in Blaenau Gwent but on one occasion there was no clean water for them, and the mistress of the house was seized with a severe pain in her leg and heard the fairies say that there was the prong of a hayfork ('pikil') in her thigh. Once inside a house, a fairy company might make merry. A Cardiganshire husbandman in the mid-seventeenth century was prepared to take his oath that 'spirits' had invaded his house one night as he lay in bed. A light had appeared in his chamber about midnight and then a dozen spirits entered in the shape of men, and two or three women with children in their arms. The spirits danced in the room and seemed to eat bread and cheese from a 'tick' or sheet spread on the floor. They smiled at him and offered him food. The frightened husbandman, 'calling to God to bless him', heard a sinister 'whisper of a voice in Welch, bidding him hold his peace'. After four hours the dancers departed and the husbandman terrified but unhurt, floundering about the chamber, woke the rest of the household.[23]

It was particularly dangerous to have fairies in a house where there was a baby. The fairies 'often attempted' to spirit away a human child while its parents slept, leaving in its stead a changeling. The fairies did not always manage an abduction, as the experience of Dazzy (Dacey), wife of Abel Walter of Glynebwy, suggested. Dazzy was nursing a child and one night awoke to find that the baby had been taken from her bed. After a search the baby was found on top of the cupboard-bed, and it was concluded that the fairies had left it there after failing to convey it any further. Changelings were of 'no growth, good appearance, or sense'. Edmund John William's son was abducted by the fairies who left 'an ideot in his stead'. Edmund Jones saw this changeling for himself, and reported that 'there was something diabolical in his aspect, but more of this in his motion and voice'. His movements were 'mad', and he made 'very disagreeable screaming sounds', which frightened passing strangers. The child's complexion was 'a dark tawny colour'. The changeling, perhaps a child with Down syndrome, survived until he was ten or twelve, which was judged longer than such children usually lived. Parents who believed that their child was a changeling might try and return it to the fairies. Pennant describes how the parents of an 'uncommonly peevish child' left it in a cradle overnight under the massive 'fairy oak' at Downing, and in the morning, finding that it was 'perfectly quiet', were convinced that their original child had been returned.[24]

The 'poor, ignorant people' were afraid of offending the fairies and being hurt by them in consequence. Iron implements were known to be offensive to the fairies and those who left them lying in the corner near the fire were sometimes hurt by visiting fairies. Those who cut down the fairies' favourite trees, particularly the monarch oak, were hurt 'even unto death' by them, although by the second half of the eighteenth century it was reported that these trees are cut down 'without any hurt'.[25] Many of those hurt by the fairies had disturbed them inadvertently by going amongst them unawares or by obstructing their path. Those who fell among the fairies were generally seized with terror. There seems to have been only one effective way of dispersing the fairies, if one was not paralysed by fear. One of Edmund Jones's narratives concerned E.T. (a 'sober' man of 'strict veracity') who when travelling by night over Bedwellty mountain was suddenly aware that there were fairies on all sides, some dancing and others (worryingly) hunting to the sound of the hunting horn. Though terrified, he recalled that 'if any person saw the fairies about him and drew out his knife', they would vanish. He did so and saw the fairies no more.[26]

Those who had been hurt by the fairies were cured only with difficulty by enchanters. Edmund Jones named two enchanters who undertook these cures: Charles Hugh of Llangybi and Rhisiart Cap Du (Richard Black Cap) of Aberystruth. These charmers were sometimes suspected of too close a connection with the fairies. Rhisiart went out to meet the fairies using a hole in his thatched roof, so it was said, although he claimed only to observe the stars through the hole. On one occasion ('as was the custom then in those days of ignorance') Rhisiart Cap Du was fetched to charm a person greatly hurt after inadvertently falling among the fairies. When Rhisiart Cap Du entered the house, the sick man flung a weight at the charmer with all his might, saying "Thou old villain wast one of the worst of them to hurt me".[27]

Encounters with fairies seem always to have been regarded as more common in the past than in the present. Fairy beliefs were expressed as a kind of cumulative historical mythology which related to the experiences of named relatives, friends and neighbours, and their ancestors, whose details could be confirmed by talking to the acquaintances of those concerned, and sometimes to the 'victim' of the story or a near relative. The narratives of fairy encounters collected by Edmund Jones have a rather prosaic, everyday quality when compared with the fairy-tales which circulated in English-language chapbooks and the stories which were embellished into a literary genre by folklorists in the nineteenth century. Fairies were encountered in everyday circumstances as people went about their usual business and some people claimed to have had numerous encounters with the fairies. As Shôn Thomas Shôn Rhydderch, otherwise

Cobler Jig, told a collector of traditions in the Vale of Neath (Jane Williams of Aberpergwm), 'I tell you that fairies were to be seen in the days of my youth by the thousand, and I have seen them myself a hundred times'.[28]

Enchanters and Fairies

Fairies were unconstrained by the ordinary limits of time, space and body, and because of this had access to knowledge ordinarily unavailable to men and women. The fairies had knowledge of many hidden things: they knew the whereabouts of lost money and concealed valuables; they knew how to cure illnesses that were beyond the expertise of physicians and surgeons; they knew about the treasures of the earth. Spirits knew the locations of hidden wealth, they had remedies for the illnesses that defeated physicians and surgeons, and they had information about the future as well as the past. Some soothsayers specialised in trying to obtain knowledge from spirits. Cunning-folk would deny that they had dealings with devils or familiars, but they might concede—or even boast—that they had consulted the fairies. John Penry, the late-Elizabethan Protestant controversialist, was quite explicit about the connection between enchanters and fairies: there were 'swarmes of southsaiers and enchanters' in Wales who professed that they walked on certain nights with the fairies 'of whom they brag themselves to have their knowledge'.[29] Enchanters claimed to meet with the fairies on particular nights of the week: Tuesdays and Thursdays according to both John Penry and Harry Lloyd. In Wales, as in England and Scotland, some enchanters claimed that they could obtain money and cures from the fairies.[30] These claims touched deep needs among the common people: the need to cure the sick, especially sick children, and the desire to be released from a poverty-stricken existence. Two rather pathetic cases from the 1630s are described here, which show how practised confidence tricksters claiming to have access to the knowledge of the fairies exploited people's vulnerability.

In 1636 two Caernarfonshire magistrates examined a complaint against Harry Lloyd of Llandygái.[31] Harry Lloyd was described as a common wanderer, but he was a vagabond with a reputation as a 'surgeon and diviner'. Harry Lloyd preferred to call himself a 'scholar', and was presumably literate, but the local constable was forthright about the sinister aspects of Harry Lloyd's reputation: 'under fayned colour & p[re]tence of surgery or phisicke [he] doth exercise wicked & unlawfull arts, (that is to say) fortune tellinge, palmistry, comon hauntinge & familiarity with wicked spirits in the night time.' Moreover, through these 'arts' Harry Lloyd had cheated several hopeful victims, and he was therefore considered dangerous to the 'inferiour sortie of people'.

The revealing examination of John David Howell, a farmer of Hirdre, Tudweiliog, has survived. In February 1635, a little before sunset, Harry Lloyd had arrived unexpectedly at his house asking for a night's lodging for 'a poore scholler borne att Bangor', meaning of course himself, and his wife. His request was granted, but once ensconced in the barn, Harry Lloyd was reluctant to leave. He had probably already spotted his next victim. In due course Harry Lloyd asked his host if he 'had a desire to be rich', adding that he could make him 'inough of gold & silver'. There was of course only one answer to this enticing question, and John David Howell predictably replied that 'he would willingly be rich if he could'. The 'poor scholar' then told John about other poor men whom he had helped to become rich. Did John know Richard y Gof, the Penmorfa blacksmith, or Evan ap Richard of Llanfaglan?

John David Howell now urgently enquired, 'How & by what meanes he made them soe rich?' Harry then imparted the secret of becoming wealthy—it was through dealing with 'familiars and spirits and certaine fairies commonly called in Welsh 'y Tyllwith Tegg'.' Harry Lloyd revealed that he regularly consulted the fairies throughout the year, meeting them on Tuesday and Thursday nights. Through Harry Lloyd's good offices, the fairies often placed a quantity of gold and silver on Richard the Smith's anvil, which he found in the morning. Similarly at Llanfaglan, the fairies and spirits regularly put gold and silver into a hole in the churchyard hedge which Evan ap Richard later gathered. These were enticing images of unearned wealth, like the money tree in the Field of Miracles in Collodi's *Pinocchio*. Harry Lloyd went on to say that he visited these wealthy beneficiaries of his skill just twice or three times a year, asking only that he should receive five or ten shillings from them on these occasions.

Having revealed his secret, Harry Lloyd went on to say that if John would give him a small sum of money, he would make him rich as well. John, 'beinge a simple man & givinge credit to Harry Lloyd's speeches', replied regretfully that he was a poor man, standing indebted to many, and had no money to spare. Harry Lloyd replied that he needed only two shillings to buy wax to make candles, explaining that when he went to meet the spirits he needed the candles to bestow on them for light. Thus encouraged, John David Howell managed to procure the money and Harry produced some wax and made candles. On Tuesday night, Harry Lloyd went out to meet the fairies but returned downcast, saying that he could not 'prevaile with the spirits' unless John gave him four shillings 'to bestowe upon the said spirits for an offer[ing]'. The remainder of the examination has been lost, but presumably Harry Lloyd persuaded John to part with more money until he realised—poor dupe—that he had been tricked.

Harry Lloyd was but one of several travelling confidence tricksters, moving from victim to victim, claiming that they could persuade the fairies to help the sick and the poor. Not long before Harry Lloyd was apprehended in Caernarfonshire, Ann Jones was committed to gaol in Denbighshire for pretending to meet with the fairies on behalf of some deluded clients. Ann's examination before a justice of the peace in November 1634 revealed the necessarily peripatetic nature of her life as she deceived one victim after another.[32]

Ann wandered up and down the country and had the reputation of being able to cure certain ailments. When asked by the magistrate whether she had any skill in 'phisicke or surgerye', Ann replied obliquely in the manner of a charmer that she was accustomed 'to helpe diverse diseases by the gift of God bestowed upon her'. Ann's remedies involved using 'dewe gathered in the moneth of Maye'. This special ingredient was unusual but probably related to Ann's reputation of being able to communicate with the fairies.

Testimony by John Lewys of Bryneglwys, Denbighshire, revealed that Ann Jones' *modus operandi* involved the heartless exploitation of parental concern. Ann Jones had called unannounced at John Lewys's house in August 1634. After gazing at John's young daughter, she gave the distressing news that, notwithstanding the appearance of perfect health, she 'hadd some disease breeding within her that might prove dangerous'. Fortunately the disease could be averted if the girl's parents would follow Ann's instructions. Ann was accustomed to conferring with the fairies in such cases. If she showed the fairies some money on which the girl had breathed, she would be freed from the sickness 'she was like to face'. John Lewys, doubtless in a distressed state, was persuaded to give Ann nine shillings in money, as well as a piece of woollen cloth worth ten shillings, which he could ill afford to lose. Ann went off with cash and cloth and never returned.

A month later, in September 1634, Ann Jones turned up at Corwen, Merioneth. Seeing that Griffith ap Owen's child was 'sicke and lame of bothe legges', Ann claimed to be 'conversant' with the fairies and knew how to cure him. Ann told Griffith that if he would lend her 'money and gould to be shewed the ffayres' she would be able to restore the child's health. Griffith, anxious for the recovery of his child, agreed to lend her 40 shillings in gold and 5s.9d. in silver. This substantial amount of money was only to be shown to the fairies and Ann promised to return it to the trusting Griffith. Ann set off with the money but, of course, never returned. Griffith, eventually realizing that he had been duped, managed to track Ann down but by then only 20 shillings was left of his money.

Ann Jones, although a practised deceiver, could not talk herself out of this tricky situation. She was committed to gaol, and indicted for cozening money from her victims under pretence of promising a cure. Ann Jones was found guilty, fined £20, and remanded in gaol for a year. The judgment of imprisonment was, as it turned out, a death sentence. Three months later Ann Jones died in gaol 'from God's visitation', as an inquest recorded.[33]

Gaining access to the knowledge of the fairies was a persistent theme of Welsh folk belief. There seem to have been people in many localities who claimed to have regular contact with the fairies. The author of *Cas Gan Gythraul* or 'The Devil's Aversion' (1711) describes an acquaintance who claimed to have met the fairies monthly over a period of eight years. He would never describe his nocturnal expeditions with the fairies in case they were angry with him. The anger of the fairies is another constant theme. Those who were familiar with the fairies courted constant physical danger and might be beaten and bruised by them. Those who revealed the fairies' secrets risked being torn to pieces.[34] However in certain circumstances fairy knowledge or abilities were transmitted to human families.

In the eighteenth century there are references to certain families believed descended from liaisons between humans and fairies who had acquired some of the knowledge of the fairies. Some of these families or their ancestors had outlandish names: 'Smychiaid',

'Cowperiaid', 'Pellings', 'Leisa Bèla'.[35] In Snowdonia the Pellings prospered through certain abilities which had come down to them from a fairy ancestor called (unusually) Penelope after whom the family were named. A member of the family ('the best blood in my own veins is this Fairy's') described how an ancestor was able to marry the fairy after abducting her from the lakeside at Llyn Cwellyn and discovering her name. Penelope consented to marriage on the condition that 'if ever he should strike her with iron, she would leave him, and never return'. One day the husband inadvertently but inevitably struck Penelope with a bridle (symbolising human control) and she abruptly disappeared. A strikingly similar story but with more circumstantial detail related to the physicians of Myddfai, a celebrated Carmarthenshire family of doctors who claimed descent from a human father and fairy mother. The ancestor of the 'Meddygon Myddfai' had married a lake-dwelling fairy after a gift of bread. His first offering of dry-baked (*cras*) bread had been rejected, as was his second offering of moist or uncooked (*llaith*) bread. Finally his offering of soft-baked bread was accepted. This is a significant episode: it is apparent that the opposition between nature (raw) and culture (cooked), and the transformation from fairy to bride, is resolved by the soft-baked bread. The fairy (unnamed) came with a dowry of cattle. The only condition of marriage was that her husband should not give her three causeless blows. Inevitably the blows occurred. After being inadvertently struck by an iron bridle she returned to the lake calling her floridly named cattle. Nevertheless her descendants retained fairy medical knowledge and rare herbs grew in Gardd Myddfai. Such was the power of the story that in 1768 a 'reputed famous Doctor and Conjouror', named William Edward, gathered 'very much money in few weeks from the Vulgar' in Cardiff after claiming to be 'one of the sons of the last Doctors of Meddvai.'[36]

Discussion

Fairy beliefs have been variously interpreted. They have often been interpreted functionally, in terms of (for example) their contribution to positive household management.[37] Robin Goodfellow in England was sometimes believed to punish the slovenly and reward the house-proud. There may well have been a cautionary element to some Welsh fairy stories: it was certainly unwise to leave babies unattended, as it was imprudent to leave sharp implements lying around at night, and so on. An earlier generation of folklorists found it helpful to think of fairies as preserving a kind of racial memory. The arresting 'odd belief' of the Welsh fairies' aversion to iron has been interpreted as a memory of 'iron-using Celtic invaders'.[38] However fairy beliefs were more complex than this and full of elements that appealed to the imagination.

It is more satisfying to think of fairy beliefs as a way of imaging society or community. More precisely, fairies were a kind of antithesis of society (an 'anti-society') displaying characteristics that were the inversion of some of the values and defining features of community. The fairies lacked the named individuality of human society or, rather, fairy names were not readily apparent to humans. The discovery of a fairy name was part of the process which integrated them—temporarily—into human society.

This seems to have been fundamental. The fairies were always referred to collectively. Indeed it is difficult in Welsh to refer to a fairy in the singular without circumlocution: the fairies are always the fair family or families. Fairies were creatures of concealment and the dark, as human society was (ideally) lived openly during the day. The fairies lived in the wild, rather than in domestic dwellings, and were sometimes associated with a subterranean or aquatic rather than terrestrial way of life. Although the fairies sometimes ventured into human habitations (as people went into the wild) they had a particular aversion to the iron implements in the house. Ideally human society was harmonious, charitable and forgiving. Fairies were quarrelsome, capricious, and malicious. Indeed, fairies seemed excited by the prospect of quarrels in human society, and were animated by them, performing serpentine dances in the air. In the Scottish-Irish tradition the inversions of the fairy and human worlds could be very strikingly expressed: when human society had scarcity, the fairies had plenty, and *vice versa*.[39] Human society was often poor and ignorant, and subject to illness. The fairies were not mortal in the way humans were, and had no need of money. They had unlimited access to hidden gold and knowledge of past and future events. Viewed in this way the fairies were an imaginative commentary on human community inverting its characteristics and highlighting its frailties, especially in relation to poverty and illness.

To return to the 'odd' belief relating to iron. The making and use of iron was regarded in some ways as a defining feature of human society; a concept which has very deep historical roots.[40] Iron repelled the fairies, sometimes dramatically so. A terrified Welshman surrounded by fairies repelled them after remembering to unsheath his knife. However, although fairies were repelled by iron, ghosts by contrast were attracted by iron. Numerous ghost stories detailed hidden or lost iron articles, often of little apparent value, which bound ghosts to the earth. Edmund Jones, our eighteenth-century observer, reported: 'That the spirits of men are troubled after death for hiding iron instruments and tools is fact proved by innumerable instances, but there is a mystery in it that cannot be understood by men upon earth.'[41] The properties attributed to iron appear to reflect an opposition between nature and culture, whereby the cultural product attracts ghosts (culture: past members of the community) but repels fairies (nature: associated with the wild). If fairies were in some ways a collective 'reversed' image of society, ghosts can be understood as images of individuals that in some ways retained the characteristics of the living. There was not an explicit 'theology' of ghosts and fairies. However, imaging the positive and negative aspects of human society through beliefs in fairies, ghosts and witches was a striking aspect of oral culture in early modern Wales. The same can be said of fairy beliefs elsewhere in early modern Europe.

12

POUQUES AND THE FAITEAUX

The Channel Islands by Francesca Bihet

The Channel Islands lie just off the coast of Normandy and have been a possession of the English crown for almost a millennium. The largest and most southerly island is Jersey.[1] Its population stands at around 100,000 with a history of immigration from France, England and more recently Portugal and Poland. English is the primary language, but Jersey French (Jèrriais) is still spoken by a small minority.[2] Further north lies the second largest island, Guernsey, with its own patois (Guernésiais). The smaller islands of Alderney, Sark, Herm, Jethou, Brecqhou and Lihou fall under Guernsey's jurisdiction.[3] Sitting between France and England the Channel Islands have a strong local identity, which is often described as 'Anglo-Norman'. Many of the place-names and laws are in French and the locals follow a unique maritime culture. Old family names and strong farming communities still play an important role in island life. The hybrid culture of the Channel Islands has produced a unique body of fairylore. Their fairies, like their culture, sit, as all fairies should, on the borders between two worlds.

Much of the material on Channel Island fairies comes from nineteenth-century guidebooks, aimed at the intrepid Victorian traveller. Examples include works such as Octavius Rooke's *The Channel Islands: Pictorial, Legendary and Descriptive*.[4] There are also collections of local folklore, written from the late nineteenth century onwards, reflecting a rising interest in the subject, in Britain more generally.[5] Regretfully, the works of two pre-nineteenth-century Jersey historians, Jean Poingdestre and Phillip Falle, contain no references to fairies.[6] In fact, the first substantial collection of fairylore was collected by Dr. Symons in the early twentieth century and later circulated by L'Amy in his book *Jersey Folklore*.[7] A comprehensive study of *Jersey Place Names* during the 1980s identified many fairy toponyms.[8] More recently, Bois compiled *Jersey Folklore and Superstitions* in two large volumes, noting parallels with other traditions.[9] In Guernsey, the nineteenth-century folklore collector and Bailiff Edgar MacCulloch recorded much of the fairylore that has been passed down to us. His manuscripts were edited by Edith Carey, who added some of her own notes and produced the seminal *Guernsey Folklore* in 1903.[10] Louisa Lane-Clarke published *Folk-Lore of Guernsey and Sark* in 1880, another key source.[11] Alongside these titles there are snippets of information from local magazines, newspapers and journals.

Pouquelayes, Ancient Monuments and Fairy Landscapes

The Channel Island fairies have distinct, often French, local names. There are no standardised spellings for many, so throughout the chapter we will give the spellings that appear in their original source. There are *les p'tites gens* or the little people.[12] The *faiteaux* are diminutive fairies apparently of 'short stature, very strong, and friendly to man'.[13] The name is sometimes said to be a form of *fée* and is sometimes connected to the Latin word *facere* (to make or do), with nods to the fairies' role as 'makers' or builders of prehistoric sites.[14] Sometimes the fairies in Jersey are just called *dames* (ladies); the road *La Rue à la Dame* in St Saviour is thought, for example, to have fairy connections.[15] In Jersey, a fairy might also be called a *bonne femme*.[16]

Fairies in the Channel Islands are also named *pouques,* which might be a deduction on the part of later local populations from the prehistoric sites that the fairies inhabit, known as *pouquelayes*.[17] These are typically prehistoric sites, such as dolmens or other megalithic structures associated with fairies and goblins.[18] Poingdestre, writing in the mid-to-late seventeenth century, mentioned how ancient monuments were called *poquelayes*.[19] Falle, meanwhile, had noted, in 1734, *pouquelaye* as 'a word I can hear of no where else, and therefore take it to be purely local [to Jersey]': *pouquelaye* appears to be used only in the Channel Islands and some parts of France.[20] However, neither mention fairylore in connection with these places. In 1841 Duncan argued the word was derived from the Celtic *pwca* fairy, and a Celtic word for place, *lles*.[21] The idea of *pouquelaye,* meaning a fairy stone or place, has remained the dominant etymology ever since.[22] It would certainly fit these sites given the connection between Channel Island fairylore and ancient monuments.

The fairylore of Jersey is tied to the landscape. Local maps show many variants of *pouquelaye* names. The most famous is the long road of *La Pouquelaye* just above St Helier. Around this area is *La Pouclée Farm*.[23] On this farm there are two fields named *Le Clos de la Pouquelaye* (the Field of the Pouquelaye) and *Le Clos de la Petite Pouquelaye* (the Field of the Small Pouquelaye), which contain some stones, supposedly the remains of a dolmen.[24] There is also a tradition that a fairy palace once stood in onc of these fields.[25] Another site bearing the name of *pouquelaye* is the beautiful and imposing dolmen of *La Pouquelaye de Faldouet* in St Martin. The road in the vicinity of this site is called *La Rue de la Pouclée*.[26] The *Mont Grantez* dolmen in St Ouen's was formerly known as *Le Creux des Faitieaux* (the Cave of the Fairies).[27] It was also called *Le Trou des Faitiaux* (the Fairy Hole), and was supposedly built by fairies.[28] There are also fields called *Les Poucquelées, Porquelées* and *Le Clos de la Pouquelaye*, near Egypt on the north coast of the island.[29]

Guernsey's landscape is also rich in fairylore, particularly Guernsey's prehistoric sites. The most famous of these is the *Creux ès Fées* (or alternatively Le Creux és Faies, the Fairies' Cave), near L'Erée in the parish of St Pierre-du-Bois.[30] This cromlech was also known as *Le Taömbé de Roué des Faïes* (the Fairy King's Tomb).[31] Much fairylore is associated with the site. Confusingly, there is also a coastal cave called *Le Creux des Fées*, between Cobo and Vazon Bay. MacCulloch claims that you can enter, through a small hole in the rock, a 'spacious hall' with 'a stone table on which are dishes, plates, drinking cups, and everything necessary for a large feast, all in stone, and all used by the fairies'.[32] The *Table de Pions*, a large round table dug out of the south-west Pleinmont headland, meanwhile, is associated with fairies too. It was originally used as a stopping place for the *Chevauchée* procession, an ancient inspection of the highways of the island.[33] Carey describes how 'on this table, tradition says, the fairies are supposed to dance'.[34] The area has become today an enchanted picnic spot.

Converging under St Saviour's church in Guernsey there is said to be a network of fairy-dug tunnels used to connect different fairy sites. De Garis notes that there are four entrances. One tunnel starts at the *Creux ès Fées* cromlech at L'Eree. The sea cave *Le Creux des Fées* forms another entrance. Tunnels supposedly start, too, at *Le Creux Mahié* at Torteval and from a cave at Saint's Bay in St Martin.[35] Lane-Clarke, meanwhile, had learnt that at *Le Creux des Fées* near Houmet Point there was a sub-terranean passage to St Saviours, said to be the work of the fairies.[36] It was from sites such as these that fairies emerged and danced during full moon. Howlett mentions that fairies came out from *Le Creux ès Fées* on a Friday night to dance at Le Catioroc, a three-footed dolmen.[37] Mont Saint was also associated with fairy dancing.[38] Carey remembered how in 1896 her aunt, a Mrs Curtis, bought some land on Mont Saint and the 'country people' told her it was unlucky to disturb the places where the fairies danced.[39] Mont Saint stands a mile from St Saviour's parish and includes a prehistoric mound of that name.[40] Guernsey has, then, a rich interconnected fairy topography, with numerous fairy caves and an entire subterranean community.

The island fairies are strongly associated with prehistoric sites.[41] MacCulloch notes that 'the best informed among the peasantry' believe that the fairies inhabited the islands before the present occupants and 'that the cromlechs were erected by them for dwelling places'.[42] Numerous sites were, in fact, according to tradition, constructed by the fairies. In Jersey the little people supposedly created the *pouquelaye* at First Tower and one at the east end of the Island, *Faldouet*.[43] Likewise, findings at archaeological sites were attributed to the fairies. For example, small flattened beads of stone were called *rouets des faikiaux* (fairy spindles).[44] In Guernsey some residents would take a bowl of milk porridge to the *Creux des Fäies* with some knitting and a supply of worsted, if they wished for some clothes to be completed swiftly by the fay folk.[45] Points on the landscape, such as standing stones, that elicited 'wonder or admiration became', in the absence of historical explanations, 'the work of the fairies'.[46] These tales allowed the locals to interact with the landscape around them.

In Guernsey there was a megalith of three upright stones supporting a horizontal one, called the *Le Gibet des Faies* (the Fairies' Gibbet) at La Hougue Patris, near *La Fontaine de Faies* (the Fairies' Fountain).[47] Upon these stones 'the last of fairies destroyed themselves'.[48] According to the story the fairies had control of L'Ancresse Common, but the witches, with their evil magic, invaded the fairies' happy haunts. The fairies congregated and decided to cure their sorrows by drinking from the fountain of forgetfulness.[49] As they were fairies, though, the spring's powers failed. The fairies, then, in despair, hung themselves on the fairies' gibbet with blades of grass and so ended the fairy race in Guernsey.[50] A parallel tradition was collected in Jersey by Symons. There was a house there, near Noirmont, where a spectre of a tiny man hanging off one of the tall Jersey Cabbage stalks could be seen.[51] It was suggested that this man was one of *Les Petit Faîtiaux*.[52] These stories fall into the general pattern of the eternally departing fairies—throughout history the fairies have been said to be leaving the land, even if they often confusedly return. This version seems rather more definite though!

Mortals who interfered with ancient monuments could be punished by the fairies. Carey notes that it was considered 'extremely unlucky' to meddle with ancient stones because the 'wrath of the spirits who inhabit this locality is incurred'.[53] Mr Hocart, who broke up the ancient stones of *La Roque Qui Sonne* at L'Ancresse for building material, was said to have been cursed.[54] As soon as his house was complete a fire broke out killing the servants. Parts of the stone were sent to Britain for sale and the ships which carried them sunk. Hocart went to Alderney and his second house was destroyed by fire.[55] He was eventually killed by some rigging that fell on his head.[56] The story of Hocart is noted in nineteenth-century guide books, with various gruesome misfortunes befalling him.[57] Whilst fairies are not explicitly mentioned, locals probably made the connection. However, it seems that not all locals were afraid of fairy retribution; Carey noted that *La Roque des Fées*, *Le Gibet des Fées* and one of the two sites known as *Creux des Fées* were 'all alas! destroyed'.[58]

La Fontaine Des Mittes stands at Belle Hougue Point on the rugged north coast of Jersey. *Mittes* possibly means 'water-nymph presiding at fountains'.[59] It is, in any case, the site of a contentious fairy legend.[60] Rooke printed the first known version of the story, which is very Victorian and sentimental in tone. He may have created it as a dedicatory legend to the beautiful spring.[61] Two fairies, Arna and Aiūna, were given an allotted time in Jersey and when this time was over God sent an angel to recall them home to a higher sphere.[62] Yet as they were sorrowful to leave their home 'from each sinless eye one pearly drop fell down, pure as themselves', and these tears became the *fontaine*.[63] Ahier claimed that the tale was a 'fabricated or made-up legend'.[64] Nevertheless, before Rooke introduced this story the spring *was* connected with healing. In *A Week's Visit to Jersey*, in 1840, the spring's healing powers for the dumb and those with sore eyes is mentioned without any accompanying legend.[65] The spring was, as it happens, still being used for healing eyes when Bois collected folklore in the late twentieth century.[66] Rooke's legend was translated into French for the *Almanach of the Chronique de Jersey* in 1891, and then re-translated for L'Amy's *Jersey Folklore*.[67]

Le Lavoir des Dames (the Fairies' Bathing Place) is an unusual square tidal pool off Sorrel Point, on the north coast of Jersey.[68] The author of *A Topographical and Historical Guide to Jersey* referred, in 1859, to this pool as *Le Lavoir des Dames* 'a Bathing Place for Ladies'.[69] L'Amy, meanwhile, recorded the local superstition that, if any man saw the fairies bathing in the pool, then he would be struck blind.[70] Bois believed that this piece of folklore was probably 'a romantic invention' for nineteenth-century guide books.[71] However, it reflects a long-standing theme of the fairies blinding individuals who witness things they are not supposed to. For example, Symons recorded one Jersey tale where a woman saw a fairy stealing a silver knife from her house. On discovering which eye the woman used to see him, the fairy jabbed his finger into that eye.[72] Or does the tradition of *Le Lavoir des Dames* reflect perhaps a cheeky parody of islanders' bathing customs?

St Brelade's Church

The beautiful parish church of St Brelade's sits in an unusual spot in the bay with the sea lapping against its graveyard walls. It is the earliest surviving church in the island and was consecrated in 1111.[73] Tradition claims that the fairies moved the foundation stones to its current location. This is, of course, a well-known folklore theme. Grinsell, an archaeologist of prehistoric monuments, remarks that '[f]ew traditions are commoner'.[74] Guernsey has similar legends. Carey notes how such stories are told of the Forest Church, of St Martin's and the Vale Churches.[75] The earliest mention of the St Brelade legend appears in 1817 in Plees' *An Account of the Island of Jersey*.[76] The author merely states that the church was intended to be built on the east side of the bay, but 'whenever any materials were collected for the purpose, on the proposed spot, fairies carried them away, together with the workmen's utensils, to the place where the church now stands'.[77] Plees suggests that the rector himself may have been the real supernatural agent, who employed people to execute his 'celestial mandate'.[78] Another early version of the tale appeared in 1836 in the *Guernsey and Jersey Magazine*, which also briefly mentioned the transportation of the stones.[79]

The legend becomes a more elaborate narrative in guide books towards the mid-nineteenth century. *A Weeks Visit to Jersey* in 1840 contained a verse account. The author claims it is a fairy legend presented 'in such doggrel verse as a prosaic embryo lawyer can tag together'.[80] We cannot tell the extent to which this poem was faithful to legends in circulation in the area. Nevertheless, it set the template for many of the future versions of the tale. Grondin, the building site overseer appeared here as a character for the first time. The men spent all day setting the foundation stones of the church. However, these stones were moved overnight to the church's current site. When the men arrived for work the next morning, the stones were missing. They spent the day working hard to find and drag the stones back to their original site. By the third night, Grondin, suspecting foul play, kept watch to discover the culprit. As the full moon rose, the fairies moved the church walls and scolded Grondin for trespassing on their dominion:

> And a legion of elfs, at the Spirit's call,
> Came dancing about and around him;
> Tore his doublet and cloak into tatters all,
> And hand and foot they bound him![81]

It was finally settled that the church site should be where the fairies had decided.

Grondin and his night-watch featured in other versions of the legend. Rooke gives an 'exceedingly verbose, flowery and hyperbolic' account of the St Brelade's Bay fairies.[82] In Rooke's version Grondin's encounter with the fairies is of note. The fairy who approached Grondin was 'a little old man in a fantastic dress'.[83] On quaffing from Grondin's flask, the man asks:

> Why do you bring all your men with their tools (taking one in his hand) and disturb the ground over which our family have held possession long before you had any recollection of anything? It is a pretty sort of proceeding to turn me out of what has for ages been in my possession.[84]

When Grondin asked the man if he was the Wandering Jew the 'little old man's face grew almost black with rage; seizing the flask, in his anger he hurled it with all his might against the nasal organ of the overseer'.[85] Rooke's version portrays the fairy man as an ancient and ambivalent being.

In the literary version of 1865, Thomas Williams includes classical and Shakespearean themes in his description of the fay folk.[86] In this poem Jersey is the last bastion for the fairies before they disappear to the moon. The folkloric theme of the fairies as a vanishing race is rendered thus:

> A little time is yet left to their race,
> Before they depart to dwell in the moon,
> Whose valleys and plains will be ready soon,
> For their people too gentle and delicate
> To live in a world of discord and hate.[87]

The poem expresses the fundamental change the island was experiencing during this period. New steamships, British tourists, the rise of English culture and language… All encroached upon the island's identity. The legend of St Brelade's Bay and the fairies echoed the challenges the islanders themselves faced.

Symons' Fairies

Jersey fairies, like many of their kind elsewhere, inhabit remote and marginal places. The wild, windswept parish of St Ouen's appears to be a favourite haunt. In a field in St Ouen's Bay stand *Les Trois Roques,* three large standing stones.[88] Symons was told that the fairies were seen carrying these rocks around in their aprons to frighten the Turks.[89] Bois assumes this is a reference to the North African pirates, who in the eighteenth century raided the Channel coast for slaves.[90] The fairies were passionate defenders of the island, a reminder of the fear of sea invasion that long blighted Atlantic coastal communities. It is a parallel to the legend of *La Longue Rocque* or *Palette ès Fées* (the Fairy Bat) at Les Paysans in Guernsey.[91] A fisherman late one night saw a lady of 'diminutive stature' walking up from the sea-shore. The lady was knitting and carrying something in her apron. Hiding behind a hedge, the man saw her take a massive stone from her apron and stick it into the ground.[92] Jersey and Guernsey fairylore share many such motifs.

Further up the hill Captain Vautier was riding past St Ouen's Manor one evening at ten o'clock. He encountered a procession of the little people carrying a small coffin. When he followed them they disappeared. They also scared his horse, who would not move until they had passed.[93] Fairy funeral processions are known, too, from Britain. Bowker in his *Goblin Tales of Lancashire* gives a similar example.[94] In this Lancashire version, one midnight, two men encounter a fairy funeral procession singing a requiem to tolling church bells. The younger man notices that the tiny corpse in the coffin resembles himself and interprets it as an omen of his death. The men follow the procession but, when trying to reach out to one of the fairies, they all vanish. About a month later, the younger man takes a fatal fall. The fairies of St Ouen's also apparently shod horses with silver shoes. James Bailhache, who farmed a property at L'Etacq, saw this with his own eyes. One day he was ploughing and the fairies changed the shoes of his horses and his plough into silver.[95] This led to the local saying 'I will have my horse shod like James Bailhache's'.[96] The local fairies were apparently very rich and lived in a cave around Thiebault at L'Etacq: their horses were also said to be shod in silver.[97] Note that in the nineteenth century there was silver mining near L'Etacq.[98]

Symons collected a story about a fairy swarm at Augerez farm in St Peter, provided by the informant Miss R. The farmer took his cart to St Ouen's Bay to collect *vraic* (seaweed fertilizer) and saw a 'cloud over the house'. He knew it was the fairies and immediately rushed back home where he found them swarming up and down in his yard. To disperse them he scattered corn from his loft and each fairy picked up a grain. His children had conjured up the fairies with a magic book and on shutting it the fairies vanished.[99] This book was probably a *Grimoire* or *Petit Albert*, which sometimes featured in Jersey witchlore.[100]

Guernsey Fairy Invasion

Guernsey has a long history of invasions and threats from the sea, and fairylore naturally reflects this. In fact, according to legend fairies themselves invaded the island. MacCulloch proposed that 'the invasion of the island by Yvon de Galles in the fourteenth century' was the historical inspiration for this legend and that 'his Spanish troops have been converted into denizens of fairyland'.[101] The basic premise of the legend, taken from Lane-Clarke's version, is that fairies from England invaded, seeking Guernsey maidens as wives. A young girl out fishing saw 'a multitude of little men dressed in green, and armed with long bows and arrows' coming to fight and make their demands. When the Guernsey men refused to hand over their womenfolk to the fairies, there was a bloody battle resulting in the defeat of the mortal Guernsey men. *La Rouge Rue* (Red Road) supposedly derives its name from the rivers of their blood.[102] Only one man and a boy who hid in an oven at St Andrew's survived the massacre. The fairies took the women of Guernsey as their wives and re-populated the island in peace. The fairies were inevitably recalled to 'the kingdom of Invisible Beings' leaving their island families behind.[103] Rooke reported the Guernsey population were 'descendants of that little race of beings, and the fact is unquestionably true, you will be told; for see the diminutive size of the pure-bred natives, even at this distant period'.[104]

Lane-Clarke includes a distant cousin of this story involving the introduction of the Guernsey lily (Nerine sarniensis). Lizzie Bailleul was a dreamy girl, who knew all the stories of the fairies.[105] One day a fairy man emerged from *Creux des Fées* and told Lizzie 'wonderful tales of a world far off down under the sea'.[106] Lizzie ran off with him. Her pining mother, then, had a dream that Lizzie was in fairy land, but that she had left a beautiful memory behind her: a 'scarlet lily, sprinkled with gold dust, whose fine curled back petals showed a golden heart', the Guernsey lily.[107] MacCulloch also includes a version of the Guernsey lily story, where this time a young Michelle De Garis was carried away to fairy land to marry a fairy man. Here her fairy lover gave her the bulb of the beautiful Guernsey lily so she might be remembered by her family.[108] The removal of girls from the island by fairy lovers matches real life courting patterns. Girls often married British men and moved to the mainland. Nevertheless, a different story recounts how a Dutch ship, wrecked on the island, brought the lily bulbs, sometime after their introduction to Paris in the 1630s.[109]

Le Petit Colin and Le Grand Colin

Two prominent Guernsey fairies bear the unlikely names *Le Grand Colin* and *Le Petit Colin*, and appear in several different fairy traditions.[110] MacCulloch collected one

Colin tale associated with *Palette ès Fées*.[111] The two Colins were fond of playing a game of ball in the fields around Paysans, using the standing stones as bats. On one occasion *Grand Colin* hit the ball so hard that it disappeared. In a fit of pique he forced his bat into the ground and refused to play further. This bat is the *Palette ès Fées* mentioned above.[112] MacCulloch reports elsewhere that the stone was alternatively believed to act as a marker when the fairies played ball.[113] Another rock, now destroyed, *La Roque des Fées* (the Fairy Rock) by Le Borg de la Forêt, was supposed to form the other boundary for the fairies' ball games.[114] As discussed above, there are island tales of fairies carrying ancient standing stones and the rock is shaped like a rustic cricket bat, suggesting the background to this unusual piece of fairylore.

MacCulloch collected another tale about the Colins' baking. In a small cottage at St Brioc a wife would sit up until the late hours spinning. One night she heard a knock at the door and a voice enquired whether the oven was hot or not. *Petit Colin* entered joining *Grand Colin*. They chatted whilst baking their bread. In gratitude a loaf was left on the kitchen table.[115] Soon her husband, accustomed to this lovely bread, wished to see the fairies. Thus, one evening, he dressed in his wife's clothes and sat pretending to spin. The fairies, enraged by this intrusion, sang:

> There's flax on the distaff,
> But nothing is spun;
> To night there's a beard,
> T'other night there was none.[116]

They left the house never to return. As with many fairy stories, a spying mortal drives the friendly fairies away.

Petit Colin also appeared in story as a fairy child living with a human mother. One night Lizabeau was aroused by 'a man of small stature but genteel appearance' asking her to attend to a sick child.[117] The man led her into a dark cavern and she soon had a sickly baby in her arms.[118] *Petit Colin* was very small and would never play with the other children. At the age of fifteen he went to work for the minister, Jean De Maresq. Twelve months after *Petit Colin* had started work, the minister walked past *La Roque où le Coq Chante* and heard a voice informing him that *Grand Colin* was dead.[119] When *Petit Colin* heard the news he bid De Maresq farewell without taking wages, for there was 'no lack of gold' where he was going.[120] That night *Petit Colin* visited Lizabeau explaining sorrowfully that he was going away. The next morning she hastened to De Maresq to discover that *Petit Colin* had disappeared. Lizabeau pined away, explaining on her death bed how she acquired *Petit Colin*. The fairy man took her to 'the cavern, which was lit with lamps of silver'.[121] Lizabeau fell into a trance and woke in her own home with *Petit Colin*.[122] Lane Clarke included this tale as *L'Histoire Du Petit Colinet* in her folklore guide.[123]

The first part of this tale resembles the common fairy nurse tale type.[124] In one Guernsey variant a woman from Houmet follows a fairy man into *Le Creux des Fées*, a 'magnificent dwelling'. However, the infant's spittle touched her eyes and she saw, instead, its true form, 'a dismal cavern, and squalor and misery'.[125] Once the infant had recovered, the woman spotted a fairy on market day. However, having witnessed what she should not, he spat in her eye and she became 'stone blind'.[126] In many stories a fairy ointment or spit allows witnesses to see the fairy world as it really is.

The changeling, as seen elsewhere in this volume, is a sick or old fairy used to replace healthy human babies that the fairies steal. A changeling will often only reveal themselves when challenged or distracted. Some of these methods are violent, yet others may be bizarre.[127] A young couple, on Guernsey, occupied a cottage at L'Erée and unbeknownst to them, their child was a changeling. While the mother cooked limpets on the fire, their young baby suddenly exclaimed:

> I'm not of this year, nor the year before,
> Nor yet of the time of King John of yore,
> But in all my days and years, I ween,
> So many pots boiling I never have seen.[128]

The mother then took the changeling and threatened to throw it on the fire, whereupon the fairy mother rushed to save her own fairy offspring and immediately returned the human baby.[129] In this case a local limpet dish has the changeling reveal itself.

The smaller island of Sark also has some fairylore. One visitor in the 1850s related a tradition that Sark's indigenous population were fairies, 'who, becoming extinct, are all buried in the ground with gold in both hands'.[130] The visitor considered that Roman coins found in the soil may have been connected with this tradition of buried fairy gold.[131] G.W. James wrote the 'conjecture is that fairies once inhabited the island, or at any rate a lilliputian race, as supposed from the minuteness of their pipes and wheels'. However, by 1845, he reported that there had been very few fairy traditions handed down.[132] MacCulloch found a tradition for the Sark fairies 'carrying their heads under their arms'.[133] This is an unusual piece of fairylore with few known parallels, except perhaps the Irish Dullahan, headless rider fairies. It is a shame that MacCulloch only briefly mentions this tradition.

Witches, Ghosts and Others
There is, as in many other places, a connection among fairy, witch, and ghost traditions in the Channel Islands. The witches are associated, like the fairies, with rites around the *pouquelayes*. For example, Howlett notes that La Pouquelaye de Mont Chinchon at Le Catioroc in Guernsey was named in witchcraft trials as the midnight haunt for witches' meetings, presided over by the Devil.[134] Some witches in Guernsey fly with bat-like wings 'by virtue of their fairy ancestry'.[135] This may be connected to traditions of the fairy invasion, where all Guernsey folk were believed to descend from fairies. We have already seen how the witches, by their evil doings,

drove the fairies to suicide on the Gibet des Faies. There is also a tenuous link between fairies and ghosts in the elusive figure of the *La Blianche Dame*, the white lady.[136] *La Dame Blanche* (the white woman) is the name of a Jersey standing stone but can also mean 'a female ghost dressed in white, encountered at night'.[137] Bois notes the 'clear lack of any relationship' between fairies and *La Blianche Dame* in local traditions.[138] Her name and associations with standing stones connect her, though, with fairylore·

In the nineteenth century fairy belief was portrayed as a dying remnant in the rural parishes.[139] MacCulloch, collecting folklore in the mid-nineteenth century, stated that fairy belief 'seems to have died out' or that 'they are no longer looked upon as beings that have any existence'.[140] Yet as late as 1912 an archaeological dig at *Les Monts Grantez* in Jersey was interrupted by an old man shouting 'Idiots! Idiots! My goodness! What sacrilege! If you disturb the fairies, you will bring trouble on the neighbourhood'.[141] De Garis in 1975 reported that Guernsey fairy tradition 'seems to have entirely vanished'.[142] Yet, in 1999, Robin Mead reported that a fairy cave on the west coast of Guernsey had been 'comfortably furnished with a mini-sized table and chairs'.[143] Another jovial take on fairies, is displayed in a miniature fairy garden hidden in a hedgerow in the parish of St Lawrence in Jersey. Clearly islanders still engage with fairy tradition, albeit in a light hearted way. There is, meanwhile, a very real belief in elemental spirits amongst the islands' neo-pagan communities. Evidence of contemporary pagan ritual practice and offerings can, indeed, be found around *pouquelayes* and ancient sites.

13
GEORGE WALDRON AND THE GOOD PEOPLE

Isle of Man by Stephen Miller

'They call them *the good People*, and say they live in Wilds and Forests, and on Mountains'.[1]
So wrote George Waldron (1687-1728),[2] in his posthumously published *A Description of the Isle of Man* (1731) of the Manx fairy folk he found, or rather, of the native Manx who encountered them in the Isle of Man.[3] Waldron did not just mention fairylore in passing, but related in depth what he found of that belief whilst living in the Island. Nor for that matter was his attention solely focussed on 'the good people,' ranging as he did over other folkloric beliefs and practices as well, and so leaving a considerable body of material, but one that has escaped serious notice to date.

Sir Walter Scott had drawn upon Waldron for background in his *Peveril of the Peak* (1822), a novel that was part-set in the Island and which used genuine characters and incidents from Manx history as part of its plot and where he introduced the 'Manthe Dog' into the plot,[4] a retelling of Waldron's *Mauthe Doog* (Manx, *Moddey Dhoo*, 'Black Dog') of Peel Castle. Whilst writers of guidebooks to the Island, responding to the developing visiting trade in the early nineteenth century, regularly picked over Waldron to fill out their passages on Manx folklore,[5] it was, above all, the 'Mauthe Doog' that caught their imagination. The consequence of this ready source was that the numerous guidebooks and directories produced throughout the nineteenth century contain little, if any, direct observations of Manx folklore, let alone fairylore, of any value.[6]

It was only towards the turn of that century that any material in depth was collected, when Karl Roeder, a German resident in Manchester, began to be active.[7] Other Manx fairy folklore remains scattered and rather than summarise it here, valuable though that would be, this chapter concentrates on Waldron alone for a number of reasons. Firstly, it is remarkably early ethnographic account of fairylore and from the same period as the Rev. Robert Kirk's better known account, for Scotland, *The Secret Commonwealth of Elves, Fauns and Fairies* (which, however, first appeared in print only in 1815). Secondly, it is a rich corpus of material that in itself provides an overview of the nature of those beliefs (as well as other Manx folklore) and published just after *Antiquitates Vulgares* (1725) by the Rev. Henry Bourne. But finally, and importantly, Waldron engages with those beliefs which is what marks him out for attention. Here we see metropole and periphery in contact, urban rationality opposed to vernacular knowledge, an English speaker encountering a community where Manx Gaelic is the everyday language. The fairy world for Waldron called for his response because it is a world so like our own but not quite our own and one not to be taken either at face value or on faith.

Manx Fairylore Collected by Waldron[8]

Fairies the Original Inhabitants of the Island

Some Hundred Years, say they, before the Coming of our Saviour, the Isle of *Man* was inhabited by a certain Species called *Fairies*, and that every Thing was carried on in a Kind of supernatural Manner; that a blue Mist hanging continually over the Land, prevented the Ships that passed by, from having any Suspicion there was an Island. This Mist, contrary to Nature, was preserved by keeping a perpetual Fire, which happening once to be extinguished, the Shore discover'd itself to some Fishermen who were then in a Boat on their Vocation, and by them Notice was given to the People of some Country, (but what, they do not pretend to determine) who sent Ships in order to make a further Discovery: That on their landing, they had a fierce Encounter with the little People, and having got the better over them, possess'd themselves of Castle *Russin*, and by degrees, as they received Reinforcements, of the whole Island.

F364* *War between fairies and mortals*

The Fairies: Their Appearance

... the Appearance of several little Figures playing and leaping over some Stones in a Field, whom, a few Yards distance, he imagined were School-Boys, and intended, when he came near enough, to reprimand, for being absent from their Exercises at that Time of the Day, it being then, he said, between Three and Four of the Clock: but when he approached, as near as he could guess, within Twenty Paces, they all immediately disappeared, tho' he had never taken his Eye off them from the first Moment he beheld them; nor was there any Place where they could so suddenly retreat, it being an open Field without Hedge or Bush, and, as I said before, broad Day.

The Fairies: Traces of their Presence

As to Circles in the Grass, and the Impression of small Feet among the snow, I cannot deny but I have seen them frequently, and once thought I heard a Whistle, as tho' in my Ear, when nobody that could make it was near me.

F261.1 *Fairy rings on grass;* F261.2 *Fairy dances in snow: no tracks left;* F262.7 *Fairies whistle*

Fairies Live amongst Mortals

… they confidently assert that the first Inhabitants of their Island were *Fairies*, so do they maintain that these little People have still their Residence among them: They call them *the good People*, and say they live in Wilds and Forests, and on Mountains, and shun great Cities because of the Wickedness acted therein; all the Houses are blessed where they visit, for they fly Vice.

C420 *Name Tabu. Prohibition against uttering the name of a person or thing;* F216 *Fairies live in forest*

Fairies and Mortals

So strongly are they possess'd of the Belief that there are *Fairies*, and so frequently do they imagine to have seen and heard them, that they are not in the least terrified at them, but on the contrary, rejoice whenever visited by them, as supposing then Friends to Mankind, and that they never come without bringing good Fortune along with them.

Fairies Interact with Mortals

If any thing happen to be mislaid, and found again, in some Place where it was not expected, they presently tell you a *Fairy* took it and returned it: if you chance to get a Fall and hurt yourself, a *Fairy* laid something in your Way to throw you down, as a Punishment for some Sin you have committed.

F391 *Fairies borrow from mortals;* F451.5.10.4 *Dwarves return what they borrow;* F361.17 *Other punishments by fairies*

Fairy Changelings (1)[9]

The old Story of Infants being changed in their Cradles, is here in such Credit, that Mothers are in continual Terror at the Thoughts of it. I was prevailed upon myself to go and see a Child, who, they told me, was one of these Changelings, and indeed must own was not a little surprised, as well as shocked at the Sight: nothing under Heaven could have a more beautiful Face; but tho' between Five and Six Years old, and seemingly healthy, he was so far from being able to walk, or stand, that he could not so much as move any one Joint: his Limbs were vastly long for his Age, but smaller than an Infant's of six Months; his Complexion was perfectly delicate, and he had the finest Hair in the World; he never spoke, nor cryed, eat scarce any thing, and was very seldom seen to smile, but if any one called him a *Fairy-Elf*, he would frown and fix his Eyes so earnestly on those who said it, as if he would look them through. His Mother, or at least his supposed Mother, being very poor, frequently went out a Chairing, and left him a whole Day together: the Neighbours, out of Curiosity, have often looked in at the Window to see how he behaved when alone, which whenever they did, they were sure to find him laughing, and in the utmost Delight. This made them judge that he was not without Company more pleasing to him than any Mortal's could be; and what made this Conjecture seem the more reasonable, was, that if he were left ever so dirty, the Woman at her Return, saw him with a clean Face, and his Hair combed with the utmost Exactness and Nicety.

F321.1 *Changeling,* F321.1.2.1 *Changeling has abnormal features or growth* / ML 5085 *The Changeling*

Fairies Attempt to Steal a Mortal Baby

A second account of this Nature I had from a Woman to whose Offspring the *Fairies* seemed to have taken a peculiar Fancy. The Fourth or Fifth Night after she was delivered of her first Child, the Family were alarm'd with a most terrible Cry of Fire; on which, every body ran out of the House to see whence it proceeded, not excepting the Nurse, who, being as much frightened as the others, made one of the Number. The poor Woman lay trembling in her Bed, alone, unable to help herself, and her Back being turned to the Infant, saw not that it was taken away by an invisible Hand. Those who had left her, having enquired about the Neighbourhood, and finding there was no Cause for the Out-cry they had heard, laugh'd at each other for the Mistake; but as they were going to re-enter the House, the poor Babe lay on the Threshold, and by its Cries preserv'd itself from being trod upon. This exceedingly amazed all that saw it, and the Mother being still in Bed, they could ascribe no Reason for finding it there, but having been remov'd by *Fairies,* who, by their sudden Return, had been prevented from carrying it any further.

F321* *Fairy steals child from cradle*

Fairies Attempt to Steal a Mortal Baby a Second Time

About a Year after, the same Woman was brought to Bed of a Second Child, which had not been born many Nights before a great Noise was heard in the House where they kept their Cattle; (for in this Island, where there is no Shelter in the Fields from the excessive Cold and Damps, they put all their Milch Kine into a Barn, which they call a Cattle House.) Every body that was stirring, ran to see what was the matter, believing that the Cows had got loose: the Nurse was as ready as the rest, but finding all safe, and the Barn-Door close, immediately returned, but not so suddenly but that the new-born Babe was taken out of the Bed, as the former had been, and dropt on their Coming, in the Middle of the Entry. This was enough to prove the *Fairies* had made a second Attempt; and the Parents sending for a Minister, join'd with him in Thanksgiving to God, who had twice delivered their Children from being taken from them.

F321* *Fairy steals child from cradle*

Fairy Changelings (2)

But in the Time of her Third Lying-in, every body seem'd to have forgot what had happened in the First and Second, and on a Noise in the Cattle-House ran out to know what had occasioned it. The Nurse was the only Person, excepting the Woman in the Straw, who stay'd in the House, nor was she detained thro' Care, or want of Curiosity, but by the Bonds of Sleep, having drank a little too plentifully the preceding Day. The Mother, who was broad awake, saw her Child lifted out of the Bed, and carried out of the Chamber, tho' she could not see any Person touch it; on which, she cryed out as loud as she could, Nurse, Nurse! my Child, my Child is taken away; but the old Woman was too fast, to be awaken'd by the Noise she made, and the Infant was irretrievably gone. When her Husband, and those who had accompany'd him, returned, they found her wringing her Hands, and uttering the most piteous Lamentations for the Loss of her Child: on which, said the Husband, looking into the Bed, the Woman is mad, do not you see the Child lies by you? On which she turned and saw indeed something like a Child, but far different from her own, who was a very beautiful, fat, well-featured Babe; whereas, what was now in the room of it, was a poor, lean, withered, deformed creature. It lay quite naked, but the Clothes belonging to the Child that was exchanged for it, lay wrapt up all together on the Bed.

This Creature lived with them near the Space of nine Years, in all which Time it eat nothing except a few Herbs, nor was ever seen to void any other Excrement than Water; it neither spoke, nor could stand or go, but seemed enervate in every Joint, like the Changeling I mentioned before, and in all its Actions showed itself to be of the same Nature.

F321.1 *Changeling;* F321.1.2.1 *Changeling has abnormal features or growth* / ML 5085 *The Changeling*

Fairies Met by Day: Fairy Abductions

A Woman who lived about two Miles distant from *Ballasalli*, and used to serve my Family with Butter, made me once very merry with a Story she told me of her Daughter, a Girl of about ten Years old, who, being sent over the Fields to the Town for a Pennyworth of Tobacco for her Father, was on the top of a Mountain surrounded by a great Number of little Men who would not suffer her to pass any further. Some of them said she should go with them, and accordingly laid hold of her: but one seeming more pitiful, desired they would let her alone; which they refusing, there ensued a Quarrel, and the person who took her part fought bravely in her Defence. This so incensed the others, that to be revenged on her for being the Cause, two or three of them seized her, and pulling up her Clothes, whipped her heartily; after which, it seems, they had no further Power over her, and she ran home directly, telling what had befallen her, and showing her Buttocks on which were the Prints of several small Hands. Several of the Towns-People went with her to the Mountain, and she conducting them to the Spot, the little Antagonists were gone, but had left behind them Proofs (as the good Woman said) that what the Girl had informed them was true; for there was a great deal of Blood to be seen on the Stones. This did she aver with all the Solemnity imaginable.

F324* *Girl abducted by fairy*

Fairies Met by Day: Transported by the Fairies

I have heard many of them protest they have been carried insensibly great Distances from home, and, without knowing how they came there, found themselves on the Top of a Mountain.

E599.12 *Human being transported by a ghost*

Fairies Met by Night: The Fairy Cavalcade

But I cannot give over this Subject without mentioning what they say befel a young Sailor, who coming off a long Voyage, tho' it was late at Night, chose to land rather than lie another Night in the Vessel: being permitted to do so, he was set on shore at *Duglas*. It happened to be a fine Moon-light Night, and very dry, being a small Frost; he therefore forbore going into any House to refresh himself, but made the best of his Way to the house of a sister he had at *Kirk Merlugh*. As he was going over a pretty high Mountain, he heard the Noise of Horses, the Hollow of a Huntsman, and the finest Horn in the World. He was a little surprised that any body pursued those kinds of Sports in the Night, but he had not Time for much Reflection before they all passed by him, so near, that he was able to count what Number there was of them, which he said, was Thirteen, and that they were all drest in green, and gallantly mounted. He was so well pleased with the Sight, that he would gladly have follow'd, could he have kept pace with them; he cross'd the Foot-Way, however, that he might see them again, which he did more than once, and lost not the Sound of the Horn for some Miles. At length, being arrived at his Sister's, he tells her the Story, who presently clapped her Hands for Joy, that he was come home safe; for, said she, those you saw were *Fairies*, and 'tis well they did not take you away with them.

F236.1.6* *Fairy in green clothes*; F241.1.0.1* *Fairy cavalcade*

Fairies and Horses: Fairies Riding Mortals' Horses at Night

There is no persuading them but that these Huntings are frequent in the Island, and that these little Gentry being too proud to ride on *Manks* Horses, which they might find in the Field, make use of the *English* and *Irish* ones, which are brought over and kept by Gentlemen. They say that nothing is more common, than to find these poor Beasts in a Morning, all over in a Sweat and Foam, and tired almost to death, when their Owners have believed they have never been out of the Stable. A Gentleman of *Ballafletcher* assured me, he had Three or Four of his best Horses killed with these nocturnal Journies.

F366.2 *Fairies ride mortal's horses at night*

Fairies and Horses: The Fairy Saddle and the Saddle Stone[10]

Not far from this [*ie*, Ballafletcher], is the *Fairies* Saddle, a Stone termed so, as I suppose, from the Similitude it has of a Saddle. It seems to lie loose on the Edge of a small Rock, and the wise Natives of *Man* tell you, is every Night made use on by the *Fairies*, but what kind of Horses they are, on whose Backs this is put, I could never find any who pretended to resolve me.

F366.2 *Fairies ride mortal's horses at night*

Fairies and Horses: The Fairy Horse Dealer

Another Instance, which might serve to strengthen the Credit of the other, was told me by a Person who had the Reputation of the utmost Integrity. This Man being desirous of disposing of a Horse he had at that Time no great Occasion for, and riding him to Market for that Purpose, was accosted, in passing over the Mountains, by a little Man in a plain Dress, who asked him if he would resell his Horse. 'Tis the Design I am going on, reply'd the Person who told me the story. On which, the other desired to know the Price. Eight Pounds, said he. No, resumed the purchaser, I will give no more than Seven; which, if you will take, here is your Money. The Owner thinking he had bid pretty fair, agreed with him, and the Money being told out, the one dismounted, and the other got on the Back of the Horse, which he had no sooner done, than both Beast and Rider sunk into the Earth immediately, leaving the Person who had made the Bargain in the utmost Terror and Consternation. As soon as he had a little recovered himself, he went directly to the Parson of the Parish, and related what had passed, desiring he would give his Opinion whether he ought to make use of the Money he had received, or not. To which he reply'd, that as he had made a fair Bargain, and no way circumvented, nor endeavoured to circumvent the Buyer, he saw no reason to believe, in case it was an evil Spirit, it could have any Power over him. On this Assurance, he went home well satisfied, and nothing afterward happened to give him any Disquiet concerning this Affair.

M210 *Bargain with devil*

Fairies and House-Water

A Person would be thought impudently profane, who should suffer his family to go to Bed without having first set a Tub, or Pail full of clean Water, for these Guests to bathe themselves in, which the Natives aver they constantly do, as soon as ever the Eyes of the Family are closed, wherever they vouchsafe to come.

No Water for the Fairy Christening: Beer Substituted[1]

Another Woman equally superstitious and fanciful as the former, told me, that being great with Child, and expecting every Moment the good Hour, as she lay awake one Night in her Bed, she saw Seven or Eight little Women come into her Chamber, one of whom had an Infant in her Arms: they were followed by a Man of the same Size with themselves, but in the Habit of a Minister. One of them went to the Pail, and finding no Water in it, cried out to the others, What must they do to christen the Child? On which, they reply'd, it should be done in Beer. With that, the seeming Parson took the Child in his Arms, and performed the Ceremony of Baptism, dipping his Hand into a great Tub of Strong-Beer, which the Woman had brew'd the Day before to be ready for her Lying-in. She told me, that they baptized the Infant by the name of *Joan*, which made her know she was pregnant of a Girl, as it proved a few Days after, when she was delivered. She added also, that it was common for the *Fairies* to make a Mock-Christning when any Person was near her Time, and that according to what Child, male or female, they brought, such should the Woman bring into the world.

ML 4025, *The Dead Child*

Fairy Music at the Funeral Wake for Mortals Held by the Fairies

A little beyond this *Den*, is a small Lake, in the midst of which is a huge Stone, on which formerly stood a Cross: round this Lake the *Fairies* are said to celebrate the Obsequies of any good Person; and I have heard many People, and those of a considerable Share of Understanding too, protest that in passing that way they have been saluted with the Sound of such Musick, as could proceed from no earthly Instruments.

F262* *Fairies make music*

Fairy Music Heard at Night

But having run so far in the Account of supernatural Appearances, I cannot forget what was told me by an *English* Gentleman and my particular Friend. He was about passing over *Duglas* Bridge before it was broken down, but the Tide being high, he was obliged to take the River; having an excellent Horse under him, and one accustomed to swim. As he was in the middle of it, he heard, or imagined he heard, the finest Symphony, I will not say in the World, for nothing human ever came up to it. The Horse was no less sensible of the Harmony than himself, and kept in an immoveable Posture all the Time it lasted; which, he said, could not be less than three Quarters of an Hour, according to the most exact Calculation he could make, when he arrived at the End of his little Journey and found how long he had been coming.

He, who before laugh'd at all the stories told of *Fairies*, now became a convert, and believed as much as ever a *Manks* Man of them all.

F262* *Fairies make music*

Stealing the Silver Cup from the Fairies[12]

One Story in particular was told me of a Man who had been led by invisible Musicians for several Miles together; and not being able to resist the Harmony, followed till it conducted him to a large Common, where were a great Number of little People sitting round a Table, and eating and drinking in a very jovial manner: Among them were some Faces whom he thought he had formerly seen, but forbore taking any notice, or they of him, till the little People offering him drink, one of them, whose Features seemed not unknown to him, plucked him by the Coat and forbad him, whatever he did, to taste any thing he saw before him; for if you do, added he, you will be as I am, and return no more to your Family. The poor Man was much affrighted, but resolved to obey the Injunction: accordingly a large silver Cup filled with some sort of Liquor, being put into his Hand, he found an Opportunity to throw what it contained on the Ground. Soon after the Musick ceasing, all the Company disappeared, leaving the Cup in his Hand; and he returned home, tho' much wearied and fatigued. He went the next day, and communicated to the Minister of the Parish all that had happened, and asked his Advice how he should dispose of the Cup: to which the Parson reply'd, he could not do better than to devote it to the Service of the Church; and this very Cup, they tell me, is that which is now used for the consecrated Wine in *Kirk-Merlugh*.

C211.1 *Tabu: eating in fairyland*; C262 *Tabu: drinking in other world*; F263* *Fairies feast*; F375* *Mortals as captives in fairyland*; F379.2 *Objects brought home from fairyland* / ML 6045 *The Drinking Cup, Stolen from the Fairies*

Mortal Musician Accepts the Fairies' Bargain to Fiddle over the Foolish Fortnight

Another Instance they gave me to prove the Reality of *Fairies*, was of a Fidler, who, having agreed with a Person, who was a Stranger, for so much Money, to play to some Company he should bring him to, all the twelve days of *Christmas*, and received Earnest for it, saw his new Master vanish into the Earth the Moment he had made the Bargain. Nothing could be more terrified than was the poor Fidler; he found he had entered himself into the Devil's Service, and looked on himself as already damned; but having recourse also to a Clergyman, he received some Hope: he ordered him however, as he had taken Earnest, to go when he should be called; but that whatever Tunes should be called for, to play none but Psalms. On the Day appointed the same Person appeared, with whom he went, tho' with what inward Reluctance 'tis easy to guess; but punctually obeying the Minister's Directions, the Company to whom he play'd were so angry that they all vanished at once, leaving him at the Top of a high Hill, and so bruised and hurt, tho' he was not sensible when, or from what Hand he received the Blows, that he got not home without the utmost Difficulty.

G303.9.5.8 *Devil takes violinist when he needs a good fiddler in hell*

George Waldron (1687-1728)

But who then was George Waldron? William Harrison, who edited the *Description* for the Manx Society in 1865, had appealed for information in the pages of *Notes and Queries* in 1864,[13] but to no avail, and the only source he was subsequently able to draw upon was a single sentence in the preface authored by Theodosia Waldron, now his widow, to *The Compleat Works* of 1731: 'As posthumous Works are generally ushered into the World with some Account of their Author, I take upon me to inform the Public, that he was a Gentleman of an ancient Family in Essex, and had the Honour to receive his Education at Queen's College in Oxford.'[14] *Alumni Oxonienses* (a source not then available to Harrison) records a George Waldron matriculating at Oxford on 7 May 1706 at the age of 16, the son of one Francis Waldron, described as a 'Gentleman of London.'[15] While this would make his year of birth to be 1690, he is now known to have been born at least three years earlier, being christened on 8 September 1687 at Saint Andrew Holborn in London. Waldron was educated at Felstead School in Essex before going up to Queen's College in 1706 to attend Oxford University. After coming down, he married Theodosia Clift in 1711, and they went on to have four children together, George (1712), Theodosia (1713), Jane (1715), and Charles (1717).

How though did Waldron come to reside on the Isle of Man? As Theodosia

Waldron herself wrote, '[t]he great many leisure Hours he had in the Isle of Man, where for some Years he resided in a Post under his late and present Majesty, gaved him an Opportunity of writing a Description of that place…'[16] Waldron was there on a watching brief as a Commissioner (or Revenue Officer) for the British Crown, actively gathering intelligence on what was then referred to in the period as the Running Trade,[17] where, in his own words, 'there is the utmost opportunity… for carrying on the Smuggling Trade.… but in this Place there is little Danger in infringing on the Rights of the Crown.'[18] Put simply, merchants made use of the Island's geographical position in the Irish Sea and its status then (as now) as not being part of Great Britain to legally import goods at extremely low rates of duty into the Island, which were then later conveyed (*ie*, smuggled) onto the coasts of Scotland and England.[19] *The Compleat Works* contains a poem dated February 1724,[20] dedicated to John Lloyd who was Governor of the Island from 1723-25, so Waldron was definitely in the Isle of Man in 1724.[21]

'Between Great Britain and Ireland': The Isle of Man
'Between Great Britain and Ireland is stretched out a considerable Island from North to South, about thirty Italian Miles in Length; but where widest, not above Fifteen in Breadth',[22] recounted Waldron, adding that, as regards the weather, 'three Parts of the Year is Winter.'[23] This was to be his home, size-wise and weather-wise, from 1723 until his death in 1728, and the period in which his *Description* came to be written. In Waldron's time, just close on fourteen thousand people lived in the Island,[24] a Manx speaking community working the land for oats and potatoes, and who all took part in the autumn herring fishery in coastal waters, its salted bounty essential to survival over the winter months.[25] This was a subsistence economy in greater part, with people working crofts and patches of land enclosed out of common land and with a scattering of larger family-held farms.

Waldron lived at Ballasalla, a village close to Castletown on the south coast, then the Island's capital and seat of government. The village, however, made little impression on him. 'Nor has Ballasalli any thing to boast of, beside a fine River running thro' it, a good Air to whiten Cloth, a Market for Fowls, where you may have the greatest Choice of any place in the Island.'[26] As regards the Running Trade, it was Douglas, on the Island's east coast, with a larger and better sheltered port than Castletown, that was at its heart with a new monied and rising merchant class of Scottish and Irish traders, as well as those native Manx equally involved, figures who Waldron was to shadow and report on their activities.[27]

This was the insular community in which Waldron found himself, definitely one as far removed from the life of the metropolis of London as was possible. As he wrote himself, 'wishing no Gentleman, who has ever known the polite Pleasures of Life, may deserve so ill of Heaven, as to be driven into this Banishment through Necessity.'[28]

'A Woman who Lived about Two Miles Distant from Ballasalli'
The person who supplied the Waldron family with butter also provided him as seen with

at least one fairy legend, a tale of attempted abduction of a young girl into Fairyland. No sooner has he finished recounting this fairy legend from his butter woman, then he starts off again: 'Another Woman equally superstitious and fanciful as the former, told me…' These set up a template for Waldron's encounters in general with Manx oral tradition: the unnamed (but often female) tradition bearer, the recounting in some detail of an item of folklore, and, above all, its demonstrable veracity as fact. Another point to be made here is that one fairy legend does not suffice for Waldron—no sooner has he recorded one, then another one follows. And they are recounted in depth as can be readily seen, or rather, narrated by Waldron in summary fashion of what has been told to him close at first-hand.

We then come to the problem of Manx. The woman who 'used to serve my Family with Butter' as Waldron recalled, would not have spoken English. She would not have had the opportunity to learn English—nor for that matter would she have ever have needed to speak English—she would have made Waldron 'very merry' with her narrative in her native Manx tongue.[29] So, the question arises, did George Waldron sit there in his cottage at Ballasalla listening to Manx but having it translated into English for him? And what about the other encounters that he had with Manx folklore, and for matter, Islanders in general as will be shown—was there always someone at his side to translate for him. Or did he come to learn and speak the language?

Waldron offers no insight into how the language issue was overcome, bar the unsatisfactory argument from silence that he makes no mention of it when he sought to 'dive into the Manners and Humour' of the Island as he put it.[30] And dive in he did, as the one thing that strikes you about Waldron from the *Description* is that he was a very sociable individual, easily moving amongst the English, Irish, and especially Manx communities in the Island, where he seems to have been a frequent guest, attending christenings, weddings, and funerals, and clearly having a circle of Manx friends who invited him on such occasions. The frequency of his dining is perhaps shown by his comment on the table manners of the Manx: 'Knives, Forks, or Spoons, are Things in so little Use with them… and as for Forks, they seem not to know what to do with them; for if a *Manks* Man or Woman, happens to be invited to an *English* Family, nothing can be more aukward than their attempting to make Use of them.'[31] Waldron's own solution was wonderfully simple: 'I carried for the future a Knife, Fork, and Spoon in my pocket.'[32] Whilst still though no closer to knowing if Waldron possessed an understanding of Manx or not, it is certainly evident that he had ever the opportunity to do so.

'Falling into Discourse with Some of the Inhabitants'
Waldron at times in the *Description* describes his encounters not just with Manx fairylore and folklore, but also those narrators themselves as well as listeners. Whilst the passages are lengthy, they do bear being quoted in full as showing Waldron's engagement with the vernacular culture of the Island and the expectation that he accept what he was being told not as belief but as creditable fact.

As at my first coming to the Island, I was extremely sollicitous in diving into the Manners and Humour of a People, which seemed so altogether new, and different from all the other *Europeans* I had ever seen; I went to Port *Iron*, the first Season for Fishery, after my Arrival: where, falling into discourse with some of the Inhabitants, I had an Account given me, which, I think, would be doing something of Injustice to the Publick to conceal.[33]

When 'accidentally falling in Company with an old *Manks* Man, who had used the Seas many Years, he told me...'[34] a tale about mermaids.[35] But, as Waldron wrote:

As I had not yet attained a thorough Knowledge of the Superstition of these People, nor the passionate Fondness for every thing that might be termed *The Wonderful;* I was excessively surprized at this Account, given with so serious an Air, and so much, and solemnly averred for Truth. I perceived they were not a little disgusted at my Want of Faith, but to make a Convert of me, they obliged me to listen to another, as odd an Adventure as the former, which they assured me was attested by a whole Ship's Crew, and happened in the Memory of some then living.[36]

Waldron, however, was not to be taken in by these credulities:

As nothing is got, by contradicting a fictitious Report, unless you can disprove it by more convincing Arguments than right Reason can suggest, but ill Words, and, perhaps worse Usage; I contented myself with laughing at them, within myself, and attempted not to lay before People, whom I found such Enemies to good Sense, any Considerations, how improbable, if not impossible, it was, that any body should give Credit to what they said.[37]

And in the end he was caught out himself when it was clear that he was to remain a sceptic:

I should, however, have doubtless heard many other Accounts of the like Nature, if, by my saying little in Answer to them, and a certain Air of Ridicule, which they observed in my Countenance, and which, in spite of my Endeavours to the contrary, I was not able to refrain, they had not perceived that it was vain to attempt bringing me over to their Side.[38]

Whilst Waldron could dismiss his butter supplier with her tales of fairy abductions and the woman who talked of fairy changelings ('Another Woman equally superstitious and fanciful as the former' as he wrote) and allow himself the indulgence to be made 'very merry with a Story' from them, one of his near neighbours was a different proposition. Described as a Gentleman, and so, in Waldron's eyes at least, a person of some social standing, he came across the fairy folk at play one day, and whilst in the past having 'affirmed with the most solemn Asseverations, that being of my Opinion, and entirely averse to the Belief that any such Beings were permitted to wander for the Purposes related of them,' this incident made even him a believer.[39]

He was not to be the only person known to Waldron who was to give him pause, however briefly, for thought: 'Another Instance, which might serve to strengthen the Credit of the other, was told me by a Person who had the Reputation of the utmost Integrity.'[40] This time it was someone who had business, unwittingly, with a fairy horse dealer. Asking for eight pounds for his horse but being offered seven, 'by a little Man in a plain Dress,' and accepting the bargain, both man and horse then sunk into the ground and disappeared into Fairyland.[41] Waldron too had a neighbour who was plagued by the *Tarroo-Ushtey* (Manx, 'Water-Bull')[42] who set out with others to hunt the beast with pitchforks, but with no effect; another so troubled used a gun, this time with success....[43]

No doubt Waldron remained a sceptical and metropolitan Englishman to the end of his days in the Island, keeping his 'certain Air of Ridicule' as he described it. Nevertheless, he still collected a remarkable body of Manx fairylore, and at an early date it must be noted, one also narrated to him in Manx. It was straitened circumstances that brought Waldron with his family in tow to the Island, but when there he clearly became fascinated with its vernacular Gaelic culture despite his clear objection to everything he was being told and asked, if not tasked, to accept that the fairy world was fact, and one that was everywhere and which you could not avoid being engaged with. No matter how well your horse would be locked up over night, the 'little Gentry' were sure to take it for a nocturnal ride.

'But having run so far in the Account of supernatural Appearances, I cannot forget what was told me by an English Gentleman and my particular Friend' wrote Waldron.[44] This particular Englishman decided to cross the river at Douglas, on horseback instead of using the bridge, and when half-way across he heard fairy music which caused his horse to stop and remain rigid for close on three-quarters of an hour until he was able to resume and complete his journey. 'He, who before laugh'd at all the stories told of *Fairies*, now became a convert, and believed as much as ever a *Manks Man* of them all.'[45]

This, however, was to be one journey that Waldron was not willing to take. It was left to be taken by another explorer of Celtic fairylore, namely Walter Evans Wentz, whose *The Fairy-Faith in Celtic Countries* (1911) contained a section on Manx fairylore collected personally by the author. This time it was to be a 'snow-bound farm-house' where fairy legends were to be recounted. Wentz came at the waning of fairylore in the Island, but came he did with no mention of Waldron who had been there some two centuries before him.

PISKIES AND KNOCKERS

Cornwall by Ronald M. James

Introduction: Rosy and the Piskeys

In 1873, William Bottrell published a legend entitled 'The Small People's Cow', set in Cornwall, a peninsula terminating at Land's End in the south-west of England. The story tells of a prosperous farm and Rosy, a dairy cow with a remarkable yield. During the evening milking, however, the cow would rush off to a remote part of the pasture before her udder was completely emptied. Eventually Rosy had a calf, and although her offspring always had its fill, Rosy continued to give copious amounts of milk.

One night a dairymaid, having gathered some grass to cushion the full bucket on her head, became aware of piskies (Cornish fairies) in the pasture. As it happened, the young woman had accidently plucked a four-leaf clover with the grass, and this gave her the ability 'to see hundreds of "Small People" (fairies) around the cow, and on her back, neck, and head.' Bottrell then adds considerable detail:

> A great number of little beings—as many as could get under Rosy's udder at once—held butter-cups, and other handy flowers or leaves, twisted into drinking vessels, to catch the shower of milk that fell among them, and some sucked it

from clover-blossoms. As one set walked off satisfied, others took their places. They moved about so quickly that the milkmaid's head got almost 'light' whilst she looked at them. 'You should have seen,' said the maid afterwards, 'how pleased Rosy looked, as she tried to lick those on her neck who scratched her behind her horns, or picked ticks from her ears; whilst others, on her back smoothed down every hair of her coat. They made much of the calf, too; and, when they had their fill of milk, one and all in turn brought their little arms full of herbs to Rosy and her calf,—how they licked all up and looked for more!'

Bottrell also noted that 'some little folks, who came late, were mounted on hares, which they left to graze a few yards from the cow.'

When the farmer's wife, Dame Pendar, looked over the hedge and called for the dairymaid, 'the Small People pointed their fingers and made wry faces at her; then off galloped Rose and the troop of small folks with her—all out of sight in a wink.' The dairymaid described what she had seen to her mistress and then added more to the narrative: 'but few of them are more than half a yard or so high [and] the women not so tall, yet they looked beautiful, all dressed like gentry; the women wore gowns as gay as a flower-garden in summer; their flaxen hair fell, in long curls, on their necks; and the men were very smart, all like sodjers [soldiers] or huntsmen.'

After hearing about the extraordinary spectacle, the mistress of the farm sought advice and concluded that she should wash the cow's udder with brine and scatter salt about it to keep the piskies at bay. At that the cow ceased to yield milk, and the fortunes of the farm failed. When the farmer decided to take the cow and her calf to market to be slaughtered, the beasts ran away and were never seen again. But by then all was lost and the once-wealthy landowner sank into impoverished obscurity.[1]

Bottrell notes that 'there are two or three versions of this story, which differ little from the above, except in locating the Small People's Cow on other farms that were dwelling-places of the Pendars in olden times.'[2] This story is echoed elsewhere, including in a book by another collector of Cornish folklore, Robert Hunt.[3] Taken together, their evidence suggests that the legend was common in nineteenth-century Cornwall. More importantly for the purposes of this chapter, the story provides details about how at least one storyteller viewed indigenous fairies.

Bottrell's account depicts these supernatural beings as having an interest in livestock. They were willing to allow people to care for and benefit from shared cattle. But the piskies were also capable of inflicting punishment when someone treated them disrespectfully. In addition, they were shorter than people, they appeared in abundant numbers, and they wore fine clothes.

Cornish Fairy Types
In 1865, Robert Hunt identified five species of Cornish fairies: the *pobel vean* or small people; spriggans; piskies (or pigseys); buccas, bockles, or knockers; and brownies. These strict categories have been criticised by everyone from Henry Jenner, an early

advocate of all things Cornish, to Simon Young, one of the editors of this volume.[4] Even Hunt remarked that when it came to the question of origins for the various species, there was possibly a shared explanation: this early collector observed that the folk may have regarded them all as being 'the spirits of the people who inhabited Cornwall many thousands of years ago—long, long before the birth of Christ.'[5] In fact, folklorists understand that while the folk had various terms for supernatural beings, definitions were usually fluid. Efforts to apply rigid taxonomies to tradition inevitably met with frustration when working with informants: one person's certainty was nearly always muddled by the vague concepts of another.

It is possible to distinguish between the supernatural beings found aboveground and the knockers—those in the mines. However, even here there is consistency in the way the Cornish perceived their extraordinary neighbours, regardless of location. The indigenous term, 'piskie', can be used generically because the collectors seem to be quoting informants who employed the term in a wide variety of circumstances. Piskie is a variant of 'pixy', now-widespread in English, but which was largely restricted to Cornwall and south-western Britain more generally. The *Oxford English Dictionary* indicates 'pixy' is of obscure origin and it cites references to the word dating back to the early seventeenth century.[6]

Of greater interest than Hunt's categories are his other observations. He pointed out that the celebrated nineteenth-century fairy authority Thomas Keightley 'entirely excluded Cornwall from consideration'. This was in spite of the fact that, as Hunt noted, 'there exists, even to the present day, a remarkable fairy mythology' in the land beyond the Tamar river. At the same time, Hunt conceded that, by the publication of his first volume in 1865, Cornish fairy folk were already dying out, thanks to 'the influences of our practical education'.[7] By way of offering a comparison with the entities in neighbouring Devon, Hunt suggests the following:

> The Piscy or Pixy of East Devon and Somersetshire is a different creature from his cousin of a similar name in Cornwall. The former is a mischievous, but in all respects very harmless creation, who appears to live a rollicking life amidst the luxuriant scenes of those beautiful counties. The latter, the piskies of Cornwall, appear to have their wits sharpened by their necessities…[8]

Hunt's perception of Devonian fairies depends, in part, on the observations of Anna Eliza Bray (1790-1883) in her much read 1836 publication, *Traditions, Legends, Superstitions, and Sketches of Devonshire on the Borders of the Tamar and the Tavy*. Without wishing to diminish the value of Bray's early attempt at collecting, her literary bent may have made her less inclined to record the dangerous aspect of the fairy world. Ultimately, Bray made a lasting impression on how Victorian England came to view fairies regardless of the county. This was particularly true of her image of 'tiny elves' amusing themselves, dancing in a circle and preferring 'solitary places, … pleasant hills and pathless woods.'[9] Bray asserted that, these dainty beings, though represented as of exceeding beauty in their higher or aristocratic order, are nevertheless, in some instances, of strange, uncouth and fantastic figure and visage: though such natural deformity need give them very little uneasiness, since they are traditionally averred to possess the power of assuming various shapes at will.[10]

While the traditions of Devon inspired Bray, similar Cornish descriptions of piskies complemented the emerging image of the Victorian literary fairy. Bottrell's 'The Small People's Cow' with its frolicking piskies, and some riding hares, were just the sort of entity celebrated in children's literature by the end of the nineteenth century. But that hardly offers a complete understanding of how the folk viewed supernatural beings. Hunt was right to question the applicability of the 'sweet' portrayal of Bray's fairies when it came to Cornwall: he realised that these creatures were typically dangerous.

Bray's characterisation of Devonian pixies likely influenced Hunt to see generous behaviour as belonging to only one of five distinct types of pixy-like Cornish super-natural beings. For example, he claimed that the *pobel vean* or small people 'are exceedingly playful amongst themselves, but they are usually demure when they know that any human eye sees them. They commonly aid those people to whom they take a fancy, and frequently, they have been known to perform the most friendly acts towards men and women.'[11]

Hunt's spriggans, on the other hand, were responsible for all sorts of misdeeds, robbing places, stealing children and cattle, and even demolishing buildings. Similarly, Hunt's piskie 'is a most mischievous and very unsociable sprite. His favourite fun is to entice people into the bogs.' He further notes that the 'Piskie partakes, in many respects, of the character of the Spriggan.'[12] In addition, Hunt's understanding of the knockers and the browney has more to do with occupation and habitat than actual differences in species.[13] This, then, is both the value and the problem with Hunt's attempt at a precise taxonomy for the Cornish fairy: while he correctly perceived differences in behaviour and location, many Cornish men and women would likely have regarded these as expressions of the same broad spectrum of similar if not identical supernatural beings.

Like pre-industrial Northern Europeans in general, the Cornish perceived fairies—regardless of the terms used—as capable of both helpful and harmful deeds. People feared fairy neighbours, but they also hoped that showing deference might win favour from these powerful beings. Attempting to attribute positive acts to 'the small people or *pobel vean*' and mischief to others creates an artificial distinction that the folk would not normally have recognized. The fact that Bray characterised her pixies as usually harmless may have inspired Hunt to see well-behaved Cornish piskies as belonging to a type similar to those of Devon. He relegated, meanwhile, detrimental behaviour to a different species.

Cornish Fairy Size
Rather than considering the Cornish piskey and its kindred as different species, it is more useful to compare them collectively with their Northern European counterparts. In this way we can understand how traditions were similar and distinct. First, petite stature is something true of all Cornish types whether above or below ground. In addition, sources often describe piskies as shrinking through time. This, it is sometimes claimed, was the price for assuming animal forms. Many thought that the piskies were destined to dwindle to the size of ants or that they would disappear altogether.

Some stories contradict, though, the idea that piskies were little: William Noy in Bottrell's 'The Fairy Dwelling of Selena Moor' thought that the 'people' he encountered were on the small side. But he only realised that they were not humans when an enslaved woman told him. In addition, numerous Cornish stories involve a human nurse taking employment in a fairy household. She believes her employer to be a normal aristocrat. Only when she washes her face with forbidden fairy bath water—intended exclusively for her young ward—does she see the supernatural world around her, including little piskies (a motif found elsewhere in this volume). Then, in those stories that end with the nurse encountering her employer at the local market, he appears as a full-sized man.[14]

Elisabeth Hartmann (1912-2004), in her 1936 treatise on Scandinavian trolls and related supernatural beings, points out that Northern European legends frequently begin with people encountering these entities and assuming that they are human. Only as the story unfolds does the protagonist comprehend the strange—and dangerous—nature of the situation. In Cornwall people entering the world of fairy are not struck by unusually sized piskies, at least at the outset. Similarly, the Irish 'wee folk' are famously small, and yet they too assume human proportions in many legends. The same is true of the equivalents of fairies in Denmark and southern Sweden. Contrasting with this, comparable supernatural beings in Norway, the rest of Sweden, and Iceland, are generally considered to be indistinguishable from people in size, except in those cases where they are actually larger than people. The diminutive stature of the Cornish piskies is not unusual then. What is noteworthy is that these entities spend more time that way than some of their counterparts elsewhere.

English or Celtic?
So, aside from their tendency to appear small, what else can be said of Cornish piskies? What about their Celtic background? Cornwall occupies a peculiar place in the cultural kaleidoscope of Britain and Ireland. The Celtic Association, a precursor of the Celtic Congress, eventually included this tiny peninsula of a mere 3,563 square kilometres as the last of its six recognized Celtic nations, shortly after the turn of the twentieth century.[15] The decline of Cornwall's indigenous language represented a

stumbling block in Cornwall's claim to be Celtic. Cornwall, indeed, is consistently seen as the most Anglicized of the Celtic countries. Nevertheless, its language is now in revival, and Cornwall's distinct roots cannot be denied.

Despite being easily eclipsed by Ireland, Scotland, and Wales, Cornwall has punched above its weight in terms of folklore. Its early collections of traditional stories were widely read in the nineteenth century. Robert Hunt and William Bottrell wanted to celebrate all things Cornish, and yet their material is often co-opted into English collections. Placing the fairy faith of Cornwall into context can be difficult, because, while some see it as distinctly Cornish, others claim it as part of wider English traditions. For example, two Oxford dictionaries, *English Folklore* and *Celtic Mythology* both have extensive references to Cornwall.[16]

Hunt demonstrated a similar ambivalence with the title of his 1865 work: *Popular Romances of the West of England or the Drolls, Traditions, and Superstitions of Old Cornwall.* Bottrell, meanwhile, asserted on the title page of his 1870 book that he was 'An Old Celt'. Although Hunt was no less enthusiastic about the unique Cornish character of Cornwall, his title speaks to the ways many have seen the distant duchy and its folklore: the most western of English counties, *and* a Celtic land, apart from the rest.[17]

Piskies

Since piskies depicted in the stories of Bottrell and Hunt seemed consistent with those of Bray from Devon, it was possible for early folklore enthusiasts to assume that these were all simply English fairies. Minor variations might occur, but it was easy to claim that they all fit into a generally homogenous larger picture. The fact that many piskey legends were shared throughout Britain—and Ireland for that matter— helped here. In fact, the Cornish fairy faith was both similar to and distinct from that of its neighbours, and this is particularly apparent when considering stories that can be catalogued as migratory legends with variants found elsewhere.

The term 'migratory legend' refers to stories generally told as true with similar plots found in different places. They were repeated over wide areas and sustained over time; much like the folktale, which people told as a form of oral, popular fiction. Norwegian folklorist, Reidar Christiansen (1886-1971), authored a catalogue of legend types drawing on the narratives of his homeland, but it was immediately apparent that many of these were also present in Britain and Ireland.[18]

For example, Bottrell's account of 'The Small People's Cow', which introduces this chapter, is perhaps tied to Migratory Legend 6055, 'Fairy Cows'. Bo Almqvist (1931-2013), a Swedish folklorist who spent most of his career in Ireland, disputed whether Irish legends about fairy cows could be classified in this way, but his concern may have been misplaced. Certainly, Cornish stories involving this motif are in keeping with those of Ireland and Wales.[19] While the Scandinavian accounts focus on how a farmer managed to capture a supernatural cow, the Celtic stories concern the cow's loss. The legends are unified by the shared motif of fairies keeping cattle, one of which joins a human farm, where it thrives, provided the cow is well tended. Either there is common ground or this was a distinct legend shared by several of the Celtic nations.

There are other migratory legends involving piskies from Cornwall. These include numerous accounts that are recognisable as Migratory Legend 7015, 'The New Suit', which is widespread throughout Northern Europe: a fairy helps a family until he is given a new suit of clothes when he abandons them.[20] At least two versions of Migratory Legend 5006*, 'The Flight with the fairies', also occur in Cornish collections: a man travels with a group of flying fairies to various locations.[21] Numerous versions of Migratory Legend 5070, 'Midwife to the fairies', appear in Hunt and Bottrell's publications. These are a variant where a nursemaid (rather than a midwife) works for a fairy family.[22] Cornish collections include two versions of Migratory Legend 6070A, 'Fairies send a Message', which describes people hearing a supernatural voice declaring that its ruler has died or that a home in the otherworldly realm is afire. In either case, a creature in the midst of the humans—an invisible entity or the household cat—declares that it must be hurrying off in response to the news. In the Cornish variant, a piskie child is cared for by a couple until he hears his father call for him, at which point he leaves.[23]

Two additional stories involving piskies warrant discussion. A group of Cornish legends come close to Migratory Legend 6045, 'Drinking Cup Stolen from the Fairies'. This is one of the most common Northern European tales and describes how a man on horseback interrupts fairies holding a feast and then steals their drinking horn. There are numerous Cornish examples that come close to the type, but there are also significant differences. Neither the drinking horn nor the horse are present in Cornwall. In the Cornish examples, the protagonist—often but not exclusively a man—interrupts piskies as they are feasting or dividing up treasure. The person steals something valuable and flees, sometimes leaving by boat. Whether this group of legends is demonstrably the same legend as 'the Drinking Cup Stolen from the Fairies' is up for debate, but the Cornish stories *are* similar to one another. At the very least, they constitute either a distinct body of legends or a regional variant of a widespread tradition.[24]

A second important story involves the idea that fairies seek to take human infants, replacing each with a changeling, one of their own who is magically imbued to appear like the stolen baby. Stories about these exchanges are common in Northern Europe and appear in Christiansen's catalogue as Migratory Legend 5085. The narrative typically describes a mother who suspects that her ill-behaved, stunted infant is actually a supernatural being, a replacement for her own abducted child. Some trick—mistreatment of the creature or performing a strange act in front of it—causes the fairies to bring back the kidnapped baby. Hunt's account of 'The Spriggan's Child' follows this legend type closely, but most Cornish references to changelings seem to describe actual infants who failed to thrive. There are details of abuse inflicted on innocent infants, whom parents suspected were not really their children but rather piskey replacements. These accounts seem to be about real events, so they cannot be linked directly to Migratory Legend 5085. Details shared by the legend and by these descriptions of real life suggest this widespread story was popular in Cornwall and that it influenced how parents treated babies with developmental problems.[25]

In all, the various legends involving piskies suggest that these supernatural beings behaved much like their counterparts in other regions. This continuity demonstrates that even a remote place like Cornwall was not that isolated. And yet, the Cornish piskies were different in their own way. Legends that describe them often exhibit a distinct local stamp. At the same time, piskies frequently appeared in nineteenth-century publications as the Victorian literary fairy, a kind of romping sprite. One should not underestimate the Cornish fairies, however, since the area's folklore collections consistently underscore the terrifying and dangerous nature of its supernatural beings. For example, Bottrell's story of 'The Small People's Cow' describes piskies that could be seen as 'cute' for a detached reader. Yet the story shows that encounters with these fairies were often perilous. Although Cornish accounts of abduction are rare, Bottrell's legend, 'The Fairy Dwelling of Selena Moor', makes it clear that the supernatural realm was best avoided.[26] To fall within the fairies' grasp meant one's immortal soul was in jeopardy, as a person became enslaved in the fairy netherworld.

Knockers

Perhaps the most famous of the Cornish piskey kindred are the underground knockers. On occasion, mining spirits elsewhere in Britain also answered to this name. Indeed, wherever people have delved into the depths they frequently believed that supernatural beings populated the mines. That said, the Cornish concept of the knocker is unusually well attested, and the tradition includes an unprecedented epilogue involving emigration.

Cornish knockers were diminutive, old, and had long beards. In keeping with the pre-industrial prohibition against women venturing underground, knockers were an all-male workforce: like aboveground piskies, they too belonged to a community, and their work habits echoed labour in the human world.[27] They could be helpful, using their rapping to lead those of good character to valuable ore. Their knocking could also warn of impending disaster. But woe to the greedy miner or to those who would watch the knockers hard at work, for the entities could also punish. Many accounts describe them as the spirits of Jews from the Roman period, sent to the mines as punishment for an imagined role in the Crucifixion. This idea provided an explanation for the underground supernatural beings, and it fit in with the common Northern European assumption that fairies were remnants of an ancient people.[28]

Accounts depict miners as being grateful for warnings of danger, but oral tradition made it clear that to incur the wrath of the knockers could prove devastating. Tom Trevorrow, a Cornish man, refused to give the knockers a bit of his meal so they ruined his luck. A man named Barker spied upon knockers as they worked, so they crippled him, giving Cornwall the phrase 'I be as stiff as Barker's knee.' Yet another legend describes an old miner who struck an agreement to leave some ore for the knockers; when his son violated the arrangement, he was left destitute as the knockers withdrew their support.[29]

Industrialisation and corporate ownership of the ever-deeper Cornish excavations affected the knocker tradition. Labourers were still concerned with their safety and appreciated supernatural indications that mines were about to collapse. But the idea of knockers leading a wage earner to wealth or punishing greed would have been anachronistic by the mid nineteenth century. It is likely, then, that most knocker legends date to the earlier time of independent tribute miners whose fortunes rose or fell on the basis of their ability to extract valuable tin.

A remarkable final chapter involving knockers occurred as the Cornish began emigrating to North America. While people brought traditions and beliefs from their homelands, most immigrant folklore fails to survive the first generation. Some few traditions persist, but they are usually localised peculiarities rather than thriving oral traditions.[30] The knocker was, however, an exception. In North America, the underground spirits became tommyknockers, and non-Cornish miners adopted them, adding legendary details of their own. The tommyknockers flourished in their new home.[31]

Research by Walter Yeeling Evans-Wentz (1878-1965) found a fading and sometimes confused fairy tradition in Cornwall prior to the Great War. He clearly demonstrates that the Cornish of the early twentieth century recalled legends that had appeared before in the nineteenth-century collections of Hunt and Bottrell. The indigenous piskies survived, even if they were diminished. Evans-Wentz shows that stories about knockers persisted into the early twentieth century in Cornwall. We know from elsewhere, meanwhile, that their North American progeny, the tommy-knocker, remained a viable tradition into the 1950s. In addition, both the knocker and tommyknocker, like piskies, feature in modern popular culture, though belief has faded away.[32]

Conclusion

The Cornish piskie provides an example of the Northern European fairy, the social supernatural beings who lived in communities and interacted with people for good or ill. Cornwall's population has always been dwarfed by the Celtic nations of Ireland, Scotland, and Wales, and yet, its piskie traditions has had a disproportionate effect on how the English-speaking world perceived fairies, thanks in part to the early collecting of Cornish folklore enthusiasts. The Cornish piskies featured in legends shared with other places. While these stories were widespread in Northern Europe, the Cornish adaptation of the narratives was unique. And finally, belief in the Cornish knockers—together with the tommyknockers—continued into the twentieth century, not least outside Cornwall.

15

PURITANS AND PUKWUDGIES

New England by Peter Muise

One cold April morning in the 1990s a woman named Joan took her dog for a walk in the Freetown State Forest, as she often did. The Massachusetts park has more than 50 miles of walking trails, so it was the perfect place for Joan and her dog to get some exercise and fresh air.

The walk didn't quite go the way Joan expected, though. As they walked down the trail her dog got agitated and led her off the path and into the trees, where Joan saw a strange person perched on a boulder.

> She described him as looking like a troll: two feet high with pale grey skin and hair on his arms and the top of his head. The monster seemed to have no clothes... His eyes were a deep green, and he had large lips and a long, almost canine nose...
> 1

The person (or was it a creature?) stared at Joan. She stared back. Finally her dog pulled her back to the trail. Joan left the park as fast as she could.

Joan was to see the strange person three more times, but not in the park. Those subsequent sightings came when she awoke in the middle of the night to see the little man staring at her through her bedroom window. The unsettling nighttime visits only stopped when Joan moved to another county far from the Freetown State Forest.

Fairies and English colonists

What Joan had encountered was a pukwudgie, one of New England's resident fairies. Surprisingly, in recent years more people have reported seeing fairies in New England than reported them in the past. During the nineteenth century most people didn't think fairies could be found there at all. They thought fairies belonged in Britain and Ireland, not in the six New England states (Maine, Vermont, New Hampshire, Massachusetts, Connecticut and Rhode Island). For example, novelist and Unitarian minister Sylvester Judd included the following passage in his 1851 novel *Margaret*: 'There are no fairies in our meadows, and no elves to spirit away our children... Our rivers harbor no nereids... Robin-Good-Fellow is unknown...'[2]

Nathaniel Hawthorne expressed a similar sentiment in his classic novel *The Scarlet Letter* (1850), as its heroine Hester Prynne watches her illegitimate daughter playing in the woods outside of seventeenth-century Boston: 'But how strangely beautiful she looks, with those wildflowers in her hair! It as if one of the fairies, whom we left in our dear old England, had decked her out to meet us.'[3] John Greenleaf Whittier, a prominent Massachusetts poet and early folklorist, made his case in even stronger terms: 'Fairy faith is, we may safely say, now dead everywhere ... It never had much hold upon the Yankee mind, our superstitions being mostly of a sterner and less poetical kind.'[4]

The stern and unpoetic superstitions Whittier alludes to were those brought by the English Puritans who colonized New England starting in the 1620s. They brought folklore about witches, magic, ghosts and the Devil with them on the long Atlantic crossing, but didn't bring any fairy beliefs. Why was this?

In his recent book *America Bewitched* (2013), historian Owen Davies suggests that British fairy folklore was tied closely to certain features of the English landscape. Fairies were associated with ancient burial mounds, old trees, or particular bodies of water. When the Puritans left the old landscape behind they left the fairies with it. However, Davies does acknowledge that English colonists in some other parts of North America, like the Canadian Maritime Provinces (see the next chapter), did bring fairylore with them. He claims this is because these settlers came from Ireland and the English West Country, which are regions with strong fairy traditions. The fairylore survived in the New World because the Maritimes are very isolated.[5]

Davies's theory could be correct. The New England Puritans came mostly from East Anglia in England and brought many East Anglian folkways with them.[6] East Anglia is rich in witch lore and was the site of England's largest and most intense witch hunts,[7] so it makes sense that New England would also be famous for witch folklore and witch hunts. East Anglia is not known for its fairylore. And unlike the Maritimes, early New England was not isolated but was a mercantile and political hub.

The early New England colonists did retain a few memories of the fairies, even though they said they left them behind. For example, Samuel Deane, a minister and vice president at Maine's Bowdoin College, included the following in his book *The New England Farmer; Or, Georgical Dictionary* (1797):

ELFSHOT or ELFSHOTTEN, a disease in horned cattle, the symptoms or concomitants of which are sluggishness and the loss of appetite. The original of the name seems to have been a superstitious opinion that cattle were shotten and wounded by elves, or fairies. The disease, however, is not imaginary. It is believed to be an opening in the peritonaeum, or film of the belly, caused by relaxation. It resembles a hole made by a bullet and may be felt through the skin...[8]

Deane apparently did not believe in fairies, but perhaps the term's continuing usage in New England suggests that some farmers still remembered the little people.

Whittier provides the following account, which is a more concrete example of how New Englanders remembered the fairies they had left behind. A man in New Hampshire ran an inn but his temperament made him poorly suited for that career. He was a 'spiteful little man' who made the inn 'so uncomfortable with his moroseness that travelers even at nightfall pushed by his door and drove to the next town.' Business suffered and it seemed likely the inn would shut down.

However, the innkeeper's wife, 'a stout, buxom woman, of Irish lineage' refused to give up hope and remained confident that business would improve. Through a small miracle it did: a group of fairies took up residence in the building. The fairies were invisible but could clearly be heard talking in the inn's main room. Word spread about the fairies and soon the establishment was filled with paying customers. They would gather in the inn's parlor to listen to the fairies: 'Small squeaking voices spoke in a sort of Yankee-Irish dialect, in the haunted room, to the astonishment and admiration of hundreds.'

Sadly for the innkeeper his guests' astonishment was short-lived. Some sceptics visiting from Massachusetts pried loose a board in the ceiling to reveal not magical fairies, but rather the innkeeper's 'three slatternly daughters' speaking in high, squeaking voices. The fairy visitation ceased abruptly after this. Rather than admit the fairies had been a hoax the innkeeper's wife instead claimed the fairies had grown tired of living 'among the Yankees, and were going back to Ould Ireland.'[9]

Whittier uses the story to demonstrate that fairies don't exist in New England, but the crowd of guests at the inn also shows that people were willing to believe they might. Unfortunately Whittier does not divulge the name of the New Hampshire town (only that it begins with an 'S') or the year the incident occurred.

Marblehead, Massachusetts is one of the few places in New England where records indicate that British fairy folklore survived. Much like the Maritimes, Marblehead is relatively isolated, and unlike other parts of New England it was originally settled by fishermen from the West of England.[10]

Joseph Story (1779-1845), a United States Supreme Court justice born in Marblehead, often told his son about the superstitions of his youth:

...Marblehead was a sort of compendium of all varieties of legend. For instance, the belief in the Pixies of Devonshire, the Bogles of Scotland, the Northern Jack o' Lanthorn was prevalent there;—and my father has told me that he was often cautioned by the fishermen, just at twilight, to run home or the Bogles would be sure to seize him.[11]

Caroline King Howard shared a similar reminiscence about Judge Story in her memoir *When I Lived in Salem, 1822-1866*:

Judge Story used to tell with great delight, that when he was a boy living in Marblehead, his mother always warned him, when he went out to pasture, to drive home the cows, to turn his jacket inside out for fear of the pixies.[12]

Judge Story would have been a child in the 1780s, but belief in pixies continued in Marblehead for at least a century more, as the following account from 1894 indicates:

I knew a woman fairly well-educated... who told me in perfect good faith that she herself had been 'pixilated' and had wandered an hour or more unable to find her home, until at last, recognizing that she was in the power of the little brown people, she turned her cloak, when the glamour vanished; in a moment she saw where she was, and was soon in her own house.[13]

Sadly, outside of Marblehead there is little evidence of British fairylore in New England from the seventeenth to nineteenth centuries. Were Whittier and the other writers correct in claiming the fairy faith was dead and the woods empty of elves? Obviously not, since Joan encountered a fairy in the 1990s. The fairies were here well before the English ever arrived, but Whittier and the others just didn't know where to find them.

Fairies and New England Indians
In 1971 an anthropologist named Susan Stevens was living on a Passamaquoddy Indian reservation in northern Maine. She had married a member of the tribe and was residing there with her husband when a strange incident occurred. In the spring of that year the local Catholic priest had given the Passamaquoddy permission to hold a dance in the church. While the Passamaquoddy looked forward to the dance they were also nervous about holding it during Lent. Dancing during the holy season somehow seemed a little unorthodox...

Stevens attended the dance, along with about 75 other people. At first the event went well, with people laughing and socializing, but shortly after it started a teenage boy reported that he had seen something lurking in the darkness outside the church. He asked his cousin if he could see anything, and the cousin said he did. It was one of the mekumwasuck.

The mekumwasuck are a type of fairy found in Passamaquoddy folklore. They are quite short (about three feet tall), have extremely hairy faces, wear outlandish clothing, and live in the woods outside human society. They sound interesting, but here's the bad part: anyone the mekumwasuck look directly at will sicken and die.[14]

The Passamaquoddy converted to Catholicism in the 1700s,[15] and the mekumwasuck had converted with them. They are ferocious guardians of the Church and punish anyone who disregards Catholic dogma. For example, a group of mekumwasuck once attacked some men stealing wine from a church. The thieves escaped by climbing out of a window, but one man became stuck and was beaten badly by the fairies before he finally escaped.[16]

Returning to Stevens's account, the boy and his cousin told the other people at the dance what they had seen outside the church. The music stopped and everyone quickly departed. It was clear the fairies were unhappy about a dance happening during Lent. From that time on no other dances were organized in the holy season.[17]

Stevens's account of the aborted dance appears in Katharine Briggs's *Dictionary of Fairies*, where it is one of the few New World entries. Briggs speculates that the mekumwasuck may actually be derived from European gargoyles that Catholic missionaries introduced to the Passamaquoddy. This doesn't seem likely, though, for two reasons.

First, Briggs writes that the Passamaquoddy also tell tales of another race of little people called the nagumwasuck. Although the nagumwasuck are ugly and don't like to be looked at they are mostly benevolent, and form a society that mirrors the Passamquoddy's. When a Passmaquoddy child is born, the nagumwasuck celebrate. When a Passamaquoddy person dies, the nagumwasuck mourn. When the Passamaquoddy built a church, the nagumwasuck built a small clay church on a lake's shore. They also make small clay cylinders that are found on beaches.[18] The nagumwasuck don't serve as church guardians, so it seems likely they are part of pre-Colonial folklore.

The mekumwasuck themselves sometimes play roles other than church guardians. For example, Charles Godfrey Leland includes a Passamaquoddy story about a mikumwess in *The Algonquin Legends of New England* (1885). In this legend a female mikumwess seduces a young hunter who dies after he leaves her for a human woman. The doomed hunter's father says, 'I know all about these female devils who seek to destroy men. Verily this was a she Mikumwess.'[19] This certainly doesn't sound like a church guardian.

Perhaps more importantly, many other American Indian groups in New England also tell stories about fairies, and many with names similar to the mekumwasuck. Rather than the mekumwasuck being derived from European gargoyles, it seems more likely the Passamaquoddy already believed in fairies, and simply adapted their existing beliefs to the new Christian religion brought by the missionaries.

American Indian groups have lived in New England for nearly 10,000 years,[20] moving into the region after the last Ice Age ended. During that time they developed rich cosmologies and mythologies that populated the landscape with a wide variety of non-human entities. Anthropologist Frank Speck wrote the following about the Penobscot, the Passmaquoddy's neighbors in northern New England, but it could easily apply to all New England tribes:

> Penobscot belief attributes existence to a host of beings, neither human nor animal in nature, whose abodes are forest depths, rocky crags and ledges, mountain tarns, outlets of lakes or deep river pools, knolls of earth, and all spots unfrequented by man and unmolested by animals. For all we are told, the fairies live on forever, unless life is interrupted by man.[21]

The Penobscot believe in two types of fairies similar to those described by the Passamaquoddy. One is dangerous, the other benevolent. The mikumweswak are short, generally male, and entice human women into the woods where they seduce them. A woman who spends time with one of the mikumweswak will never marry a human man. The mikumweswak can sometimes be helpful, but are more often dangerous. In fact, they are said to remove the brains from hunters they find sleeping in the woods. Needless to say, the operation is always fatal.[22]

More benevolent are the wanagemeswak, whose faces are so narrow (like the blade of an axe) that they can only be seen in profile. The wanagemeswak are shy but friendly towards the Penobscot and warn them of impending attacks by enemies. They also create figurines of humans and animals from river clay. Anyone who finds one of these small sculptures will have good luck.[23]

In 1835, four Penobscot men reported coming upon an entire village made of clay on the shores of an isolated lake during a hunting trip. The clay village included buildings, animals, and furniture, and its fairy creators were nearby. When the wanagemeswak saw the hunters in their village they fled into the lake. Determined to learn more about the little people, one of the hunters was buried under the sandy shore by his companions. When the wanagemeswak returned to their village the hunter emerged from hiding and captured two of them. They tried to hide their faces from the hunters, who were amazed to see that they were long and exceedingly narrow. The captive fairies told the hunters that the wanagemeswak are divided into twelve tribes, each ruled over by a gigantic king. The kings' main source of sustenance is children who have fallen into the lake. At this point the wanagemeswak led the hunters to their tribe's monarch, who was sleeping a short distance away. The hunters hastily departed upon seeing the terrifying giant.[24]

Speck describes several other Penobscot fairies as well, including the alembeg-winosis, which he translates as 'underwater dwarf man.' The alembegwinosis is usually male, stands about three feet tall, has long hair and lives in deep pools along riverbanks and in lakes. They eschew clothing and tend to avoid humans. Seeing an alembegwinosis is usually an omen that someone will soon drown.[25]

An alembegwinosis will grant wishes if humans aid it in a time of need, but the wishes usually do not turn out well. Speck tells how one day after a large thunderstorm an injured alembegwinosis was found lying on the beach by a husband, his wife, and their son. The family nursed the little man back to health; in return he granted them three wishes. Several days later the family went to a local trading post to trade some animal furs. The wife saw a well-made broom and said, 'Wow! I wish I had that broom.' Instantly it was hers. Realizing she had just wasted a wish, the husband shouted angrily, 'I wish that broom was stuck up your anus!' Instantly it was. Happily, the son used the third and final wish to remove the broom.[26]

The Penobscot told Speck about several other fairy-like beings, including the nudemkenowet, a half-fish, half-human creature that harasses women bathing alone, and the swamp woman Skwaktemus, who is clad only in moss and her long hair. Poor lonely Skwaktemus tries to lure children and hunters to her boggy home, from which they will never return. The forests are also haunted by the eskudait, the will-o'-the-wisp, a floating ball of light that is an omen of misfortune.[27]

Further west, in Vermont, the Abenaki also tell stories about fairies. They call them manogemassak, which they translate simply as 'little people.' They live in rivers, have long narrow faces like axe blades, and speak with squeaky voices. The manogemassak travel in stone canoes and try to avoid being seen by humans. They spend their nights making clay sculptures, like the round clay balls found at Lake Champlain's Button Bay. The Abenaki also say the swamps are haunted by a being known simply as the swamp spirit, which lures children to their doom with its lonesome cries.[28]

As these examples show, the American Indians of northern New England have a rich tradition of stories about fairies. Across the region they share similar names and traits. Although Indian fairylore has undoubtedly changed over time through European contact, only among the Passamaquoddy are the fairies associated with the Catholic Church, and it seems almost certain the fairies existed in Indian lore long before the first Europeans arrived in New England.

Northern New England was colonized late and relatively lightly by the English, and parts of it are still sparsely populated. On the other hand, southern New England—Massachusetts, Connecticut and Rhode Island—was heavily colonized in the early 1600s by the English, and those states remain the most densely populated today. The Indian tribes in southern New England were decimated first by European diseases, and then by a series of wars with the English. Despite these calamities, some American Indian tribes still live in southern New England, and still have lore about fairies.

For example, the Mohegan of Connecticut tells stories about fairies called makiawisug, who dwell underneath Mohegan Hill in Montville, Connecticut. According to the Mohegan medicine woman Gladys Tantaquidgeon, the makiawisug are small, bulky and born directly from the earth itself. They have lived under the hill since before humans arrived in Connecticut.[29] In 2012, the Mohegans petitioned to stop a housing development from being built on Mohegan Hill. Their petition claimed:

> The sacred stone piles on Mohegan Hill are a critical feature of the traditional landscape of Mohegan Hill; they were created by the 'Little People' who live deep within the ground of Mohegan Hill. These 'Little People' or Makiawisug are the ancient culture heroes of this region. These stone piles also possess powers that protect the Mohegan people from outsiders...[30]

Tantaquidgeon, who died in 2005, gave the following advice for interacting with the makiawisug:

> Do not look directly at the makiawisug. If you do, they will point their finger at you and become invisible. They will then steal your possessions.
>
> To gain their favor, leave baskets full of berries and cornbread outside for the makiawisug. They sometimes like offerings of meat as well.
>
> Do not talk about the makiawisug in summer. This is when they are the most active. If they hear you talking about them they will become offended and steal your possessions.

According to Tantaquidgeon, the Makiawisug are led by Granny Squannit, an old woman with very long hair.[31]

Granny Squannit is also known to the Wampanoag tribe of Cape Cod. Also called Ol' Squant, the Wampanoag say her face is hidden by her long hair. Different accounts claim Granny Squannit has either eyes like a cat, square eyes, or just one single eye in her forehead, and she takes offense at anyone who looks directly at her face.

Granny Squannit can be kind or malevolent. She taught humankind the use of medicinal plants, and will provide healing herbs if left an offering (she prefers dumplings, cakes, liquor and tobacco set out on a plate covered with a napkin or leaves). She also provides food for people who are shipwrecked, and will even grant wishes (for reasons I explore below).

On the other hand, she sometimes causes shipwrecks, and likes to kidnap boys and men. She takes offense if talked about, and will point her finger at anyone who sees her and then turn invisible. Like the makiawisug once she is invisible she will steal. Granny Squannit combines positive and negative aspects in one being, and has the traits of many of the fairies already discussed. She may in fact be a survival of the pre-Colonial Indian goddess Squauanit, the women's goddess, who was mentioned by Roger Williams in *A Key Into The Language of America* (1643).[32]

To sum up, while the early English settlers and their descendants claimed there were no fairies in New England, the American Indians who live here described a variety of fairies. These are known by several names, many of them similar, and some of them share traits such as extremely long hair, unusual facial features and concern about being seen by humans. Other shared traits include invisibility, granting wishes, and capturing or luring humans to them. They can also be malevolent, so visitors to the New England woods should follow Gladys Tantaquidgeon's suggestions!

Fairies and New England's Contemporary Dominant Culture
On December 15, 1956, a man name Alfred Horne was harvesting Christmas trees near Derry, New Hampshire. The late autumn woods were very quiet, and Horne was alone.[33]

Well, at least he thought he was. As he went about his work Horne realized that someone was standing nearby. Or perhaps some*thing* would be a better word: he was being watched by a two-foot tall, green-skinned humanoid with floppy ears like an elephant. The creature had only tiny holes for a nose, and like a snake its eyes were covered with nictitating membranes. Even stranger, its hands were simply stumps and its feet lacked any toes.

Horne watched the creature for about twenty minutes. Realizing no one would believe his tale without evidence, he decided to capture it. He grabbed hold of it, but as soon as he did the creature emitted a blood-curdling shriek. Horne was so terrified that he ran off, leaving the creature behind.[34]

Horne kept the encounter secret for several years, until he described it in two letters to the Boston astronomer and UFO researcher Walter Webb. Horne thought Webb might be able to explain what he had seen in the woods. Of course, rather than an extraterrestrial the creature might have been an elf, given the season and Horne's work harvesting Christmas trees. This seems even likelier when one considers where it happened. Derry, New Hampshire is home to a legendary fairy.

Nineteenth-century authors like Whittier would have been surprised to learn that a New Hampshire town had a resident fairy, but the number of fairy sightings and legends in New England has actually grown in the twentieth and twenty-first centuries. American Indian tribes always had fairylore, but in recent years it has increasingly appeared in the dominant New England culture as well. Ghosts, Bigfoot and UFOs are still more widely known in contemporary New England, but more fairies are being reported now than in the nineteenth century.

There are several reasons for this. First, large numbers of immigrants from areas with fairylore, like Ireland, settled in New England, particularly in the nineteenth century. Second, the mass media has popularized New England fairies in ways that were not possible in the past. Stories about New England fairies can be found on the Internet, on television, and in documentaries. Finally, paranormal investigators and cryptozoologists have drawn attention to the legendary creatures of this region in recent years.

In some cases, the contemporary New England fairies are simply Old World fairies transplanted into a new setting. For example, the author Joseph Citro tells of a successful New England businessman of Irish descent who heard the wailing of a banshee on two occasions. The first was when his grandfather died, and the second was at the death of John F. Kennedy, America's first president with Irish ancestry.[35]

In other cases, the modern fairies are the result of the dominant European culture using Indian culture in new ways. That seems to be the case in Derry, New Hampshire, which was originally founded by Scots-Irish families and incorporated as the town of Londonderry in 1729. Named after the city in Northern Ireland, New Hampshire's Londonderry eventually split up into several smaller towns, including Derry.[36]

The Scots-Irish settled on the shores of a small lake whose official name is Beaver Lake, but which is also called Tsienneto. This is allegedly an Indian word that means 'sleeping in beauty.'[37] The lake's beauty was the subject of several poems, and in 1907 Derry resident Robert N. Richardson wrote *Tsienneto: A Legend of Beaver Lake*, a short pamphlet describing how a powerful Indian medicine man named Tsienneto created some of the lake's natural features. According to the pamphlet, the story was told to Richardson by a 'little, old gray-visaged wood nymph.'[38]

Richardson's pamphlet was perhaps just poesy, but the legend of Tsienneto continued to grow. Mary MacMurphy, the wife of Derry's Episcopal minister, claimed Tsienneto was actually the name of a fairy queen who lived in Beaver Lake. Tsienneto liked to help people in distress, and 1697 came to the aid of Hannah Duston, an English settler who was kidnapped during an Indian raid on Haverhill, Massachusetts. Duston was brought north into New Hampshire, but managed to scalp and kill her captors (Duston did indeed kill and scalp ten Indians, and statues commemorating her bloody deed can be found in Massachusetts and New Hampshire). According to MacMurphy, Tsienneto put Duston's captors into a deep sleep so they could be killed.[39]

Alfred Horne's 1956 encounter with the little green man has been interpreted in the light of these earlier Derry fairy stories. The Derry legend illustrates several of the major influences on modern New England fairylore: non-English immigrants, American Indian lore (whether or not it is authentic), and paranormal investigators (like Walter Webb).

Rise of the Pukwudgies

Some of these influences can also be seen in the folklore surrounding pukwudgies, who are positioned to become the most widely recognized modern New England fairies. Pukwudgies are mentioned in many books on the paranormal, including Joseph Citro's *Passing Strange* (1996),[40] Christopher Balzano's *Dark Woods: Cults, Crime and The Paranormal in the Freetown State Forest* (2008),[41] George M. Eberhart's *Mysterious Creatures: A Guide to Cryptozoology, Volume Two* (2010),[42] and Loren Coleman's *Monsters of Massachusetts* (2013).[43]

Pukwudgies have also been featured on several television shows that cater to viewers interested in paranormal phenomena, like Destination America's *Monsters and Mysteries in America*[44] and Animal Planet's *Freak Encounters*,[45] and they are discussed in the documentary film *The Bridgewater Triangle*.[46] By comparison, traditional American Indian fairies, like the makiawisug, get very little mention in the media.

Pukwudgies are slowly becoming known outside the paranormal community as well. For example, a brewing company in Massachusetts produces Pukwudgie Pale Ale, while a Pukwudgie Mountain Bike Race is held in that state's Freetown State Forest. J.K. Rowling has even incorporated pukwudgies into her fictional Harry Potter universe.[47]

How did the pukwudgies become so popular? Surprisingly, Whittier was one of the first people in New England to mention them. He was apparently unaware of the fairylore from the New England Indians, but *was* aware of fairylore from the Ojibwa Indians who live in the Midwest region of the United States: 'It is a curious fact that the Indians had some notion of a race of beings corresponding to the English fairies.' Whittier notes that the Ojibwa call them puckweedjinees, which he translates as 'little vanishers.'[48]

Henry Wadsworth Longfellow, one of America's most popular nineteenth-century writers and a resident of Massachusetts, also wrote about pukwudgies in his epic poem *Song of Hiawatha*. The poem was inspired by Ojibwa legends, and includes a section titled 'The Death of Kwasind,' which tells how fairies called puk-wudjies jealously kill a human hero.[49]

Whittier and Longfellow both lived in New England, but neither claimed the pukwudgies did. That changed when Thomas Weston incorporated elements of 'The Death of Kwasind' into his book *A History of The Town of Middleboro* (1906).[50] Weston inaccurately presented the story as a traditional Indian legend from southeastern Massachusetts, thereby connecting the pukwudgies to New England.[51]

Two Wampanoag Indians from Mashpee, Massachusetts solidified that connection. In the 1930s author Elizabeth Reynard was collecting Cape Cod legends for an upcoming book. Eager to include local Indian legends, Reynard consulted with Chief Red Shell (Clarence Wixon) and Chief Wild Horse (Clinton Haynes). The two Wampanoag men provided Reynard with many stories, some of which included elements drawn from other Indian groups (like the Ojibwa) and from written sources.[52]

One of the stories, 'The Battle with The Pygmies,' describes how heroic giant Maushop, his wife Quaunt, and their sons battled against the malevolent pukwudgees.

These pygmies, or Little People, were called Pukwudgees. Only a handful of them were in each band, yet so potent was their magic (even a common Pukwudgee had charms greater than those of the tribal medicine men), so terrible were their miracles, that Maushop and his sons and his wife could not always prevail against them.

Maushop's sons are poisoned by the pukwudgies, and he and his wife depart from

Cape Cod, leaving it to the pukwudgies.[53] This story was later made into an illustrated children's book, *The Good Giants and the Bad Pukwudgies* (1982).[54]

The pukwudgies have a variety of magical powers. They can transform themselves into animals, and can vanish into thin air. They also send will-o'-the-wisps (here called Tei-Pei-Wankas) to lure humans into swamps. They use their powers to harass human women and girls, and also to lure humans off cliffs or shoot them with poisonous darts.[55] Some of these characteristics are similar to those exhibited by the traditional New England Indian fairies already discussed, but pukwudgies seem to lack the benevolent side that some of those beings show. Pukwudgies do not heal, they do not bring luck, and they do not warn of impending enemies.

People who encounter pukwudgies generally find the experience frightening. For example, a *YouTube* video titled 'When Pukwudgies Attack' shows a woman apparently possessed by a pukwudgie. The possession ends when the Christian Trinity is invoked.[56] Joan's encounter with a pukwudgie (described on the first page of this chapter) was unsettling, as was another encounter described in Balzano's book.[57]

In 1990, a Raynham, Massachusetts man named William Russo encountered a pukwudgie. One night while walking his dog near the woods Russo saw a small, hairy humanoid creature standing under a streetlight. The creature beckoned to Russo, saying 'Ee wa chu. Ee wa chu. Keer. Keer.' Russo quickly departed. He later realized the creature was saying, 'We want you. We want you. Come here. Come here.'[58] Further north, pukwudgies are said to haunt the Vale End Cemetery in Wilton, New Hampshire, where they chase visitors at night[59] and have been blamed for the death of a paranormal investigator.[60]

Less ominous but still disturbing, a four-year-old child walking in Newington, New Hampshire's Great Bay National Wildlife Refuge with his family told his father the following:

> He said something like, 'So daddy, I saw a little man over there. He had a basket of candy around his neck, and he wanted me to reach in and take some. But I said no, and that I had to come back to talk to you.'

The father could find no sign of the little man (described by the child as gray in color), and realized later it was most likely a pukwudgie.[61]

Most of these stories show the pukwudgies' sinister side, but at least one online commenter thinks they may just be misunderstood. In response to someone seeking advice for her haunted home, the commenter suggested her problems might be caused by pukwudgies, and that offering them strawberries or planting fruit trees might propitiate them.[62] The advice is similar to that offered by Gladys Tantaquidgeon for dealing with the makiawisug.

Still More Contemporary Fairies

Although pukwudgies currently are the most widely known New England fairy, several other types have been and continue to be reported in modern times. A few examples are given below.

In the early twentieth century a man named Perry Boney lived in Connecticut's rural Great Basin area. Boney was somewhat eccentric. His neighbors weren't sure where he came from, but he operated a very tiny one-room general store deep in the woods. Boney never made a profit, since he sold all his goods for the same price he bought them. He always had a strange distant expression on his face, and children thought he could talk with the fairies that lived in the streams and creeks. Boney also was able to speak with a local raccoon. He disappeared as suddenly as he appeared, and local lore suggests he returned to the fairy realm from whence he came. The Great Basin has since been flooded to make a reservoir, which adds to Boney's mystique.[63]

In the 1980s, journalist Neil Hogan wrote about Connecticut fairies, calling them the Old Men of the Mountains in his column for *The New Haven Register*. These robe-wearing creatures live in caves in the hills near Canaan. They tend to avoid humans except when they are hungry or need help, and will reward those who feed them with triangular metallic coins covered in strange symbols.[64]

Around the same time, two women in Somerville, Massachusetts hired a psychic to exorcise their home. They thought a ghost was haunting it because objects kept moving around unaccountably. The psychic explained their problem was not a ghost, but was instead a troll associated with a stream under their cellar. She banished the small hairy creature.[65] It may have not gone far, though. A friend of mine who lived across the street twenty years later reported similar unexplained activity in his house!

Middlebury, Connecticut is home to a dilapidated and haunted fairy village. Originally built as a tourist attraction on a now defunct trolley line, local legend currently claims a man built the miniature houses to please his fairy-plagued wife. She demanded he build houses for the fairies to live in, and a throne for herself, for she believed herself to be Queen of the Fairies. Purportedly, she angrily killed her husband when he sat on her throne and then committed suicide in remorse. A stone structure said to be the throne still remains. Anyone foolish enough to sit in it is doomed to die within seven years, though it is unclear whether fairies or the wife's ghost commit the deadly deed.[66]

I'll end this chapter on a more upbeat note. Several respondents to the Fairy Census reported encountering fairies in New England. They included a strange six-fingered man sitting on a boulder, a small humanoid made of vegetation, and tiny fairies with dragonfly wings.[67] One of the nicest responses came from a Wiccan priestess, who saw shimmering shapes in a pine tree as she presided over a wedding ceremony. She and the bride both believed these were fairies that had come to join in the festivities. A fairy-blessed pagan wedding here in New England is something the original Puritan settlers would have never imagined.

BANSHEES AND CHANGELINGS

Irish America by Chris Woodyard

Irish Fairylore in the New World

Stories of banshees, changelings, and fairies were an integral part of Irish life and lore. This chapter will consider the question: Did belief in those fairy entities accompany Irish emigrants to America? We will see what evidence for transplanted Irish fairylore may be found in the popular America press and examine in detail a unique nineteenth-century case of 'taken by the fairies,' reported from the Irish community in Dubuque, Iowa.

There has never been a consensus about the status of fairies in America: were some home-grown or did certain fairies come to America with emigrant believers? Did British and Irish fairies arrive at all?

Most folklorists would say that they did not. Only one, Wayland Hand, offered an extensive catalogue of American fairy beliefs in his article 'European Fairy Lore in the New World.'[1] However, his entries are somehow generic, abstract, and bloodless, devoid of actual encounters with the Gentry and focused on belief and superstition, rather than experiences.

Conversely, Richard M. Dorson flatly denied that European fairylore arrived in the United States at all:

These beings cavorted and made mischief throughout the isles of Britain, but failed to take passage with the emigrants sailing for America. One explanation may be that they were absorbed in the new environment by the stronger figures of witches, ghosts and devils with which they were closely associated in the folk mind…a still more compelling reason exists for the nonmigration of fairy beings. No European, African, or Asian people entering American shores have brought with them the folk creatures of their *Heimat,* the spirits rooted in the soil—as Devil, witch, and ghost were not—of the homeland. The water nymph, the mountain troll, the garden gnome, belong irrevocably to the old culture and the Old Country.[2]

There is a general impression among scholars that while European immigrants managed to smuggle the odd banshee, kobold, or gnome, the brownie, the leprechaun, and the trooping fairies were left behind on the pier, waving a sad farewell to those bound for the Land of Opportunity.

Perhaps the New World was just that—too new to sustain the old gods and guardian spirits. The fairies of the auld sod were literally inhabitants of that sod. Across the water, there were no raths, no hedged fields in which to pixilate mortals, and no greenswards for fairy rings and dancing.

Owen Davies argues that the New World did not have the topographical memory to sustain fairies:

> One obvious reason for the weakness of fairy lore is that in Western Europe the fairies were rooted in local geographies and popular interpretations of the ancient landscape. They inhabited liminal places, physical and metaphysical boundaries between the past and present, this world and other realms, natural features that represented portals between different states of being. So we find fairy legends and sightings focused around prehistoric earthworks and burial mounds, and landscape features such as venerable trees, streams and bridges. Now, all these features could also be found in the North American landscape of course. The difference is that in the old world landscape associations with fairies had their roots in centuries of accumulated tradition and experience. The fairies lost their relevance once divorced from these long-held associations….[3]

And yet, around North America, there are intriguing traces of Ireland's Good People in the popular press, half-hidden, like the entrance to a fairy fort. These traces are often obscured by disclaimers about superstition, which was seen as a characteristic of the poor, the uneducated and the unassimilated immigrant.

Newspapers of the nineteenth and early twentieth century often took a mocking and sceptical tone towards supernatural encounters of all kinds. While many ethnic groups were pilloried for their superstitious beliefs in the press, there were particularly relentless attacks on the Irish, ranging from ethnic jokes and painful dialect stories to condescending commentary about ignorant customs and folk beliefs. It is easy to see how Irish immigrants thus attacked would abandon, moderate, or hide their belief in fairies. Americanisation, with its proud, anti-superstition mandate, was urged on all immigrants. Thaddeus Russell states:

> Through the nineteenth century and into the twenties, Irish American community leaders waged a remarkably successful campaign of assimilation with the goal, as the Irish newspaper the Boston Pilot put it, to create 'calm, rational, and respectable Irish Catholics of America.' The movement was led at the grassroots by Irish Catholic priests such as Archbishop 'Dagger John' Hughes of New York and Archbishops John Joseph Williams and William Henry O'Connell of Boston, who used the power of the church and Christian mortality to make immigrants adopt the ways of their new country.[4]

According to historian Kerby Miller, most Irish priests during this period 'reflected both their church's concerns for order, authority, and spiritual conformity and their middle-class parents' compatible obsessions with social stability and their children's chastity.' They therefore 'condemned tradition wakes, fairy belief, sexually integrated education, crossroads dancing, and all other practices which threatened either clerical or bourgeois hegemony...' This 'iron morality' helped make the post-Famine Irish the world's most faithfully practicing and sexually controlled Catholics, but in the process it crushed many old customs which had given color and vitality to peasant life. In America, the Church's worldview merged seamlessly with a ruthless determination by many Irish immigrants to make themselves one with their new nation'.[5]

It has also been suggested that much fairylore and belief had been lost before emigrants even disembarked.

> Among the genres of Irish songs to perish during the Great Famine were songs of the supernatural. Fairy lore was an indigenous feature of Irish-speaking communities, whose songs acted as natural carriers of that tradition. The work of Petrie and O'Curry gives extensive coverage to songs of fairy abduction, changelings, and musical exchanges with the fairies. Both testify to the ardor of these beliefs among rural communities throughout the west of Ireland.[6]

As early as 1856, a practical reason for the lack of fairylore in America was suggested in a newspaper article entitled, 'Why Have We No National Fairy Lore?'

> There is one thing which our national literature will lack when it 'comes to years of discretion; ' and in the history of our people, at least as far as the little folks are concerned, if not the 'children of larger growth', it will be felt as a serious loss. We have no National Fairy Lore. Alas! we began to be a people too late in the day for the least shadow of morning romance still to linger through the broad light of prac-

ticality—*we have too much common sense!*[7]

Supernatural Irish Entities in America

If we ignore the sceptics and the folklorists alike, and stubbornly seek evidence of the fairy faith in North America, what sorts of fairies are we likely to find? To begin with, there are shape-shifting spook lights reminiscent of bogey tricksters and giant, leaping fiends with luminous eyes, as well as tantalising will-o'-the-wisps. While there are apparitional women in white, perhaps an echo of stately fairy queens, there seem to be no household brownies. One finds the odd leprechaun story, typically in a compilation of Irish superstitions or associated with tales of buried treasure. Occasionally, a leprechaun will appear in the guise of a ghostly dwarf, such as this one, reported at New Haven, Connecticut by three Italians, a Swede, and an Irishman named Owen McNulty.

[These men] employed in the brickyard, were going home about 7 o'clock in the evening. Suddenly there appeared in the road before them the figure of a man about three feet high, dressed in black velvet clothes of the fashion of 100 years ago. The coat was trimmed with fur, and on his head was a cocked hat. McNulty had a spade on his shoulder. He said: "Boys, I guess I'll stop the chap," and so saying he made a thrust at the figure with his spade, but it passed through and the dwarf vanished. The men were much frightened and crossing themselves, fled for home. They went the next day to see if their senses had played them false, when the figure appeared again in the full light of day. McNulty again lunged at the object with his spade and cut it in two. It went up into the air about forty feet and the pieces reunited with lightning rapidity and then vanished into the air. They then went home and told the woman with whom they boarded. She said that it was not strange, and that many other people had seen the same thing. All five are industrious men, who positively assert that the story is true in every particular. The diminutive ghost carried a lantern when it was first seen at night; but the next day its hands were empty. There is a tradition that many years ago a sailor of dwarfish stature sailed up the Quinebec [Quinebaug] River, his boat was capsized and he drowned.[8]

Although most European dwarf traditions were left behind in the Old Country, there is a tendency in these rare miniature entity stories, to turn the creature into a traditional ghost of a baby or a dwarf individual. Such entities almost invariably wear 'antiquated' costumes, such as the Connecticut 'sailor' dwarf.

Fairy changelings were one of the rarest of New World émigrés. While the term 'changeling' was frequently cited in the American popular press, it was almost always employed in the context of vacillating politicians. It was used in the fairy sense primarily in stories of changeling abuse back in Ireland, with headlines or commentary expressing horror at this 'appalling superstition.' For many years there were rumours of a New York City changeling murder, telling of a child thrown into the fire by its parents. While there was a debate over whether this was merely an apocryphal libel, the story has at last been located and appears to be genuine.[9] Critics of Irish immigration would have seen in it confirmation of their worst fears about immigrant superstition and criminality.

Ghosts, Banshees, and Fairies
Owen Davies suggests that ghosts took the place of fairies in the New World, which is consistent with the Irish belief that some of the dead inhabited fairyland.

> The dead consort with fairies, and mothers have sometimes heard the voices of their children singing the old Irish songs far down beneath the raths or funeral mounds where the fairies dwell.[10]

Certainly stories of fairies were conflated with other supernatural narratives.

A classic wife-changeling story appeared alongside tales of local ghosts, jack-o-lanterns, and a sinister black dog in an article entitled 'Something About Ghost Stories, People Who Believed in the Supernatural', by James Magness. The proverbial Oldest Inhabitant of Coshocton, Ohio, Magness wrote articles about life on the Ohio and Erie Canal during the early pioneer days. The influence of the Irish, who built the canal, as well as other local Irish settlers, may be seen in this tale:

> Another man, we are told, lost his wife in child bed. She was a beautiful woman in life, but in death looked haggard and cadaverous. He buried her, but afterwards a spectre haunted him which purported to be the ghost of his wife, telling him she was not really dead, but was living; and that haggard figure he had buried was not his wife, but was substituted by some fairies for her. This spectre haunted him nightly, claiming to be his wife, and one night, to convince him more fully, she let the babe she had left with him nurse at her breast, and dropped a few drops of breast milk on the bed-clothes, which was plainly visible in the morning. The husband believed it an illusion but couldn't get rid of the phantom. He told the matter to his pastor who told him it was an illusion and to shake it off if he could. But the man never fully got rid of it[11]

The only fairy entity that consistently accompanied Irish emigrants to America was the banshee. The memory of *An Gorta Mór*, the Great Famine, was more than enough reason for the banshee to stalk the decks of the coffin ships and keen over the canals of America, where, it was said, 'for every mile of canal an Irishman is buried.' Death walked closely with the Irish. The banshee, if terrible, was at least familiar.

The banshee was also a matter of familial pride; a way to assert one's distinguished lineage, even if the clan had fallen on hard times. Stories were told of men consulting doctors or being taken for mad when they claimed they heard their family banshee, a certain token of death. Political writer and editor Thomas Devin Reilly, of Washington D.C., for example, told his family that he 'heard the Banshee of his clan wailing along the shores of the Potomac,' and died shortly thereafter.[12] It was reported that the

O'Reillys and O'Neills of St Louis were descendants of 'banshee' families. 'No doubt many other Irishmen in St Louis can truly lay claim to the distinction of aristocracy conferred by "having a banshee in the family".'[13]

Carrying the fairy faith to its logical conclusion, there is the question of fairy logistics. Fairies do not like salt or iron and cannot cross running water. Crossing the sea on an iron-ribbed boat might have presented insoluble difficulties. One author felt safe in asserting, 'The Banshee never comes to America. She is afraid to cross the ocean, but there are plenty of ghosts and spirits in New York without her.'[14]

Elliott O'Donnell had a different view:

The Banshee, however, as Mr McAnnaly [author of *Irish Wonders*] says, does, sometimes, travel; it travels when, and only when, it accompanies abroad one of the most ancient of the Irish families; otherwise it stays in Ireland, where, owing to the fact that there are few of the really old Irish families left, its demonstrations are becoming more and more rare...[15]

The term 'banshee' eventually ceased to signify a warning spirit attached to a family and became a generic token of death.

Fairy belief was most prevalent in New England and in the East Coast Irish communities. Lynn Hollen Lees writes:

The belief in witches and fairies seems to have declined after migration, but it did not vanish. The Irish who came to the United States brought fairy lore with them and used it creatively to shape and to comment upon their social experiences. In Paterson, New Jersey, Irish residents dubbed a local well the Dublin Spring. An Irish fairy was said to have brought the water for it from the lakes of Killarney in her apron. Fairies were declared to walk in the streets of Paterson, usually in the guise of an old woman with a cane begging. Irish residents of New York as late as fifty years after migration believed in the banshee and in the presence of ghosts and spirits in the city.[16]

Away with the Fairies in Iowa

Eastern coastal cities, including New York and Boston, were known for their large Irish enclaves. Yet the American West had much appeal for the Irish immigrant as well. Iowa was touted as an Irish paradise, offering cheap, fertile farmland, steady work in the lead mines, and a strong Catholic presence. Catholic officials in Iowa actively recruited the Irish for their state. Bishop Mathias Loras wrote to the Eastern newspapers, appealing for more Irish settlers to move beyond the Eastern cities to Iowa. The vicar general of the Diocese of Dubuque, the Rev. Terence Donaghue, also wrote to priests in Ireland for immigrants and said that the new immigrants must 'be smart, for we are get-ahead people here.'[17]

By 1850, Dubuque was one-quarter Irish, while the First Ward neighbourhood became known as 'Dublin' or 'little Dublin.'[18] While there was no official place in Iowa for the superstitious shanty Irishman, stories of fairy folklore from the Old Country continued to be told.

Early in 1870, *The Dubuque Daily Times* published some Irish fairy stories, including 'Pat Doogan and the Fairies,' which told of Pat's wife Cathleen who was stolen by the fairies and how he failed to get her back.[19] Another story, 'What a Fairy Can Do', told of a man whose sick wife wasted away to a skeleton. The only thing that kept her alive was a daily pot of milk boiled by her husband and drunk at midnight. When the husband accidentally spilt the milk, his real wife, restored to health, was returned to him by the fairy that had taken her place.[20]

In 1875 and 1876, in Dubuque newspapers we find various references to fairies in poems, declamations in school exercises, theatrical entertainments, and this intriguing snippet about damage from a wind storm: 'Elsewhere the mischief was greater. In the county hay stacks were lifted from their foundations and scattered broadcast just as the fairies used to do in Ireland'.[21] Fairy belief, if not boldly riding its ponies down the high street, was at least rustling around in the bushes.

While there are many stories from Britain, Ireland, and elsewhere in Europe of wives and children taken by the fairies, there are practically none in the United States. Let us look at a rare story of an alleged fairy abduction in the heartland.

In 1876 the Dubuque papers printed this jocularly sceptical report, without identifying the participants:

What Fairies Did.
It is not likely that anyone will doubt that fairies are wonderful little fellows when the climate agrees with them, but it is more than likely that some incredulous people will feel like questioning the truth of the following story, which was told for a fact, yesterday, by the father of the girl himself. He lives near Holy Cross, in this county. Among other children he had a daughter 22 years of age, who was subject to fits. To get relief from the fits she was taken to the Brothers' Monastry [sic], where she was cured after a short stay. When her father was taking her home, at one point in the timber, she called his attention to a large number of finely dressed people, dancing to music and enjoying themselves very much. The father was unable to see any crowd of dancers, at which she was very much surprised. When she got home, she told her sister with whom she slept that the fairies would carry her off soon. During the same night she arose from her bed, and since then has not been seen, although a four weeks' search has been made for her. Reporters have an accommodating nature, are disposed to believe almost anything, but try as we might, a look of incredulity got possession of our countenance in spite of our herculean efforts to keep it down. An old gentleman who discovered this eased us by telling us several things about the fairies that he had seen "with his own eyes." If he saw them with his own eyes it would be altogether inexcusable for us to doubt further, although we still do think those little red coated fellows are wonderful for their size. They must have

tremendous muscle when they can lift a big woman out of bed and carry her off and then put her back again without hurting her. These American fairies might not handle a person so carefully.[22]

Perplexingly, the story of the girl's disappearance was most widely circulated a full decade after it occurred. It is possible that a lengthy story about the mysterious disappearance of Mrs Louis Bruns and her 17-year-old daughter Nina, which appeared in the *Des Moines Register* the day before Kittie Crowe's story, triggered a retelling of Dubuque's most sensational disappearance.[23]

Stolen by Fairies

A Marvelous Story That Comes from the Bounding West.

Dubuque, Ia., March 28. Andy Crowe is a well-known and prosperous farmer, living in Center township, Dubuque county. Some years ago he had a daughter, the sole remaining member of his family living at home. The girl, just approaching womanhood, was afflicted with a strange malady that baffled the skill of physicians. He finally concluded to take the girl to Father Bernard of the New Melleray monastery, who, on account of his well-known piety and self-abnegation, had established quite a reputation far and wide as a restorer to health of persons afflicted with physical or mental diseases. The good father prayed over the girl and prescribed medicines for her cure. On her way home from the monastery the girl told her father that all that was done for her by Father Bernard would not help her in the least and that she would go away in a year from that time to live with the fairies. Her father paid no attention to what the girl said; in fact, he forgot all about it until just a year from that night he woke up in the morning and found his daughter gone. A candle was burning in her room, and all her clothes were left behind except one calico dress. On reporting her disappearance and what the girl had told him, the neighbors became very suspicious, and charged the old man with making away with her. The neighboring creek was dragged for her body, and the woods and fields subjected to a close search, but no trace of the missing girl was found. In just a year from her disappearance she returned home and related a wonderful tale regarding her absence. She said she had been off with the fairies, with whom she had lived in the most splendid style. They had everything that heart could desire, and spent most of their time in traveling incog. over the country. She had traveled with them and rode in the cars, invisible to mortal eyes. They heard of the suspicions attaching to her father on account of her disappearance, and, at their command, she had returned home to clear up the old gentleman. A grand feast was held in honor of her return, which was attended by all the neighbors, to whom she related her wonderful experience. Two days later she came to Dubuque to visit her sister, who is married to a man named James Hayes, a teamster, residing on Thirteenth street. On the third day after coming to Dubuque she came down stairs and informed Mrs Hayes that she had to go, that two of the fairies had come for her and that they were now upstairs waiting for her.

Mrs Hayes followed the girl upstairs, and there, to her amazement, she saw two queer-looking beings resembling men dressed in antiquated black costumes, and with them the girl left the house. Mrs Hayes followed them to the door and watched them go up the street, when, after going half a block, all three suddenly disappeared in the air, since which nothing has ever been heard of the missing girl. Such is the story that has been repeatedly told by Andy Crowe, always with tearful eyes and impassioned voice, and most of his neighbors, many of whom are well posted in the legendary tales regarding the fairies in Ireland, implicitly believe the same.[24]

The same story above appeared first in the *Des Moines Register* for 26 March 1886, under the misspelt headline: 'Beyond Belief: The Wonderful Story of a Dubuque Girl, Alleged to Have Been Abducted by Fairies'.[25] Two days later the Des Moines paper let rip with the following:

The Fairies of Dubuque
At last Dubuque has got ahead of Des Moines. The aspiration of its later life has been realized. It has something that Des Moines has not. It has something that has been read about in song and story, and some thing nearly all people are supposed to dream about under the inspiration of hasheesh or the refined essence of the poppy. It is something that every city might have had, we suppose, but which no city in Iowa at least, has ever had but Dubuque. Therefore the city founded on the basis of galena [the lead mines] and the beneficence of Julian Dubuque is ahead of every other Iowa city in one thing. Therefore Dubuque is greater than any other Iowa town. Therefore hurrah for Dubuque!

It is fairies that Dubuque has got. It doesn't know exactly what they are, but it has them. Like all other fairies, these fairies are very queer. A year ago they took Miss Kittie Crowe, the pretty daughter of Mr Andy Crowe, made her invisible, and carried her away with them. She has just returned. She would not have returned at all, she said, only because of her mysterious disappearance the neighbors of her father, with the usual kindness of neighbors, began to account for her strange disappearance by saying he had murdered her. The fairies had heard of this, and so sent Miss Kittie back to save the old gentlemen from the present terrors of neighborhood gossip, and the possible terrors of Judge Lynch. Very fittingly a grand feast was spread in honor of Miss Kittie's return. All the neighbors came in, just as they always do in the stories about fairies, to welcome Miss Kittie, and to hear her tell of the wonders of her year's experience in Fairyland. According to her report they don't do at all in Fairyland as we have thought. They don't live in the cups of flowers, dance on the sunbeams, play hide and seek in the meshes of milady's hair, nor sip the honey of the sunshine, nor dance in the coliseum of the lily by moonlight, nor do any of the elfish and gnomish things that all good fairies are popularly supposed to do. Instead, Miss Kittie says, that in her year with them they spent the time traveling incog. over the country, riding in railway cars, invisible to mortal eyes. If this is true, it be very disenchanting, and fairies are no better off than we poor mortals. But Miss Kittie doubtless told the truth. For Dubuque people always do, except when they are talking of Des Moines.

Three days Miss Kittie staid away from the fairies. On the third day she told her married sister that she had to go again, that the fairies could do without her no longer. The sister followed her upstairs, and according to a Dubuque dispatch, "saw two queer looking beings, resembling men, dressed in antiquated black, and with them the girl left the house." She saw them go up the street. "After they had gone half a block all three suddenly disappeared in the air. Since which nothing has been heard of the missing girl." There the story ends, so far as the outside world is given to know.

None of us can compete with these things. We hasten on behalf of Des Moines to throw up the sponge and say at once that we will not even try to compete with Dubuque in this respect. Who would have thought it of Dubuque—the practical, so worldly, and with not a poet to its name since McCreery left it.[26]

Since it has gone at things in this way we warn all the cities competing with it for the Soldiers' Home to look out for it. For if it has all the fairies with it, who can be against it? It has been invincible heretofore. What will it not be now[27]?

The sarcasm was heightened by the long-time rivalry between Dubuque and Des Moines, Iowa's capital, over the title of 'largest Iowa city.' But the Des Moines paper clearly mistook 'the old gentleman's' reminiscences for a current event. The 1886 story did not have an unusually large syndication; available databases show only a handful of papers repeated the story, with nearly all of them clustered in late March 1886.

Miss Kittie Crowe and the 'Fairies'

As to the facts of the story, New Melleray Abbey is a Trappist/Cistercian community that still exists. There were two Father Bernards, one of whom was briefly Prior, but no mention of healing is made in the monastery's history, which is not unusual; singularity was not encouraged or documented. While the usual strict enclosure was kept, the Crowes still could have visited the monastery. One of the features of Cistercian life is hospitality to guests. For example, one of the mayors of Dubuque went to the monastery for a 'rest cure' when he was facing a court case. It is not inconceivable that the father could have brought his daughter with her strange, physician-baffling malady to look for a miracle among the monks.

It is interesting to note that, in Irish belief, Kittie's sickness was consistent with being 'away with the fairies.'

Ireland has scores of stories of people who are said to be 'away,' which is the euphemism for this thraldom. Being 'away' means that *while in this world,* and even at times pursuing their ordinary avocations, people in this state are also in the power of the Sidhe. In most cases the person who is 'away' is tired and languid, or perhaps subject to fainting fits. The belief is that at certain times the Sidhe—or the 'gentry,' as they are often called—have control over the affected person, who has to take nocturnal journeys with them.[28]

Was this improbable yarn just a squib to sell newspapers or was it a touch of the blarney about people who never existed? On that score, the existence of the main characters can be confirmed in census reports. In 1860 Catherina Crow (rather than Crowe), age five, born in Iowa in 1855, was living in Jefferson Township with Andrew Crow, 55, Jane Crow, 40, (both born in Ireland), Martin, nineteen, Mary Ann, seventeen, Jenny, ten, and John, eight. In 1870 Kittie's sister Mary Ann, age 27, was living in Dubuque, Ward 3, with her husband James Hayes, teamster, and four children under the age of eight. Her parents were living in Center Township with three sons and 'Katy' age fourteen. By 1880 Andy/Andrew was 80 and described as a widower, but there was also another Jane in the household, age 21, described as 'wife,' who is more likely to have been daughter Jennie. Kittie/Katy/Catherina is nowhere to be found, having vanished from the record into marriage, death, a Fate Worse than Death, or, possibly, the world of the fairies. Her brother Martin was listed as 'idiotic' and 'insane,' and by 1910 was likely living in the St Joseph Sanatorium, an insane asylum.

Martin was briefly something of a celebrity when this story was reported in many Midwestern papers in 1894.

Dubuque, Ia., July 20. For 18 years Martin Crow has lain in the county jail awaiting an examination by the insane commissioners on the charge of insanity. To every grand jury visiting the jail during this time he has pleaded for release in vain. The commissioners finally decided to investigate his case with the idea of releasing him. On examination he was found to be insane on one point, insisting his father was not dead, and the commissioners decided to remove him to the Independence asylum.[29]

Perhaps Martin believed his father was not dead, but in Fairyland.

Although humans cannot fathom the motives of the fae, it is not recorded that those taken by the fairies were ever sent home for an altruistic reason such as saving Father from the gallows. The Good People were just not that good. While the notion of the fairies riding trains is a diverting one, the story is ambiguous when speaking of 'invisible to mortal eyes'. One pictures Kittie and her friends avoiding the yard bulls as they hopped freight trains around the country. We might theorize that Kittie fell pregnant or ran away with the help of a sweetheart or plausible procuress. If the story unfolded as told, she must have had help. A single calico dress would not have taken her far, unless she had pilfered the household allowance and the theft was kept quiet.

Another reading of this story is a sordid one. The word 'fairy' was a term used for prostitutes, as we see in *The Green Book, or, the Gentleman's Guide to New Orleans, Listing the Principal Maisons de Joie: Names of Madames, Angels, Nymphs, and Fairies, Color and Nationality*.[30] Did Kittie find herself leading a luxurious life as a soiled dove in a nearby town? Or had she eloped with that horror, a Protestant? Perhaps she had access to local gossip from clients or newspapers and returned home to clear up the matter of her disappearance. She could not stay; life was good with the 'fairies' and she would not want to risk her secret being exposed. The community was, as the articles note, full of citizens familiar with the Irish lore of fairies and abductions. Spinning such a story would be a face-saving gambit for everyone.

But what of the 'two queer-looking beings resembling men dressed in antiquated black costumes'? Did these 1880s Men in Black call themselves fairies? If the sister's story can be credited, they pulled off an Oliver Lerch-like disappearance in broad daylight. (Does 'in the air' mean they actually went up in the air?) This is where the pleasant logic of the prostitution/Protestant story breaks down. Oddly enough, there are earlier historic stories of Iowan Men in Black.[31]

The story is puzzling enough; the reprinting of the story a decade later is even more baffling. False, fantastical stories are quite common in the American papers of the nineteenth century. Strangely, at least to the modern mind, these tales frequently included the names of genuine individuals, often prominent citizens, perhaps to lend credence to the unlikely stories or perhaps simply to sell papers. Yet editors were sometimes sued or horsewhipped for printing libellous or defamatory pieces about renowned local personalities. Why did these prominent citizens not complain about their inclusion in stories involving superstition, monsters, ghosts, or a daughter taken by the fairies? There seems to be a missing subtext and it is frustrating to scholars using journalistic sources.

The obvious explanation is that the young woman ran away or was sent away to conceal a scandal or a pregnancy and a story was made up to account for her disappearance. 'Visiting an aunt in Chicago' would have been the more usual and credible excuse, but needs must when the Tuatha Dé Danann drives...

It is also conceivable that, given young Kittie's prior mystery illness and her brother's subsequent 'insanity' that she, too, was sent to an asylum because of mental illness or epilepsy. It may be that the death of Jane Crowe, Kittie's mother, who died in 1875, the year before Kittie disappeared, triggered the girl's flight from family drudgery. Whatever the enigmatic truth, perhaps a fairy tale, an Irish fairy tale following the well-worn paths of the Gentry, was the perfect solution.

As Peter Narvaez writes, 'Fairy explanations could be used by participants to mask actual deviant behaviours such as extreme tardiness, premarital sexual relations, infidelity, incest, child molestation, wife battering, and sexual assault. The possibility of concealing scandal through fairy alibis must be considered when approaching enigmatic narratives...'[32]

Andrew Crowe died in 1892. There is no mention of Kittie in his obituary. She might not have survived him or she might have been dead to him. Or she could have been considered as one of the departed, a kind of Schrodinger's fairy: dead, yet not-dead, in the twilight purgatory that was the Irish fairyland. She had returned once by the graces of the Good People; she could not return again.

17

FAIRY BREAD AND FAIRY SQUALLS[1]

Atlantic Canada by Simon Young

Introduction

Most of Canada has no fairy traditions, save for fragments of Amerindian lore.[2] However, a notable exception are the isolated coastal settlements out east, in New Brunswick, Nova Scotia, Prince Edward Island, Labrador, north-eastern Quebec and, above all, Newfoundland.[3] A story, collected in the 1980s in Nova Scotia had, for example, a young woman in love with a fairy or 'fallen angel'.[4] Earlier in the century a doctor from Labrador reported that on Belle Isle Strait 'fairies or devils' would try to wreck ships by appearing as bright lights on some haunted cliffs.[5] There is a recently recorded tale, meanwhile, from Newfoundland about the fairies pulling out a man's tongue, gouging out his left eye and removing his fingernails.[6] No wonder that misbehaving children were often told, in this province, 'the fairies will get you'...[7] Of course, Canadian fairies were not always so, well, diabolical: sometimes they limited themselves to more innocent sports, misleading folk in the woods or racing around in whirlwinds. But there is no question that these Maritime and Newfoundland and Labrador fairies were terrifying, even by the standards of their European *confrères*. This was possibly because of the Irish and Highland background of many of the settlers in the east; Ireland and the Scottish Highlands having, of course, a bigger share of frightening supernatural beings than England, another country that provided many settlers.

More remarkable than their malignity, though, is the way that these fairies hid so long and so artfully. By the time they emerge fully into our records, in the later twentieth century, they had been entrenched in small towns and villages, for perhaps two centuries. Yet you will be hard pressed to find records of them from before the 1960s. For example, there are two fine folklore collections from Nova Scotia in the 1930s. Yet one has no significant reference to fairies, while the other dedicates several pages to fairy tales from Scotland; there are only two short fairy stories about Nova Scotia itself.[8] Had the fairies almost vanished from Nova Scotia at this date? Probably not. There is a similar absence of mentions in folklore writing about Newfoundland from the pre-war period[9]: yet as we shall see fairylore was still thriving there in the later twentieth century. The suspicion is that fairies were, for folklore collectors or for the 'folk' themselves, a medieval hangover in the New World and hence an embarrassment. Most Canadians subscribed, instead, to the idea that this was virgin land, waiting to be bent to the will of the British Empire. Here is a description from the northern forests in 1842, set among the pines of Kipling's 'Recessional':

As to ghosts and spirits, they are totally banished from Canada. This is too much a matter-of-fact country for such supernaturals to visit. Here are there no historical associations—no legendary tales of those that came before us. Fancy would starve for lack of marvellous food to keep her alive in the backwoods. We have neither fay nor fairy, ghost nor boggle, satyr nor wood-nymph—our very forest disdain to shelter dryad or hamadryad. No naiad haunts the rushy margin of our lakes, or hallows with her presence our forest rills. No Druid claims our oaks; and, instead of poring with mysterious awe among our curious limestone rocks, that are often singularly grouped together, we refer them to the geologist, to exercise his skill in accounting for their appearance; instead of investing them with the solemn characters of ancient temples or heathen altars, we look upon them with the curious eye of natural philosophy alone. Even the Irish and Highlanders of the humblest class seem to lay aside their ancient superstitions on becoming denizens of the woods of Canada.[10]

It was not, of course, that there was no interest in fairies among Canadian readers: newspaper stories on fairylore and fairy books appeared as often in Canada as in Britain; fairies, also, appeared in Canadian plays and pantomimes.[11] However, these fairies were either the generic fairy of children's fiction or folklore fairies from Britain or Ireland. They were not the fairies of the Atlantic provinces. In fact, the only Canadian author who, in the 1800s, celebrated east coast fairy traditions was John Hunter Duvar. Duvar wrote a five-thousand word comic poem entitled the 'Emigration of the Fairies', describing how a family of English fairies were washed across the Atlantic on a lump of peat, arriving on Prince Edward Island, finding everything there 'upon a larger scale'. The poem ends with this verse:

> Thus have I told the true tale, as I find
> Writ in our annals, how the fairy folks,
> Unwitting driven by fate—fate is not blind —
> Now dance 'neath maples 'stead of English oaks,
> And how, obeying Colonization's law,
> The genial Fairies came to Canada.[12]

The poem, as this extract hints, has far more to tell us about attitudes to the settlement of the New World, than fairy traditions: 'Colonization's Law' is a gentler but, nevertheless, remorseless 'manifest destiny'. The poem does, though, presuppose nineteenth-century fairy beliefs in Prince Edward Island itself, something that, as we shall see, can also be glimpsed in other sources.

Fairy Evidence
There are scattered records from the Canadian Atlantic coast, which give us a sense of what we have lost. We have for example this Scottish-Canadian fairy legend from the years just before the First World War. The tale was collected in Scotland, but it includes Nova Scotia, the 'New Scotland' in Canada, in its unhappy coda.

> My grandmother, Catherine MacInnis, used to tell about a man named Lachlann, whom she knew, being in love with a fairy woman. The fairy woman made it a point to see Lachlann every night, and he being worn out with her began to fear her. Things got so bad at last that he decided to go to America to escape the fairy woman. As soon as the plan was fixed, and he was about to emigrate, women who were milking at sunset out in the meadows heard very audibly the fairy woman singing this song:
>   What will the brown-haired woman do
>   When Lachlann is on the billows?

Lachlann emigrated to Cape Breton, landing in Nova Scotia; and in his first letter home to his friends he stated that the same fairy woman was haunting him there.[13]

Another story, from 1902, is from Prince Edward Island. The island had an important number of Highland settlers, as, indeed, did much of the Maritimes. 'Some of them firmly believed in the existence of fairies. They believed that the power of wizards and witches to do mischief, far exceeded common belief.'[14] Perhaps Roderick, the hero of this anecdote, came from among nineteenth-century Highland settlers? Our author recalls, in any case, how Roderick, who had a reputation for supernatural powers, had invited his neighbours to a dance. At a certain point Roderick had vanished and the party-goers followed his footprints in the snow to where Roderick had started to run and then mysteriously disappeared, his footprints ending on the top of a fence. Roderick eventually returned four hours later and described what had happened to him.

> O... those cursed fairies have been after me again. They plague me incessantly. I cannot rid myself of them by any means. To-night, just as I was coming in, two of them seized me, compelled me to drop my lantern, and then took me off to some foreign land. I think it must have been across the Atlantic ocean, for I never saw so much water before. After hurrying me through many strange places they at last turned westward again: and crossing that vast ocean, one of them who seemed to be the leader asked if I would go with him the next time he came. I told him no, and all at once I was immersed in the billows beneath me; and each time I refused his request he ducked me in the briny ocean, and threatened me with many and more terrible punishments, until at length I was fain to give in, and tell him yes I would go again.[15]

This story is one of the very few to be handed down to us from Prince Edward Island. By the time serious folklore collecting had begun between and after the wars we only have anemic afterthoughts of a dying or dead fairy tradition. For example, one book on the supernatural beings of the island gives a single paragraph to fairies, with fairies plaiting horses' manes and fairy rings in the grass:[16] we are a long way from Roderick being chased through the drifts by swooping furies.

The best evidence for Atlantic Canadian fairies is unquestionably from Newfoundland. Several early Newfoundland newspapers have now been digitized and here and there, in the newsprint of a century or a century and a half ago, there are lived fairy stories.[17] Some of these stories are jokey in tone but still give us precious insights into how fairies were seen in the second half of the nineteenth century. For example, in 1863 a hunter warns his friend not to speak disrespectfully of the fairies: the friend does and they get lost.[18] In 1865 there is an account of a man, a Mr Lundy, who wished to hire a cart in Carbonear. It was dark when he arrived, though, and '[n]obody was bold enough to invade the dominion of the fairies and threats and entreaties were like in vain'.[19]

In St Johns, Newfoundland in 1881 three young women went for a walk in the city centre, only for one of the three to suddenly disappear. The two survivors 'began to blame the fairies' and were about to go home when they discovered their companion had fallen down a coal chute![20] It is a silly tale, but it is interesting that the fairies were an obvious cause for a missing woman, in the centre of the largest town on the island, and that the two companions, instead of looking for their friend, chose to beat a hasty retreat. Another story, from 1897, describes a missing pig that suddenly reappeared. How could this strange event be explained? The owner opined 'that either he or the pig must have been with the fairies'.[21] 'To be in' or 'to be with the fairies', meaning to be dreaming or absent, is a Newfoundland equivalent of the Irish 'to be away with the fairies'.

However, there are also more serious stories. In 1880, for instance, some Newfoundland fairies found themselves in court. A man had missed several days of work and had not been paid.

This was accounted for by the plaintiff, who contended that he left his home two hours before dawn for the purpose of going to work, and that all he remembered was seeing a funeral, when he lost his senses and was carried away by the fairies. A witness deposed that he discovered the plaintiff, three days afterwards, lying speechless on the ground. The defendant did not deny the allegation concerning the interference of the fairies, but submitted that the lost time should be made up.[22]

Romantics will be glad to learn that the man kidnapped by the fairies won his case.

Fairies kidnapping Newfoundlanders was evidently a relatively common event. Consider this instance from 1900:

A resident of this city, who is subject to extraordinary hallucinations, was the other night, as he seriously states himself, 'again carried off by fairies'. He left Water Street about 8 pm, having done his Xmas shopping and turned up Adelaide Street to go home, but, before he had reached New Gower Street, was surrounded by an army of fairies who hustled him along eastward. Though he passed hundreds of people, he could not see anyone until he reached Mount Carmel Cemetery. At this point he saw two men approaching and asked them with tears rolling down his cheeks to be kind enough to accompany him home. Having heard the man's story the good Samaritans saw him safely with his wife and family. Strange as these facts may appear, they are not the less true. But stranger still is the knowledge that the subject of these few lines is a steady, sober and industrious man, and in conversation expresses himself most intelligently, with sound, sensible remarks. Some time ago, before the cold weather set in, he was similarly afflicted, being led away in the Black Marsh Road directions, through bogs, marshes, rivers and heavy woods. On that occasion he was found by a farmer in an exhausted state. On the last occasion he barely had strength to reach home.[23]

One interesting point about this article is its treatment of the victim, who in most of the English-speaking world, had he appeared in a newspaper, would have been mocked. Yes, the writer states he was 'subject to extraordinary hallucinations' (habitually or the two kidnappings?), but he was also 'steady, sober and industrious'. Being kidnapped by fairies was not necessarily, then, in Newfoundland, a cause for a prolonged stay in an asylum.

Other evidence for fairies in Atlantic Canada comes from place-names. Sometimes place-names are related indirectly to fairies. So Fox Hole at Butlerville, Newfoundland is the place where the fairies keep stolen babies, and sometimes they can be heard crying.[24] At other times we have names with the word 'fairy' in them. One scholar has reported a dozen fairy names from Newfoundland including: Fairyland, Fairy Hill, Fairies' Marsh, Fairy Rock, the Fairy Grounds, Fairy Run, Fairy Path, Fairies Field,

Fairy Ridge and Fairy Break.[25] Other names are reported in the Maritimes. Nova Scotia, for example, has a Fairy Hill at Dartmouth[26] and a Fairy Hole on Kellys Mountain. Fairy holes in England (where the place-name originated) tend to be small caves[27]: the Nova Scotian Fairy Hole is on a New World scale with the entrance alone measuring some thirty feet; wider than many English fairy holes are deep. This impressive site was connected with an Amerindian god, Gluskap, and was called by the Mi'kmaq 'Gluska' bewi'gwom' (Gluskap's Wigwam). The Mi'kmaq believed that the cave was the gateway to a land of stone dwarfs: was this perhaps the inspiration for the English name?[28]

Newfoundland: A Fairy Melting Pot

The scattered evidence, gathered together in the previous paragraphs, are so many bread crumbs in the wood of fairy: they are difficult to follow and they lead, on their own, nowhere. However, a far more significant collection of fairy accounts, and the basis for the rest of the chapter, was made in Newfoundland in the later twentieth century. Beginning in the mid-1960s, Newfoundland's Memorial University gathered records of fairylore and experiences. These were collected, in the first instance, by two of the greatest folklorists of their generation, John Widdowson and Herbert Halpert; but, crucially, also by local students who would write reports on the beliefs and experiences of their own families and neighbours.[29] Memorial has, thanks to this happy alliance of teachers and students, one of the best fairy collections in the world; second only, in fact, to Ireland's remarkable fairy archives. Then, in the late 1980s, a gifted young American folklorist, Barbara Rieti, took this material and, with extensive field work of her own, wrote one of the best fairy books of the last century—*Strange Terrain* (published in 1991)—describing the fairies of Newfoundland, with many original reflections on storytelling and belief.[30]

Barbara Rieti encountered some familiar names for the fairies including: elves, good people, bad people, little people, lutins, leprechauns, devil's angels, and co-pixies (see the Dorset chapter).[31] But there were also many unusual forms, which are much more difficult to explain, including darbies, the little-johns, dalladadas, hollies, jackies, mickadenies and the dawnies.[32] One of these words is French, some have a Gaelic inspiration and some are English, for example, the archaic 'co-pixies'. However, even more confusing than the origin for this or that form is the sheer range. There is a long tradition of not saying the word 'fairies' (a word that irritates the fey) and of finding alternative names: e.g. 'the gentry' or 'the good neighbours'.[33] But, even taking this into account, there would be perhaps five or six names in an equivalent area of Ireland or Britain. Here we have more than a dozen. What does this range tell us? Well, Newfoundland was, put simply, a fairy melting pot. Here British, Irish and French colonists came together and settled in close proximity. Some brought fairy traditions with them, and some did not. In some areas fairy traditions took root, in some areas they failed to. Where fairy traditions took root they took on different characteristics depending on the mix of the community. For example, Barbara Rieti describes two close Newfoundland towns where the names and the character of the fairies varied: Avondale with a Gaelic Catholic history and Bishop's Cove that was British protestant in origins.[34]

Fairy traditions, naturally, came from different parts of the Old World. For example, there was the Newfoundland tradition of carrying bread to stop the fairies misleading you. Now being misled by the fairies is reported in many parts of Britain and Ireland, but the only area where bread is recorded as an antidote to fairy meddling was Devon, in south-western England. There were many settlers from the south-west of England in Atlantic Canada: it is very possible that they brought this custom with them. There are other traditions that do not sound English at all. There was, for instance, the idea of fairy paths, and the belief that it was unlucky to build on them: children born in houses constructed on fairy paths typically died or suffered from serious illnesses.[35] This is a tradition only reported in Ireland in modern times. It presumably crossed to Newfoundland with Irish settlers in the early 1800s. Another Gaelic-sounding fairy tradition is the 'fairy squall', a phrase still used today in Newfoundland, the notion that the fairies sent any sudden gusts of wind: in Ireland and Scotland there was the idea, indeed, that the fairies travelled in these gusts.[36] However, the word 'fairy squall' is not known in British or Irish sources and is probably a local adaptation of a Gaelic phrase.[37] References to fairies plaiting horses' manes, meanwhile, seem to cluster in French-speaking areas and such traditions were certainly known in France.[38]

When we look at fairies in Newfoundland we see, then, a *minestrone* of different traditions with ingredients coming from different parts of the Old World: fairy paths from Ireland, fairy plaiting from France, bread from south-west England…. Another striking feature of these ingredients, though, is their age. Take, here, the use of bread carried in the pocket to protect travellers. I noted above that this is a tradition associated with the south west of England. But the truth is that we have only two references—one certainly and one probably from Devon—and both of these are from the seventeenth century.[39] Nothing further is recorded from Britain in the eighteenth century: hardly surprising as very few fairy traditions are recorded in the 1700s. However, it is strange that nothing is recorded in the tens of thousands of words given over to south-western or, indeed, English folklore in the 1800s. The natural supposition would be that this bread-based tradition had died out in the intervening years. Yet in Newfoundland we have records of people carrying bread so as not to get lost in the 1960s. A custom, then, that was vanishing in Britain at the time of the Glorious Revolution was still being used in Newfoundland, three hundred years later, at the time of the Cuban Missile Crisis. Presumably early south-western settlers brought a dying tradition with them and it was revived in a land where being misled could mean death in the wilderness, as opposed to a wet and miserable night on a Devon moor.

There are also, it must be said, delightful Canadian touches to some of the stories. For instance, a well-known Irish and Scottish fairy story includes an attempt by a family to rescue a member kidnapped by the fairies from a cavalcade of fairy horses. The same story is told in Newfoundland, but family members have to drag their kidnapped brother from a sledge rather than from a horse.[40] Another tale has fairies in Northern Quebec—the tale is told by a Labrador man—saving a traveller who is lost in a blizzard by leading him to safety with chiming bells: the exact opposite of what European fairies do with their tunes and wiles, in, admittedly, less extreme weather conditions.[41] Back in Newfoundland one story has a man trying to fend off fairy attacks by carrying silver bells: unfortunately the bells are not 'real' silver so the fairies pounce.[42] I know of no European equivalent to this. But bells are carried in Canada to keep bears away… Canadian friends ridicule the idea, but is it possible that bear precautions and fairylore have got mixed up here?

The Last Traditional Fairies?

Another important point about the fairy melting pot on the east coast of Canada and particularly in Newfoundland was the liveliness and strength of fairy belief there. Folklorists are reluctant to measure the depth of fairy beliefs among different populations. They note that storytellers are, forever, talking about the death or the disappearance of the fairies[43]: indeed, one of the best attested fairy tales describes the fairies leaving a given corner of the land after centuries of residence, observed by a stunned human witness.[44] Yet fairies are stubbornly present, often decades or generations after they were supposed to have disappeared. Katharine Briggs referred, with good reason, to fairies as 'the Vanishing People', but an even better phrase might be 'Flickering Folk'. To pronounce the fairies dead on the basis of a fairy flit tale is the equivalent of chopping down an oak because its leaves turn brown. A much better way to judge the extent to which fairies are present in the life of a given population is to look at the depth of fairylore.

In what follows, I am going to offer for Newfoundland (the area with the best folklore accounts) a fairy barometer: a simple 1-3 scale for fairylore. Level one is that of *sensing* fairies: fairies are seen dancing, fairies are heard playing music, we even have one case where fairies are smelt.[45] Level two is *low level interaction* without lasting consequences for humans. Here the witness might be misled or their horse might be rode by the fairies at night or the fairies might steal food. The third level is *intense interaction* with fairies, with lasting consequences for any humans involved. This interaction includes, humans marrying fairies, humans being kidnapped or 'changed', magical contracts in which fairies give a sorcerer's powers to humans, or servile relations in which fairies do farm or house work. In areas with weak fairy traditions, for example, south-eastern England in the nineteenth century, only level one experiences are reported. In areas with intermediate fairy traditions, like, say, Devon in the 1800s, levels one and two will feature. Then, in areas with strong fairy traditions all three levels will appear. An example here might be Ireland in the same period, where changed children were reported in newspapers, and where fairy doctors trafficked with 'the good people' for occult powers.[46]

How does Newfoundland score on this scale in the data harvested from the 1960s to the early 1990s? In what follows I will limit myself to witnesses who believed that these experiences had happened to them. This means that, in the case of elderly witnesses, we are in a band of time stretching back to the First World War. In this arc of time, level one was certainly reached and fairies were seen and sometimes heard. There was, for example, a sighting reported by three Newfoundland brothers of fairy women singing the first verse of Abide by Me. (My guess would be that the brothers, the Kelloways, had stumbled upon a small group of eccentric travellers…: one of the Kelloways, remembering his childhood experience, commented that the fairies were 'as big as the wife there but not quite so fat').[47] Some fairies were reported as being malovelent-looking: like two women, dressed in black, seen carrying buckets of water.[48] Some were, instead, joyous like the colourfully-dressed women spotted running across a barren common.[49] Some were carrying on, instead, like their human neighbours: two little girls out berry picking turned to see six fairies doing exactly the same thing.[50]

There were also level two experiences. Men and women found evidence of fairies in their stables: a classic proof here is that the manes of horses had been plaited as if by minute hands[51]; or there was the man who got caught in a violent fairy squall.[52] Much more numerous are the Newfoundlanders who have been misled by fairies when out in the woods. In itself getting lost is a normal part of travelling through wilderness areas, particularly while hunting or berry picking. However, many of these reports have unusual features. For example, the young girls running into trees barring their way on a familiar road[53]; or people travelling impossible distances in short times ('how I got there I don't know, I guess I got lifted up and brought down').[54] Of course, there are many possible explanations for these kinds of experiences and not all involve fairies: neurological episodes, freak meteorological conditions and alcohol might also feature.[55] But what matters is that many of those who talked about being led astray did so with reference to the fairies and were still doing so in the late 1980s.

Level three experiences—strong interaction between fairies and humans—are more difficult to come by in post-war Newfoundland, but they are there. There are stories of kidnapped human beings, including one from the late 1960s: 'my cousin's mother disappeared into the hills one afternoon and she was never seen again. Many of the old people… said that the fairies took her'.[56] There are many stories of humans being changed, but most of these are remembered, in fantastic terms, from the late nineteenth or early twentieth century. However, one adolescent recounted how his uncle and aunt received a changeling in 1968![57] A much better attested form of fairy interaction is the 'fairy blast', where the fairies injure someone who has broken their rules. In 1972, for example, one collector had talked with a woman who had been hurt by fairies before the war: '[t]he fairies did it, don't you fool yourself',[58] while Barbara Rieti interviewed another woman in the late 1980s who had, as a teen, been fairy whipped.[59]

A final level-three fairy experience is absent from contemporary Newfoundland accounts. Those claiming to traffic magic favours with the fairies. From the Middle Ages we have records of men and women who used friendships with the fairies, to hurt and to heal their neighbours: fairies often took on the role of, in witchcraft terms, 'familiars'.[60] There are few people matching this description in England after 1600, and none after about 1700. In Wales and Scotland such figures vanish after 1800, and in Ireland shortly after 1900. Yet, in Newfoundland they were still operating in the early twentieth century. In St John's, for example, there was one Stuart Taylor 'known to the small boys as the 'fairy man' or 'changeling', who played incessantly on a tin whistle'. Stuart Taylor seems to have been mentally unbalanced and a figure of fun and fear as much as of wizardry.[61] Others took more conscious efforts to cultivate the fairies in public. One contemporary of Taylor, Dr. Richard Dunn, a Newfoundland quack, was famous for giving fairies a ride on his carriage, as he went around the island.[62] Mr Kelly from Holyrood was, meanwhile, a seventh son of a seventh son, who was called into deal brutally with changed children.[63]

On this evidence Newfoundland scored, in the period 1960-1990, perhaps two and a half out of three on the fairy scale. Witnesses had seen fairies; there had been light interaction; and there were some memories of more serious and sometimes more deadly experiences with the 'good folk'. It is easy to nod at this information and then move on. But this score needs to be put in a wider context. It is doubtful that, in the late 1960s, there was any area of England or Wales that could reach two on the scale; and only a few regions of Ireland and Scotland.[64] Yet Newfoundland was, at the same date, hovering between two and three. There is a case to be made, in fact, that Newfoundland was the area in the Anglo-Saxon or Celtic world where fairylore was best preserved by the late twentieth century. Indeed, the only area in the north Atlantic that could have put up a claim for comparable levels of fairy belief at this date was Iceland.

Why was it that Newfoundland fairylore proved so persistent? It is true, first, that Newfoundland is relatively isolated: and it is certainly true that Newfoundlanders are visited by fewer tourists than other fairy strongholds like the Hebrides or the west of Ireland. But Newfoundlanders were and are far travelled: whether we are thinking of early Newfoundlanders heading for work in New England; or the cod fishers passing up and down the Great Banks. Another factor is perhaps the dangerous landscapes that Newfoundlanders have to work and travel in: fairies are often the personification of the wilds. Though this begs the question why other North American regions with perilous landscapes did not attract their own fairy populations: where, for instance, are the fairies of Alaska?[65] A final factor is surely the lack of scholarly interest in Canadian fairies before the 1960s: the stories were told quietly, without any sense that they were worth recording. The only reason we have such good records, after all, is because of the happy quirk that Memorial University invested in folklore and that collectors went out with notebooks and tape-recorders. This begs the question of how strong fairy belief was and, indeed, *is* in nearby regions, which did not benefit from the same level of attention: Labrador, North Eastern Quebec or northern Nova Scotia, say.

Fairies Talk

1 Thomas Crofton Croker, *Fairy Legends and Traditions of the South of Ireland*, 3 vols. (London, 1825-1828), III, xiii-xiv.
2 Anon, 'Pallasgrean Petty Sessions', Monday', *Freeman's Journal and Daily Commercial Advertiser* (4 Jan 1838), 4 excerpted from the *Limerick Star*.
3 Anon, 'The Tipperary Witch', *The Spectator* (1864), 1067-1068; Anon, 'Witchcraft in Carrick-on-Suir', *Waterford Mail*, 12 Sep 1864, 2.
4 Angela Bourke, *The Burning of Bridget Cleary: A True Story* (London, 2006).
5 Richard Green, *Elf Queens and Holy Friars: Fairy Beliefs and the Medieval Church* (Philadelphia, 2017), 5.
6 John Aubrey, *Three Prose Works* (Fontwell, 1972), 196.
7 5, 5: 'but till 'tis one o clock/ Our dance of custom round about the oak/ Of Herne the Hunter, let us not forget.'
8 Marjorie Johnson, *Seeing Fairies: From the Lost Archives of the Fairy Investigation Society* (San Antonio, 2014), 128.
9 Elise Innes, *The Elfin Oak of Kensington Gardens* (London, 1930).
10 Johnson, *Seeing Fairies*, 35.
11 Katharine Briggs, *The Fairies in Tradition and Literature* (London, 2002 [1967]), 157.
12 Fairy Census: 'England (London) Female; 1980s* ['1990s']; 21-30; in woodland; with several other people, some of whom shared my experience; 3 am-6 am; two to ten minutes; never or almost never has a supernatural experience.'
13 Johnson, *Seeing Fairies*, 41.
14 Chapter on Yorkshire.
15 Chapter on Atlantic Canada.
16 Chapter on Devon.
17 Chapter on Irish America.
18 Chapter on Cumbria.
19 The data from almost 500 of these sightings has now been processed and will be released on Simon Young's academia.eu site in January 2018. For further sightings fairyist.com/survey/.
20 Fairy Census: 'England (London).Chapter on Worcestershire.
21 Fairy Census: 'England (London).'Ireland (Co. Dublin). Male; 1990s; 21-30; in open land (fields etc); with one other person who shared my experience; 9 pm-12 am; one to two minutes; never or almost never has supernatural experiences'.
22 'US (Texas). Female; 1970s; 0-10; in woodland; on my own; can't remember time; many hours; regular supernatural experiences.'

{1} *Fairy Queens and Pharisees / Sussex by Jacqueline Simpson*

1 Annabel Gregory, 'Witchcraft, Politics and "Good Neighbourhood" in Seventeenth-Century Rye', *Past and Present*

133 (1991), 33-66. See also Annabel Gregory, *Rye Spirits: Faith, Faction and Fairies in a Seventeenth Century English Town* (London, 2013). See Rye Corporation MSS 13/25.
2 Diane Purkiss, *Troublesome Things* (London, 2000), 116-23.
3 G. Slade Butler, 'Appearance of Spirits in Sussex', *Sussex Archaeological Collections* 14 (1862), 25-34. See Harleian MSS 358, art. 47, fol. 188.
4 Gregory, 'Witchcraft', 36; Butler's version merely says (p. 28) that 'then she looked and they were gone'.
5 Gregory, 'Witchcraft', 45.
6 Emma Wilby, *Cunning Folk and Familiar Spirits* (Brighton, 2005), 17.
7 Purkiss, *Troublesome Things*, 24-8.
8 Anon, *The Brideling, Sadling and Ryding of a rich Churle in Hampshire*, cited in *The Oxford Book of the Supernatural*, ed. D. J. Enright (Oxford, 1994), 491-2; cf. Wilby, *Cunning Folk*, 24.
9 Purkiss, *Troublesome Things*, 118.
10 Gregory, 'Witchcraft', 46.
11 Reported in Allan Cunningham's 'Life of Blake' in his *Lives of the Most Eminent Painters, Sculptors and Architects* (London, 1830), vol. 2, 142-79; and in Alexander Gilchrist, *The Life of William Blake* (London, 1880), 160 1.
12 Charlotte Latham, 'Some West Sussex Superstitions Lingering in 1868', *Folk-Lore Record* 1 (1878), 1-67 at 28.
13 M. A. Lower, *Contributions to Literature: Historical, Antiquarian, and Metrical* (London, 1854), 158-63.
14 Lower, *Contributions to Literature*, 160-1.
15 W. D. Parish, *Dictionary of Sussex Dialect* (Lewes, 1875), 41.
16 Latham, 'Some West Sussex Superstitions', 28-9.
17 Arthur Becket, *The Spirit of the Downs* (London, 1909), 283.
18 ML 7005, 'The Heavy Load', Reimund Kvideland and Hemming K. Sehmsdorf, *Scandinavian Folk Belief and Legend* (Minneapolis 1988), 240-1.
19 *Oxford English Dictionary*.
20 *Place Names of Sussex*, 214, 233, 203, 308, 387, 415. See also H. C. P. Smaill, 'Puck in Sussex Place-Names', *Sussex County Magazine* 14 (1940), 369.
21 ML 7005, 'The Heavy Load', 240-1.
22 A. A. Evans, 'A Countryman's Diary', *Sussex County Magazine* 14 (1940), 313-14.
23 Latham, 'Some West Sussex Superstitions', 29.
24 L. N. Candlin, 'Sussex Sprites and Goblins', *Sussex County Magazine* 17 (1943), 97.
25 ML7015 in R. Th. Christensen's catalogue, and F381.3 in the AT motif index.

{2} *Pucks and Lights / Worcestershire by Pollyanna Jones*

Further Reading
Jabez Allies, *On the Ancient British, Roman, and Saxon Antiquities and Folk-lore of Worcestershire* (London, 1852)
Roy Palmer, *The Folklore of Hereford & Worcester,* (Hereford, 1992)
1 Katharine Briggs, *A Dictionary of Fairies* (London, 2011), 336-7.
2 Jabez Allies, *On the Ancient British, Roman, and Saxon Antiquities and Folk-lore of Worcestershire* (London, 1852), 308, 338, 340, 380, and 424.
3 *Ibid.,* 409.
4 *Ibid.,* 418.
5 Jabez Allies, *Observations on certain curious indentations in the old red sandstone of Worcestershire and Herefordshire: considered as the tracks of antediluvian animals: and the objections made to such an hypothesis refuted* (London, 1846), 55-58.
6 Allies, *On the Ancient*, 410.
7 Personal Communication 2003, C. Jones and D. Partington. Consider also this sighting: "I was driving down the dual carriageway towards Bromsgrove (A448) and had just reached the spot by the railway bridge, just past Finstall. There was a glowing white mist on the bank near the bridge on the side of the road. I saw it as I was driving towards it and wondered what it was. It didn't appear to move, and was shaped like a large puff of smoke. It was dark, on a winter's night, and it had been a rainy day, although it wasn't raining on the night. I saw something similar a few years later on Hewell Lane (B4096) near Burcot, driving from the Tardebigge direction." Personal communication, T. Hughes, 1997. Note that the locations of the Burcot and Bromsgrove *ignis fatuus* are only 1.5 miles apart, as the crow flies. Whilst the land is no longer marshland, there are several pools in the area which consist mostly of fields and woodland.
8 Allies, *On the Ancient*, 435-6; J. O. Halliwell, *Fairy Mythology of Shakespeare* (London, 1845), 200.
9 Briggs, *Dictionary*, 222-3; Bruce Dickens, 'Yorkshire Hobs', *Transaction of the Yorkshire Dialect Society* 7 (1942), 9-23.
10 Allies, *On the Ancient*, passim but particularly 413.
11 Roy Palmer, *The Folklore of Hereford & Worcester* (Almeley, 1992), 107; Andrew Morton, *Tolkien's Bag End* (Studley, 2009), 24-5.
12 Act 2, 1.
13 T. F. Dyer, *Folk-lore of Shakespeare* (New York, 1884), 22-3, 88-90.
14 Wirt Sykes, *British Goblins* (London, 1880), 20-4.
15 Allies, *On the Ancient*, 448.
16 *Ibid.,* 418.
17 *Ibid.,* 204-5.
18 Local superstition, passed down orally among children. Fairly common to this

day.

19 For example, Whitlenge Gardens, Halesowen, Worc. This is a modern phenomenon: fairy doors are sold at craft fairs and in craft shops and some end up on trees in the woods.

20 bl.uk/onlinegallery/onlineex/illmanus/h arlmanucoll/ m/011hrl000000055u00001000.html (Accessed 1 December 2016)

21 Alaric Hall, 'Getting Shot of Elves: Healing, Witchcraft and Fairies in the Scottish Witchcraft Trials', Folklore 116 (2005), 19-36.

22 Palmer, Folklore, 125.

23 This paragraph is based on personal communications from Val Herlihy and her friends recorded 1995-1997. They had learnt these traditions from their own parents in the early twentieth century.

24 Personal communications from Val Herlihy and her friends recorded 1995-1997, with Palmer, Folklore, 125.

25 Allies, On the Ancient, 418.

26 See, for example, the chapter on Cumbria or on Sussex.

27 Allies, On the Ancient, 308.

28 Ibid., 308.

29 John Lindow, Trolls: An Unnatural History (London, 2014), 53-4.

30 Allies, On the Ancient, 459.

31 Graham Seal, Outlaw Heroes in Myth and History (London, 2011), 38.

32 Cassandra Eason, "The Wild Hunt" cassandraeason.com/folklore_legend/the-wild-hunt.htm (Accessed 1 December 2016)

33 Palmer, Folklore, 132.

34 Personal communication, August 2006, the day after the sighting.

{3} Pixies and Pixy Rocks / Devon by Mark Norman and Jo Hickey-Hall

1 In the old West Country dialect it was common for pairs of letters to be transposed. For example, in the local dialect you would 'aks' a question rather than 'ask'; hence piskey instead of pixie. Piskie is still very common in Devon.

2 Theo Brown, Devon Ghosts (Norwich, 1982), 129.

3 Carole G. Silver, Strange and Secret Peoples (Oxford, 1999), 48-9.

4 J. Jones, 'Description of a Cavern Near Chudleigh in Devonshire', The Philosophical Magazine 39 (1812), 161-4 at 164.

5 Lady Rosalind Northcote, 'Devonshire Folklore', Folklore 11 (1900), 212-17 at 213: Northcote says that 'toes' may have been 'toads'!

6 Mrs Bray, A Peep at the Pixies (London, 1854), 149.

7 Nigel Sadler, Ottery St Mary Through Time (Stroud, 2013), 43.

8 Ibid., 44.

9 Simon Young, 'Pixy-Led in the South West', Transactions of the Devonshire Association 148 (2016), 311-336 at 320-321.

10 A View of Devonshire in MDCXXX with a Pedigree of Most of its Gentry (Exeter, 1845), 433.

11 G. Pycroft, 'Devonshire Folklore', The Western Antiquary 3 (1884), 28-29, 37-38 at 28: this was allegedly extracted from two numbers of the Weekly Mercury.

12 Anna Eliza Bray, A description of the part of Devonshire bordering on the Tamar and the Tavy; its natural history, manners, customs, superstitions, scenery, antiquities, biography of eminent persons etc. in a series of letters to Robert Southey, Esq., III vols. (London, 1836), III, 171.

13 Jeremy Harte, Explore Fairy Traditions (Avebury, 2004), 74, paraphrasing Bray. While these types of folklore were frequent for the era, the disciplinarian fairy acting as a stick to lazy servants had its original roots in the tales of 'Robin-good-fellow' and Charles Perrault's much loved French peasant folk tales, such as Cinderella and Sleeping Beauty. See further Diane Purkiss, Troublesome things: A History of Fairies and Fairy Stories (London, 2000), 165.

14 William Crossing, Tales of the Dartmoor Pixies: Glimpses of Elfin Haunts and Antics (London, 1890), iii.

15 Crossing, Tales, 71-3.

16 Ibid., 52-6.

17 Ibid., 36; Harte, Explore, 48.

18 Sir John Bowring, 'Devonian Folk-lore Illustrated', Report and Transactions: The Devonshire Association for the Advancement of Science, Literature and Art 2 (1868), 70-85 at 77-8.

19 Quoted in Charles W. Wood, The Argosy 58 (1894), 413.

20 Bowring, 'Devonian Folk-lore Illustrated', 79-80.

21 A.S. Hurd, 'Dartmoor: The Highlands of Devonshire' The Windsor Magazine: an illustrated monthly for men and women (Dec 1996), Vol. 5, 740-47.

22 G.M. Herbert, 'Pixies', Devonshire Association for the Advancement of Science, Literature and Art. (Barnstaple, July 1867) (London), Vol. 2 Part 1, 80.

23 Sir Arthur Conan Doyle, The Coming of the Fairies (London, 1921), 130-31.

24 Daniel Codd, Paranormal Devon (Stroud, 2013), 124, citing Morning Post (19 Nov 1930).

25 Joyce Chadwick, 'Fairies are not Dead', John O'London Weekly (21 Mar 1936), 986.

26 Codd, Devon, 124, undated news report.

27 D.A. Macmanus, Irish Earth Folk (New York, 1959), 38-40.

28 Ruth St Leger-Gordon, The Witchcraft and Folklore of Dartmoor (Stroud, 1983), 23-24.

29 Marjorie T. Johnson, Seeing Fairies (San Antonio, 2014), 43.

30 Katharine Briggs, The Fairies in Tradition and Literature (London, 2002), 164-5, citing Ruth Tongue's collecting.

31 Pers. Comm. 26 February 2016.

32 Sarah Hewett, Nummits and crummits: Devonshire customs, characteristics, and folk-lore (London, 1900), 38.

33 Diana Mullis, West Country Faerie (Ilkley, 2005); Pers. Comm. 16 July 2016.

34 M.A. Howard, The Book of Faerie (Taunton, 2014), 30.

{4} Fairy Magic and the Cottingley Photographs / Yorkshire by Richard Sugg

1 Richard Sugg, A Century of Supernatural Stories (CreateSpace, 2015), 205-207.

2 Sugg, Century, 199-200.

3 William Henderson, Notes on the Folklore of the Northern Counties (London, 1879), 274, n.12.

4 'Occasional Notes', The Cornishman (23 April 1896).

5 'Record Shows Death by Frying Pan', BBC News, 30 Nov 2006 news.bbc.co.uk/1/hi/england/cumbria/6157611.stm

6 Forty Years in a Moorland Parish: Reminiscences and Researches in Danby and Cleveland (London, 1891), 52.

7 Examples of Printed Folk-lore concerning the North Riding of Yorkshire, York and the Ainsty, ed. E. Gutch (London, 1901), 131.

8 Examples of Printed Folk-lore, 130.

9 Mr T. London, Leeds Mercury (2 Oct 1886). The hill was in fact an ancient burial mound, as was revealed when the landowner, Lady Frankland Russell, had it excavated in August 1855.

10 The common 'hob' (as in 'hobgoblin') is a shortform of 'robert'; gryma an Anglo-Saxon word for 'goblin' or 'demon'; and skratti an Old Icelandic word meaning 'wizard', 'goblin', or 'monster'.

11 Richard Blakeborough, Wit, Character, Folklore & Customs of the North Riding of Yorkshire (London, 1898), 143.

12 Wit, Character, Folklore, 142.

13 J. Cocksedge, 'Local Notes and Queries', Leeds Mercury (11 Oct 1884).

14 Forty Years, 52-54.

15 Charles C. Smith, 'Fairies at Ilkley Wells', The Folk-Lore Record 1 (1878), 229-231, at 229-231. For further discussion and a more detailed account of the sighting, see: Simon Young, 'Three Notes on West Yorkshire Fairies', Folklore 123 (2012), 223-230, at 225-227.

16 Marjorie T. Johnson, Seeing Fairies (San Antonio: Anomalist Books, 2014).

17 Coming of the Fairies, 12, 57, 21; 'Dundee Lecturer and Existence of Fairies', Dundee Courier and Argus (1 Feb 1921).

18 'Conan Doyle's Latest', Daily Mail (10 April 1923); Case of the Cottingley Fairies, 35.

19 'Dundee Lecturer and Existence of Fairies', Dundee Courier and Argus (1

February 1921).

20 *Coming of the Fairies*, 50-51.

21 *Westminster Gazette* (12 Jan 1921), cited in *Coming of the Fairies*, 69.

22 Cf. *Case of the Cottingley Fairies*, 27 (though this wrongly gives her age as seventeen).

23 *Coming of the Fairies*, 50; first reproduced in *The Strand*, Nov-Dec 1920.

24 David Hewson, 'Secrets of Two Famous Hoaxers', *The Times* (4 April 1983).

25 Steve Fairclough, 'Fairtyale Ending [sic] for the Fantasy Photographs that Fooled Generations', *The Times* (8 October 1998).

26 Hewson, *The Times* (18 March 1983); *Case of the Cottingley Fairies*, 142.

27 *Case of the Cottingley Fairies*, 132.

28 *Case of the Cottingley Fairies*, 147; Hewson, *The Times* (4 April 1983).

29 *Case of the Cottingley Fairies*, 56, 17-18.

30 *Case of the Cottingley Fairies*, 171.

31 *Case of the Cottingley Fairies*, 52.

32 'Fairies, Folklore and Forteana', *Fortean Times* 356 (Aug 2017), 27.

33 David Hewson, 'Cottingley Fairies a Fake, Woman Says', *The Times* (18 March 1983).

34 Elsie was born 19 July 1901. If she was actually sixteen when the first photograph was taken, then that fateful day must have been either 21 or 28 July—the only two July Saturdays after her sixteenth birthday, on Thursday 19 July.

35 Steve Fairclough, 'Fairtyale Ending [sic] for the Fantasy Photographs that Fooled Generations' *The Times* (8 October 1998).

36 *Case of the Cottingley Fairies*, 169.

37 Mark Branagan, Steven Jones, *Daily Mirror* (15 Jan 2017).

38 *Case of the Cottingley Fairies*, 24.

39 *Case of the Cottingley Fairies*, 169. The image, by Claude A. Shepperton, was from *Princess Mary's Gift Book*.

{5} *Fairy Barrows and Cunning Folk / Dorset by Jeremy Harte*

1 S 508 (dated 946) in the Electronic Sawyer, esawyer.org.uk/ (Accessed 2016).

2 David Mills, *The Place-Names of Dorset*, English Place-Name Society 52, 53, 59/60 & 86-7, 1977-2010), 1.243.

3 *Ibid*, 1.185.

4 *Calendar of the Charter Rolls* (HMSO, 1903-27) 2.243; *The Dorset Lay Subsidy Roll of 1327* (Dorset Record Soc. 6, 1980) 77, 80, 82, 94.

5 Mills, *Place-Names of Dorset*, 3.207 (*ersc*), 3.100 (*hæg*), 1.192, 214, 328 (*pytt*), 4.249 (*wella*), 1.80 (*mersc*), 3.54, 98 (*mōr*), 1.38, 4.205, 386 (*lacu*), 3.149 (*lane*), 1.185 (*beorg*), 1.49 (*stān*).

6 John Gover, Allen Mawer and Frank Stenton, *The Place-Names of Wiltshire* (English Place-Name Society 16, 1939), 465.

7 John Hutchins, *The History and Antiquities of Dorset*, 1st edition (London, 1774), 1.217.

8 Mills, *Place-Names of Dorset*, 1.272.

9 Albert Hugh Smith, *The Place-Names of Gloucestershire* (English Place-Name Society 38-41, 1964-5) 3.64; Gover, Mawer and Stenton, *Place-Names of Wiltshire*, 495; Aileen M. Armstrong *et al*, *The Place-Names of Cumberland* (English Place-Name Society 20-22, 1950-2), 1.lxxv.

10 Mills, *Place-Names of Dorset*, 4.35.

11 Except in Shropshire, which has several local names with *goblin*: H.D.G. Foxall, *Shropshire Field-Names* (Shropshire Arch. Soc., 1980), 67.

12 Mills, *Place-Names of Dorset*, 3.225.

13 There is a map in Sarah Semple, *Perceptions of the Prehistoric in Anglo-Saxon England* (Oxford, 2013), 180-1.

14 *Pyrs* appears once in Dorset (Mills, *Place-Names of Dorset*, 1.238) apparently with the sense of 'giant' rather than 'fairy' as it is compounded with *dic*, an element often associated with *eoten*, 'giant'.

15 *The Examination of John Walsh* 1566, ed. G.J. Davies, *Touchyng Witchcrafte and Sorcerye* (Dorset Record Soc 9, 1985), 54-67 at 62.

16 Keith Thomas, *Religion and the Decline of Magic* (London, 1971), 26, 317, 727.

17 Cecil l'Estrange Ewen, *Witchcraft and Demonianism* (London, 1933), 378.

18 A map of c.1791 in the Ilchester papers at the Dorset Record Office; the barrow is at SY 583.864.

19 Mills, *Place-Names of Dorset*, 1.28, 3.226. There is also a Grimbury Marsh in the neighbourhood of Christchurch at SZ 167.916, according to a supplement published by Dorset Environmental Records Centre in 1998 to their gazetteer of Dorset place-names.

20 Mills, *Place-Names of Dorset*, 1.278, 3.96, 4.33, 221.

21 Charles Warne, *Celtic Tumuli of Dorset* (London, 1866), 1.

22 H. St George Gray, 'Report on the Wick Barrow excavations', *Proc. of the Somerset Nat. Hist. & Arch. Soc* 54 (1908), 1-77 at 76.

23 Elizabeth Otter, *A Southwell Maid's Diary* (Dorland, 1930), 32. Neddyfield is the Nether Field of the old strip system; another instance of fairies haunting arable land.

24 For Cadbury, see J.A. Bennett, 'Camelot', *Proc. of the Somerset Nat. Hist. & Arch. Soc* 36 (1890), 1-19; for Withypool, F.J. Snell, *A Book of Exmoor* (London, 1903), 254. Katharine Briggs discusses the type: *A Dictionary of Fairies* (Harmondsworth, 1976), 95.

25 John Hutchins, *The History and Antiquities of Dorset*, 3rd edition (London, 1861-73), 2.653; the story is not found in earlier editions.

26 *The Antiquary* 19 (1889), 73.

27 Richard Warner, *Topographical Remarks,*

Relating to the South-Western Parts of Hampshire (London, 1793), 2.201.

28 Kingsley Palmer, *Oral Folk-Tales of Wessex* (Newton Abbot, 1973), 46. The tale type is ML 7060.

29 *The Apophthegmes of Erasmus, translated into English by N. Udall*, ed. Edwin Johnston (Boston, 1877), no. 99; Bart van Es, *Shakespeare in Company* (Oxford, 2013), 167.

30 Francis Grose, *A Provincial Glossary* (London, 1787), *s.v.*

31 John R. Wise, *The New Forest: Its History and its Scenery* (London, 1863), 175.

32 John Brand, *Observations on the Popular Antiquities of Great Britain*, ed. Henry Ellis (London, 1893), 2.513.

33 Mills, *Place-Names of Dorset*, 1.94.

34 Thomas Westcote, *View of Devon* (Exeter, 1845), 433.

35 Lucy Franklin in *Medieval Devon and Cornwall*, ed. Sam Turner (Macclesfield, 2006), 144-61 at 154; Jack Hurley, *Legends of Exmoor* (Dulverton, 1973), 32.

36 'Songs of the Pixies', in *The Collected Works of Samuel Taylor Coleridge: Poetical Works I*, ed. J.C.C. Mays (Princeton, 2001), 106-8.

37 Phil Quinn, 'A toast to the recently departed fairy faith in the Bristol region', *3rd Stone* 26 (1997), 21-3.

38 William Barnes, *Poems of Rural Life in the Dorset Dialect* (London, 1844), 363-4.

39 *Dorset Year Book* 1949-50, 41.

40 Thomas Hardy, *Return of the Native* (1878), chapter 3; *Mayor of Casterbridge* (1886), chapter 44.

41 George Roberts, *The History and Antiquities of the Borough of Lyme Regis* (London, 1834), 252.

42 Barbara Rieti, '"The blast" in Newfoundland fairy tradition', in *The Good People*, ed. Peter Narvaez (Lexington, 1991), 284-97.

43 William Barnes, *Poems*, ed. Bernard Jones (Arundel, 1962), 1.133.

44 Tony Hunt, *Plant Names of Medieval England* (Woodbridge, 1989) 87.

45 William Barnes, *Poems, loc cit*.

46 There is a hint here of the 'the King of France's cellar' tale-type, discussed by Briggs, *Dictionary of Fairies*, 149, which also features the predicament of someone who has been drinking with the fairies and cannot escape. But Barnes could have picked this up from written sources, not Dorset tradition.

47 Henry Moule, 'Dorset folk-lore', *Folk-Lore Journal* 6 (1888), 115-9 at 116.

48 J.S. Udal, 'Dorsetshire folk-speech and superstitions relating to natural history', *Proc. of the Dorset Nat. Hist. & Arch. Soc.* 10 (1899), 19-46 at 23-4.

49 A good firsthand account can be found in H. Colley March, 'Dorset folklore collected in 1897: I', *Folk-Lore* 10 (1899), 478-489 at 483.

50 George Roberts, *The Social History of the Southern Counties of England* (London, 1856), 530.

51 T. Worthington, *Chideock: Historical and Other Notes* (Bridport, 1880), a copy annotated by C.V. Goddard, in Dorset County Museum.

52 E.J. Begg, 'Cases of witchcraft in Dorsetshire', *Folk-Lore* 52 (1941), 70-2.

53 Melissa Harrington spoke on elfknots at the 2013 annual conference of the Folklore Society.

54 Thomas Hardy, *The Woodlanders* (1887), chapter 28.

55 *The Complete Poems of Thomas Hardy*, ed. James Gibson (London, 1978), 814 (no. 796); it was originally published in 1925.

56 John Symonds Udal, *Dorsetshire Folk-Lore* (Hertford, 1922), 261, 330.

57 Samuel Menefee, 'Circling as an entrance to the Otherworld', *Folklore* 96 (1985), 3-20.

58 Leonard Tatchell, *The Heritage of Purbeck* (Dorchester, 1954), 151; he has another fairy pool at 63.

59 Palmer, *Oral Folk-Tales*, 120.

60 Aubrey L. Parke, 'The folklore of Sixpenny Handley, Dorset', *Folklore* 73/4 (1962-3), 481-7 at 482.

61 Arthur Conan Doyle, *The Coming of the Fairies* (London, 1922), 134-5.

62 Ralph Wightman, *Portrait of Dorset* (London, 1965), 169; *Evening Echo Holiday Guide* July 1977.

63 Llewellyn Powys, *Dorset Essays* (London, 1935), 115-21.

64 Initially in Sean Street, *Tales of Old Dorset* (Newbury, 1992), 50-3.

65 Robert J. Newland, *Dark Dorset: Fairies* (Privately, 2006). The novelties appear at 19, 20, 21, 27, 33-4, 52, 53, 56, 65.

{6} *Fairy Holes and Fairy Butter / Cumbria by Simon Young*

Further Reading

Alan Cleaver and Lesley Park, *The Fairies of Cumbria* (Whitehaven, 2011)

Marjorie Rowling, *The Folklore of the Lake District* (London, 1976)

Jeremiah Sullivan, *Cumberland & Westmorland, ancient and modern; the people, dialect, superstitions and customs* (London, 1857)

1 In writing this article I benefitted from the heroic online cataloguing work of Alan Cleaver: several Cumbrian fairies would have escaped me without Alan's help. I would also like to acknowledge the advice in this article of David Higginson-Tranter, Lesley Park, Stu Spencer and Chris Woodyard.

2 Geoffrey Hodson, *Fairies at Work and at Play* (London, 1925), *passim*.

3 Marjorie T. Johnson, *Seeing Fairies* (San Antonio, 2014), 91-2.

4 *Ibid.*, 125.

5 Francesca Williams, 'Underwater garden

gnomes hidden in Lake District', *BBC News* (26 Oct 2012), bbc.com/news/uk-england-cumbria-20066683 (Accessed 24 July 2016).

6 Anon, 'Granddad creates fairy garden in west Cumbria', *News & Star* (9 Jul 2014), newsandstar.co.uk/news/Granddad-creates-fairy-garden-in-west-Cumbria-c632257a-bb17-4498-950c-5d144375d5b9-ds (Accessed 24 July 2016).

7 Alan Cleaver and Lesley Park, *The Fairies of Cumbria* (Whitehaven, 2011), 40-5.

8 For the chimney wing, John Briggs, *The remains of John Briggs* (Kirkby Lonsdale, 1825), 217-218; for the poem, W P-T, 'The Spinners', *Carlisle Journal* (10 Nov 1804), 4.

9 Briggs, *The Remains*, 223-4.

10 *Ibid.*, 224.

11 Anon, 'A ride from Keswick to Penrith on the Orton Ghost', *Kendal Mercury* (13 Oct 1849), 4. Chris Woodyard points out to me that there is some satire in this...

12 A. Craig Gibson, 'Ancient Customs and Superstitions in Cumberland', *Transactions of the Historic Society of Lancashire and Cheshire* 10 (1858), 97-110 at 108.

13 Rev. S. Taylor, 'Daily Life—and Death—in 17th Century Lamplugh', *Transactions of the Cumberland and Westmorland Antiquarian and Archaeological Society* 44 (1944), 138-141 at 139. Note that the undated document seems to be early eighteenth century (in terms of calligraphy), but it purports to be a list of deaths in the parish from 1658-1663. There are some reasons to doubt its reliability: Cleaver and Park, *Fairies*, 25-6.

14 J[eremiah] Sullivan, *Cumberland & Westmorland, ancient and modern; the people, dialect, superstitions and customs* (London, 1857), 138. For fairies and railways in Cumbria see also Anon, 'Carlisle, Langholm and Howick Railway', *Carlisle Patriot* (7 Nov 1857), 8. For fairies and steam engines generally: Simon Young, 'Fairies and Railways: A Nineteenth-Century Topos and its Origins', *Notes and Queries* 59 (2012), 401-403.

15 H. 'A Tramp in Derbyshire', *Ashton Weekly Reporter* (9 Nov 1867), 2.

16 J.C[lose], 'Little Tom, the Giant of Helgillow', *Once a Year: Tales and Legends of Westmorland* (Kirkby-Stephen, 1862), 93-94 at 94.

17 Anon [Eliza Lynn Linton], 'The Fairy Howk', *The New Monthly Magazine* 86 (1849), 1-16. Linton was of course a Cumbrian writer and describes her tale as a 'Legend of Cumberland', 1. See folklore motif: F301.2.

18 Bulkeley, 'Some East Cumberland Superstitions', *Cumberland and Westmorland Antiquarian and Archaeological Society Transactions* 8 (1886), 225-232 at 227.

19 'Cumbrian Fairy Place-Names' (submitted for publication).

20 W.D., 'Recollections', *Cumberland Pacquet* (18 Sep 1827), 4.

21 Alaric Hall, 'Are there any Elves in Anglo-Saxon Place-Names?', *Nomina* 29 (2006), 61-80 at 77; Folklore motif: F211.

22 Mary C. Fair, 'Notes on Recent Finds in Eskdale', *Cumberland and Westmorland Antiquarian and Archaeological Society Transactions* 13 (1913), 218-224 at 219.

23 I cannot find a pre-war reference to this tradition though. Indeed, it is striking how even quite detailed descriptions do not mention this challenge, e.g. Anon, 'Silverdale and Fairy Steps', *Lancashire Evening Post* (8 Jun 1933), 9. 7 Jul 2017 I took two of my daughters, 6 and 9, to the steps. We established that a child can climb up without touching the sides, but only, with a bottom push at one point.

24 Anon, 'A Fairy!', *Carlisle Journal* (13 Apr 1844), 2.

25 Anon, 'A Local Tragedy', *Carlisle Patriot* (30 Jun 1871), 4.

26 J. Close, *Once a Year: Tales and Legends of Westmorland* (Kirkby-Stephen, 1862), 63.

27 *Ibid.*, 74.

28 Hector Maclean, 'Caerthannoc or Maidencastle, Soulby Fell', *Cumberland and Westmorland Antiquarian and Archaeological Society Transactions* 12 (1912), 143-145 at 145.

29 W. G. Collingwood, 'Who was King Eveling of Ravenglass?', *Cumberland and Westmorland Antiquarian and Archaeological Society Transactions* 24 (1924), 256-259.

30 Bulkeley, 'Superstitions', 227.

31 William Hutchinson, *Excursion to the Lakes in Westmoreland and Cumberland, August 1773* (London, 1774), 104-5: 'if [the traveller] advances, certain genii who govern the place, by virtue of their supernatural arts and necromancy will strip it of all its beauties, and by inchantment transform the magic walls upon his approach.' Or is this just a conceit...? Molly Lefebure, *Cumberland Heritage* (London, 1974), 212-3.

32 Henry Swainson Cowper, *Hawkshead (The Northernmost Parish of Lancashire): Its History, Archaeology, Industries, Folklore, Dialect etc., etc.* (London, 1899), 230.

33 Bulkeley, 'Superstitions', 227-8.

34 Anon, 'Local Superstitions', *Carlisle Patriot* (26 Feb 1886), 6.

35 Bulkeley, 'Superstitions', 227.

36 Eta, 'Traditions and Superstitions of the Olden Times: Witches, Fairies &c', *Kendal Mercury* (1 Jan 1859), 6.

37 Frank Warriner, *Millom People and Places* (Beckermet, 1937), 44.

38 James P. Morris, *A Glossary of the Words and Phrases of Furness (North Lancashire)* (London, 1869), 31. For some examples and a picture: *Varii*, 'Fairy Pipes', *The Monthly chronicle of North-country lore and*

legend (1889), 561-2.

39 Daniel Scott, *Bygone Cumberland and Westmorland* (London, 1899), 137; Bulkeley, 'Superstitions', 227: see folklore motif F384.1.

40 Briggs, *The Remains*, 224. See F271.1.

41 Cowper, *Hawkshead*, 308.

42 Jennifer Westwood and Jacqueline Simpson, *The Lore of the Land* (London, 2005), 242-243 and 773-774.

43 Jeremy Harte, *Explore Fairy Traditions* (Loughborough, 2004), 81.

44 Mrs Hodgson, 'On some Surviving Fairies', *Transactions of the Cumberland and Westmorland Antiquarian and Archaeological Society* 1 (1901), 116-118 at 116.

45 I thank David Higginson-Tranter for help with this section.

46 Alaric Hall, 'Getting Shot of Elves: Healing, Witchcraft and Fairies in the Scottish Witchcraft Trials', *Folklore* 116 (2005), 19-36.

47 Bishop of Barrow-in-Furness [sic!], 'Bishop Nicolson's Diaries: Part IV', *Transactions of the Cumberland and Westmorland Antiquarian and Archaeological Society* 4 (1904), 2-70 at 58.

48 Sullivan, *Cumberland*, 138. Stuart Spencer kindly writes: 'The description seems to cover several distinct morphologies: a hollow, circular form; an elongated, solid form; and a plate and cup form. The first is consistent with a crinoid ossicle.'

49 Marjorie Rowling, *The Folklore of the Lake District* (London, 1976), 86-9. note that Cumbria had four lucks, Scott, *Cumberland*, 147-153.

50 Glyn Davies, 'New Light on the Luck of Edenhall', *Burlington Magazine* (Jan 2010), 4-7.

51 Katharine Briggs, *A Dictionary of Fairies* (London, 2003), 140: folklore motif F352.

52 *Ibid.*, 42-3: F338.

53 Eta, 'Traditions', 6.

54 Hodgson, 'On some Surviving Fairies', 117.

55 Briggs, *Dictionary*, 66-8. Folklore motif F485.5.5(0).

56 Cowper, *Hawkshead*, 307

57 Briggs, *Dictionary*, 296-298: F235.4.6.

58 The normally very good Marjorie Rowling caused confusion here by claiming that the event had taken place in 1857: *Folklore*, 31!

59 Sullivan, *Cumberland*, 137; no grandson in 'The People and Dialect of Cumberland', *Kendal Mercury* (17 Feb 1855), 3.

60 Briggs, *Dictionary*, 94-96: folklore motif F388.

61 Joseph Ritson, *Fairy tales, now first collected* (London, 1831), 57.

62 E.g. Johann Georg Kohl, *Travels in Ireland* (London, 1844), 62.

63 William Dickinson, *Cumbriana: Fragments of Cumbrian Life* (London, 1876), 130-1.

64 E.g. Thomas Booth, 'A Morning Ramble into the Pennine Range', *Burnley Express* (19 Jul 1884), 6.

65 Dickinson, *Cumbriana*, 131.

66 Briggs, *Dictionary*, 330.

67 Dickinson, *Cumbriana*, 131.

68 L.F. Newman and E.M. Wilson, 'Folklore Survivals in the Southern 'Lake Counties' and in Essex: A Comparison and Contrast, Part IV', *Folklore* 63 (1952), 91-104 at 93.

69 John Richardson, *Cummerland Talk: Being Short Tales and Rhymes in the Dialect of that County: Together with a Few Miscellaneous Pieces in Verse* (London, 1871), 99-100.

70 Dickinson, *Cumbriana*, 137-138.

71 Anon, 'Devonshire Folklore', *Reports and Transactions of the Devonshire Association* 24 (1890), 49-54 at 52-53.

72 The best general account remains Anon [James Briggs?], 'Soutra Fell', *The Lonsdale Magazine* 2 (1821), 423-425. The earliest appeared in *The Gentleman's Magazine* (1747), 523-525 with a diagram of the route taken by the phantoms. Note that there is much confusion of the dates, particularly the last. The final sighting was 1744 not 1745.

73 Simon Young, 'The Supernatural Warriors of Castle-an-Dinas in Cornwall', *Journal of the Royal Institution of Cornwall*, 2017, pp. 95-104.

74 John Harland and T.T. Wilkinson, *Lancashire Folk-lore Illustrative of the Superstitious Beliefs and Practices Local Customs and Usages of the People of the County Palatine* (London, 1867), 111.

75 Briggs, *The Remains*, 223-4.

76 William Pearson, *Letters, Papers and Journals of William Pearson* (London, 1863), 7 (in the second part of the book: there are two sets of pagination).

77 Rev. James Simpson, 'Relics of Olden Times in Westmorland', *Kendal Mercury* (22 Nov 1856), 3.

78 Sullivan, *Cumberland*, 138.

79 Hodgson, 'Fairies', 116.

80 Eta, 'Traditions', 6.

81 Medium, 'The Spiritualists', *Carlisle Journal* (18 Nov 1864), 6.

82 Anon, 'On Thursday Evening', *Cumberland Pacquet* (24 Dec 1867), 5.

83 Anon, 'May Festival at Moor Row', *Cumberland Pacquet* (2 Jun 1892), 6.

84 Anon, 'Children's Fancy Dress Ball in Carlisle', *Carlisle Patriot* (22 Jan 1897), 6.

85 Anon, 'Concert in St Stephen's School Carlisle', *Carlisle Patriot* (26 Nov 1897), 5.

{7} *Ferishers and Hikey Sprites / East-Anglia by Francis Young*

1 Robert Forby, *The Vocabulary of East Anglia* (London, 1830), vol. 2, 387.

2 Alaric Hall, *Elves in Anglo-Saxon England* (Woodbridge, 2007), 64-5; Francis Young, *Suffolk Fairylore* (Norwich, 2018), 23-5.

3 Young, *Suffolk Fairylore*, 96-7.

4 The National Archives, Kew, PROB 11/14/367. I am grateful to Neil Langridge for this reference.

5 Keith Briggs, pers. comm., 4 May 2019.

6 Young, *Suffolk Fairylore*, 75-6.

7 Young, *Suffolk Fairylore*, 13-14.

8 Young, *Suffolk Fairylore*, 16.

9 Walter Rye, *Scandinavian Names in Norfolk* (Norwich, 1920), 31.

10 Simon Young, pers. comm., 12 August 2020.

11 Simon Young, pers. comm., 14 December 2020.

11 *A Guide to the Branch Railway from the Eastern Counties Line at Ely and Peterborough* (Norwich, 1847), 15.

12 Forby, *Vocabulary of East Anglia*, vol. 2, 431.

13 Forby, *Vocabulary of East Anglia*, vol. 2, 352. For discussion of Suffolk dialect terms of possible significance to fairy belief see Young, *Suffolk Fairylore*, 80-1.

14 On the translation of *faunus* as 'fairy' see Richard Firth Green, *Elf Queens and Holy Friars: Fairy Beliefs and the Medieval Church* (Philadelphia, 2016), 82.

15 Thomas of Monmouth, *The Life and Miracles of St William of Norwich*, ed. A. Jessopp and M. R. James (Cambridge, 1896), 79-85.

16 Johann Stilting et al. (eds), *Acta Sanctorum Octobris* (Antwerp, 1765), vol. 1, 677-8.

17 Francis Young, *A History of Exorcism in Catholic Christianity* (Basingstoke, 2016), 81.

18 Ralph of Coggeshall, *Radulphi de Coggeshall Chronicon Anglicanum*, ed. J. Stevenson (London, 1875), 120-1. Translation by the author. For a detailed discussion of the Malekin story see Young, *Suffolk Fairylore*, 48-51.

19 Katherine Briggs, 'The English fairies', *Folklore* 68 (1957), 270-87, at 280.

20 William of Newburgh, *The History of English Affairs: Book I*, ed. P. G. Walsh and M. J. Kennedy (Warminster, 1988), 114-17; Ralph of Coggeshall, *Chronicon*, 118-20. For a detailed discussion of the Green Children and fairylore see Young, *Suffolk Fairylore*, 31-44.

21 Briggs, 'The English fairies', 280; Katherine Briggs, *British Folk-Tales and Legends: A Sampler*, 2nd edn (London, 2002), 186; Enid Porter, *The Folklore of East Anglia* (London, 1974), 76-7.

22 Christopher Harper-Bill (ed.), *The Register of John Morton, Archbishop of Canterbury 1486-1500. Vol. 3: Norwich sede vacante, 1499* (Woodbridge, 2000), 215-16.

23 Green, *Elf Queens*, 18-19.

24 A confusion first recorded in the Woodbridge area in the early nineteenth century (see Edward Moor, *Oriental Fragments* (London, 1834), 456 n.1).

25 A. Gibbons (ed.), *Ely Episcopal Records* (Lincoln, 1891), 37.

26 William Bullein, *Bulleins bulwarke of defence against all sicknesse, soarenesse, and woundes that doe dayly assaulte mankinde* (London, 1579), fol. 56v.

27 Owen Davies, *Popular Magic: Cunning-Folk in English History*, 2nd edn (London, 2007), 184.

28 Peter Elmer, *Witchcraft, Witch-Hunting and the State in Early Modern England* (Oxford, 2015), 29-30.

29 Emma Wilby, *Cunning Folk and Familiar Spirits: Shamanistic Visionary Traditions in Early Modern British Witchcraft and Magic* (Eastbourne, 2005), 50-7.

30 Cecil L'Estrange Ewen, *Witchcraft and Demonianism* (London, 1933), 146-7.

31 Malcolm Gaskill, *Witchfinders: A Seventeenth-Century Tragedy* (London, 2005), 44.

32 Ewen, *Witchcraft*, 287.

33 Lois Fison, *Brother Mike: An Old Suffolk Fairy Tale* (Norwich, 1893), 30.

34 Eveline Gurdon, *County Folk-lore Printed Extracts No. 2: Suffolk* (London, 1893), 191-2.

35 Enid Porter, *Cambridgeshire Customs and Folklore* (London, 1969), 164.

36 Charles Whitehead, *Lives and Exploits of English Highwaymen, Pirates and Robbers* (London, 1834), vol. 1, 329-30.

37 Thomas Keightley, *The Fairy Mythology*, 2nd edn (London, 1850), 306.

38 I am grateful to Neil Langridge for this information.

39 Arthur Hollingsworth, *The History of Stowmarket* (Ipswich, 1844), 248.

40 For a detailed discussion of the Stowmarket fairies see Young, *Suffolk Fairylore*, 82-6.

41 Walter Rye, 'Norfolk Superstitions' in John L'Estrange (ed.), *The Eastern Counties Collectanea* (Norwich, 1872-3), 2-4, at 3.

42 Daniel Rabuzzi, 'In Pursuit of Norfolk's Hyter Sprites', *Folklore* 95 (1984), 74-89; Jacqueline Simpson and Jennifer Westwood, *The Lore of the Land* (London, 2005), 502.

43 Rabuzzi, 'In Pursuit of Norfolk's Hyter Sprites', 79.

44 Peter Tolhurst, *This Hollow Land: Aspects of Norfolk Folklore* (Norwich, 2018), 198.

45 Ray Loveday, *Hikey Sprites: The Twilight of a Norfolk Tradition*, 2nd edn (Norwich, 2014), 11.

46 Loveday, *Hikey Sprites*, 34-5.

47 Young, *Suffolk Fairylore*, 88-92.

48 William Camden, *Britannia*, ed. Richard Gough (London, 1722), vol. 2, 90.

49 Porter, *Folklore of East Anglia*, 75-6.

50 Francis Young, *Witches and Witchcraft in Ely* (Ely, 2013), 15-19.

51 Charles Partridge, 'Fairies in East Anglia', *East Anglian Notes and Queries*, New Series 10 (1903-4), 242-3.

52 Joan Forman, *Haunted East Anglia* (London, 1974), 60-1.

53 Hollingsworth, *History of Stowmarket*, 248.

54 Young, *Suffolk Fairylore*, 98.

55 Simpson and Westwood, *Lore of the Land*, 68.

56 On modern encounters with fairies see Marjorie T. Johnson, *Seeing Fairies* (San Antonio, TX, 2014).

{8}   *The Sidhe and Fairy Forts / Ireland by Jenny Butler*

Further Reading

Angela Bourke, *The Burning of Bridget Cleary* (London, 1999)

Eddie Lenihan with Carolyn Eve Green, *Meeting the Other Crowd: The Fairy Stories of Hidden Ireland* (Dublin, 2003)

Patricia Lysaght, 'Fairylore from the Midlands of Ireland' in *The Good People: New Fairylore Essays*, ed. Peter Narváez (Kentucky, 1997), 22-46

Ríonach uí Ógáin and Tom Sherlock, eds., *The Otherworld: Music and Song from Irish Tradition* (Dublin, 2012)

1 Bernhardt Maier, trans. C. Edwards., *Dictionary of Celtic Religion and Culture* (Suffolk, 2000), 248.

2 Tomás Ó Cathasaigh, 'The Semantics of "Síd"', *Éigse: A Journal of Irish Studies* 17 (1977-1979), 137-155 at 137.

3 James MacKillop, *Oxford Dictionary of Celtic Mythology* (Oxford, 2004), 129-130.

4 Dáithí Ó hÓgáin, *The Lore of Ireland: An Encyclopaedia of Myth, Legend and Romance* (Cork, 2006), 211.

5 Katherine M. Briggs, 'The Fairies and the Realms of the Dead', *Folklore* 81 (1970), 81-96 at 81.

6 Gearóid Ó Crualaoich, 'The "Merry Wake" and Popular Resistance to Domination in Early Modern and Modern Ireland' in *Irish Popular Culture 1650-1850*, eds. J. S. Donnelly Jr. and K. A. Miller (Dublin, 1998), 173-200 at 179.

7 Dáithí Ó hÓgáin, *The Lore of Ireland*, 210.

8 *Ibid.*, 210.

9 William Neilson, *An Introduction to the Irish Language: In Three Parts* (Dublin, 1808), 57.

10 Peter Harbison, *Ancient Irish Monuments* (Dublin, 1997), 22; 24.

11 Patricia Lysaght, 'Fairylore from the Midlands of Ireland' in *The Good People: New Fairylore Essays*, ed. Peter Narváez (Kentucky, 1997), 22-46 at 30.

12 Carole G. Silver, *Strange and Secret Peoples: Fairies and Victorian Consciousness* (Oxford, 1999), 43.

13 Lawrence J. Taylor, *Occasions of Faith: An Anthropology of Irish Catholics* (Dublin, 1997), 74.

14 Niall Mac Coitir, *Irish Trees: Myths, Legends and Folklore* (Cork, 2003), 52.

15 It has been suggested that since *trimethylamine*, a chemical found in hawthorn blossom, is the same chemical present in the early stages of decay of animal tissue, the association with the smell of death

and rot is what has given rise to this belief that the tree causes death. However, beliefs about fairies and otherworldly connections with hawthorn abound and not all of this lore has negative connotations. Thus, it would seem that attempting to explain the unluckiness of the tree by way of the presence of a chemical is rather reductionist and unsatisfactory with regard to the range of other beliefs attached to the tree. However, it is interesting to note this further association with death.

16 Niall Mac Coitir, *Irish Trees*, 53.

17 *Ibid.*, 4.

18 Sean McMahon and Jo O'Donoghue, *Brewer's Dictionary of Irish Phrase and Fable* (London, 2004), 380.

19 Angela Bourke, *The Burning of Bridget Cleary* (London, 1999), 28.

20 See further Jenny Butler, 'Changelings', in *Spirit Possession around the World: Possession, Communion, and Demon Expulsion across Cultures*, ed. Joseph Laycock (Santa Barbara, 2015), 68-71.

21 William Butler Yeats, ed. *The Book of Fairy and Folk Tales of Ireland* (London, 1994), 55.

22 Emyr Estyn Evans, *Irish Folk Ways* (London, 2000, 1957), 272.

23 Evans, *Irish Folk Ways*, 56-58.

24 Evans, *Irish Folk Ways*, 55.

25 'Second Sight' is a term in both Ireland and Scotland for psychic or clairvoyant powers. Along the same lines of meaning, the term 'clairvoyant' comes from the French word *clair*, via Latin *clārus* 'clear', and the French word *voir* from Latin *vidēre* 'to see'; the suggestion in this etymology is also a special kind of 'sight', one that allows contact with the spirit realm.

26 Nancy Schmitz, 'An Irish Wise Woman: Fact and Legend', *Journal of the Folklore Institute* 14 (1977), 169-179 at 172.

27 Gearóid Ó Crualaoich, *The Book of the Cailleach: Stories of the Wise-Woman Healer* (Cork, 2003), 94.

28 Diane Purkiss, *Troublesome Things: A History of Fairies and Fairy Stories* (London, 2000), 126.

29 Richard P. Jenkins, 'Witches and Fairies: Supernatural Aggression and Deviance among the Irish Peasantry', in *The Good People: New Fairylore Essays*, ed. Peter Narváez (Kentucky, 1997), 302-335 at 318.

30 Silver, *Strange and Secret Peoples*, 34.

{9}   *The Seelie and Unseelie Court / Scotland by Ceri Houlbrook*

Further Reading

Margaret Bennett, 'Balquhidder Revisited: Fairylore in the Scottish Highlands, 1690-1990', in *The Good People: New Fairylore Essays*, ed. Peter Narváez (Lexington, 1991), 94-115

Lizanne Henderson and Edward J. Cowan, *Scottish Fairy Belief* (East Linton, 2004)

Robert Kirk, 'Secret Commonwealth', in *Folk-Lore and Legends: Scotland*, ed. Anonymous (London, 1889)

1 Ross and Cromarty Sheet XC.03. 1907. County Series 1: 2500.

2 John Arnott MacCulloch, 'The Mingling of Fairy and Witch Beliefs in Sixteenth and Seventeenth Century Scotland', *Folklore* 32 (4) (1921), 227-44 at 231-32.

3 Lizanne Henderson and Edward J. Cowan, *Scottish Fairy Belief* (East Linton, 2004), 9.

4 Surveyed in 1904. Anonymous. *Folk-Lore and Legends: Scotland* (London, 1889), 186.

5 *Ibid.*, vi.

6 Henderson and Cowan, *Scottish Fairy Belief*, 2.

7 *Ibid.*,31, 12n.

8 Robert Kirk, 'Secret Commonwealth', in *Folk-Lore and Legends: Scotland*, ed. Anonymous (London, 1889), 154-169 at 154.

9 Margaret Bennett, 'Balquhidder Revisited: Fairylore in the Scottish Highlands, 1690-1990', in *The Good People: New Fairylore Essays*, ed. Peter Narváez (Lexington, 1991), 94-115 at 100-101.

10 Emma Wilby, 'The Witch's Familiar and the Fairy in Early Modern England and Scotland', *Folklore* 111 (2) (2000), 283-305.

11 Henderson and Cowan, *Scottish Fairy Belief*, 16.

12 Robert Pitcairn, *Criminal Trials in Scotland*, volume 1 (Edinburgh,1833), 49-58.

13 MacCulloch, 'The Mingling of Fairy and Witch Beliefs', 234.

14 *Ibid.*; Diane Purkiss, *At the Bottom of the Garden: A Dark History of Fairies, Hobgoblins, and Other Troublesome Things* (New York, 2000), 85-157; Wilby, 'The Witch's Familiar'; Ronald Hutton, 'The Global Context of the Scottish Witch-Hunt', in *The Scottish Witch-Hunt in Context*, ed. Julian Goodare, (Manchester, 2002), 16-32 at 27-32; Alaric Hall, 'Getting Shot of Elves: Healing, Witchcraft and Fairies in the Scottish Witchcraft Trials, *Folklore* 116 (1) (2005), 19-36

15 Francis James Child, *The English and Scottish Popular Ballads* (Northfield, 2001).

16 James Augustus Henry Murray, *The Romance and Prophecies of Thomas of Erceldoune: Printed from Five Manuscripts; With Illustrations from the Prophetic Literature of the 15th and 16th Centuries* (London, 1875); Child, *English and Scottish Popular Ballads*, 430-45.

17 Thomas the Rhymer, Walter Scott, *Sir Tristrem: A metrical romance of the thirteenth century* (Edinburgh, 1819).

18 Walter Scott, *Minstrelsy of the Scottish Border: Consisting of historical and romantic ballads, collected in the southern counties of Scotland with a few of modern date, founded upon local tradition* (Edinburgh, 1810); Walter Scott, *Letters on Demonology and Witchcraft* (Cambridge, 1830[2011]); Alex Owen, "Borderland Forms': Arthur Conan Doyle, Albion's Daughters, and the Politics of the Cottingley Fairies', *History Workshop Journal* 38 (1994), 48-85 at 51.

19 Henderson and Cowan, *Scottish Fairy Belief*, 142-170.

20 Henderson and Cowan, *Scottish Fairy Belief*, 2.

21 *Ibid.*,14.

22 Kirk, 'Secret Commonwealth', 154.

23 Henderson and Cowan, *Scottish Fairy Belief*, 15-16; Katharine Briggs, *Abbey Lubbers, Banshees & Boggarts: A Who's Who of Fairies* (Harmondsworth, 1979), 16-17.

24 David MacRitchie, *Fians, Fairies, and Picts* (London, 1893); Briggs, *Abbey Lubbers*, 128; Owen, 'Borderland Forms', 53-54; Henderson and Cowan, *Scottish Fairy Belief*, 19.

25 Kirk, 'Secret Commonwealth', 154.

26 Wilby, 'The Witch's Familiar', 291-2.

27 Anonymous, *Folk-Lore*, 10.

28 Kirk, 'Secret Commonwealth', 154.

29 Juliette Wood, 'Filming Fairies: Popular Film, Audience Response and Meaning in Contemporary Fairy Lore', *Folklore* 117 (3) (2006), 279-296 at 285.

30 MacCulloch 'The Mingling of Fairy and Witch Beliefs', 229.

31 Henderson and Cowan, *Scottish Fairy Belief*, 56.

32 Anonymous, *Folk-Lore*, 187.

33 Wilby, 'The Witch's Familiar', 287.

34 Anonymous, *Folk-Lore*, 187.

35 Kirk, 'Secret Commonwealth', 160.

36 Bennett, 'Balquhidder Revisited', 107.

37 Briggs, *Abbey Lubbers*.

38 Kirk, 'Secret Commonwealth', 161.

39 Briggs, *Abbey Lubbers*, 141.

40 Kirk, 'Secret Commonwealth', 160.

41 Anonymous, *Folk-Lore*, 10.

42 Child, *English and Scottish Popular Ballads*, 452-83.

43 Anonymous, *Folk-Lore*, 187.

44 *Ibid.*,187-188.

45 *Ibid.*,188.

46 Wilby, 'The Witch's Familiar', 290.

47 Anonymous, *Folk-Lore*, 99-100.

48 *Ibid.*,98-99.

49 Wilby, 'The Witch's Familiar', 298.

50 Scott, cited in Henderson and Cowan, *Scottish Fairy Belief*, 18.

51 Henderson and Cowan, *Scottish Fairy Belief*, 14.

52 MacCulloch, 'The Mingling of Fairy and Witch Beliefs', 229; Hall, 'Getting Shot of Elves'.

53 Anonymous, *Folk-Lore*, 186.

54 Henderson and Cowan, *Scottish Fairy Belief*, 47.

55 Anonymous, *Folk-Lore*, 151-153.

56 *Ibid.*,151.

57 Henderson and Cowan, *Scottish Fairy Belief*, 44.

58 Wilby, 'The Witch's Familiar', 292.

59 Thomas the Rhymer, Walter Scott, *Sir Tristrem*.

60 Richard Bovet, *Pandaemonium, or The Devil's cloyster* (London, 1684), 172-5; Wilby, 'The Witch's Familiar', 292.

61 Robert Pitcairn, *Criminal Trials in Scotland*, volume 3 (Edinburgh, 1833), 602-12.

62 Katharine Briggs, *The Fairies in Tradition and Literature* (London, 1967), 120.

63 Ernest Walker Marwick, *The Folklore of Orkney and Shetland* (London, 1975), 34.

64 Kirk, 'Secret Commonwealth', 159.

65 Briggs, *Fairies in Tradition*, 115.

66 Anonymous, *Folk-Lore*, 23.

67 Edwin Sidney Hartland, *The Science of Fairy Tales: An inquiry into fairy mythology* (London, 1891), 101.

68 *Ibid.*,98.

69 *Ibid.*,93-94.

70 Anne Ross, *The Folklore of the Scottish Highlands* (London, 1976), 98.

71 Marwick, *Folklore of Orkney and Shetland*, 83.

72 Ross, *Folklore of the Scottish Highlands*, 98.

73 Hartland, *Science of Fairy Tales*, 109.

74 Marwick, *Folklore of Orkney and Shetland*, 82,

75 John Firth, *Reminiscences of an Orkney Parish. Together with old Orkney words, riddles and proverbs* (Stromness, 1922), 76; George Calder, *Highland Fairy Legends: Collected from oral tradition by Rev James MacDougall* (Ipswich, 1978), 18; Briggs, *Abbey Lubbers*, 10.

76 John Gregorson Campbell, 'The Gaelic Otherworld', in *John Gregorson Campbell's Superstitions of the Highlands and Islands of Scotland and Witchcraft and Second Sight in the Highlands and Islands*, ed. Ronald Black (Edinburgh, 2005), 19.

77 John Arnott MacCulloch, Incense, in *Encyclopaedia of Religion and Ethics*, ed. James Hastings *et al.* (Edinburgh, 1914), 201-205 at 202; John Mercer, *Hebridean Islands: Colonsay, Gigha, Jura* (Glasgow and London, 1974), 192; Campbell, 'The Gaelic Otherworld', 19.

78 Henderson and Cowan, *Scottish Fairy Belief*, 99.

79 Walter Evans-Wentz, *The Fairy-Faith in Celtic Countries* (London, 1911), 91; Joyce Underwood Munro, 'The Invisible Made Visible: The Fairy Changeling as a Folk Articulation of Failure to Thrive in Infants and Children', in *The Good People: New Fairylore Essays*, ed. Peter Narváez (Lexington, 1991), 251-283 at 256.

80 Hartland, *Science of Fairy Tales*, 97; Evans-Wentz, *Fairy-Faith*, 58; Calder, *Highland Fairy Legends*, 18.

81 Ann Helene Bolstad Skjelbred, 'Rites of Passage as Meeting Place: Christianity and Fairylore in Connection with the Unclean Woman and the Unchristened Child', in

The Good People: New Fairylore Essays, ed. Peter Narváez (Lexington, 1991), 215-223 at 216.

82 Kirk, 'Secret Commonwealth', 161.

83 Hartland, *Science of Fairy Tales*, 95.

84 Firth, *Reminiscences of an Orkney Parish*, 76.

85 Evans-Wentz, *Fairy-Faith*, 120.

86 Sheila MacDonald, 'Old-World Survivals in Ross-Shire', *Folklore* 14 (1903), 368-384 at 371-372.

87 Evans-Wentz, *Fairy-Faith*, 87.

88 Ross, *Folklore of the Scottish Highlands*, 111.

89 Firth, *Reminiscences of an Orkney Parish*, 75-76; Marwick, *Folklore of Orkney and Shetland*, 84.

90 MacCulloch, 'The Mingling of Fairy and Witch Beliefs', 359.

91 Hartland, *Science of Fairy Tales*, 98.

92 Munro, 'Invisible Made Visible', 256.

93 Keith Thomas, *Religion and the Decline of Magic* (London, 1971), 731-2.

94 Anonymous, *Folk-Lore*, 9-10.

95 Ross, *Folklore of the Scottish Highlands*, 16.

96 Bennett, 'Balquhidder Revisited', 113.

97 *Ibid.*,105.

{10} *Trows and Trowie Wives / Orkney and Shetland by Laura Coulson*

Further Reading

Ernest Marwick, *The Folklore of Orkney and Shetland* (London, 1975)

Tom Muir, *The Mermaid Bride and Other Orkney Folk Tales* (Kirkwall, 1998)

Jessie M. E. Saxby, *Shetland Traditional Lore* (Edinburgh, 1932)

Shetland Folklore Development Group, *Da Book O' Trows* (Lerwick, 2007)

1 I would like to thank Sigurd Towrie for creating and maintaining the extremely informative Orkneyjar website (orkneyjar.com), which originally piqued my interest in the Trows of Orkney. The Shetland Folklore Development Group also deserve a special mention for publishing their wonderfully titled *Da Book O Trows*, leading me to new sources I would never have otherwise found, and their CD of trow songs provided the perfect soundtrack for my trip to Orkney. I would also like to thank Sarah Beeson and Tom Marley for their help in translating the Latin of the Jo Ben manuscripts, and Newcastle Library for kindly letting me access the Shetland and Orkney books in their research reserve. Finally, a big thank you to my very patient and understanding husband Richard for driving me all over Orkney in search of trows.

2 Biot Edmondston and Jessie M.E. Saxby, *Home of a Naturalist* (London, 1888), 189.

3 Alan Bruford, 'Trolls, Hillfolk, Finns, and Picts: The Identity of the Good Neighbors in Orkney and Shetland', in *The Good People: New Fairylore Essays*, ed. Peter Narváez (Kentucky 1997), 116-141

at 119.

4 Ernest Marwick, *The Folklore of Orkney and Shetland* (Edinburgh, 2011), 33.

5 John Brand, *A Brief Description of Orkney, Zetland, Pightland Firth, and Caithness* (Edinburgh, 1701), 789.

6 William Smith, 'Sandwick Trows', *Orkney and Shetland Miscellany Old-Lore Series 4* (1911), 2-3 at 3.

7 Samuel Hibbert, *A Description of the Shetland Islands* (Edinburgh, 1822), 565.

8 G.F. Black, *Witchcraft And Witchcraft Trials In Orkney And Shetland* (s.l., 2011), 46.

9 Jessie M.E. Saxby, *Shetland Traditional Lore* (Edinburgh, 1932), 150.

10 Eliza Edmonston, *Sketches and Tales of the Shetland Islands* (Edinburgh, 1856), 21.

11 Marwick, *Folklore*, 39.

12 Tom Muir, *The Mermaid Bride and Other Orkney Folk Tales* (Kirkwall, 1998), 175: Tape TA/590.

13 Ernest Marwick, *An Orkney Anthology: selected works of Ernest Walker Marwick* (1990-2012), 2 vols, I, 270.

14 D.S., 'Orkney Mound-Lore', *Orkney and Shetland Miscellany Old-Lore Series 4* (1911), 116-7 at 116.

15 Marwick, *Anthology*, I, 267.

16 Arthur Edmondston, *A View of the Ancient and Present State of the Zetland Islands* (London, 1809), 76.

17 J. J. Haldane Burgess, 'Some Shetland Folk-Lore', *Scottish Review* 25 (1895), 91-103 at 101.

18 John Bremner, *Hoy, The Dark Enchanted Isle* (Kirkwall, 1997), 94-5.

19 Marwick, *Anthology*, vol. 1, 270.

20 Edmondston and Saxby, *Home*, 213.

21 John Spence, *Shetland Folk-Lore* (Lerwick, 1899), 38-9.

22 Hibbert, *Description*, 588.

23 Jessie M.E. Saxby, *Shetland Traditional Lore* (Edinburgh, 1932), 16.

24 Edmondston and Saxby, *Home*, 203.

25 Saxby, *Lore*, 130.

26 Edmondston and Saxby, *Home*, 208.

27 Katharine Briggs, *A Dictionary of Fairies* (London, 2011), 127.

28 John Spence, 'Klik Mills, Birsay and the Fairies', *Orkney and Shetland Miscellany Old-Lore Series 2* (1909), 129-132 at 131.

29 Burgess, 'Folk-lore', 102.

30 H. Marwick, 'Antiquarian notes on Stronsay', *Proceedings of the Orkney Antiquarian Society* 5 (1926-27), 61-83 at 71.

31 Jakob Jakobsen, *The Dialect and Place Names of Shetland* (S.L., 1897).

32 John Nicolson, *Some Folk-tales and Legends of Shetland* (Edinburgh, 1920), 32.

33 Marwick, *Folklore*, 33.

34 Edmondston and Saxby, *Home*, 202.

35 Robert Menzies Fergusson, *Rambles in the Far North* (Paisley, 1884), 232.

36 Saxby, *Lore*, 128.

37 *The Scotsman* 1893, cited in Marwick, *Folklore*, 36.

38 Saxby, *Lore*, 192.

39 Nicolson, *Folk-tales*, 45.

40 *Ibid.*, 43.

41 Bruford, 'Trolls, Hillfolk, Finns, and Picts', 117.

42 Marwick, *Folklore*, 162.

43 Hibbert, *A Description*, 447.

44 Spence, *Shetland Folk-Lore*, 166.

45 Edmondston and Saxby, *Home*, 217.

46 *Ibid.*, 215.

47 John Nicolson, *Folktales and Legends of Shetland* (Edinburgh, 1920), 38.

48 G. F. Black and Northcote W. Thomas, *Examples of Printed Folk-Lore concerning the Orkney & Shetland Islands* (London, 1903), 153-4.

49 Burgess, 'Shetland Folk-Lore', 101.

50 Edmondston and Saxby, *Home*, 189-191.

51 Burgess, 'Shetland Folk-Lore', 101.

52 www.tobarandualchais.co.uk/, track ID 31923 & 77263 (Accessed 1 Sep 2016).

53 Burgess, 'Shetland Folk-Lore', 100.

54 Edmondston and Saxby, *Home*, 209.

55 Nicolson, *Folktales*, 36.

56 Edmondston and Saxby, *Home*, 211-12.

57 Spence, *Shetland Folk-Lore*, 149-51.

58 Black and Thomas, *Examples*, 21.

59 Hibbert, *A Description*, 449.

60 Saxby, *Lore*, 65.

61 Nicolson, *Folktales*, 14.

62 Muir, *Bride*, 48.

63 Nicolson, *Folktales*, 18.

64 Saxby, *Lore*, 66.

65 Jakobsen, *Dialect*, 116.

66 Saxby, *Lore*, 65.

67 Nicolson, *Folktales*, 29.

68 Edmondston, *A View*, 76.

69 Hibbert, *A Description*, 450.

70 Marwick, *Anthology*, 276.

71 Edmondston and Saxby, *Home*, 192.

72 Nicolson, *Folktales*, 20.

73 Burgess, 'Shetland Folk-Lore', 102-3.

74 Nicolson, *Folktales*, 28.

75 Fergusson, *Rambles*, 222-3.

76 Nicolson, *Folktales*, 21.

77 Hibbert, *A Description*, 451.

78 Nicolson, *Folktales*, 23.

79 Hibbert, *A Description*, 447.

80 Edmondston and Saxby, *Home*, 211.

81 Nicolson, *Folktales*, 37.

82 Edmondston and Saxby, *Home*, 136.

83 Nicolson, *Folktales*, 12.

84 Edmondston and Saxby, *Home*, 139.

85 *Ibid.*, 141-3.

86 *Ibid.*, 143-4.

87 tobarandualchais.co.uk/, track ID 47639) (Accessed 1 Sep 2016)

88 Saxby, *Lore*, 86.

89 Edmondston and Saxby, *Home*, 193.

90 Edmonston and Saxby, *Home*, 146.

91 Edmondston and Saxby, *Home*, 281.

92 Spence, *Shetland Folk-Lore*, 93-4.

93 *Ibid.*, 165.

94 *Ibid.*, 122.

95 Edmondston, *A View*, 76.

96 Marwick, *Folklore*, 37.

97 Ibid., 36.

98 Anon., 'Extracts from a journal kept during a coasting voyage through the Scottish islands', The Edinburgh Annual Register (1812), 431-46 at 434.

99 Marwick, Folklore, 37.

100 Da Book O Trows (Lerwick, 2007), 133.

101 Da Book, 125, gives original source as Shetland News, 7 Mar 1903.

102 Fergusson, Rambles, 230-1.

103 Ibid., Rambles, 230.

104 Edmondston and Saxby, Home, 202.

{11} The Fair Family and Enchanters / Wales by Richard Suggett

Further reading

Edmund Jones, A Geographical, Historical, and Religious Account of the Parish of Aberystruth (Trevecka, 1779; Cowbridge, 1988).

Edmund Jones, The Appearance of Evil: Apparitions of Spirits in Wales, ed. John Harvey (Trevecka, 1780; Cardiff, 2003).

T. Gwynn Jones, Welsh Folklore and Folk-custom (1930; Woodbridge, 1979).

John Rhŷs, Celtic Folklore Welsh and Manx (2 vols, Oxford, 1901).

Richard Suggett, A History of Magic and Witchcraft in Wales (Stroud, 2008).

1 John Penry, Three Treatises Concerning Wales (Cardiff, 1960), ed. D. Williams, 33.

2 Melville Richards, 'The supernatural in Welsh place-names' in Studies in Folk Life, ed. Geraint Jenkins (London, 1969), 303-13.

3 These spirits are discussed in the standard accounts of Welsh folklore, especially T. Gwynn Jones, Welsh Folklore and Folk-custom (Woodbridge, 1979).

4 For 'practical religion', see Richard Suggett, A History of Magic and Witchcraft in Wales (Stroud, 2008), 138-42.

5 Keith Thomas, Religion and the Decline of Magic (London, 1971), 606-7.

6 As W. J. Gruffydd suggested, Folklore and Myth in the Mabiniogion (Cardiff, 1958), 5-7.

7 Text and translation in Helen Fulton (ed.), Selections from the Dafydd ap Gwilym Apocrypha (Llandysul, 1996), 120-21.

8 William Salesbury, A Dictionary of Englyshe and Welshe (London, 1547), s.v.

9 Penry, Three Treatises Concerning Wales, ed. Williams, 33; Robert Kirk, 'The Secret Commonwealth' in The Occult Laboratory, ed. Michael Hunter (Woodbridge, 2001), 79.

10 Geraint H. Jenkins, 'Popular beliefs in Wales from the Restoration to Methodism, Bulletin of the Board of Celtic Studies 27 (1978), 443; Charles Edwards, Y Ffydd Ddi-ffuant (1677), ed. G. J. Williams (Cardiff, 1936), 238; Edmund Jones, A Geographical, Historical, and Religious Account of the Parish of Aberystruth (Trevecka, 1779), 84-6.

11 Bibliographic discussion in Simon Young,

'Two notes on Edmund Jones's Relation of Apparitions', Archaeologia Cambrensis 163 (2015), 237-9.

12 Hunter (ed.), The Occult Laboratory, 12-21; 77-106.

13 Jones, Account of the Parish of Aberystruth, 75; Edmund Jones, The Appearance of Evil, ed. John Harvey (Cardiff, 2003), 83.

14 Jones, Account of the Parish of Aberystruth, 69-70.

15 Crofton Crocker (ed.), Fairy Legends and Traditions of the South of Ireland. The New Series (London, 1828), 232.

16 John Wynn, The History of the Gwydir Family and Memoirs, ed. J. Gwynfor Jones (Llandysul, 1990), 51.

17 Bodleian Library, Oxford, MS Ashmole 1814 (1), f. 248 (letter from William Baxter to Edward Lhuyd, n.d.).

18 Jenkins, 'Popular beliefs in Wales', 445. By the C19th in the Ceiriog Valley they wore knee britches, white waistcoats, green coats (cot las), white stockings, and always had red caps: NLW, Gwenith Gwyn MS 245.

19 Jones, The Appearance of Evil, ed. Harvey, 86-7.

20 Jones, Account of the Parish of Aberystruth, 77-8; Thomas Pennant, The History of the Parishes of Whiteford and Holywell (London, 1796), plate 2.

21 Richard Baxter, The Certainty of the World of Spirits (London, 1691), 133-4; J. H. Davies (ed.), The Morris Letters (2 vols, Oxford, 1907-9), I, 321-2.

22 The Diary of William Thomas, ed. R.T.W. Denning (Cardiff, 1995), 437.

23 Jones, Account of the Parish of Aberystruth, 77; Baxter, The Certainty of the World of Spirits, 130-1.

24 Jones, Account of the Parish of Aberystruth, 79-80; Pennant, The History of the Parishes of Whiteford and Holywell, 5-6.

25 Jones, Account of the Parish of Aberystruth, 77.

26 Jones, The Appearance of Evil, ed. Harvey, 95-6.

27 Jones, Account of the Parish of Aberystruth, 70-1.

28 Crocker (ed.), Fairy Legends and Traditions of the South of Ireland, 208.

29 Penry, Three Treatises Concerning Wales, ed. Williams, 33.

30 Cf. Thomas, Religion and the Decline of Magic, 608-9; 613-14.

31 Caernarfonshire Record Office, Quarter Sessions Records 1632, 1636/7; Cf. J. Gwynfor Jones, 'Y tylwyth teg yng Nghymru'r unfed a'r ail ganrif ar bymtheg', Llên Cymru VIII (1964-5), 96-9; A.L. Bier, Masterless Men: The Vagrancy Problem in England, 1560-1640 (London, 1985), 104.

32 NLW, Great Sessions 4/21/3/21, 32, 40.

33 NLW, Great Sessions 4/21/3/59,74 (indictments); 4/21/4/95 (inquest).

34 T.P., Cas Gan Gythraul. Demonology, Witchcraft and Popular Magic in Eighteenth-century Wales, ed. Lisa Tallis (Newport, 2015), 108-10.

35 John Rhŷs, Celtic Folklore Welsh and Manx (2 vols, Oxford, 1901), I, 64-70.

36 William Williams, Observations on the Snowdon Mountains (London, 1802), 37-40; Rhŷs, Celtic Folklore Welsh and Manx, I, 48, 68-9; Diary of William Thomas, ed. Denning, 203.

37 Thomas, Religion and the Decline of Magic, 612-13.

38 Gruffydd, Folklore and Myth in the Mabiniogion, 12-13; cf. Rhŷs, Celtic Folklore Welsh and Manx, II, 659-88.

39 Kirk, The Secret Commonwealth, 67-8.

40 James Frazer noted numerous instances of aversion to iron in The Golden Bough (London, 1925 edn), 224-6.

41 Jones, The Appearance of Evil, ed. Harvey, 113.

{12} Pouques and the Faiteaux / Channel Islands by Francesca Bihet

Further reading

Dorothy Collings, Folk-Tales of the Channel Islands (London, 1955)

Erren Michaels, Jersey Legends (Stroud, 2015)

Heather Sebire, The Archaeology and Early History of the Channel Islands (Gloucestershire, 2005)

Marguerite Syvret and Joan Stevens, Balleine's History of Jersey (Chichester, 2011)

1 Peter Hunt, A Brief History of Jersey (Sussex, 2006), 4.

2 Hunt, History of Jersey, 5.

3 Hunt, History of Jersey, 4.

4 Octavius Rooke, The Channel Islands Pictorial, Legendary and Descriptive (London, 1856).

5 Richard Dorson, 'The Founders of British Folklore' in Folklore Studies in the Twentieth Century: Proceedings of the Centenary Conference, ed. Venetia Newall (Woodbridge, 1978), 7-13 at 8.

6 Jean Poingdestre, Caesarea or A Discourse of the Island of Jersey (Jersey, 1889); also Philip Falle, Caesarea or an Account of Jersey (London, 1734).

7 John L'Amy, Jersey Folklore (Wiltshire, 1983), 17-28; also Société Jersiaise, Lord Coutanche Library, MS CUL/L/9, Symons Jersey Folklore Notes, n.d.

8 Joan Stevens, 'Jersey Place Names', Nomina 4 (1980), 24-6.

9 Jaqueline Simpson, 'Review of Giles Bois, Jersey Folklore and Superstitions', Folklore 122 (2011), 329-350 at 349.

10 Charlotte Burn, 'Review of Edgar MacCulloch, Guernsey Folklore', Folklore 15 (1904), 119-123 at 119.

11 Louisa Lane-Clarke, Folk-Lore of Guernsey and Sark (Guernsey, 1880).

12 Marie De Garis, Folklore of Guernsey (Guernsey, 1975), 146.

13 L.Q., 'The Hougue-Bie Jersey', *The Guernsey and Jersey Magazine* 2 (1836), 364-369 at 367.

14 Charles and Joan Stevens and Jean Arthur, *Jersey Place Names: Volume One The Dictionary* (Jersey, 1986), 214.

15 L'Amy, *Jersey Folklore*, 26.

16 Stevens and Arthur, *Jersey Place Names*, 218.

17 De Garis, *Folklore*, 155.

18 Stevens and Arthur, *Jersey Place Names*, 431.

19 Poingdestre, *Caesarea*, 8.

20 Falle, *Caesarea*, 256.

21 Jonathan Duncan, *History of Guernsey with Occasional Notices of Jersey, Alderney and Sark* (London, 1841), 372.

22 Edgar MacCulloch, *Guernsey Folklore*, ed. Edith Carey (London, 1903), 110; also Edith Carey, *Guernsey Folklore: Lecture Delivered at the Ladies' College* (Guernsey, 1909), 1; also L'Amy, *Jersey Folklore*, 18.

23 F. J. Willy, 'Excavations at La Pouclée, St Helier, 1996', *Société Jersiaise Annual Bulletin* 92 (1966), 233-237 at 233.

24 Willy, 'La Pouclée', 236.

25 *Ibid.*, 237.

26 Stevens and Arthur, *Jersey Place Names*, 431.

27 *Ibid.*, 218.

28 E. Toulmin Nicolle, R. Gardner Warton and J. Sinel, 'Report on the Exploration of the Dolmen at Les Mont Grantez, St Ouen', *Société Jersiaise Annual Bulletin* 38 (1913), 315-325 at 321.

29 Stevens and Arthur, *Jersey Place Names*, 431.

30 MacCulloch, *Guernsey Folklore*, 112.

31 De Garis, *Folklore*, 158.

32 MacCulloch, *Guernsey Folklore*, 138.

33 Edith Carey, *Channel Island Folklore: A Lecture Delivered in Jersey* (Guernsey, 1909), 4.

34 Carey, *Ladies' College Lecture*, 7.

35 De Garis, *Folklore*, 166.

36 Lane-Clarke, *Folk-Lore*, 12.

37 C.J. Howlett, *Guernsey Street and Road Names* (Guernsey, 1983), 5.

38 MacCulloch, *Guernsey Folklore*, 124.

39 *Ibid.*, 124.

40 De Garis, *Folklore*, 158.

41 Edith Carey, *The Channel Islands* (London, 1904), 9.

42 MacCulloch, *Guernsey Folklore*, 202.

43 Société Jersiaise, Symons Jersey Folklore.

44 Carey, *Jersey Lecture*, 2.

45 MacCulloch, *Guernsey Folklore*, 203.

46 Duncan, *History of Guernsey*, 372.

47 Howlett, *Road Names*, 27.

48 Duncan, *History of Guernsey*, 571.

49 MacCulloch, *Guernsey Folklore*, 222.

50 *Ibid.*, 223.

51 Société Jersiaise, Symons Jersey Folklore.

52 L'Amy, *Jersey Folklore*, 28.

53 Carey, *Channel Island Folklore*, 14.

54 MacCulloch, *Guernsey Folklore*, 114.

55 *Ibid.*, 115.

56 *Ibid.*, 117.

57 Frank Dally, *The Channel Islands* (London, 1860), 59.

58 Carey, *Jersey Lecture*, 1.

59 Stevens and Arthur, *Jersey Place Names*, 359.

60 Sonia Hillsdon, *Jersey Witches, Ghosts and Traditions* (Norwich, 1987), 8.

61 Rooke, *Channel Islands*, 64.

62 *Ibid.*, 64-5.

63 *Ibid.*, 65.

64 Philip Ahier, 'La Fontaine de Mirtre', *Jersey Reporter* (29 July 1966), 9.

65 *A Week's Visit to Jersey* (Jersey, 1840), 162.

66 Giles Bois, *Jersey Folklore and Superstitions: Volume One* (Milton Keynes, 2010), 253.

67 Ahier, 'La Fontaine de Mirtre', 9; also L'Amy, *Jersey Folklore*, 63-4.

68 L'Amy, *Jersey Folklore*, 65.

69 James Graves, *Topographical and Historical Guide to the Island of Jersey* (Jersey, 1859), 74.

70 L'Amy, *Jersey Folklore*, 65.

71 Giles Bois, *Jersey Folklore and Superstitions: Volume Two* (Milton Keynes, 2010), 92.

72 Société Jersiaise, Symons Jersey Folklore.

73 Chris Lake, 'The Legend of St Brelade's Church', *Jersey Evening Post* (27 April 1984), 30.

74 L.V. Grinsell, 'Some Aspects of the Folklore of Prehistoric Monuments', *Folklore* 48 (1937), 245-259 at 253.

75 MacCulloch, *Guernsey Folklore*, 221.

76 W. Plees, *An Account of the Island of Jersey* (London, 1817), 341-342.

77 *Ibid.*, 341-342.

78 *Ibid.*, 341-342.

79 L.Q., 'Hougue-Bie', 368.

80 *Week's Visit to Jersey*, 201.

81 *Week's Visit to Jersey*, 204.

82 Philip Ahier, *Stories of Jersey Seas, of Jersey's Coast and of Jersey Seamen* (Huddersfield, 1955), 261.

83 Rooke, *Channel Islands*, 51.

84 *Ibid.*, 51.

85 *Ibid.*, 51.

86 Thomas Williams, *Jersey Legends in Verse* (London, 1865), 29-39.

87 *Ibid.*, 34.

88 L'Amy, *Jersey Folklore*, 27.

89 Société Jersiaise, Symons Jersey Folklore.

90 Bois, *Volume Two*, 79-80.

91 De Garis, *Folklore*, 159.

92 MacCulloch, *Guernsey Folklore*, 126.

93 Société Jersiaise, Symons Jersey Folklore.

94 James Bowker, *Goblin Tales of Lancashire* (London, 1883), 83-97.

95 Société Jersiaise, Symons Jersey Folklore.

96 L'Amy, *Jersey Folklore*, 28.

97 Société Jersiaise, Symons Jersey Folklore.

98 R.A. Ixer and C.J. Stanley, 'Mineralization at Le Pulec, Jersey, Channel Islands', *Mineralogical Magazine* 43 (1980), 1025-1029 at 1025.

99 Société Jersiaise, Symons Jersey Folklore.

100 Tony Bellows, *Channel Islands Witchcraft* (Raleigh, 2009), 30.

101 MacCulloch, *Guernsey Folklore*, 199. Carey supported MacCulloch in this. See Carey, *Ladies' College Lecture*, 2.

102 Lane-Clarke, *Folk-Lore*, 13.

103 *Ibid.*, 14.

104 Rooke, *Channel Islands*, 8.

105 Lane-Clarke, *Folk-Lore*, 48-53.

106 *Ibid.*, 51.

107 *Ibid.*, 52.

108 MacCulloch, *Guernsey Folklore*, 221-222.

109 William Curtis, 'Amaryllis Sarniensis', *The Botanical Magazine* 9 (1795), 294.

110 Howlett, *Road Names*, 21.

111 MacCulloch, *Guernsey Folklore*, 127.

112 *Ibid.*, 127.

113 *Ibid.*, 126.

114 *Ibid.*, 128.

115 *Ibid.*, 217.

116 *Ibid.*, 218.

117 F. Clarke, 'The Fairy Child', *Clarke's Monthly Illustrated Journal* 1 (June 1872), 4-5 at 4.

118 *Ibid.*, 4.

119 *Ibid.*, 5.

120 *Ibid.*, 5.

121 *Ibid.*, 5.

122 *Ibid.*, 5.

123 Lane-Clarke, *Folk-Lore*, 15-21.

124 Jeremy Harte, *Exploring Fairy Traditions* (Avebury, 2004), 84-5.

125 MacCulloch, *Guernsey Folklore*, 208.

126 *Ibid.*, 209.

127 Harte, *Fairy Traditions*, 117.

128 MacCulloch, *Guernsey Folklore*, 220.

129 *Ibid.*, 220.

130 S.B., 'A Visit to Sark', *The Home Friend: New Series* 2 (1855), 467-476 at 470.

131 *Ibid.*, 470.

132 G. W. James, *The Sark Guide* (London, 1845), 87.

133 MacCulloch, *Guernsey Folklore*, 200.

134 Howlett, *Road Names*, 4.

135 T.L.L. Teeling, 'Guernsey Folklore', *The Gentleman's Magazine* 293 (1902), 168-177 at 174.

136 L'Amy, *Jersey Folklore*, 64.

137 Stevens and Arthur, *Jersey Place Names*, 95.

138 Bois, *Volume Two*, 86.

139 MacCulloch, *Guernsey Folklore*, 223.

140 *Ibid.*, 198.

141 L'Amy, *Jersey Folklore*, 26.

142 De Garis, *Folklore*, 167.

143 Robin Mead, 'Island of fairies and Fantasy', *In Britain* 9 (1999), 38.

{13} *George Waldron and the Good People / Isle of Man by Stephen Miller*

Further Reading

Walter Yeeling Evans-Wentz, *The Fairy Faith in Celtic Countries* (London & New York, 1911)

Stephen Miller, ed. *Charles Roeder: Skeealyn Cheeil-Chiollee, Manx Folk-Tales* (Onchan, 1993)

George Waldron, 'A Description of the Isle of Man', in *The Compleat Works, in Verse and Prose, of George Waldron*, ed. Theodosia Waldron (London, 1731), 91-191

1 To this day in the Isle of Man the Fairies

are never referred to as such, and naming them is taboo. Instead, they are known as 'The Little People' or 'Themselves.'

2   Elizabeth Baigent, *Waldron, George (1689/90-1726x31)*, ODNB entry (Oxford, 2004). Baignet is in error over the length of time Waldron lived in the Island, too readily accepting the 'near Twenty Years residence there' mentioned on the title page of the 1744 printing of the *Description*.

3   George Waldron, 'A Description of the Isle of Man,' in *The Compleat Works, in Verse and Prose, of George Waldron*, ed. Theodosia Waldron (London, 1731). The *Description* was separately printed in London in 1744, with the title changed. George Waldron, *The History and Description of the Isle of Man* (London, 1744). In 1865, William Harrison edited this printing for the Manx Society. It uses, however, the title of the 1731 printing and adds the preface. Punctuation and capitalisation were silently modernised. George Waldron, *A Description of the Isle of Man*, Manx Society, vol. xi, ed. William Harrison (Douglas, 1865).

4   Discussed in the commentaries in Walter Scott, *Peveril of the Peak*, The Edinburgh Edition of the Waverley Novels, ed. Alison Lumsden, vol. 14 (Edinburgh, 2007).

5   For an example of the sales such guides could command, even in this early period, see the Introduction to *Jefferson's Isle of Man New Guide* (1840): 'The rapid sale of four editions of 'Jefferson's Guide through the Isle of Man,' consisting of 10,000 impressions, is a convincing proof of the estimation in which this little work has been held by the public...' *Jefferson's Isle of Man New Guide* (Douglas, 1840), iii.

6   Even by the 1860s, fatigue (for some at least) had set in as seen in William Peacock's *Everybody's New Guide... to the Isle of Man* (Manchester, 1863): 'I do not intend to occupy these pages with those worn-out legends, which have been printed year after year in the Guide books, until the very mention of them becomes distasteful.' He further stressed, '[b]e pleased to observe that I have in this chapter, given *living* examples.' Emphasis as in the original. See Chapter 14, 'Manx Belief in the Supernatural,' in Peacock, *Everybody's New Guide*, 63; 67. The popularity of Waldron is shown in Henry Jenkinson's *Practical Guide to the Isle of Man* (London, 1874), 44: 'The home of the following story of a mermaid, which ends rather simply, is Port Erin; but as other guide writers have inserted it when speaking of Port Soderick, we suppose we must do likewise, or some readers might be disappointed.'

7   Some of that material has appeared, though without commentary or motif index, in *Charles Roeder: Skeealyn Cheeil-Chiollee, Manx Folk-Tales*, ed. Stephen Miller (Onchan, 1993).

8   Motifs taken from Stith Thompson, *Motif-Index of Folk-Literature: A Classification of Narrative Elements in Folk-Tales, Ballads, Myths, Fables, Mediæval Romances, Exempla, Fabliaux, Jest-Books and Local Legends*, Revised and enlarged ed., 6 vols. (Copenhagen, 1955-58). Parallel motifs are given in parentheses. Searched using MOMFER <momfer.ml>. For its extension to Irish material, see Tom Peete Cross, *Motif-Index of Early Irish Literature*, Indiana University Folklore Series, vol. 7 (Bloomington, Indiana, 1952). Motifs marked with an asterisk are taken from Cross. For Migratory Legends (ML), see Reidar Th. Christiansen, *The Migratory Legends. A Proposed List of Types with a Systematic Catalogue of the Norwegian Variants*, FF Communications, vol. 175 (Helsinki, 1958).

9   Séamas MacPhilib, 'The Changeling (ML 5058): Irish Versions of a Migratory Legend in their International Context', *Béaloideas* 59 (2013), 121-131.

10   For the present-day Saddle Stone, see Stephen Miller, 'The Saddle Stone in the Isle of Man,' *FLS News* 71 (2013), 14-15a.

11   For further discussion, see Stephen Miller, 'Norwegian Dead-Child Legends in Mann (ML 4025)', *Béaloideas* 69 (2001), 107-114.

12   Such fairy cups are often known as 'Lucks,' of which the most well known is the Luck of Edenhall, now in the Victoria and Albert Museum in London. A recent study is Glyn Davies, 'New Light on the Luck of Edenhall,' *The Burlington Magazine* 152 (Jan 2010), 4-7.

13   William Harrison, 'George Waldron,' *Notes & Queries* 5 (3rd ser.) (1864), 384.

14   George Waldron, *The Compleat Works, in Verse and Prose, of George Waldron*, ed. Theodosia Waldron (London, 1731), vii.

15   Joseph Foster, *Alumni Oxonienses: The Members of the University of Oxford 1500-1714*, vol. iv. Sabery-Zouch, 4 vols. (Oxford & London, 1892), 1555a.

16   Waldron, *The Compleat Works, in Verse and Prose, of George Waldron*, vii.

17   For background, see R.C. Jarvis, 'Illicit Trade with the Isle of Man, 1671-1765,' *Transactions of the Lancashire and Cheshire Antiquarian Society* lviii (1947 [for 1945-46]), 245-67.

18   Waldron, *The Compleat Works, in Verse and Prose, of George Waldron*, 102.

19   This activity collapsed in large part in 1765 with the passing of the Revestment Act by the British parliament that placed the Island's customs and excise regime under Crown control.

20   'HONORANDO / JOHANNI LLOYD / INSULÆ MANNIE GUBERNATORI, / IN ANGLIA COMMORANTI, CALEND FEB. 1724.' Waldron, *The Compleat Works, in Verse and Prose, of George Waldron*, 264-71.

21   For evidence of his search for advancement by favour and his descent into penury, see the letters to Sir Hans Sloane, BL Sloane 4061, fol. 316 (n.d.) and Sloane 4061, fol. 244 (13 December 1722). Reproduced in Stephen Miller, '"My Misfourtunes press so hard upon me": Letters from George and Theodosia Waldron to Sir Hans Sloane,' *Proceedings of the Isle of Man Natural History and Antiquarian Society* xi.4 (2007 [for 2003-05]), 560.

22   Waldron, *The History and Description of the Isle of Man* 1. The 1744 edition is used hereafter due to ready access to a digital facsimile.

23   *Ibid.* 3.

24   A census organised by Bishop Wilson using the clergy recorded a population of 14,006 in 1726. William Harrison, ed., *A Description of the Isle of Man* (Douglas, 1865), 93.

25   '[T]he natives in general, both Rich and Poor, and all the Irish who inhabit in the Island, living almost wholly on Herrings and Potatoes; the former of which, are pickled up in the Season, and last the whole Year.' Waldron, *The History and Description of the Isle of Man*, 125.

26   *Ibid.* 29.

27   *Ibid.* 14-15.

28   *Ibid.* 153.

29   Bishop Hildesley wrote in 1763 to the antiquarian Richard Gough that 'Amongst 3 or 400 Adults of both Sex in each of ye Country Parishes, there are not 5 p cent of ye Natives, take one Congregation with another, that can make sense of an English Chapter of Sermon; which ye listening Flocks often hear to their great loss, notwithstanding [my] repeated Injunctions to ye Contrary.—Numbers read ye English Bible, & that well & Intelligibly to English hearers, and at ye same time scarce understand a sentence themselves.' Letter from Bishop Hildesley to Richard Gough, 2 December 1763, 'Collections Relating to ye Isle of Man,' Bodleian MS Gough Islands 1, fol. 33v [p.66]. The language shift to English was to occur only in the 1850s.

30   Waldron, *The History and Description of the Isle of Man*, 105.

31   *Ibid.* 93-94.

32   *Ibid.* 94-95.

33   *Ibid.* 105.

34   *Ibid.* 105.

35   Motifs: B81. *Mermaid. Woman with tail of fish. Lives in sea;* B81.13.11.1. *Mermaid caught by fishermen;* B81.9.2. *Mermaid has large breasts;* B82.6. *Merman caught by fisherman (released).*

36   Waldron, *The History and Description of the*

Isle of Man, 108.

37 *Ibid.* 113-14.

38 *Ibid.* 114.

39 *Ibid.* 66.

40 *Ibid.* 67.

41 *Ibid.* 67.

42 Motif: B184.2.2.2 *Magic cow (ox, bull) from water world*. See, Bernhard Maier, 'Beasts from the Deep: The Water-Bull in Celtic, Germanic and Balto-Slavonic Traditions,' *Zeitschrift für celtische Philologie* 51.1 (2009), 4-16.

43 Waldron, *The History and Description of the Isle of Man*, 85-85.

44 *Ibid.* 72-73.

45 *Ibid.* 72-73.

{14} *Piskies and Knockers / Cornwall by Ronald M. James*

Further Reading

William Bottrell, *Traditions and Hearthside Stories of West Cornwall*, 2 vols, (Penzance, 1870-1873)

William Bottrell, *Stories and Folk-Lore of West Cornwall* (Penzance, 1880)

Walter Yeeling Evans-Wentz, *The Fairy Faith in Celtic Countries* (Oxford, 1911)

Robert Hunt, *Popular Romances of the West of England or the Drolls, Traditions, and Superstitions of Old Cornwall* (London, 1903)

Ronald M. James, *The Folklore of Cornwall: The Oral Tradition of a Celtic Nation* (Exeter, 2018)

Enys Tregarthen, *Pixie Folklore and Legends* (New York, 1996)

1 William Bottrell, *Traditions and Hearthside Stories of West Cornwall* (Penzance, 1873, second series), 73-76.

2 Bottrell, *Traditions*, 76.

3 Robert Hunt, *Popular Romances of the West of England or the Drolls, Traditions, and Superstitions of Old Cornwall* (London, 1903, combined first series, 1865 and second series, 1865), 107-9.

4 Hunt, *Popular Romances*, 80-81. On Jenner see Walter Yeeling Evans-Wentz, *The Fairy Faith in Celtic Countries* (New York, N.Y. 1990; originally 1911), 164-5; Simon Young, 'Against Taxonomy: The Fairy Families of Cornwall', *Cornish Studies: Second Series, Twenty-One*, ed. Philip Payton (Exeter, 2014), 223-37; Young argues that Hunt, being influenced by the sciences, employed a rigid taxonomy but that Bottrell's idea of 'types' is more fluid. He also maintains that Bottrell's approach is more like the one that would have been found among the folk. The inclination to shun strict categories is echoed by others: see Elisabeth Hartmann, *Die Trollvorstellungen in den Sagen und Märchen der Skandinavischen Völker* (Tübingen, 1936), for example. Young's observation is appropriate here because his focus is on Cornish material.

5 Hunt, *Popular Romances*, 80-81. In her private notebooks, Enys Tregarthen mentioned an alternative Cornish explanation for the origin of piskies, namely that they were the descendants of the unwashed children of Eve, hidden from the Lord who had come to visit. Tregarthen's reference to this story, classified as ATU 758, is an isolate and consequently difficult to evaluate. See Enys Tregarthen collected by Elizabeth Yates, *Pixie Folklore and Legends* (New York, 1996; originally published as *Piskey Folk: A Book of Cornish Legends, Pixie Folklore and Legends*), 11-12. See also Hans-Jörg Uther, *The Types of International Folktales (Part I)* (Helsinki, 2011), 415-6.

6 OED on CD Rom 4.0, based on second Edition (1989) with additions: *vox* 'pixie'.

7 Hunt, *Popular Romances*, 79; Thomas Keightley, *The Fairy Mythology* (London, 1860); on Keightley, see Richard Dorson, *The British Folklorists: A History* (Chicago, 1968), 52-57.

8 Hunt, *Popular Romances*, 80. For a treatment of Anna Eliza Bray and the influence of her writings on the popular image of the pixey, see Paul Manning, 'Pixies' Progress,' from eds. Michael Dylan Foster and Jeffrey A. Tolbert, *The Folkloresque: Reframing Folklore in a Popular Culture World* (Boulder, Colorado, 2016), 81-103. Bray's birth year also appears as 1789. See her *Traditions, Legends, Superstitions, and Sketches of Devonshire on the Borders of the Tamar and the Tavy*, volume 1 (London, 1836). Her second volume on Devonian folklore was equally influential: *A Peep at the Pixies* (London, 1854). On the Victorian-era perception of folklore, see ed. Jack Zipes, *Victorian Fairy Tales: The Revolt of the Fairies and Elves* (London, 1987), xiii-xxix.

10 Bray, *Traditions, Legends, Superstitions, and Sketches of Devonshire*, 172-3; see Manning, 'Pixies' Progress,' 82 for his use of this quote.

11 Hunt, *Popular Romances*, 81.

12 *Ibid.*, 81.

13 *Ibid.*, 82. 'Browney' is likely an imported term; it is not used consistently in Cornish legendary material. Elsewhere in Britain, the term is often associated with Migratory Legend 7015, 'The New Suit', which describes a spirit who does chores in a barn or elsewhere on a farm. In Cornwall, the supernatural actor in this legend type is typically called a piskey.

14 Bottrell, *Traditions*, 95-102; Hunt, *Popular Romances*, 83-85, 111-8, and see Evans-Wentz, *The Fairy Faith in Celtic Countries*, 175-6; 182.

15 Amy Hale, 'Rethinking Celtic Cornwall: An Ethnographic Approach', *Cornish Studies: Second Series, Volume Five*, ed. Philip Payton (Exeter, 1997), 100-11.

16 Jacqueline Simpson and Steve Roud, *A Dictionary of English Folklore* (Oxford, 2000); James MacKillop, *A Dictionary of Celtic Mythology* (Oxford, 1998).

17 Bottrell, *Traditions*.

18 Reidar Th. Christiansen, *The Migratory Legends: A Proposed List of Types with a Systematic Catalogue of the Norwegian Variants* (Helsinki, 1958). Migratory legends are also called 'testimonial legends'. See Christiansen's article, 'Some Notes on the Fairies and the Fairy Faith', *Béaloideas*, 39/41 (1971-1973), 95-111.

19 Bo Almqvist, 'Crossing the Border: A Sampler of Irish Migratory Legends about the Supernatural', *Béaloideas* 59 (1991), 209-17, 219-78, especially 272. Almqvist cites Séamus Ó Catháin, 'A Tale of Two Sittings—Context and variation in a fairy legend from Tyrone', *Béaloideas* 48-49 (1980-1981), 135-47. For Irish variants, see Brian Earls, 'Supernatural Legends in Nineteenth-Century Irish Writing', *Béaloideas* 60-61 (1992-1993), 93-144, especially 134; for a discussion of Welsh variants of 'The Fairy Cow', see Robin Gwyndaf, 'Fairylore: Memorates and Legends from Welsh Oral Tradition', from ed. Peter Narváez, *The Good People: New Fairylore Essays* (Lexington, 1997), 189-90, and see Wirt Sikes, *British Goblins, Welsh Folk-lore, Fairy Mythology, Legends and Traditions* (London, 1880), 37-38. In addition, Evans-Wentz, *The Fairy Faith*, 143, 147 and 203-4, mentions fairy cattle in Welsh tradition and in Brittany.

20 Hunt, *Popular Romances*, 129-30. Hunt quotes from a tale told by Thomas Quiller Couch in *Notes and Queries*. The story of 'The New Suit' has enjoyed a lengthy history thanks in part to its publication in the collection of the Brothers Grimm: see their story number 391.

21 Hunt, *Popular Romances*, 88-90. Katharine Briggs, *Folk Tales of Britain: Legends* (London, 2011; originally 1971), 484; Briggs classifies this as ML 5006*. It is reminiscent of Christiansen's Migratory Legend 6050, 'The Fairy Hat'.

22 Hunt, *Popular Romances*, 83-85, 109-18. See also Evans-Wentz, *The Fairy Faith*, 175-6 and 182. For an academic treatment dealing with the history of this migratory legend, see Críostóir Mac Cárthaigh, 'Midwife to the Fairies (ML 5070): The Irish Variants in their Scottish and Scandinavian Perspective', *Béaloideas* 59 (1991), 133-43. The article draws on an unpublished dissertation. The midwife motif appears in Jonathan Couch with additions by T. Q. Couch, *History of Polperro* (Truro, 1871), 138-9 and in Tregarthen, *Pixie Folklore and Legends*, 77-88, but these examples may be borrowed from Bray, *Traditions, Legends, Superstitions, and Sketches of Devonshire*, 183-8. Tony

Deane and Tony Shaw reproduced Couch's story without attribution in their Folklore of Cornwall (Stroud, 2003), 63.

23 Hunt, Popular Romances, 95-96; Couch, History of Polperro, 134-5. The legend also appears in the folktale type index as ATU 113A, 'Pan is Dead'. The migratory legends cited in this paragraph are treated fully by Ronald M. James, The Folklore of Cornwall: The Oral Tradition of a Celtic Nation (forthcoming).

24 Cornish stories frequently substitute a boat for a horse found in other countries. See, for example, Ronald M. James, 'Curses, Vengeance, and Fishtails: The Cornish Mermaid in Perspective,' Cornish Studies Third Series, Volume 1, ed. Garry Tregidga (Exeter, 2015), 42-61; and Ronald M. James, "The Spectral Bridegroom": A Study in Cornish Folklore,' Cornish Studies 20, ed. Philip Payton (Exeter, 2013), 131-47.

25 Hunt, Popular Romances, 91-95; Séamas Mac Philib, 'The Changeling (ML 5058): Irish Versions of a Migratory Legend in their International Context', Béaloideas 59 (1991), 121-31; Simon Young, 'Five Notes on Nineteenth-Century Cornish Changelings', Journal of the Royal Institution of Cornwall (2013), 51-79. See also his 'Some Notes on Irish Fairy Changelings in Nineteenth-Century Newspapers', Béascna 8 (2013), 34-47. The abduction of infants is comprehensively treated by Hartmann, Die Trollvorstellungen. The motif found expression in literature at least as early as the first century: see Titus Petronius Arbiter, The Satyricon, as discussed by Ronald M. James, 'Two Examples of Latin Legends from the Satyricon', Arv: Scandinavian Yearbook of Folklore 35 (1979), 121-5.

26 Bottrell, Traditions, 95-102.

27 The well-known Cornish 'bal maidens' worked in the mining industry —possibly even before the industrial period—but they were usually assigned to surface tasks. 'Bal' is a Cornish word for a mine.

28 Ronald M. James, 'Knockers, Knackers, and Ghosts: Immigrant Folklore in the Western Mines', Western Folklore Quarterly 51 (April 1992), 153-76; for an imaginative treatment of the Jewish motif, see Paul Manning, 'Jewish Ghosts, Knackers, Tommyknockers, and other Sprites of Capitalism in the Cornish Mines', ed. Philip Payton, Cornish Studies: Second Series, Thirteen (Exeter, 2005), 216-55.

29 On Trevorrow see Bottrell, Traditions and Hearthside Stories of West Cornwall (1873), 186-93. On Barker, see Hunt, Popular Romances, 88. This legend is echoed in Elizabeth Mary Wright, Rustic Speech and Folk-Lore (New York, 1913), 199; on the third story, see Bottrell, Traditions and Hearthside Stories of West Cornwall (1873),

186-93.

30 Peter Narváez, 'Newfoundland Berry Pickers "In the Fairies": Maintaining Spatial, Temporal, and Moral Boundaries Through Legendry,' from ed. Narváez, The Good People, 336-69; Barbara Rieti, Strange Terrain: The Fairy World in Newfoundland, (Newfoundland, 1991).

31 James, 'Knockers, Knackers, and Ghosts.' Caroline Bancroft, 'Folklore of the Central City District, Colorado', California Folklore Quarterly (October 1945), 315-42; James C. Baker, 'Echoes of Tommyknockers in Bohemia, Oregon, Mines', Western Folklore 30 (1971), 121-2; Wayland Hand, 'California Miners Folklore: Below Ground', California Folklore Quarterly 1 (1942), 127-53.

32 See Evans-Wentz, The Fairy Faith in Celtic Countries, 163-82. For the persistence of the North American tommyknocker, see F. D. Calhoon, Coolies, Kanakas and Cousin Jacks: and Eleven Other Ethnic Groups who Populated the West during the Gold Rush Years (Sacramento, 1986), 320-1; and for an account of a tommyknocker from the 1950s by a Portuguese-American miner, see James, The Folklore of Cornwall.

{15} Puritans and Pukwudgies / New England by Peter Muise

1 Christopher Balzano, Dark Woods: Cults, Crime and the Paranormal in the Freetown State Forest (Atglen, Pennsylvania, 2008), 107-109.

2 C. Grant Loomis, 'Sylvester Judd's New England Folklore,' The Journal of American Folklore 60: 236 (Apr.-Jun., 1947), 151-158.

3 Nathaniel Hawthorne, The Scarlet Letter (New York, 1950), 235.

4 John Greenleaf Whittier, Prose Works of John Greenleaf Whittier, Vol.2 (Boston, 1866), 237.

5 Owen Davies, America Bewitched. The Story of Witchcraft After Salem (Oxford, 2013), 37-38.

6 David Hackett Fisher, Albion's Seed: Four British Folkways in America (Oxford, 1989).

7 Malcolm Gaskill, Witchfinders: A Seventeenth Century English Tragedy (Cambridge, 2007).

8 Samuel Deane, The New England Farmer; Or, Georgical Dictionary (Worcester, 1797), 97-98.

9 Whittier, Prose Works, 239-240.

10 Samuel Roads, History and Traditions of Marblehead (Boston, 1880), 7.

11 William Wetmore Story, Life and Letters of Joseph Story, Vol. I (Boston, 1851), 29. See also Peter Muise and Simon Young, 'Pixy-Lore in Massachusetts?', Devon and Cornwall Notes and Queries (Spring 2015), 205-207.

12 Caroline King Howard, When I Lived in Salem, 1822-1866, (Brattleboro, 1937), 197.

13 Sarah Bridge Farmer, 'Folklore of

Marblehead, Mass,' The Journal of American Folklore 7: 26 (Jul. - Sep. 1894), 252-253.

14 Katharine Briggs, Dictionary of Fairies (London, 1976), 268-270.

15 Passamaquoddy Tribe @ Indian Township, Passamaquoddy.com, 'Culture and History' (Accessed 14 August 2016).

16 Briggs, Dictionary, 268-270.

17 Ibid., 268-270.

18 Ibid., 268-270.

19 Charles Godfrey Leland, The Algonquin Legends of New England, (Boston, 1885), 295-299.

20 William Scranton Simmons, Cautantowwit's House. An Indian Burial Ground on the Island of Conanicut in Narragansett Bay (Providence, 1970), 5.

21 Frank Speck, 'Penobscot Tales and Religious Beliefs,' The Journal of American Folk-Lore 48: 187 (Jan - March 1935), 12-13.

22 Ibid., 15.

23 Ibid., 22.

24 Harley Stamp, 'The Water Fairies,' The Journal of American Folklore 28: 109 (Jul - Sep. 1915), 310-316.

25 Speck, 'Penobscot Tales,' 13.

26 Ibid., 84.

27 Ibid., 14-15.

28 William A. Haviland and Marjory W. Power, The Original Vermonters. Native Inhabitants, Past and Present (Hanover, 1981), 191.

29 Melissa Jayne Fawcettt, Medicine Trail: The Life and Lessons of Gladys Tantaquidgeon (Tucson, 2000), 31-33.

30 Ellyn Santiago, 'Mohegan Tribe's Cultural Boundary Reduced But Could Still Block Affordable Housing,' Montville Patch, September 24, 2012, online edition.

31 Fawcett, Medicine Trail, 31-33.

32 William S. Simmons, Spirit of the New England Tribes (Hanover, 1986), 242-243.

33 Richard Holmes, 'Tales of Old Derry: The Legend of the 'Derry Fairy,' Derry News, Nov. 13, 2008, online edition.

34 Joseph Citro, Joseph, Passing Strange. True Tales of New England Hauntings and Horrors (Boston, 1996), 145.

35 Citro, Passing Strange, 149.

36 Richard Holmes, 'History of Derry,' Town of Derry website, derry.nh.us (Accessed August 19 2016).

37 Henrietta Frost, 'Tsienneto,' Granite State Magazine 4 (July - Dec. 1907), 19.

38 Richard Holmes, 'Was Tsienneto An Indian Seer or a Fairy Queen?', Derry News, March 8, 2012, online edition.

39 Eva A. Speare, New Hampshire Folk Tales (Littleton, 1932), 193.

40 Citro, Passing Strange, 142.

41 Balzano, Dark Woods, 102-113.

42 George M. Eberhart, Mysterious Creatures: A Guide to Cryptozoology, Volume Two (Bideford, 2010), 468.

43 Loren Coleman, Monsters of Massachusetts.

Mysterious Creatures in The Bay State (Mechanicsburg, 2013), 63-66.

44 *Monsters and Mysteries in America*, 'New England', aired 22 December 2013.

45 *Freak Encounters*, 'Pukwudgie', aired 14 December 2010.

46 *The Bridgewater Triangle*, documentary directed by Aaron Cadieux and Manny Fanoleire, 2013.

47 J.K. Rowling, 'Ilvermorny School of Witchcraft and Wizardry,' pottermore.com/writing-by-jk-rowling/ilvermorny (Accessed 19 August 2016).

48 Whittier, *Prose Works*, 241.

49 Henry Wadsworth Longfellow, *The Song of Hiawatha* (London, 1860), 173-177.

50 Thomas Weston, *A History of The Town of Middleboro* (Boston, 1906), 424-426.

51 Simmons, *Spirit*, 216.

52 *Ibid.*, 215.

53 Elizabeth Reynard, *The Narrow Land. Folk Chronicles of Old Cape Cod.* Second Edition (Boston, 1934), 27-29.

54 Jean Fritz, *The Good Giants and The Bad Pukwudgies* (New York, 1982).

55 Reynard, *Narrow Land*, 27-29.

56 YouTube video, 'When Pukwudgies Attack', uploaded 21 August 2008 (Accessed 19 August 2016).

57 Balzano, *Dark Woods*, 109-111.

58 *The Bridgewater Triangle*, documentary, 2013; *Monsters and Mysteries in America*, 'New England,' aired 22 December 2013.

59 Eric Stanway, 'Spirits and Hauntings and Pukwudgies, Oh My,' *The Nashua Telegraph*, October 10, 2010, online edition.

60 Fiona Broome, '(NH) Wilton - Vale End Cemetery, Wilton—Possible Demons,' http: //encounterghosts.com/possible-demons-at-vale-end-cemetery/, posted 17 March 2008 (Accessed 19 August 2016).

61 Anonymous commenter, 'Interlude: 'Tis A Magic Place,' Secret Sun blog, http: //secretsun.blogspot.com/2015/06/inte rlude-tis-magic-place.html, posted 25 June 2015 (Accessed 19 August 2016).

62 Anonymous commenter, 'Weymouth Massachusetts Ghost Sightings—PAGE 3,' Ghosts of America website, ghostso-famerica.com/0/Massachusetts_Weymo uth_ghost_sightings3.htm, undated (Accessed 31 October 2015).

63 Iveagh Hunt Sterry and William H. Garrigus. *They Found A Way* (Brattleboro, 1938), 144-159.

64 Citro, Passing Strange, 145-146.

65 Arthur Myers, *The Ghostly Register. Haunted Dwellings. Active Spirits. A Journey to America's Strangest Landmarks* (Chicago, 1986), 186-200.

66 Ray Bendi, 'Little People's Village, Middlebury,' Damned Connecticut website, damnedct.com/little-peoples-village-middlebury/, posted April 2009 (Accessed 7 June 2016).

67 'Fairy Sightings: New England Fairies,' *Fairy Investigation Society Newsletter* 4, New Series, July 2016, 6-10.

{16} *Banshees and Changelings / Irish America by Chris Woodyard*

1 Wayland D. Hand, 'European Fairy Lore in the New World', *Folklore* 92 (1981), 141-148.

2 Richard M. Dorson, *America in Legend: Folklore from the Colonial Period to the Present* (New York, 1973), 14-15.

3 Owen Davies, *America Bewitched: The Story of Witchcraft after Salem* (Oxford, 2013), 37-38.

4 Thaddeus Russell, *A Renegade History of the United States* (New York, 2010), 151.

5 Russell, *A Renegade History*, 151-152.

6 Gearoid O HAllmhurain, 'The Great Famine A Catalyst in Irish Traditional Music Making,' in *The Great Famine and the Irish Diaspora in America*, ed. Arthur Gribben (Amherst, 1999), 112.

7 'Why Have We No National Fairy Lore?', *Sandusky [OH] Register* (15 Mar 1856), 3.

8 'An Accommodating Ghost', *Kansas City [MO] Star* (14 Jan 1886), 3.

9 Simon Young, 'Five Notes on Nineteenth-Century Cornish Changelings', *Journal of the Royal Institution of Cornwall*, 87-116 at 57 for the story so far. On 10 September 2016, I found the original story, 'A Remarkable Case of Hallucination'', *New York [NY] Times* (18 Mar 1863), 8.

10 'Concerning the Dead', *Daily Yellowstone Journal* [Miles City, MT] (9 Jul 1887), 4.

11 James Magness, 'Something About Ghost Stories, People Who Believed in the Supernatural', *The Democrat and Standard* [Coshocton OH] (12 May 1903), 5.

12 'Thomas Devin Reilly, Reminiscences', *Irish Citizen* [New York NY] (18 Jan 1868), 5.

13 'Some Animal Ghost Stories', *The Cincinnati [OH] Enquirer* (29 Apr 1911), 11.

14 Elsa Goldina Herzfeld, *Family Monographs: The History of Twenty-four Families Living in the Middle West Side of New York City* (New York, 1905), 22.

15 *The Banshee* (London, 1920), 12.

16 Lynn Hollen Lees, *Exiles of Erin: Irish Migrants in Victorian London* (Manchester, 1979), 188.

17 Lyn Jerde, 'The Irish of Dubuque, Iowa', *Irish America Magazine* (March/April 1995), 72, celticcousins.net/irishiniowa/dubuque.ht m (Accessed 19 Sep 2016)

18 'Irish', *Encyclopedia Dubuque*, encyclope-diadubuque.org/index.php?title=IRISH (Accessed 19 September 2016)

19 'Pat Doogan and the Fairies', *Dubuque [IA] Daily Times* (13 Feb 1870), 4.

20 'What a Fairy Can Do', *Dubuque [IA] Daily Times* (9 Feb 1870), 4.

21 'The Big Wind', *Dubuque [IA] Daily Times* (17 Dec 1876), 8.

22 'What Fairies Did', *Dubuque [IA] Daily Times* (4 Jun 1876), 8.

23 'Mysterious Disappearance. A Mother and Daughter, Having Relatives in Des Moines Strangely Missing', *The Des Moines [IA] Register* (27 Mar 1886), 2.

24 'Stolen by the Fairies', *Plain Dealer* [Cleveland, OH] (29 Mar 1886), 2.

25 'BEYOND RELIEF The Wonderful Story of a Dubuque Girl, Alleged to Have Been Abducted by Fairies', *Des Moines [IA] Register* (26 Mar 1886), 3.

26 'There is No Death', *YesterYear Once More*, (31 Mar 2011), yesteryearsnews.wordpress.com/tag/john -luckey-mccreery/ (Accessed 19 Sep 2016)

27 'The Fairies of Dubuque', *The Des Moines [IA] Register* (28 Mar 1886), 4.

28 Vere D. Shortt, 'The Fairy Faith in Ireland', *The Occult Review* 18 (1913), 70-78 at 72.

29 'Waits Eighteen Years for Examination', *Lincoln [NE] Daily News* (20 July 1894), 3.

30 Anonymous, *The Green Book, or, the Gentleman's Guide to New Orleans, Listing the Principal Maisons de Joie: Names of Madames, Angels, Nymphs, and Fairies, Color and Nationality* (New Orleans, 1895). Cited in Marion S. Goldman, *Gold Diggers & Silver Miners: Prostitution and Social Life on the Comstock Lode* (Ann Arbor, 1981), 187.

31 Chris Woodyard, 'The Men in Black: Two Nineteenth-century Accounts', hauntedo-hiobooks.com/wp-admin/post.php?post=1661&action=edit (Accessed 20 Sep 2016); 'Very Strange If True! Two Ghosts in Wapello County!', *Burlington [IA] Hawk Eye* (31 Oct 1863), 2.

32 Peter Narvaez, 'Newfoundland Berry Pickers "In the Fairies": Maintaining Spatial, Temporal, and Moral Boundaries Through Legendry', in *The Good People: New Fairylore Essays*, ed. Peter Narvaez (Lexington, 1991), 336-367 at 357.

{17} *Fairy Bread and Fairy Squalls / Atlantic Canada by Simon Young*

1 I would like to thank Dale Jarvis, Peter Muise, Barbara Rieti, John Widdowson and Chris Woodyard for help and inspiration with this chapter. I dedicate it to my grandfather Ted Mullin, a Canadian and a resident of Comox, Vancouver Island, who died just before the publication of this article, aged 97.

2 E.g. A. F. Chamberlain, *Notes on the history, customs, and beliefs of the Mississaguas* (Cambridge, 1888), 157-8; Charles G. Leland, *The Algonquin legends of New England; or, Myths and folk lore of the Micmac, Passamaquoddy, and Penobscot tribes* (Boston, 1884), 18.

3 Newfoundland, it should be noted, was a dominion until the late 1940s. For convenience I refer throughout to Newfoundland as being part of Canada: readers might wish to remember, though, that Newfoundland had its own proud history prior to confederation in 1949.

4 Margaret Bennett, *The Last Stronghold* (Edinburgh, 1989), 124-5.

5 Wilfred Thomason Grenfell, *A Labrador Doctor The Autobiography of Wilfred Thomason Grenfell* (Cambridge, 1919), 270-1.

6 Lisa Wilson, *Folk Belief and Legend of the Bay Roberts & Area* (St Johns, 2014), 33. A story collected by a high school student was this perhaps exaggerated?

7 John Widdowson, *If You Don't Be Good: Verbal Social Control in Newfoundland* (St Johns, 1977), 123. Among supernatural figures only Boo Man and the Black Man were more popular as bogies.

8 Arthur Huff Fauset, *Folklore from Nova Scotia* (New York, 1931); Mary L. Fraser, *Folklore of Nova Scotia* (s.l: s.n., s.a [registered in the British Library 1932]), 69-77.

9 George Patterson, 'Notes on the Folk-Lore of Newfoundland', *Journal of American Folklore* 8 (1895), 285-90; Anon, 'Superstitions in Newfoundland', *Journal of American Folklore* 9 (1895), 222-3; Patrick Kinsella, *Some superstitions and traditions of Newfoundland: a collection of superstitions, traditions, folk-lore, ghost stories, etc., etc.* (s.l.: s.n., 1919).

10 Anon, 'Impressions of Canada upon Emigrants', *Kendal Mercury* (24 Dec 1842), 1.

11 For an Irish fairy, Anon, 'Phil Carney and the Phooca', *Evening Telegram* (9 Nov 1895); for theatre, Anon, 'An Hour in Fairy Land!', *Evening Telegram* (23 Dec 1895).

12 John Hunter Duvar, *De Roberval, A Drama; also The Emigration of the Fairies and the Triumph of Constancy: A Romaunt* (St John, 1888), 151-172 at 172.

13 W.Y. Evans-Wentz, *The Fairy Faith in Celtic Countries* (London, 1911), 112-3.

14 Ewan Lamont, *A Biographical Sketch of the Late Rev. Donald McDonald* (Charlottetown, 1892), 23.

15 J.M.K., 'How Roderick Visited Europe', *The Prince Edward Island Magazine* (June 1902), 136-140 at 139.

16 Julie. W. Watson, *Ghost Stories & Legends of Prince Edward Island* (Willowdale, 1988), 97.

17 Canada lacks a central database of scanned newspapers. For the east coast the best sites are library.mun.ca/cns/webresources/links/newspapers/ (Newfoundland, buggy and difficult interface, reasonable sample); islandnewspapers.ca/islandora/search/ (Prince Edward Island, excellent interface,

one newspaper 1890-1957). Both are free of charge.

18 Anon, 'Beset by the Fairies', *Harbor Grace Standard* (14 Oct 1863).

19 Anon, 'The Fairies of Carbonear', *Harbor Grace Standard* (23 Sep 1865).

20 Anon, 'While three young ladies…', *Evening Telegram* (10 Oct 1881).

21 Anon, 'The Missing Pig', *Evening Telegram* (8 Feb 1897).

22 Anon, 'Central District Court', *Evening Telegram* (1 Oct 1880).

23 Anon, 'Carried off by Fairies', *Evening Telegram* (26 Dec 1900).

24 Wilson, *Folk Belief*, 31.

25 Barbara Rieti, *Strange Terrain: The Fairy World in Newfoundland* (St Johns, 1991), 66-67.

26 Helen Creighton, *Bluenose Magic: Popular Beliefs and Superstitions in Nova Scotia* (Toronto, 1968), 102.

27 See also the chapter on Cumbria for instances.

28 Anne Christine Hornborg, *Mi'kmaq Landscapes: From Animism to Sacred Ecology* (Aldershot, 2008), 89-90.

29 Rieti, *Strange Terrain*, xv.

30 The second part of this chapter is, as the notes show, overwhelmingly based on Barbara Rieti's work, though, with different emphases.

31 Rieti, *Strange Terrain*, elves (20), good people (20), bad people (124), little people (20), leprechauns (118), devil's angels (124), and co-pixies (74 and 230): for lutins see Gary R. Butler, 'The Lutin Tradition in French-Newfoundland Culture: Discourse and Belief', in ed. Peter Narváez, *The Good People* (Lexington, 1991), 5-21.

32 Rieti, *Strange Terrain*, darbies (24-5), the little-Johns (18 and 218), dalladadas (78), hollies (82), jackies (147), mickadenies (238) and the dawnies (239).

33 Katharine Briggs, *A Dictionary of Fairies* (London, 2003), 127: motif c433.

34 Rieti, *Strange Terrain*, 122.

35 Dermot Mac Manus, *The Middle Kingdom: the Faerie World of Ireland* (Gerrards Cross, 1973), 99-117.

36 Mac Manus, *The Middle Kingdom*, 94-6.

37 G.M Story, W.J Kirwin and J. D. A Widdowson (ed.), *Dictionary of Newfoundland English* (Toronto, 1990),168.

38 Butler, 'The Lutin Tradition'. Dale Jarvis, 'Fairies, Horses and the Mane Event', *The Telegram* (19 Apr 2010), makes the point that mane plaiting is rarer in English-speaking communities, but that it is attested

39 Simon Young, 'Four Neglected Pixy-Led Sources from Devon', *Devon Historian* 85 (2016), 39-49 at 42-44.

40 Rieti, *Strange Terrain*, 55.

41 Grenfell, *A Labrador Doctor*, 328-9.

42 Wilson, *Folk Belief*, 37.

43 Katharine Briggs, *The Vanishing People* (London, 1978), 7-8.

44 Motif F333.

45 Marmaduke Morris, *Yorkshire folk-talk; with characteristics of those who speak it in the North and East ridings* (London, 1911), 340.

46 Angela Bourke, *The Burning of Bridget Cleary: A True Story* (London, 2006), 24-38.

47 Rieti, *Strange Terrain*, 87.

48 *Ibid.*, 21.

49 *Ibid.*, 80.

50 Peter Narváez, 'Newfoundland Berry Pickers 'In the Fairies': Maintaining Spatial, Temporal, and Moral Boundaries Through Legendry', in *The Good People*, ed. Peter Narváez (Lexington, 1991), 336-367 at 344.

51 Rieti, *Strange Terrain*, 65-6.

52 *Ibid.*, 71-2.

53 *Ibid.*, 17.

54 *Ibid.*, 101.

55 Simon Young, 'Pixy-Led in the South West', *Transactions of the Devonshire Association* 148 (2016), 311-336..

56 Rieti, *Strange Terrain*, xvi.

57 *Ibid.*, 46.

58 *Ibid.*, 206.

59 Barbara Rieti, '"The Blast" in Newfoundland Fairy Tradition', in *The Good People* ed. Peter Narváez (Lexington, 1991), 284-297 at 284-5 (see also 289).

60 Emma Wilby, *Cunning Folk and Familiar Spirits* (Brighton, 2010), 112-20.

61 Rieti, *Strange Terrain*, 170-1.

62 *Ibid.*, 164.

63 *Ibid.*, 40.

64 It would be interesting to compare strength of belief in the 1930s school survey in Ireland duchas.ie/en, with the Memorial fairy archives from the 1960s.

65 In a personal communication in Sept 2016 Dale Jarvis writes: 'this doesn't quite ring true to me, as the vast majority of fairy stories I've heard here don't take place in wild spaces, but rather in borderland spaces (berry picking spots, paths, wood cutting places, ends of gardens)—those spaces that are halfway between wild and civilized places.'